The Banquet
of Esther Rosenbaum

Penny Simpson

ALCEMI

First impression: 2008

© Penny Simpson, 2008

*This book is subject to copyright
and may not be reproduced by any means
except for review purposes
without the prior written consent of the publishers*

Published with the financial support of the Welsh Books Council

Editor: Gwen Davies

ISBN: 9 780 95552 723-4

Printed on acid-free and partly-recycled paper.
Published by Alcemi and printed and bound in Wales by
Y Lolfa Cyf., Talybont, Ceredigion SY24 5AP
e-mail ylolfa@ylolfa.com
website www.alcemi.eu
tel 01970 832 304
fax 832 782

The best and most extraordinary artists will be those who every hour snatch the tatters of their bodies out of the frenzied cataract of life, who with bleeding hands and hearts hold fast to the intelligence of their time.
Huelsenbeck: *Dada Manifesto*, 1917

I know that new ideas can only be executed by the hungy and the discontented.
George Grosz

Prologue

" " Glass chandeliers have melted in the heat of the flames, forming chains as fine as spun sugar. Walking through the auditorium, they clink eerily above my head. Theatr Hoffmann is littered with tiers of scorched velvet seats and the bodies of dismembered plaster angels. Pigeons eye me balefully from the nests they have constructed in the crumbled ruins of the stalls. Occasionally, a bird flies up from the burnt floorboards, its wings setting into motion the glass threads of the chandeliers. The last time I visited, the air was filled with the noise of applause. Clapping hands, beating wings. The first night of *Green Phoenix*. Kaya's blond beauty as fragile as melted glass; her words burning our hearts. Now, it's the sugar chain chandeliers whispering and cracking above my head.

The floorboards of the stage are dangerous to negotiate. I crawl my way across its uneven surface to the prompt corner where I sit up on my heels and survey the scene. The sun has settled directly overhead and it's scorching hot inside the burnt-out theatre, as if the place were still stuck in the eye of a bomb's conflagration. I carry a bag made out of coarse felt strapped around my body. I loosen the belt ties and pull out a flask of water and a sheaf of manuscript paper. I no longer wear my tapestry skirts and my old neighbour Esau Jakoby is dead. We last met in a snow-filled wasteland, our eyes smarting from the spirals of black smoke that pumped out from the row of chimneys behind us. Esau was a smudge of tears, soot and falling snow.

"It's Esther Rosenbaum, who else? Taller than the tallest Junker in the land."

I lip read his words at a distance and I believe this is what he told me, but a line of barbed wire was coiled across his lips. Then he was gone, down into the ground where he settled like a stone. This is what happened to exiles in those days of snow and death. Our ammonite bones the only story in that blasted wasteland. I pulled my blanket over my head and crouched down in the snow, a curled heap that might, just might be overlooked by the men in the watch towers. I cupped snow in my hands and licked moisture from the clumped flakes. No tapestry skirts to find out my stories, just piles of bones.

My eyes are sharp. One blue, one green; the sea and the forest.

My father told me my first stories and encouraged me to tell my own. I didn't disappoint him, I hope. My stories just whispers at night. Faces pressed so close in their bunks, words melted in dehydrated throats. A woman of worth, at last, "*clothed in strength and dignity.*" Well, there was precious little else clothing us. The snow, the rain. Sunshine as bright as a gold coin, wedged in a sky as grey as my skin. Threadbare people, until night fell and I drew on the floor of the hut with pieces of charcoal rescued from the wood stove. I told stories and I fed imaginations that were as greedy as hollow stomachs. Scheherazade in her soot-coated rags. Once, I invented recipes inspired by the stories of my world, but it was rubbed out as easily as the charcoal pictures under my bare feet. My listeners could only feed on the memories of my story-recipes: clock cakes served up on plates of bone; a jugged hare resting inside a hollowed-out toy drum; pastries twisted up like a Renaissance plait. And a magical clock that played out the lives of its creators: *the metal from a father's belt buckle; feathers from an old woman's mattress; even a cheap candlestick that lit up a first love affair…*

By the end, I had become a voice and little more. Each morning, hands reached out and rubbed my boney feet, forcing me awake. A pulse of heat travelling slowly up my frozen body –

I shall bring my last story full circle sitting in the ruins of Theater Hoffmann. The sun is my only spotlight, my chorus the pigeons who fly around its charred interior.

The stage is set –

bone girl

berlin, 1915

The crisis blows up in the early hours of the morning, shortly before Purim gets underway. It's five o'clock in the morning and the stove in the apartment kitchen is burning hot, releasing the smell of baking hamantaschen. Every spare surface is hidden under baking trays lent by our neighbours. I'm kneading dough in the kitchen alongside Mama when Benjamin finally arrives. He's not wearing either his wig, or his costume, just his everyday moleskin trousers and a green frock coat that dwarfs his scraggy body. He barely glances in my direction, but calls out for Pappa, who is lurking in the bedroom next door. Pappa emerges in a fluster, his black coat flapping at his heels and his prayer shawl unravelling. He is wearing his wig, which I made for him out of old strips of newspaper and parcel string.

"You didn't paint over the dragon, Esther," he chides me, simultaneously ushering Benjamin through the bedroom doorway. "Your backcloth would look better draped over a Christian altarpiece than shown at our Purimspiel."

"It's too late to change anything now."

As usual, Benjamin comes to my defence. I hope it's a good sign, that he's still going to play heroine in the Purimspiel, but the truth is there's been no word from him for days and that's why Pappa has been so tetchy. The dragon I've painted on my backcloth, wreathed round a fig tree, is a mere sideshow. Pappa is convinced his lead actor hasn't learnt his lines, but I think something more is at stake. Benjamin is our next-door neighbour in the mietskasernen and, every year, plays the role of Queen Esther in the Purimpsiel Pappa writes and directs with relish – sporting a very daring wig, red as a battle scar. Truth to tell,

9

with no Benjamin, there's no Purimspiel. But this year, there's a new threat from beyond our borders: war has broken out and rumour bites hard into our lives. There have been constant food shortages, which means days spent queuing in the streets frozen by late frosts, blowing on numb fingers. We can only celebrate Purim, because everyone has rallied round to supply Mama with brown paper bags full of flour and handfuls of eggs. The rumours are many and varied, but rumours of call-up papers being issued to the Jews of the Scheuenviertel has caused a particular stir. Pappa has been shut away in the bedroom writing his playscript for the last couple of weeks and so is completely out of touch with the latest news, but Mama and I hear everything on the stairwells where neighbours gather and barter what little is left of precious stocks – slivers of olive soap, handfuls of ersatz coffee and the sheets of brown paper which we use to replace broken glass. They also whisper the names of sons and fathers who have enlisted. Benjamin Stein's name hasn't been added to the roll call as yet, but I dread it. Although he is a violinist of rare skilll – and one recognised as such beyond the Scheuenviertel for his talent – that means little now war has broken out and music and dancing have become a guilty secret along with luxuries, like scented soaps and fresh eggs.

The door to the bedroom is slammed shut and Mama and I are left to bake the hamantaschen, little three-cornered cakes, stuffed full of poppy seeds, which will be distributed to the refugees in the hostel at Auguststrasse later this evening after the Purimspiel. The thought of these cakes makes me lick my lips, but they taste only of sweat. I'm greasing baking trays, my ears alert to the slightest sound from behind the closed bedroom door, when suddenly it flies open again and Pappa stamps out.

"Explain to Ida and Esther what you have just explained to me," he demands.

Please God, I whisper under my breath, let Benjamin have only forgotten his costume – it wouldn't be the first time.

"Tell them why you have to go and fight. Go on."

He drags Benjamin into the kitchen by the sleeve of his coat and thrusts him down on a milk churn, the only available seat.

"Ach, doesn't one blow just lead to another?"

It's true then, Benjamin has gone to enlist and that's why he's been so elusive in recent days. My friend looks over to me, the expression in his eyes like that of a lost dog. He's not finding explanation easy, but why should he?

"I get to wear a uniform and fight for the Kaiser. It shows I'm as good as the next man."

"You need to kill to prove that?" Pappa asks, incredulous.

We all understand what he means – why does a Jew have to go to such lengths to prove his value? A musician who carries a gun is an anomaly, not proof of how we should live alongside our Christian neighbours.

"You should be playing my daughter's namesake, not an idiot," Pappa sneers.

"What do you think, Esther?" Benjamin retaliates. "Will you wish me well, at least? I wanted to make a quick getaway, but I couldn't do that, not after all we have shared as neighbours…"

"Like a burglar?"

I'm snide in my response, because I'm frightened. Benjamin grabs his collar as if under arrest and pretends to hoist himself up off the floor, but I can't laugh at his antics like I usually do.

"You're staying to do the Purimspiel, aren't you?"

Pappa snorts and turns on his heel, back into the bedroom. The door is slammed shut for a second time. Mama follows him and I can hear her trying to calm him down as only she knows how. Benjamin stays sitting on the milk churn.

"I don't know if I can pretend any more, Esther. Take a look at the world out there and then tell me if putting on a dress and playing heroine is going to help? It's a nonsense, isn't it? We have real enemies to fight, but not with words."

There is a long pause, after he has spoken. If I accept this argument, it means losing my friend. So much for the power of the spoken word. Benjamin tries to recruit me to his cause one more time.

"We are old friends, aren't we? Surely we can trust each other to do what is right?"

Saying this, he plucks a parcel wrapped in newspaper from out of his coat pocket. It's my Purim gift, which he hands over with a typical cavalier flourish. Inside, there's a palm tree modelled out of dough. Benjamin has always bought me gifts of sweets and savouries – wrapped up in tissue paper when times were better – claiming they would take the sting out of my growing pains. Fifteen years old and seven feet tall in my stockinged feet. Many a time, he has made my outsized limbs seem no more threatening than a sneeze. I look at the palm tree lying adrift in my big paw and smile. It's hard to contradict my friend when his very name seems like a place in my heart where everything can be talked into being. He takes the newspaper wrapping back and folds it up into the shape of a bird, then slots his fingers inside its wings and flies it in circles around my head.

"But what about the Purimspiel?" I try again.

"I really don't know, Esther."

He gives me the paper bird and then he walks out of the apartment – away to a war, or to a bierkeller, who knows? My world seems to have tipped upside down, like a soup plate on an unsteady tray. I usually confide in Pappa when something worries me, but today is different. We share a worry and a huge doubt. Pappa has always said doubt can be a force for good, if it leads to questions. *Teach thy tongue to say I do not know* is his favourite rabbinical quotation, but this morning there are too many doubts surfacing for comfort. Mama returns to the kitchen, looking tearful. Pappa is evidently beyond reasoning with and I don't want another argument about my backcloth.

"We need to find Frau Frankl," Mama announces.

Business as usual, even if there is a war on and Benjamin is absconding. Frau Frankl and her husband are the best bakers in Gipstrasse and they can be relied on to source spices and other scarce ingredients in these times.

"If she's not at the bakery, she'll be at the hostel, Esther. And take these to haggle with."

She thrusts a handful of porcelain chips into my pocket. Each chip is as round as a thumbnail and has been marked up with a number matching the seats in the Oranienburgerstrasse synagogue. There are far too few seats, particularly on holidays, so the chips are raffled, but Pappa is cantor and this Purim he has obviously given Mama some of his hidden supply to help her obtain saffron and cinnamon. I make my way down the stairwell, cautious in the gloom. The stone steps are worn down from overuse (it's like treading on a ladder made out of crescent moons) and they are often crowded with people trading bread and gossip. The savagely cold winter we have just endured saw our cramped apartments and winding staircases overrun by rats, who crawled inside to escape the cold. Their fried bodies still litter the tops of the exposed water pipes, emitting a terrible stench which follows me down into the courtyard. Actually, courtyard is too grand a word for such a squalid place – it's little more than a dirty big puddle fed by open drains.

Our apartment faces out on to Gipstrasse and the wider world, but backs on to dozens of near identical courtyards, an endless brick maze for those not born within its walls. Each courtyard is a dim shaft where the sun tries to penetrate, but more often than not fails. You can barely turn round, because it's always a squash on a day like today when everyone is out and about parading in their holiday finery, children anchored to their hips. I should be celebrating too, because my birthday coincides with Purim, but Benjamin's news has shaken me and I don't feel like decorating my hair with lilac sprigs as I usually do. I'm wearing the new skirt I've been given by Mama, stitched out of one of Esau Jakoby's old tapestries. Esau is one of the Scheuenviertel's many street traders, and a Purimspiel regular. Ever since I started accelerating towards the sky, he's had a lot of business from Mama.

His friend Agnes, the flowerseller, sits (as she always does) at the entrance to our courtyard, selling bunches of brightly coloured stocks. She's blind and her eyes have the texture of boiled eggs. She identifies me with no trouble, because I throw such a huge shadow over her.

"Is Frau Rosenbaum baking hamantaschen? I'll give you flowers for a cake, liebe."

"Yes, Agnes, she is. I'll bring you some when I get home."

I make my promise and leave the dark confines of the courtyard for the chaos that is the Scheuenviertel; past the bookshops, publishing houses and printers on Grosse Hamburgerstrasse where my father buys prayer books and the scholarly texts he uses in his classes at the Academy for Jewish Studies (and in the lessons he gives to me, much

13

to many people's disgust). Past Toynbee Hall where he gives free lectures on religion to Jews who are too poor to even buy a book; past the synagogue which is modelled on the Alhambra and boasts a magnificent dome covered in gilded buttresses. This is one of the few buildings in the district to have central heating and gas lighting. We crowd inside to feed on its light and warmth and marvel at the huge glass skylights adorned with sacred texts. They run over the walls and around the painted cast iron pillars. What we gaze on and pray for is always more than just a gesture, even away from the synagogue.

"Life is religion; religion is life," Pappa says. "They are as close as the hand inside the glove."

I write his lessons down on my hands and maybe this is what our Rabbis do too in their private study? Over time, their many words have run together and formed elbow-length gloves. The hand in the glove, buried in sayings, submerged in meaning. I'm no different. Doctors from all over Berlin have hunted me out to measure my growing bones. They pinch my skin and quarrel between themselves over my terrifying height. Sometimes, I yearn to be invisible, but that has a cost all of its own as I've discovered from the Russian refugees who are pouring into the city for sanctuary.

Their temporary home – an old cotton equipment factory in Auguststrasse – is where I'm heading. Frau Frankl works as a volunteer in the women's dormitory and that's where I find her, flitting between the narrow beds which are slotted in at odd angles between pieces of discarded machinery, evidence of the business that was once run in here. The hostel is a crumbling blister from the outside; inside, it's a claustrophobic, overheated warren, stretching up five storeys. Its walls are mapped with restless shadows, which exceed even my extraordinary height. The furnishings are provided by our neighbours under supervision from the Board of the Jewish Community, including the wooden clothes pulleys which swing dangerously close to my ears. Frau Frankl sees me the minute I enter the dormitory, and charges over to my side. Her cheeks are flushed and her sheitel has slipped on her head, disguising the solitary black eyebrow which cuts across her forehead like a whiplash.

"What's all this I've been hearing from Esau?"

She steers me towards an empty bed, obviously under the impression it will take my weight better than a conventional chair. She opts for a three-legged stool opposite me.

"The Purimspiel is to take place right here and not in your apartment, that's what," she continues in her rapid-fire manner. "And can you tell me who might be expected to organise everything, as if I couldn't guess?"

It looks as if I'm going to have to make peace with Frau Frankl, before trying to bargain with her. Pappa only announced the change in venue last night.

"The men's dormitory might work," I suggest. "My backcloth could hang between the wood stoves. What do you think, Frau Frankl?"

"I think your father is a genius, whatever the stage he appears on."

She looks up at me from her little footstool and smiles. The truth of the matter is, she doesn't mind a challenge and she has always admired my father, a scholar and a teacher of the faith that sustains her whenever human enterprise gets beyond her control. Frau Frankl is a round, untidy woman with a habit of wearing little leather notebooks, in which she makes her many lists, tied to her skirt belt.

"I hear he plays Haman again – and with a new beard."

My turn to smile. It's the moment I've been waiting for – the moment I can change the subject and produce the synagogue tickets, which clink satisfyingly as I pour them in and out of my palms. Frau Frankl's eyes light up. She knows she'll have no trouble bartering them for assistance in setting up the new Purimspiel stage. We make a pretence of haggling and then she presents me with three paper bags she has already prepared for Mama – one filled with strands of precious saffron, the others with cinnamon sticks as fragile as the charcoal I use to sketch the Purimspiel backcloths.

"Herr Rosenbaum's choice of subject is sadly an apt one in these times," Frau Frankl muses, rattling the chips between her fingers. "A woman who prevented a bloodbath just by talking down her enemy Haman at a banquet. Imagine that."

I have never found it hard to imagine my namesake. She would resemble the actresses I see photographed in the newspapers – women like Kaya Tucholski, one of the major stars of the Bebelsberg Studio. When war broke out last year, she volunteered to work as an auxiliary nurse in the city's hospital wards. I've kept a photograph showing her on her rounds dressed in a nurse's cap – and a floor-length, sable fur coat. Kaya Tucholski is a china doll of a woman who inhabits a world I doubt I will ever enter, but that doesn't stop me dreaming that I might one day paint backcloths for the Schauspielhaus, or the Bebelsberg Studio. And what if Kaya Tucholski were ever to play Queen Esther? What a moment that would be – but our Purimspiel only casts my father's students from the Academy and several of our more extrovert neighbours like Benjamin Stein.

No doubt, there will also be competition from the flocks of pigeons which regularly escape through the attic ceiling to scavenge for bread warming up on the dormitory stoves. I hate the pigeons' scabby eyes and querulous manners. So small, so vulnerable, but ignorant of their plight – unlike the Russian exiles. They have lost everything, even their names have been extinguished in the pogrom fires. There's one such stranger hiding under my dormitory bed, as I sit bartering spices and advice with Frau Frankl. It's the girl we call Rachel. Frau Frankl pulls her out by her leg, and she emerges reluctantly. Her name is a borrowed one, like many of the other names used by the hostel residents, but in Rachel's case it's because she's a mute. No one has been able to guess her age either, because she's so thin she could be a pale thread worked up against the dark wood of the dormitory walls. Rachel hides under Frau Vishniac's bed – one of the older hostel residents – because she's scared she might otherwise remind her of her dead babies. Frau Frankl searches in her pockets and finds a bag filled with figs.

"Ach, that those two would only find hope in one another," she says, offering the fruit to Rachel on the tips of her fingers.

It might well be Frau Frankl's wish, but it's not one shared by Frau Vishniac. I've often seen her creeping along the dormitory walls, tapping them in a bid to wake her children who she's convinced lie hidden beneath them. I try and keep to the spirit of the festival occasion when I reply, however.

"Well, anything's possible, as Queen Esther proved all those years ago."

Rachel has finished the figs, something Frau Frankl takes as a sign to finish our conversation. She crunches up the empty paper bag, as if twisting my words with it. I know she sees things differently, that what she believes possible are the hundred kinds of cruelty of this world, foremost being forced into exile, like Frau Vishniac and little Rachel. "Exile" was a word I once recognised only in my history books. I had never realised before the strangers came that it could exist in my present, outside my reading. Visiting the hostel, I hear stories I can scarcely believe. Frau Frankl says it's as if people are constantly in the process of redrafting their statements for a court hearing, but what court can possibly bring them back to the safety of their old world? So much has been destroyed and torn apart, as easily as a brown paper bag, so what point in stories that say otherwise? Except that Frau Frankl is a woman of faith, and faith decrees at Purim that we trust in a miracle in which a woman rights the world with a few choice words. Frau Frankl shooes Rachel away from her side, like she would one of the more persistent pigeons, and turns her attention back to the Purimspiel preparations. She consults her latest list in her notebook and recites its contents, as we make our way back down the stairs to the entrance hall. "Chairs – three dozen; nails for the backcloth – a handful; candles – maybe a hundred, if we can borrow enough; trestle tables for the hamantaschen. Ach, Esther, I shall see you at curtain up. Get along now and find Esau. You must tell him he's to bring your backcloth here the minute he can. "

Storm

I eat Benjamin's palm tree and give the paper bird away to a neighbour's daughter on my return to the courtyard. Hovering at the foot of the stairwell, I wait on Esau. Just inside the courtyard's entrance, someone else stands waiting, a heavily pregnant woman dressed in worn out clothes, her grossly extended stomach mocking the rest of her starved body. The stranger holds a dirty chemise in one hand and rests the other on top of her belly. I realise we are waiting for the same person. Shortly after propping myself against the courtyard wall, a familiar figure lurches into view from the direction of Auguststrasse. It's Esau, struggling between the shafts of his shabby little cart like an ant trying to push along an orange box. The stranger takes a few tentative steps forwards, but doesn't display the chemise and I think she must be shy of trading so blatantly on the street.

Esau lugs his cart past Agnes and her baskets of dying flowers and comes to a halt in front of the pregnant woman. He tips back his top hat by way of greeting. Esau usually wears his hat pulled down low over his brows to disguise the wrinkles that have opened up across his forehead, like a fan. The woman hands him the chemise quickly, looking around her as she does so, as if she were trading a gun, or a nugget of Forget-Me-Not for some wild-eyed addict. Esau's eyes are red rimmed, but they are sharp. The chemise is as ragged as the rest of the woman's wardrobe, so he only offers a few pfennigs in exchange. Before I know it, I've produced a few strands of saffron that have escaped into my pocket and I give them to the woman.

"Sell these as well," I instruct her.

She sniffs up the strands I've put in her hand and bursts into tears.

18

God knows what memories are let loose for her by the smell, but maybe it's just the confusion she feels at being rescued by a giantess and a monkey in a top hat? The deal done, she walks back down the street, hugging her belly and occasionally taking another sniff at the precious saffron.

"A Purim gift, Esau," I say, before he can tick me off. "Now, listen: there's a job for you to do. Frau Frankl wants the backcloth taken over to the hostel at once."

He smiles his snaggle-toothed smile and shakes his head, but not unkindly. He's traded with the Rosenbaums long enough to forgive our many eccentricities.

"I hope your mother has prepared a dish of something by way of thanks."

"Mama's making enough to feed an army."

"So, Frau Rosenbaum is turning soldier too," he sighs. "It would seem I'm the only one to be left driving a cart and not a tank these days."

He levers his cart to the bottom of the stairwell and follows me up the stairs. We live on the seventh floor of the mietskasernen and it's a steep climb. I look back over my shoulder to ensure Esau is keeping up with my long legged stride and catch him resting against the wall.

"Ach, I walk in straight lines, Esther. This endless winding up and down is fit only for snakes."

Mama consoles Esau with a dish of orange segments when we finally arrive in the kitchen. He shares them with me sitting at the old deal table, which has already been cleared of the first batch of hamantaschen by volunteers living on our stairwell. The table is very old, its surface scarred by dozens of chopping knives. Pappa joins us after a short while, but he is edgy and doesn't contribute much to the conversation. Esau lifts a segment of orange discreetly from the plate, before risking a question that might well lead to his evacuation from the premises.

"And what about Benjamin, Herr Rosenbaum? I saw his costume hanging on the bedroom door as I came in, but no sign of its wearer."

His question hits the rest of us hard, like a bullet. Pappa moans and

Mama drops the baking tray she has just removed from the oven.

"This is not the time, Esau," she begins, but Pappa is quick to intervene.

"So, when exactly is the right time, Ida? The show due to start at seven and Benjamin already on board a troop ship."

Mama instinctively puts her hand on my shoulder.

"He might be hunting out ribbons for his costume, Isaac…"

Pappa sighs heavily. He must save the day and he can't do that sitting on a milk churn. He offers to help load Esau's cart and they exit over the pile of damaged cakes littering the floor. Mama goes down on her knees and starts picking up the crumbs. Her vertebrae puncture the back of her dress, like beads, and there is a large patch of sweat tucked in between her protruding shoulder blades.

"He really has gone, hasn't he?"

"You can never second-guess such a man, Esther."

I decide there and then not to go the Purimspiel, but Mama chivvies me along. She says the walk will do me good, if nothing else, so I leave her packing up the unspoilt hamantaschen and make my way out. My journey to Auguststrasse is slow, but I'm glad to have my hair loose and my stockings rolled up in my pockets, enabling me to feel the soft leather of my shoes against my skin. In sight of the hostel, I bump into Herr Rosenfeld, who is off to Frau Jacob's to borrow some pins for the costume making. His shoes I can't help notice are little more than leather threads, stuck together with mud and probably a lot worse from the cobbled streets. He is as pale as a winter candle.

"Your backcloth is up, Esther," Herr Rosenfeld informs me. "It's been judged a big success. Certainly, it's more of a success than the acting company. Eli Mendelssohn hasn't put in an appearance as yet and he's supposed to be bringing Haman's sword. Your father is most put out."

"But apart from Eli?" I interrupt.

"Does it matter?"

Yes, it does matter. I'm fifteen today, but what kind of celebration is this? I slam the hostel door shut behind me, but I've barely made my entrance when a pile of newspaper lands at my feet. It's Pappa's wig.

"We can't continue with this charade," he shouts to someone lurking in the shadows behind him. "A villain, but no hero? It's a travesty."

So, it's true. Benjamin really has abandoned us – and on my birthday too. I sink down on the bottom stair, legs pulled up to my chin. I'm blocking Pappa's route, but I don't move. He gently nudges me with his toe.

"Maybe you could be our understudy, Esther?"

The idea is so preposterous, I burst out laughing. Women don't act in the Purimspiel, but I'm a giantess. Dispensation, or desperation? I can hardly tell from Pappa's expression. His burnt cork beard swamps his mouth and his eyes are mere shadows in the dark, dank stairway.

"I can't," I reply, surly and ashamed, because what else can I say?

I don't want to be stared at. It happens all the time out in the street and in the courtyards and I've had my fill of living on a stage every waking minute. Pappa shrugs and turns around to talk to the stage manager. The men's dormitory is packed to the rafters. Nearly sixty people have been crammed in around the wood stoves. Pappa is reluctant to disappoint them by cancelling the show. The stage manager seems to think it's the best course of action. The attic dormitory is not only overcrowded – there are also problems with a leaking roof and rotten floorboards. The deafening crash of a heavy rainfall drowns out their voices and I fail to hear the end of their argument. I put my hands over my ears and close my eyes, as the storm booms on overhead. I only gradually become aware that it's raining indoors. Opening my eyes, I find Benjamin standing in front of me, decked out in Mama's old dress, now heavily embroidered with wool and coloured paper. The rain is sliding off his bridal veil.

"You'll miss the show, Esther."

"Benjamin! I thought you'd gone."

"A change of plan," he concedes. "One more performance from Benjamin Stein and then it's away to war."

Confusion and happiness dart around inside my brain, like drunken mayflies. I want to hug my friend, but I'm stalled by a tuneless trumpet fanfare being played high up in the building.

"That's my cue," he says, bunching up his skirts and hurtling up the first flight of stairs.

I glimpse his work boots as I follow at his heels. Bursting into the men's dormitory on the attic floor, there are startled cries from the audience and several of the younger children burst into tears at the sight of a man in a muddy bridal veil and a wheezing giantess.

"Am I too late, Isaac?"

Benjamin flicks his tulle veil back from his face and flashes a grin the width of the room. Pappa scowls, then smiles. He has obviously cast himself as saviour of a dire situation, but, as usual, with Benjamin around, he's been upstaged.

"Welcome, Herr Stein."

"Just call me Majesty," Benjamin retorts.

His boots clomp dangerously close to young hands that stretch out along the floor. Braver souls pull the wool loops on his dress, hindering his less than regal progress to the stage. The acting arena has been marked out by a row of empty tins filled with candles. My backcloth hangs between the two wood stoves, the dragon curling above Pappa's head. A round of applause as Benjamin makes it safely to his wedding day. Only Judith, his wife, remains unimpressed. She rolls her eyes and mutters something to her neighbour.

Judith Stein: a shoehorn of a woman who slips in and out of the mietskasernen, always ready to relieve people of their secrets. She is like one of the hostel pigeons, her eyes quick and alert for any stories to feed on. Judith claims the charities handing out turnip bread in our courtyard are staffed by communists trying to win our votes and that the Frankls who run the district bakery are as bent as a butcher's hook. When she first heard an organ play in our synagogue, she fainted clean away with shock at such a break with tradition.

She loathes the fact that her husband dresses up with brightly rouged cheeks and a horsehair wig wobbling on top of his black curls. She blames Pappa for this outrage, because he writes the scripts for the Purimspiels. She blames me for assisting in the costume making. She blames me, full stop, because her husband remains my constant friend – in spite of my strange looks. Judith Stein doesn't think it appropriate that her neighbours grow as tall as trees. She finds it even less appropriate that they befriend her husband when they are half his age. She says as much to anyone who will listen (and many do).

She's still scowling when the play begins with Queen Esther and King Ahaseurus exchanging their wedding vows. A plate of Purim oranges stands in for the feast that will celebrate their nuptials, except, of course, it's no celebration because Haman is in attendance, his exaggerated false eyebrows folded up in a vicious frown. He wants the King to issue a proclamation that will see every Jew in the empire put to the sword.

"A nation of deceivers and murderers has infiltrated the tribes of the world," he warns in dark tones, as the wedding banquet gets underway.

The guests, made up of residents drawn from our stairwell, mutter and shake their heads in concern. The King bangs his tankard in support of Haman, unaware that his new bride was born a Jew.

"A nation who put their own laws up against those of every other nation. A nation that will willingly disobey our royal decree and so destroy the unity of the empire."

"Treason!" roar the wedding guests, warming to Haman's theme, and jumping to their feet, overturning crockery, glasses, figs and oranges.

"What nation is this, Haman?" they chorus.

"The Jews," he replies.

The audience falls silent. A few stray oranges tumble against the skirting boards, but otherwise nothing. Haman is usually greeted with jeers and catcalls and the shaking of dozens of rattles, but the audience is silent. The scenario is simply too close to recent events in their lives.

"To the grave with all of them," Herr Frankl, the baker, shouts, his cardboard beard slipping down his chest. "Shake to dust the star of Judah!"

The wedding guests have become a baying mob. Fingers run across throats; eyes roll. Thunder cracks in the distance. Haman slinks offstage and the scene changes swiftly. One of the student actors holds up a piece of cardboard. On it is written: "*Queen Esther's Bedroom.*" Mama's best candlestick and a silver mirror suffice as props. Benjamin's Queen paces the floor between the two wood stoves, shedding bouquet and veil. Her guardian Mordecai argues that she must go and plead with the King.

"You can save everything, Esther," he observes with chilling accuracy, "because you have nothing to lose and yet you can win the survival of God's people. There is a glimmer of a chance, if you believe enough in the King's love for you."

"But dare I gamble on it?" Benjamin's Queen asks, flinging his arms up in a tragic pose. "I shall pray and fast for three whole days and nights and then I will know what to do to meet this threat."

The refugees move in closer, anxious to catch his every word. They shiver, because they remember only too well the feel of a hollow belly. They remember eating the roots of plants, hiding in holes dug in forest grounds. Benjamin knows this, Pappa knows this. The script – written out on scraps of paper torn from the margins of students' essays – echoes their predicament, not just that of a Biblical heroine. Benjamin rushes over to the wood stove and smears himself in ashes. I know he's no longer playacting: he's gone deep inside the tragedy. His fingers claw through the ashes, smudging the grey rouge on his cheeks and lips. We all hold our breath. An audacious miracle, but here is Queen Esther inspiring belief in us all over again, thanks to a miracle that we know as well as we do our neighbours. A story about a Jewish Scheherazade, who used words alone to secure victory over her enemy.

An extraordinary silence follows Benjamin's encounter with Mordecai. The thunder eases for a minute, no birds sing, no trees sweep against the hostel windows. Even the children around me stop squealing and pinching each other. Mama lights the candles which stand in old tins around the stage, but they are soon eclipsed by flashes of pale green lightning. It fills the room, its dancing fingers plucking at our upturned faces. The thunder returns and it seems even louder than before, roaring over our heads and obliterating all other sounds.

Benjamin stands frozen against my backcloth, his next speech lost in the storm's racket. The rain drops like a curtain and the open windows let us breathe in its acrid smell. Suddenly, the floor beneath my feet begins to shake. Mama grabs hold of Rachel and hugs her to her chest.

"Blessed be the true Judge!" she screams, before they both slip through the disintegrating floorboards, as easily as a sheet of paper inside its envelope.

Instinctively, I reach out to Benjamin, but he seems tiny in the rapidly changing dimensions of the attic dormitory. Large cracks have opened up the walls, big black fingers that taunt the bright lightning. They dance together. Cracks and crackles of light and noise. The floor tips up and we move with it. We've gone overboard – down, down, into the guts of the upended hostel. An explosion of sound, followed by a terrible motion of sinking into the bowels of the earth. Several dozen people tumble down along with me, spinning like flies trapped in a jam jar. A blanket of bricks holding me as I bounce down into something unseen, unknown. Darkness presses against my eyelids.

The hostel has been whisked away like a piece of cloth. I open and shut my eyes; I listen to my drumming heart. My body is obstructed by a tremendous weight which presses against my chest and my breath whistles through fragments of plaster. Each part of my body is bearing this rubble up in a magnificent balancing act, but each time I draw breath, I'm bringing it still closer to my skin. My body is going to destroy me, after all. A transgressor in a world of pygmies. Hadn't I always known it? I cling to sound, as a means of escape: the pulse of my blood, the tick of my heart, even the scraping of my hair against brick, but finally there is something else too, a footfall, a voice, and then a small patch of light breaks into my world.

"Esther? Where are you?"

It's Benjamin. He has organised a rescue party, who ease me out of my brick cell and into the cold air that is the morning after the storm. Benjamin tells me I have been buried for over seven hours. His hands press down over my eyes in order to screen them, only letting them slip away when I've been lowered on to safe ground. It's a while before my eyes stop stinging; the sunlight is so intense that at first I glimpse nothing but smudges of colour which metamorphose into an ugly sprawl of upended furniture, discarded clothing and limbs frozen in flight, trapped under piles of masonry, even the occasional head poking out of the sea of moving rubble. The refugee hostel has folded down to the ground, like a concertina's belly. Benjamin kneels beside me, rubbing my hands between his dust-covered fingers.

He struggles to speak, but his wife Judith is not so easily cowed. I can see her hopping from one pile of rubbish to another, rescuing a broken toy, a torn dress, a bloody brick, a loose nail, a letter. This latest catastrophe has brought life only to her lined face and crooked shoulders.

"Not even time to finish a letter," she calls out to whoever is within earshot. "Look, neighbours, the writing stops just here. A word starts and then the building must have fallen…"

Benjamin ignores her and tries to comfort me. He turns my hands over and over, as if an explanation might have etched itself on to my palms. Judith spots us and darts over. "God have mercy!" she screams, prodding at my body in a vicious inspection. "What evil has she caused us this time?"

A noisy crowd surges up behind her. I can scarcely make out individual faces, but I sense the atmosphere turn electric, although all I have done is let Benjamin comfort me. He is up on his feet, pushing away the crowd who have edged in so close, one of them even manages to stand on my hand.

"Have you no pity?" Benjamin yells. "Her parents dead, but all you can do is stand and watch like vultures? Get a stretcher over here – and be quick."

"Shut up, you fool," Judith shouts back. "A stretcher for someone who has bought this disaster on us? A curse is what she deserves – may she follow the coffins of her children to their graves."

Benjamin pushes her to one side and, ignoring the shouts of the other bystanders, begins to organise a speedy exit for me. I'm bundled up into a pile of knotted coats and carted away, Benjamin's terrible revelation about my parents' fate still ringing in my ears. My eyes are screened by a stranger's hat. When we arrive at the Nursing Hospital of the Jewish Congregation, the doctors tuck me up like a curl of hair across two beds. Benjamin removes the hat from my eyes, but only after the windows of the ward have been blocked out with scraps of rags, leaving no natural light.

I open my eyes slowly, blue first, then the green, searching in vain for my parents in the dimness. A mouse scuttles down the side of the bed, but it doesn't frighten me; if it dares brush against me, I'll imagine it's Mama's hand stroking me back into sleep after a nightmare. Benjamin sits beside me, still dressed in his bloodstained Purimspiel costume, but I'm unable so much as to reach out and stroke his exhausted face.

Esau

We sleep; we wake. I notice one morning that Benjamin's forehead is raw as a slab of meat. He had beaten his head against a pile of stones when he discovered my father, but he only tells me this much later. I sleep for a fortnight and when I first sit up, I discover I'm numb from head to foot. My injuries? I have two broken ribs, torn ligaments in my legs and a very black right eye.

"When did they bury Mama and Pappa?" I croak, my voice cracking from lack of use.

Benjamin pours me a glass of water. He's giving himself time to think how best to break the news.

"On a day that was as cold as you can imagine," he finally reveals. "The courtyard was jammed full. I put a stone on their graves for you, but you must visit when you are better." Benjamin looks away, as if he can't bear to see my distress. "They sleep beneath trees," he adds quietly.

"Chestnut trees?"

The next time he shows, Benjamin brings me a selection of leaves gathered from my parents' grave. Chestnut tree leaves. I press them against my sore eyes and wonder if they were picked from the tree under which my parents first met? Mama was on her way to the Oranienburgerstrasse synagogue and Pappa tried catching her attention by reciting a benediction for a horse chestnut tree standing in front of him. Eventually, she joined in, oblivious to the gawkers surrounding them. I imagine them now standing together under the tree's boughs, Pappa swaying underneath, keeping in time with the windswept branches above him; Mama trying to hide her blushes with the back of her hand. Spring. Celebration. A faith as warm as a gloved hand on a red cheek, but where had it led them, after all?

I shake my head, trying to dislodge such thoughts. Small fragments of worse memories work loose: a pile of rubble, a child's face gripped by a necklace of brick, bloodstained teeth catching the light... I run through these scenes time and time again, twisting them this way and that, like one of my tapestry skirts, and find new horrors everywhere. Benjamin's presence is the only thing that consoles me. He visits me each day and updates me on the news from the courtyard. Everybody is in uproar, but it's not just the news of war that preoccupies my old neighbours. They are debating the aftermath of the storm and finding portents in every detail. Benjamin is careful, I notice, to avoid any mention of Judith in his reports.

"There is all kind of talk about the absentee landlord," he explains one afternoon. "The authorities made a mistake, you see, trusting a man from outside the community to run the hostel. Frau Frankl has found it all out. This man's agent was a cocky fellow with a real gold watch and tie pin. He used to swagger into the bakery and demand his rolls be baked in front of his eyes. Frau Frankl says he told her rents were deliberately kept cheap, because the refugees were without regular work. They simply packed more in to make up their profits. It must have seemed like a dream come true at the time, but their dreams have failed them in – even in exile. The foundations under their feet were loose as an old man's teeth..."

Benjamin is sidetracking. He can barely look me in the eye.

"You're hiding something, aren't you?" I finally interrupt. "Please Benjamin. You must tell me. The doctors think I can go home soon. I must know what to expect."

His head shoots up when I mention "home." He takes a deep sigh and edges forwards in his chair. His hands loop round mine and he gives them a gentle squeeze.

"The world has turned upside down. That much is certain, Esther. There is more, you're right. But what I'm going to tell you, I don't believe a word of it, not for a minute. You understand?"

"Go on."

He takes another deep breath. "Our neighbours are fickle, but you know that already. They forget the agent and claim *you* are responsible for pulling the hostel down around our ears. They wonder that you were spared and so many others killed, or injured. They think you have magic powers. There is talk you will soon be excommunicated by the Board. Achje, you've not spoken a word in your own defence, Esther, and they think that proof enough. Everyone's claiming it's your guilt that silences you."

"What chance have *I* had to make my case, lying here in hospital?"

Another squeeze of my hand. Benjamin has tears in his eyes. I have no doubt he is simply repeating Judith's ugly claims and not his own views. He runs his hands through his hair, then inspects his fingers carefully as if worried the colour might have come off on his fingers.

"There is something else, liebe. A stranger is living in your father's apartment. He says he's a long distant cousin and he's made a claim on your home with the Board. I've been round to see him, but it was a waste of time. I managed to rescue some of your clothes though and Esau is looking after them until you…"

"Until I what? Make my home in the gutter?"

"Please Esther. Don't joke about such matters." Benjamin is distressed by my response. He shades his eyes with his hands, which have also been scarred in his rescue attempts.

"But who will help me now?" I ask in what I hope is a more conciliatory tone.

"Well, there's Esau for a start – he argues with anyone who condemns you. He puts me to shame."

"You have performed miracles," I contradict him. "Without you, I would have been lynched."

He doesn't argue with me and nor does Esau when he comes to visit later. He hears the full story not just the tidbits that are fed to Benjamin, who is married, after all, to my main accuser.

"Frau Stein thinks the storm is God's punishment because you seduced Benjamin under her very own nose and in her very own bed," Esau reveals. "Yes, that's what everyone is talking about: how did you manage to knock out the heart of a man twice your age?"

Esau smells of the streets, of mud, smoke, rotten fruit, dead meat, and I start crying at the thought of facing that world once more, my card marked, my silent grief misinterpreted as guilt. Worse, I really don't have family left alive. Esau whips out a handkerchief and mops my face.

"Tender as a hatched chick," he sighs, before returning the handkerchief to his pocket. "But look, what do you say about coming to stay with me until you find work?"

"Mud sticks, Esau."

"It certainly does."

He shakes his trouser leg and large chunks of dried mud fall on to the floor. Esau tells me he has been banned from the Oranienburgerstrasse Synagogue, because he challenged Judith in the women's gallery of all places. He was asked to apologise, but refused, and now trade is falling off fast.

"But what do I care what is said about me?" he says, shrugging. "I've lived in this city's shadows for so long, my heart is a stone."

And so it is, a month after the hostel's collapse, I move into Esau's apartment in Linienstrasse. He lives in a world of soft edges – and unexpectedly low ceilings – each of his two rooms filled to the brim with second-hand clothes. I ransack them to make a bed and my world reduces down to the size of a cufflink. I care nothing for the streets outside now, because they only contain enemies like Judith Stein, who raps on the windows of my new home and curses me. I shrink even further under my ragged covers, but she's not put off. In the end, Esau has to chase her away with a broken umbrella.

"All this nonsense about black magic," he sighs, a couple of months after my arrival. "You would think they were peasants living in a rundown shtetl with nothing beyond their horizon but an early grave. Achje, Esther, you've been brought to ruin by a freak storm. Since when was that a crime? And as for that wretch, Judith Stein!" He takes a few minutes to compose himself. "You have nothing but the clothes you refuse to stand up in. Well, let us turn this to our advantage. I will write to a cousin of mine. He's a tailor in Augsburg who might well have work for you. What do you say?"

"He won't want to hire me, not when he finds out about me."

"You only have to stay until you are fully recovered," Esau persists.

"I'll think about it."

I can't keep eating Esau's ersatz spinach (stewed nettles with salt) and Benjamin will be martyred if he continues to help me. I must swallow pride, grief and despair and head for Augsburg, a place I have never heard of before, to work for a man I have never met. Early in September, I put on one of Esau's second-hand hats and head for the cemetery off Schonhauser Allee where my parents lie buried. I have to hold on to the street lamps as I walk in order to steady my swaying body after such a long hibernation.

I lay stones on each of their graves. I see that the headstones are stained, and, using the hem of my skirt, I scrub away a layer of mud and grit only to discover it's my tears doing the damage. I lie down on the path that runs between the gravestones and watch the sky through my blue eye. Clouds the colour of smudged charcoal break out across its watery surface. I open up my fingers and let my green eye pierce the view. Nothing changes. The clouds still hang in shreds around the sun, like the peeled fingers of silk gloves. Other visitors tut loudly as they walk past my tall, unburied corpse. They know who I am and they disapprove.

Who will show me any charity? I pull myself up from the ground very slowly. My shoes have rubbed, so I take them off and hide them in my skirt pockets. I want my feet to pick up the mud of the streets; I want to root myself in the place which has turned its back on me.

Retracing my steps to Linienstrasse, I catch sight of Frau Frankl on the other side of the street. She crosses over and hands me the wicker basket she's carrying – it contains a saucepan full of Sabbath cholent.

"A gift for you both," she says. "Besides, you will starve, if you don't eat something soon. And what would your mother have to say about that? Ach, what a woman she was. She made a hat out of leaves once. Wore it to synagogue. The heat from the candles melted the glue and the leaves tumbled about her shoulders. It was like Autumn in a minute."

Frau Frankl sees the tears in my eyes and pats my wrists. She invites me to go and drink coffee with her and Herr Frankl when I feel better, then she is away and I head back to Esau's where I find him absorbed in a reply he has received from his cousin. The good news is that Michael the Tailor is in need of a housekeeper and cook, but in the postscript he announces he's glad Esau didn't make a request for money, because business is slack and he is tightening his belt.

"He has done well for himself, in spite of this warning about tight belts," Esau sighs. "And there's hope for you, Esther, with such a position at Michael's. You're fifteen, you can make a new life for yourself."

But in exile, living amongst strangers? I remember Rachel and her shaking limbs, the pregnant woman selling her clothes for food and, suddenly, I feel hollowed out, like an empty egg shell. Force of habit encourages me to turn to Benjamin for help. I send him a note and ask him to join Esau and myself for supper that evening, trusting he will once again be able to rescue me. I have never cooked without Mama's guidance before – so it's with some apprehension I unearth Esau's little stove from under a pile of of ragged clothes. I'm going to bake a loaf of braided bread baked to Mama's recipe, which I will coat with egg yolk dipped on the end of a feather, just as she taught me. A dish of dried herrings and bowls of spinach soup complete the frugal meal, but Benjamin declares it is a banquet. When I serve him "potage" he throws up his hands in mock horror. Apparently, the local restaurants have all dropped the use of French names on their menu cards since the outbreak of war.

"Le potage is now Die Suppe – that's if it's available. If nothing else, we are learning to eat the words of a new vocabulary. But where will it end? You know, Judith tried to buy a turnip only this morning, but the last one was sold three days ago. Achje, you have herrings and spinach in plenty, Esau. You're a good housekeeper."

"I know a lot of people who need shirts."

"This war has everything back to front," Benjamin consoles, wiping my cheeks with the back of his jacket sleeve. "It may well be safer outside the city for the foreseeable future."

He is solicitous and I am wary.

"What about you, Benjamin?" I ask, as casually as I can. "What does the future hold for you?"

"I've got a clean bill of health," he says, taking his medical papers out of his pocket. "I can begin training next week."

"Why take the risk?" I interrupt him.

Benjamin's scowling face is all warning, but Esau plunges in after me, regardless.

"I must confess, I don't know what to make of it all," he muses. "One kills a reputation dead with her spite, another must shoot his brother in a hole in the ground. I fail to understand these rules of combat. I want only to close the next deal. Buy a new handcart..."

The dangers Benjamin faces signing up are all too real, but it's the idea of my exile to Augsburg which really frightens me. I thought I could survive it while I still had my two friends living in the Scheuenviertel, ready to welcome me back the minute it was safe for my return. But Benjamin's decision betrays that hope. I walk out on my friends and hide away in my improvised bed. For several weeks after this botched encounter, Esau begs me to make it up with Benjamin but I insist he come to me, clutching an olive branch. He stays away. Only at the very last minute, on the eve of my departure to Augsburg, does he send his Purim crown over by way of apology.

"Benjamin says when he comes back, he will play actor again," Esau reports. "But there is a war to fight in the meantime."

I put the crown on my head. I'm to be an exiled Queen, after all.

bats and peacocks

I leave for Augsburg the very next morning, dressed in my favourite peacock skirt. Michael the Tailor is a master craftsman and I'm no charity case, even if I do travel with a single carpet bag. Esau packs it into his handcart and we set off on foot for Zoo railway station. I am afraid Benjamin may have left Berlin without saying goodbye. I have a faint hope that I might bump into him on the same station platform, dressed in his uniform. But I discover only a lecherous train guard armed with a posy of winter greenery. My fame has, apparently, spread beyond the confines of the Scheuenviertel thanks to the newspapers which have picked up on the sensational story of an orphaned giantess. The train guard shows far too much curiosity. My reputation seemingly is this: I seduce men old enough to be my father.

"We are honoured, Fräulein Rosenbaum," he says with a leer. "There's a bottle of sekt on ice for you in the restaurant car, courtesy of the management."

Esau grabs the bouquet and throws it out of the train window.

"These newspaper stories about you are neither kind nor truthful," he warns. "You must be careful, even in Augsburg."

So my sanctuary is already a tainted place. I can hardly speak, I'm so sick with grief and confusion. Esau kisses my cheeks and hugs my torso as best he can with his delicate monkey frame. He smells of mothballs and there is stale egg yolk splattered on his waistcoat. As far as I know, Esau has never kissed anyone before, let alone a giantess going into exile. Then he is gone. I peek through the blind and I see him glance back. He's crying and I feel cruel, because I have no tears left inside me. The guard's whistle blows and the train moves away from the platform. As it picks up speed, I hear a voice calling my name. I wrench up the blind, expecting to see Esau, but discover Benjamin running to keep up with the train. He is wearing his threadbare green frock coat. I kneel down on the floor so I can better see his face. His beautiful hands pluck imaginary chords out of the air and his mouth opens and shuts, like a film actor's. What is he trying to tell me? All these days of shamed silence. We have been as bad as each other. ·

I reach out through the window towards Benjamin, who has become a blur of colour. My hands fall back against the side of the train door. I think I hear the familiar sound of a violin. Maybe Benjamin has strapped his violin case to his back and he's pulled it free to play me a last tune? I imagine the notes of a Purimpsiel song filtering through the air, as I sink down on the carriage floor and watch my old world disappear in a rush of cloud and steel.

I'm a felled pine tree. I'm cherry blossom lying in a gutter. I'm a dovecote fallen into disrepair. I glimpse these things out of the train window on my way into exile. The train's wheels pound strange rhythms inside my head: pine, cherry, dove; dove, cherry, pine. The train travels through rain soaked pine forests and tiny villages where the tiled roofs of houses slope down to the ground. A ruined castle on a hill welcomes me with a flag – Rapunzel's tower shrunk to the size of a thimble. Children play around a disused well hidden under a thicket of trees; old men tend allotments by a river. The trees fringing watery fields smudge their surfaces grey, green and blue. Women twirl their umbrellas dry on Leipzig railway station. I'm halfway to Augsburg and I try to remember my life before this journey, but I fail. I'm the felled tree. I'm the man cycling through the fields, holding an umbrella in his hand. I'm the rain. I can't remember Esther Rosenbaum.

Was this how the strangers felt when they came to Berlin, their lives packed up in brown paper parcels? I have my carpet bag, filled with tapestry skirts and pastries Esau has given me for the journey – all this and his winter coat-enveloping love, but everything else I've had to leave behind. I shuffle my skirt and try and find a picture that will help me tell the story of my flight, but it's all a blur through my tears. What use are stories now?

I arrive in Augsburg late in the evening. I uncurl from my seat, only after everybody else has left the train. I negotiate my way out of the compartment, stooping so low I almost fall out on my hands and knees. A fellow traveller runs up to help, but when he sees my full length he stands back, perplexed. Then a smile breaks out on his face. He has two teeth, like a baby's, and a lizard tongue that jumps out of his mouth.

"You with the circus people, lady?"

"No. I've come to stay with Michael the Tailor in Halderstrasse. Can you give me directions, sir?"

He puffs up his chest, pushes back his cap and begins considering my best option.

"You on foot?' he conjectures. "Well, it's not far from here. Five, ten minutes at a guess. Family are you?"

"Friend."

"Well, take a left past the tram stop, Fräulein, and you'll soon be in Halderstrasse. You can't miss it, as it happens. Building a synagogue up there. Follow the row of houses you'll see leading away from the building site and you'll find Jakoby's house at the end. Watch out for a pair of tall gates – he's holed up behind those." He takes another look at me, from the toes of my boots to the knot of hair I've tied up on top of my head. "And good luck, Fräulein."

I pull up the hood of my cloak and turn left as instructed. I immediately find myself in the middle of a building site where workmen in newspaper hats are busy with wheelbarrows and ladders. I glimpse the smudged outline of a large dome through the rain, which has got heavier as I move into Halderstrasse. The sky is pressing down on the building site, like a big fat thumb. The edge of the pavement is clogged with wet sand and fallen leaves. On I go, past a row of six-storey houses, which thread their way in the opposite direction to the synagogue. These houses are built on a grand scale, decorated with all kinds of marbles and artificial columns carved into their facades. Apart from the synagogue workers, there is no one else around. It is a far cry from the Scheuenviertel where there would be dozens of street peddlers hawking their wares from the boxes they carry on their backs; there are no angry altercations, gossiping friends, no Esau and his barrow, no refugees huddled in doorways repairing their shoes with old rags.

I find the gates eventually. They are covered in rust and lean up in a lopsided fashion against two ivy coated door posts. The stonework has crumbled badly, like a dry bread loaf, and the two big urns sitting on top of the posts are buried under a pile of leaves. I can't see a house and wonder if I might have come to a back entrance by mistake.

"Fräulein Rosenbaum?" a shrill voice demands.

It's a short, dark-haired man, dressed in an embroidered skull cap and a black velvet smoking jacket over overalls. He stands at my hip level, his fingers threaded through the bars of one of the gates.

"Herr Jakoby?" I reply, but I know the answer already just by looking at the man.

He has the same features as his cousin: dark brown eyes, a thin mobile mouth and hands with veins so close to the skin they look like worms surfacing from the soil. Studying me, his head stretches back and his brow wrinkles up. He has sideburns that have grown to a quite ridiculous length down his sheep-like face. I'm on my guard.

"You'd better come in, I suppose," he says. "Wait there."

He disappears from view and I stand waiting outside the gates. I feel like a beggar hoping for charity from the master of the house. A few minutes pass and Michael reappears, this time outside the gate. He must have made his way out from another entrance concealed in the shrubbery. Coming up to me, he grabs hold of my skirt and slaps at his forehead with his free hand, as if in great pain.

"Who is responsible for such terrible stitching, Fräulein?" he barks. "A herringbone as wayward as this is a disgrace."

How dare he: my peacock skirt is a masterpiece – isn't it? My courage fails me. It's all been a terrible mistake. I'll buy a ticket home, but where exactly is home?

"There are two things you must consider if you intend staying," he warns. "First, never speak of your race. And secondly, you must never, ever, dress in such shabby city *finery*." The sneer placed on the last word releases my tears. I'm going to cry for ever, big, fat tears which try to tell Michael about the storm, about my parents' deaths and my reluctant exile. "Oh, there's a third," he adds, relentless. "Don't waste emotion on me, Fräulein."

He turns on his heel and I look to see where he is heading. A faint outline of a pathway leads under a tangle of lilac and rhododendron to the left of the iron gate. Follow I must, although I'm almost on my knees again. Michael takes me in a circular direction until we arrive at another small gate, which he unlocks with a key he wears on his watch chain. I find myself ankle deep in an overgrown garden – purple clovers, clock flowers, daisies and dandelions sweep over my feet. The garden is beautiful even though it has been badly neglected. I look up and find another six-storey house, topped with a gable roof. Michael opens the door and we walk straight into his ground floor workshop. There is only one garment on display that evening, a three-quarter length evening coat, but proof enough that Herr Jakoby deserves his reputation as a master tailor – the coat simply blazes colour, even in the dim light. The coat is a deep Prussian blue, with an ostrich feather collar and a lining covered in tiny gold stars. I walk up to the dummy to take a closer look.

"Don't touch!" Michael shouts. "It's a couture garment that you must treat like you would the Kaiser's jewels. There is to be no meddling in here, you understand?"

He fidgets with the coat and I notice his supernaturally long hands, like a pianist's. All of his actions are quick, but measured. This is a man who is used to sizing up a piece of fabric and understanding in an instant how best it will cut and fold. He makes a few adjustments to the coat's collar, but they are invisible to my untrained eye. Before I can ask who the coat is for, he bundles me out of the workshop and in to a dining room furnished with a large gate-legged table and an enormous sideboard. One pillar is much taller than the rest and ends in a lily pad. I'm on eye level with it. There is a chaise longue drawn up under the window sill opposite the dresser and this I learn is to be my new bed.

"Blankets and so on in the chest," he offers by way of explanation. "I will be up at sunrise. That's when my working day begins. I'll want the fire laid in the workshop and a pot of coffee left on the sill. Can you manage that?"

I nod, although I have no idea where to find coals, or coffee. I assume Michael will tell me in the morning. He scuttles away into the workshop, leaving me with a plate of bread and cheese and a smoky candle. The moon has already risen, a fat yellow orb which shines so brightly I dispense with my candle. I perch on my improvised bed and discover it's far too small. I start thinking about Esau and wonder if I might ever see him again. I've got this idea I'll never see anything familiar ever again. Michael's apartment will never feel like home. I sleep badly, bunched up like an untidy ball of string on top of the chaise longue. It seems no time at all, before the sun rises – and Michael the Tailor with it. I'm horribly disorientated, after such a dismal start to my new life in Augsburg. Michael comes to show me the kitchen and I'm instantly on my guard again. It is a low-ceilinged room, barely the width of my outstretched arms, containing little more than a tiny wood stove, a few pots and pans and a pile of logs wedged up under the butler skin.

Michael waves his arm in the direction of a single shelf on which is stored a bag of coffee, some sugar and a wooden box with a loaf of bread. A small pantry next door has a few more stores, but it could never be mistaken for Ali Baba's cave of riches. Michael has an urgent commission to work on and suggests I go out and "get my bearings", after making his coffee. He declines to eat, claiming he prefers to do that after a morning's sewing. He offers little more in the way of guidance, so I decide to keep the cathedral as my compass point, and sniff out any route I can.

I walk in circles, sometimes squeezing myself through the narrow passageways that run alongside the canals, which criss-cross the city, at other times presenting myself to the world at large in the elegant Maximilianstrasse. I feel as though I am walking through an opera set in anticipation of meeting a frock-coated man servant, who will whisk me away to a chicken and beer supper. I'm tall enough to see into the top storeys of these houses. I even manage to rescue a dog that has backed off a first-floor window sill. I pick him up and hand him back to his startled owner, a boy with hair as red as my own.

I believe this city must be dusted and polished overnight, because it is so neat. Threading my way up to the Rathaus, I pass through winding streets where the leaves of weeping willows brush against my arms. The city is full of little parks and imposing red brick houses with delicate white paintwork. A café owner greets me, as he shakes out his tablecloths. The sun is bright and warm and it feels like spring already. I pull off my hat and, turning the next corner, come across a man sitting on a stool playing the spoons.

"A pfennig a song, Fräulein," he cries out between tunes. When his spoons tumble to his feet, he whistles me a song instead. My very own tune, what a bargain. I feel the sun on my bones and wish I could sing, or play the spoons and make people laugh as they go about their daily business. In the Hofgarten, statues peer out from behind lilac bushes. A nun in a white cap, secured with a big bow under her chin, calls out a blessing when I sneeze into my sleeve. I sit down on a bench and watch a woman in a black beret read her way through a newspaper.

Returning to Michael's apartment, I pause to watch the builders at work on the synagogue site. Two of the workmen sit outside a makeshift office, constructed out of old planks of wood. They drink cups of coffee and seem preoccupied by the small stones they have laid out in the sand at their feet. It's only when I step closer, I realise they are plotting a design for a mosaic. Both men wear newspaper hats and their overalls are thick with plaster and dust. One's about fifty, stocky as a bear with a zig-zag nose; his companion no older than me, wiry and gangly with enormous feet that look as if he might find them impossible to lift. The young man spots me first. His mouth drops open and he spills his coffee. This alerts his friend.

"It's only the giantess I told you about," he remarks casually, before returning to the mosaic at his feet.

I realise then it's the man I met on the station platform. He has been transformed by his coat of plaster.

"Fräulein Rosenbaum," I reply, holding out my hand. The young man hesitates then stands up, cleans his hand on his trouser leg and offers it to me.

"Good morning, Fräulein Rosenbaum," he says. "I'm Frank Smolin and this is the site foreman Wilhelm Grass. We are at your service." He jerks forwards in a little bow, causing Wilhelm to laugh out loud. "Are you planning to turn butler then?" he mocks. "The boy is a noodle. You found Herr Jakoby's place then?" he asks, after a short pause. I remember his warning about going to the tailor's when we first met. I think he does too. He fiddles with a few pieces of mosaic and then returns his attention to me.

"I did, thank you, Herr Grass."

"You'll not thank me soon enough," he retorts. "Jakoby is a miser and a cheat. I wouldn't trust him any more than I would an Englishman."

Frank is searching in his hod bag, whilst this exchange goes on. He produces a blue and white striped paper bag full of apples and offers me one. "You must visit the market as early as you can to get fruit, like this," he says, evidently trying to switch the subject.

"Jakoby eats boiled turnips, not fruit," Wilhelm immediately thwarts him.

"I've not been given any menus yet, Herr Grass.'

"Menus?" Wilhelm's eyebrows shoot up his plaster forehead forming two little V's. "You'll have a long wait, Fräulein Rosenbaum," he reveals. "A pan of boiling water; a peeled turnip. That's all you'll be needing in that household. And nerves of steel."

"Why do you dislike him so much?" I ask, intrigued by his angry dismissal of my new employer.

"Sacked my wife to take you on," he explains – without pulling his punches. "He told her you would be cheap, because you were desperate for work."

I blush, although I can hardly be blamed for my employer's actions. Frank gives me a concerned look. I don't think he can be much more than fifteen and he doesn't look very robust, unlike his colleague. He offers me another apple and invites me to come back to the site in order to view the elaborate fixtures and fittings that are going to be set into place soon.

"It will be the most brilliant synagogue people have ever seen," he enthuses. "Gold candelabras as big as you are, Fräulein Rosenbaum, and hundreds of crystal lights. We're designing mosaics for the cupola and the back wall of the women's gallery..."

"He's new to this business," Wilhelm interrupts. "He sees a bag of gravel and he wants to discuss it with his mother."

He knocks Frank's hat off and ruffles his hair. I remember Pappa then and my eyes prickle with tears. Right now, he seems as fantastical to me as a gold candlestick must be to poor Frank. My evident distress brings both men up short. Frank looks to Wilhelm, but Wilhelm looks at my shoes. The soles have come loose and sand from the site has leaked in.

"We must get you a pair of boots, if you mean to come back," Wilhelm observes, holding my gaze.

I realise he is a generous man beneath his gruff exterior. A week after my arrival, Wilhelm organises a whipround and commissions a shoemaker to make me a pair of black leather boots. He draws round my feet on a piece of cardboard to make sure the fit is right. I soon have a pair of button boots with little wedge heels and laces that thread up like spiders' webs. Before long, I'm able to make regular visits to my new friends. When work commitments allow, we sit together outside the makeshift office, drinking tea and studying the technical drawings which Wilhelm and Frank must create in bricks and mortar.

The first thing I concoct in my new home is a boot-shaped cheesecake topped with honey coated apples slices – for Wilhelm and Frank. I'm gaining confidence. No family, or Benjamin, to talk me into a good humour, but Frank and Wilhelm's quips and compliments. If I took more, would I be greedy? Those first few months in Augsburg I settle for a half-empty belly.

The year turns and its nearly Easter, before I come across another Augsburg resident with a reputation. Frau Brecht is the first woman in the city to drive a motor car, and she has quickly won notoriety. She manages to drive over one of the altar griffins left propped by Wilhelm's office, and causes further uproar. By the time I arrive, the arguments have dwindled and Frau Brecht sits resplendent behind the wheel of her car, which is battered and scratched from a dozen or more such confrontations. She wears leather gauntlets and a pair of goggles, which give her the appearance of a bug-eyed nightfly. When I loom into view, she removes the goggles and replaces them with an ornate pair of opera binoculars.

"Good lord!" she booms. "Why are you so tall, Fräulein? You should have been born a man, I think. But there we are, this world was not invented to give us what we most want in life. If it were, I would be a jockey, you know."

I'm so struck by this idea of Frau Brecht on a racing horse I fail to feel offended by her candid remarks about my appearance. Her lack of contrition for the damage she has done is staggering – and admirable. I warm to her as she sits ignoring calls for a policeman to be summoned to adjudicate. Maybe I can thread her onto my necklace of friendship?

"Stand upright, Fräulein!" Frau Brecht commands. "No good ever came of walking about with your nose to the floor. You'll miss all the action I provide in this hell of a place."

With this, she honks her car horn and reverses away from the smashed griffin. She knocks down a couple of fence posts, squashes a cardboard box and ricochets back on to the road. Wilhelm leads the round of applause from the site workers.

"Bravo," he calls out after Frau Brecht. "The mad old bat didn't manage to kill anyone this time."

grandmother Brecht
takes the upper hand

augsburg, 1916

T he Easter holiday might be upon us, but Michael the Tailor is in a most unseasonal mood. He has misplaced a blouse and the buyer is due any minute.

"But if I lost her custom, Esther, would it be such a tragedy?" he ponders. "She has a reputation, you see."

"What for, Herr Jakoby?"

"Eccentricity," Michael confirms. "Normally, I wouldn't do business with such a woman, but a sale is a sale, and I make many sales with Frau Brecht. A good thing too, as I'm a poor tailor with a gargantuan cuckoo-in-the-nest to feed."

"But we've already met at the building site," I explain. "She ran over a statue."

"Only a statue?" Michael snorts. "We should offer up prayers. She's a complete menace on the road – and everywhere else come to think of it."

"She said she would like to be a jockey."

"She's a gambler, Esther. Beware."

I'm not sure whether to leave the workshop and so avoid the menacing gambler, or to stay put and search for the missing blouse. I'm still dithering when Frau Brecht suddenly appears by my side, stopping abruptly like a dog fighting its choking chain.

"Didn't I warn you before, Fräulein?" she shouts in the direction of my ear. "Head up, chin up."

Seen at close range, Frau Brecht is a dumpy and untidy woman, with

45

large grass stains all over her car coat. She wears her opera binoculars around her neck, hanging from a string of ebony beads. Much to my amazement, she sits down on Michael's workbench uninvited, leaving him silenced (although he does have several dressmaking pins wedged between his teeth). He is hunched up working intently on a piece of silk. His fingers pluck at the fabric, as gentle as an insect's wings. Frau Brecht sits swinging her legs to and fro, stopping only to study one of his sketches through her binoculars.

"This is a splendid coat, Herr Jakoby," she concludes. "I would wear it myself, if I ever went anywhere other than the races."

"You visit your son, Frau Brecht," Michael replies, removing the pins momentarily.

"When we are on speaking terms, but luckily that's a rare enough occurrence these days," she replies with a wink in my direction.

She starts to quiz Michael about what she describes as "my intriguing arrival." Michael raises his eyebrows and stabs even more viciously at the piece of cloth he is working. As they parry, I pick out threads of Frau Brecht's history. She has a son living in Holbeinstrasse who she argues with constantly, largely because he disapproves of her behaviour on and off the racecourse. He buys materials for a local paper factory, and is motivated by very little beyond his accounts ledger. She ignores him and lavishes her devotion instead onto Bertolt, her grandson. He is a regular visitor to her home in Hinterer Lech, a street flanked by one of the city's canals and close to the celebrated Café Voltaire.

"Have you eaten there yet, Esther?" she asks.

"No, I have work to do, the cooking, the accounts, the orders…"

"Work?" she asks, incredulous at such a suggestion. "Cooking and cleaning for this spindly legged man? Ach, how can that be a life? You should come and taste one of Schwarz's cakes and then you would understand all about baking. He is a master konditor who trained in Berlin and is nothing less than a genius."

I'd like to know more about a fellow cook, but Frau Brecht shifts topics as fast as a card shuffler.

"Do you drive?" she fires at me next. "Ach, of course not. You will be preserving your reputation – God knows why. How you behave, frankly, should be your own affair and no one else's. Take my example: I drive myself round, as you know, and my son is furious. He thinks women should sit still and watch him steer. The very idea. And to think I gave birth to him."

I giggle but Frau Brecht has another favour to ask of me – one that has the potential to make Michael swallow all his pins at once in shock.

"Will you come and drink chocolate with me at Café Voltaire, Esther?"she asks. "I have a table booked. They're waiting for me." Michael splutters, but Frau Brecht is an astute woman. She follows up her unusual request by ordering a new car coat, a tactic she must know will result in my boss failing to argue about the propriety of being seen out drinking with a servant. Much to my concern, however, she then announces we will drive to Café Voltaire. I fold myself up on the back seat and as we shoot off down the road my worries mount. Frau Brecht plays absentmindedly with her accelerator pedal, as if her actual speed bore no possible relation to the terrain we pass through. She keeps swivelling her head round to ask me questions, honking her car horn at the same time.

On reaching Café Voltaire (miraculously unharmed), we assemble around a marble table set up on the cobblestones. Frau Brecht sits on the table, so she can "look me in the eye". She is as nosy as a judge. The rest of the café's clientele are sitting indoors. They watch in barely disguised disbelief our arrival outside. One man by the window adjusts his pince-nez and fixes me with his beady eye. He shakes his head and makes some comment to his companion. The waiter who hurries out to take our order also does a doubletake. I realise this will be a daily occurrence in my new home.

"Two hot chocolates and two of whatever Schwarz has baked in the way of a special today, please, Erich," Frau Brecht orders.

Erich disappears back inside the café and is mobbed by the two men in the window seat. Frau Brecht raps on the glass and breaks up their conversation, which I know I am the subject of. When she's satisfied Erich has set about his duties, she climbs back onto the table.

"Herr Jakoby tells me you bake a good cheesecake, but Schwarz could probably teach you new tricks."

She continues singing Schwarz's praises, as we wait for our hot chocolates to arrive. Erich finally brings them, served up in two big bowls, each one topped with whipped cream that curls up like bonfire smoke. The cakes follow swiftly. They are towering edifices made out of pastry and sponge cake and echo the shape of the city's onion-domed cathedral. Herr Schwarz has devised a deceptively simple method of construction, alternating four layers of shortcrust pastry and sponge. Each of the layers are soldered together with thin layers of orange cream. I pick up the onion dome and discover a chocolate praline pineapple hidden inside. Each subsequent mouthful convinces me I must meet with its creator, but Frau Brecht has bad news. Peter Schwarz is an albino. He rarely walks outside, because his eyes are so delicate. And he's supposedly extremely shy of strangers.

"But I'm a cook too, Frau Brecht," I point out.

"Can you possibly be in his league, though?" she reflects. "This man has made cakes for the Kaiser in the shape of Schloss Sanssouci – every window, every statue, every rosette recreated down to its last detail." She peers up at me and smiles mischievously.

"Served it up on a plate the size of this table along with a pair of binoculars so that you could inspect the accuracy of his reproduction."

Such achievements stun me, particularly as I barely have enough to make an omelette. Michael has me running around boxing orders and chasing up late payments, so I find myself cooking less and less. My job description has expanded into a full-time clerk–cum–accountant. We often eat bread and cheese and the little stove stays unlit for days at a time. I'm jealous of this cook, and wonder if I can take a peek at him. Frau Brecht sends a message via Erich, but we are rebuffed. Peter the Albino has gone home early. His eyes are not good – they have reacted badly to the afternoon's strong sunlight. His sincere apologies, etcetera, etcetera. Come back another day soon. I somehow doubt Frau Brecht will waste many more afternoons chatting with her tailor's cook. I'm disappointed. Frau Brecht spots this in a minute.

"I'll have words when I next see him," she reassures me. "He's susceptible to flattery. He's a man, just as much as he is a master konditor." I trust Frau Brecht to keep her promise. She will pin it up in her tatty grey bun and pull it out, like a conjuror does his rabbits, when she next has a dull day to fill. She tells me her days are very boring out of the racing season. I confess I've never been to the racetrack and Frau Brecht has to steady herself against the table.

"Never raced! My dear Esther, we must get you an education."

She makes another memo to herself and pins it up in her hair, alongside the willow leaves that seem to be permanently lodged up there. Then we part and I watch as her car scrapes its perilous way back down a crowded Steingasse. Luckily, Frau Brecht proves to be more reliable as a friend than a chauffeur – we take to drinking hot chocolate in Café Voltaire on a regular basis and she grills me about my life. She cries when she hears about the refugees and the aftermath of the storm. I want to gloss over it, but she insists I spell it out.

"People who hate the Jews are just narrow minded," she states, prodding the air with a pastry fork. "Minds narrow most when people fail to eat cake and debate. In this respect, my grandson Bertolt is a particular credit to me. He came into the world halfway through a debate with himself and he's never stopped since and that, I can vouch, is a good thing."

"I'm not sure I'm very good at debating," I venture. We are eating another of Schwarz's masterpieces: a sugar-spun willow tree with marzipan leaves.

"The trick is this, Esther: never argue on an empty stomach. A habit I have kept to for a lifetime and I can still cut the mustard, so to speak. I want to argue, I slice the cake."

There's no question Frau Brecht has many more arguments, after she takes up with me. Augsburg is shocked at what it sees. Frank keeps me up to date with the gossip. He's left the building site and joined up to fight a war that has already claimed the life of his younger brother. His regiment is heading for the trenches and he's busy calling on his various relatives.

"My aunties have never really liked Frau Brecht," he muses when we meet for a farewell coffee at Café Voltaire. "They don't like the fact she refuses to wear a hat; they moan because she's always tramping grass from the racecourse on to their carpets. As for her friendship with you, that's considered a step too far."

"Why should be being tall deny you friendship?" I ask.

Frank looks embarassed. "They are stupid and they don't think how they might hurt someone with their comments."

I blush. The army hasn't knocked compassion out of Frank, even if it has built up his shoulders and put a strain on the seams of his uniform jacket. Frank will be able to build walls with no trouble when he comes home on leave. But in the meantime, I need to build a wall of my own against the disputes erupting around me and Frau Brecht. She saves me in the end by asking me to join her household. A cook is a respectable position, after all. She even promises to buy me an apron and a cap when she makes her offer over hot chocolate and cake one afternoon in Café Voltaire. It's both a job offer and a birthday gift, she points out.

"Sixteen years old!" she sighs. "You have your whole career ahead of you, so Herr Jakoby will probably ask for compensation when you leave. But I shan't pay through the nose. I shall offer him the price of two new suits and no more. What do you say, Esther?"

I don't waste time on words. I walk out of Michael's life and into Frau Brecht's waiting car – she times me with the stopwatch she uses at the races.

"Five minutes flat," she remarks. "The speed of a true thoroughbred."

This is recommendation enough for a woman like Frau Brecht and it's not held against me when I boil the potatoes dry later that evening. What can I say, other than at last Augsburg feels like a home, a place I have come to from choice and not because I have been hounded away. I sleep in the attic, a large, airy room with a roof that points up like a Gothic church spire making it easy for me to stand up comfortably in its centre. I sleep on velvet and brocade cushions filched from a recent production of *Salome* in the local theatre.

The basement kitchen is equipped with everything a chef might need – even one like me who has been plunged into its boiling heat, like an overgrown lobster. Frau Brecht possesses a solitary cookbook, but I ignore that and turn to experiment. In the soft steam of the canalside kitchen, I find inspiration and turn alchemist. I work pans and griddle rack; big copper basins and a whisk the size of witch's broom.

I gradually find my voice again – in the dishes I cook up. These are my new stories – dishes that would not shame the banquets embroidered on my skirts. The secret of the culinary arts? A cook plays with the senses; he surprises, seduces, nurtures and cossets, just like the best storytellers do. I achieve all this when I join the Hinterer Lech household and finally feel at liberty to experiment in my new role. Better still, Frau Brecht likes what I serve up.

"Schwarz will have to watch his step," she crows. "You're catching him up with every new menu you create."

Our household is small: it consists of Frau Brecht, Mimi, the maid, and occasionally Bertolt. He is a skinny runt of a man, with closely cropped hair and bad teeth, but I take to him at once, because he's articulate. We barter words and I feel like a wine taster, rolling his words on my tongue and finding rare subtleties in their many flavourings. Bertolt is able to thread conversations up into extraordinary word necklaces, which I wear with growing pride. He sometimes helps me at the weekends when he's free from his duties as a tutor. He likes to pour boiling water over the ants that scuttle across the kitchen's stone-flagged floor.

"It's like a scene from the battlefields in Flanders," he observes one ant-killing day. "People are being murdered there with the same lack of concern. They die choking in mud holes."

I feel guilty about the ants and guilty about the men being shot down in their hundreds, but I don't really know that much about the war. I'm a cook, wreathed in perfumed steam. I might know by name many of the sons of Frau Brecht's neighbours who have been killed or wounded on the Western Front but I don't actually know them. These people haven't touched me. I pray for them in the newly opened synagogue though, a place of such calm you can scarcely believe in the idea of men choking to death in the trenches. Here, visitors are sheltered by a cupola-shaped heaven made out of thousands of pieces of blue and yellow ceramic. Stories and songs bind me to my fellow Jews, as tight as a ring on a swollen finger. They are invisible, but alive in the words that speak down the centuries. This is what Bertolt believes in too: the power of words. He just uses them in a different way to a synagogue cantor.

"I'm writing a play, Esther," Bert tells me one day. "Watching it will be like having your tooth pulled."

I tell him about the Purimspiels we staged in the Scheuenviertel. He is curious. He even makes me a Purim crown out of dandelions. I sit on the doorstep, drying my hair in a tea towel whilst he reads me his strange poems, full of brilliant, terrible words. He writes about poet murderers who seduce and abandon women and generally snub their noses at the authorities. Sometimes, he sings his poems in Gabler's Tavern, or in brothels. Pappa spent hours with his books, Bertolt no time at all. He's so busy shoe-horning the world into his songs, he doesn't even wash. His mouth is stained with tobacco and the lilac coloured ink he favours. To be blunt, he smells, but Frau Brecht warns me not to dismiss genius simply on the grounds of a lack of soap.

"We're at war," she points out. "He's saving vital resources."

She reads his poems when the races aren't running. The minute she finds a line she likes, she shouts the house down. We are all urged to assemble in her bedroom and listen to her read out the relevant pithy phrase, except for Mimi who busies herself rearranging boxes of jewellery on the dressing table.

"It don't make any sense," she objects.

"It's not supposed to," Frau Brecht chides.

"Well, what should it do then?"

"Bugger sense, that's what," Frau Brecht fumes. "This war has stripped us clean of reason. Hundreds of thousands killed to reclaim pieces of land no bigger than my garden. How do you write about that sensibly?"

In late October, we discover that Frank has become one of the missing. He is lost in some far off land in service to the Kaiser. Bertolt tells me I should write a poem instead of grieving. I hesitate. It's been a long while since I made up a story – let alone attempted to compose a poem. I start scribbling words down on the back of an old flour bag. I remember Frank rearranging my hair, because he thought it wrong that I tied it up in a knot and secured it with a fork or whatever came to hand when I left the house. He liked a woman's hair to be as elaborate as one of his drawings; pinned, plaited and secure. Now, Frank is dead in a hole in the ground, his own hair a tangle of muddy knots. Ach, it's unbearable. What good are words? My new world shakes and rattles as badly as the old. There are no stars, no heaven, no words that can knot us up, like a ring on a finger. I throw the flour bag away, but Bertolt rescues it. He rubs it flat with the palms of his filthy hands and smiles at my feeble verses.

"It should read like skin peeling off a wound," he says. "If that's what it feels like, then that's what you should write."

In the end, Bertolt steals Frank's story away in a song which he performs at Gabler's Tavern. It's a brutal, ugly song and doesn't reflect the Frank I knew, so I decide to bake a cake in his memory instead, filled with apples and knotted up like a plait of hair. Frank's Apfelkuchen is my first story-recipe, each ingredient and the method of its execution a reminder of something precious. Later, I help myself to a pearly button from one of Frank's work shirts left hanging on a nail in the makeshift office. I bury it under a tree which stands in a corner of the synagogue's courtyard. Frank was not a Jew, but he loved this building. He is in so many ways already buried here – he *is* the sunlit cupola's mosaic. And he's always remembered in our household whenever I serve up Frank's Apfelkuchen with a bowl of fresh cream.

ant men/moth women

Where to turn when my world spins like an autumn leaf? I assume Benjamin is overseas – his destination unknown – and Esau couldn't read an SOS even I sent him one. There is no consolation from the past, so I anchor myself in my kitchen and unleash a culinary onslaught.

I concoct a sense of purpose – a pinch of imagination, a dash of optimism – which punctures my grief when I least expect it to. Bertolt loves the cooking of his father's household. Tastebuds can do more than a photograph, or a letter, to conjure up life as it was, he argues. I don't disagree. He has succeeded in deferring the draft by getting appointed as a tutor and arrives at my lair most weekends. I'm not sure what he teaches, but he lends me dozens of American thrillers in translation. He also plays his guitar out on the kitchen steps for hours at a time and manages to persuade me back into the world, that is to say, back to Café Voltaire. He feeds me cake on the end on a pastry fork and I tell him all about Peter The Albino, my invisible rival. Bertolt begs an audience for me, but the shy konditor continues to elude me.

"You'll have to lie in wait, like a thief," Bertolt advises. "When he leaves the café, knock him out cold and tuck him up under your arm. Bring him back to the house for questioning. Oma will demolish his resistance."

"You read too many thrillers, Bertolt. Besides, I'd make a lousy thief. And how could I hide anywhere?"

"We need good old-fashioned luck," he suggests.

But luck, as I know to my cost, is not in the habit of cosying up to me. But Peter has had some luck in his life, so says Erich, who turns

54

out to be head waiter at Café Voltaire.

"Herr Schwarz was excused service in the Kaiser's army because of his raspberry-coloured eyes," he explains. "He only came here, after trying out his luck here, there and everywhere else. He says it's temporary, mind, because he's going back to Berlin when the war ends."

When the war ends. The spell we all repeat in desperation that the fighting will one day come to a halt and there will be no more ants crawling into cracks of blistered earth to die.

"How does Herr Schwarz create such wonderful cakes with all the food shortages?" I ask Erich.

He busies himself sorting out an unravelling napkin and fails to reply. I'm about to repeat my question, but Bertolt decides to answer for him.

"Herr Schwarz has patrons, Esther. And he knows how to play the black market better than most. Oma is a "patron". She's been stealing herbs from your kitchen garden for ages. That's why we don't drink ersatz coffee when we come here."

We may drink real coffee, but I still fail to win an audience with Peter the Albino. He does, however, makes his presence felt in my life in a very distinctive fashion. After Frank goes missing, I start receiving small cardboard boxes in the post, each one filled with tiny, handmade chocolates, all intricate as a piece of jewellery. I know instinctively that they are gifts from Peter and I'm flattered. He has heard I am a chef too. Sometimes, his chocolates are flavoured with spirits, sometimes with fresh cream. Such luxurious ingredients when so many lack even twisted, rotten vegetables for their supper! I feel guilty touching such masterpieces, but Bertolt has no such qualms. He scoops them up in his ink-stained fingers and swallows them down in one go. There are lines of poetry inside the boxes, concealed behind the tissue paper lining, which Bertolt reveals are from poems written by Baudelaire, Mallarmé and Rimbaud. He approves, if only because these are his own role models.

"A pastry chef with a love of poetry," he declares admiringly. "What more can a girl want?"

Do I write him a list here and now? Maybe I should, but Bertolt is keen to get to the races. The Challenger Cup meeting in Böcklin looms and the household in Hinterer Lech is in uproar. "Oma is determined to take you to the races with us," Bertolt warns. "You haven't lived in her opinion until you've placed a bet."

I'm intrigued, in spite of myself. It's Purimspiel all over again with a mock Gothic pavilion as backdrop, laced inside and out with black timbers. The pavilion's hall is dominated by an enormous chandelier, which spills candle grease from its many sconces onto the floorboards below. I can feel the nubbly texture through the soles of my boots. There is a large fireplace at the far end of the hall, decorated with plaques and cups won by champion horses whose old iron shoes line the entrance doors opposite. Inside the pavilion, I encounter a cluster of women in unusual, eye catching attire. They look like Benjamin did as Queen Esther: powder pale, with orange and purple lips; their dresses as thin as a moth's wing. They smoke and drink as fast as the racehorse owners and their friends, who scatter bank notes over them like confetti. Bertolt spots them too. He lights a cigar and hands it over to me.

"They are whores, Esther," he points out.

I blush, not because of his crudity, but because I'm plain, and being plain is the real crime here, not the scams worked by the bookies and the horse owners. You don't get to wear tissue dresses and feather boas being plain is what Bertolt actually means. I lack the rounded cheeks and dimpled chins of the cocottes; my face is far too long and my cheekbones collide with my mouth, which is as thin as a pencil.

"You've got a strong face, Esther," Bertolt consoles. "You shouldn't despair. You look like one of Oma's old lovers, you know, the one we must never mention." He takes another puff on his cigar and drops his voice to a conspiratorial whisper. "Maybe she hasn't told you about him yet? A Junker no less with shoulders so broad, you could hang off them like a bat." He's trying to make me laugh, but I'm wrapped up in this new challenge, sparked off by the sight of real women.

"I used to climb trees, Bertolt, but when I got so tall I thought what is the point? I can see everything I need to see just by standing up."

"Nothing every really comes from swinging about on trees," Bertolt points out. "Stand tall and to hell with all the rest."

"But when you're as tall as I am, it just feels as if you're committing a crime."

"Well, now you mention it, how on earth are you going to win a kiss?" he says in a jokey manner which I know is meant to mollify me, but I blush instead.

I'm nearly seventeen years old and I've never really been kissed by a man, well, not unless you count Pappa and Benjamin – and Frank. He once took my hand and kissed it. Would there ever be anyone who would want to kiss such a hollow face as mine? I think back to the courtyard in Gipstrasse. The boys assaulted me and chanted ugly rhymes whenever I walked past. I made friends with the squirrels and the birds who lived in the parks instead. Later, I got to know Benjamin Stein, but look where that has landed me: into boiling hot water. I'm just like one of the pathetic ants I kill in my kitchen. I have that much value in a world which judges me solely on my appearance and on nothing I might have to say.

I'm interrupted in my line of thought by one of the moth-dress women. She walks up to me stinking of smoke, a shred of tobacco resting on her top lip. She climbs up on a nearby chair so we are nearly at eye level. I hear her friends, and the racehorse owners shriek with laughter in the distance.

"They've made a bet with me, Fräulein," she sneers. "They've dared me to come over and talk to you." I stare at the woman's orange mouth and cry without saying a word. The stranger suddenly ducks her head forwards and licks up a stray tear. What does grief taste like, I want to ask her?

"I suppose if you own a mirror you must cry all the time," the stranger observes.

I can't move, I can't speak. The intruder stays standing on her chair, smoking and taunting me in turn. I push her off her perch and she ends up a long way down, sprawled like an upturned ant. It's my turn to laugh, but I can't make my mouth work. Bertolt curses, I stand crying, whilst the woman with the tobacco mouth struggles to her feet. Her shoes have come off in her fall, tiny pink mules decorated with glittering beads. Bertolt picks them up. He throws one of the shoes at the woman as she runs away, but I pluck away its pair. It looks like a doll's shoe lying inside my big paw. I could never wear such beautiful, tiny shoes. If they were mine, they would have to be as big as boats. Bertolt is at my hip. I look down on his cropped head and I want to kiss it in gratitude, but I know I'll topple over if I try. Boat shoe woman with her trapped kisses. They beat at my mouth, like a horde of butterflies.

Later that same night, I make a study of myself in the dancer's mirror that stands in my attic room. I kneel down in front of it and try and unravel my body's distorted proportions: my nipples are two large buttons set in ponds of wrinkled skin; my hip bones punch out of my sides like clenched fists. My stomach is swollen like it is each month, giving me the contours of a woman but only for a short while. I shut myself away and hide under my cushions. I curl up and wait for the tension to ease. I'm a storm waiting to break – electric, brooding, my imagination dancing over possibilities, like a bird over rocking waves. I stroke myself all over; bone erupts through skin. A bone of longing.

Rumours multiply during my cloistered absence from the world at large: the war is about to end. Frau Brecht is at the hub of things, driving over to Malkeston's, an infamous café-kabarett in Munich, to plot revolution over glasses of Mampe Halb und Halb, her favourite brandy. Speakers from Berlin come down to talk about the Republic they will set up in Bavaria to free people cut off from hope of change. The rumours wash over me, a wave that rolls and subsides. Unseen, unheard, except by the man who continues to send me chocolate boxes decorated with handwritten poems. I try and flesh out this invisible admirer in my daydreams. I skulk in the kitchen and order Mimi to go to the market for supplies instead of me. The months pass and Frau Brecht and her grandson conspire to lure me out of doors. They describe in loving detail the new cakes being cooked up in Café Voltaire; they tease me about missing my chance of meeting with Peter the Albino.

"You'll never be his match," Frau Brecht argues. "None of us can eat dreams and that's all you're concocting these days."

She frets over Mimi's ability to shop – she's always coming home with the wrong ingredients, or the wrong change. Frau Brecht issues me with an ultimatum: either I pitch in to the running of the household as I used to do, or I go back to Michael the Tailor's. She's adamant and brooks no discussion. I take several weeks plucking up courage to open the front door. The hum of voices in the street, the noise of the canal seem unbearably loud. I take a few tentative steps out of the door and into Hinterer Lech where I'm nearly flattened by someone who rushes past in the opposite direction. I sense a flash of colour – white and green – and the squeak of well-oiled boots. Watching the stranger gallop down the road, I wonder over his odd gait. His walk is more like an insect's flight, a translucent lacewing maybe, fluttering in a harsh current of air.

Frau Brecht is waiting for me on the steps when I return. She's almost dancing with excitement.

"You know who that was, don't you?" she calls out, before I've even started mounting the little set of steps leading to the door. "That was Peter the Albino. Didn't you see him?"

"Only briefly," I reply.

My first impression wasn't really that favourable.

"He looked very old with that white hair of his, Frau Brecht. How old is he?"

"He's an Albino, you fool," Frau Brecht sighs.

A few days later, I venture out again, but I don't bump into any more white-haired chefs. Truth telling, I'm disappointed. That pale, lacewing figure of a man has started me daydreaming all over again. I manage to walk as far as the synagogue where I sit for a while in the courtyard and remember my old friends Benjamin Stein and Esau Jakoby; before I know it I feel as solitary as Frank's buried shirt button.

The day I finally meet with Peter the Albino, it's like fate calling. A threat of rain is stinging the air and I'm forced to take shelter under a chestnut tree near Café Voltaire. I watch Erich through the leaves as he rushes the tables back inside the café. He's interrupted by a tall man with a shock of white hair who strides up to him from the direction of Hinterer Lech. The stranger is wearing a green eyeshade and an odd collection of patched military greatcoats with an old leather cartridge bag slung over his shoulder. He looks as if he has been hidden under a stone for centuries, his skin is so pale. I retreat into my leafy shelter, suddenly shy, but Erich pops up amongst the foliage and I'm chivvied out of my hideaway.

"Come and shelter inside the café, Fräulein Rosenbaum," he calls up to me. "Herr Schwarz insists. He's off to Munich to get his eyes tested and officially we're closed, but he says you're welcome to join him before he catches his train."

I'm surprised by Peter's offer, but I quickly follow Erich back into the café where he leaves me alone in what I think is an empty room. The evening breeze whips my hair out of its loose knot and this is how Peter first sees me: bent over double, my hair hanging down like a curtain. I throw my head back and it's like a piece of lightening which he catches, winding it up over his arm, before holding it in close to his eyes. His eyeshade bobs down and I glimpse a fringe of white hair. Then I realise he's actually smelling my hair.

"Camomile," he announces. "You wash your hair in flowers." He looks up at me. I think he might climb up to my eyes on my rope of hair, but he lets it drop. "Please take a seat, Fräulein Rosenbaum," he says, ushering me towards the one table that has yet to be stacked with chairs.

I opt to sit on the floor and Peter sits on a bar stool in front of me. Erich serves us real black coffee and then disappears into the kitchen. I feel less self-conscious in his absence and begin to inspect my host more fully. I see he has rubies for eyes and his eyelashes are long and feathery, like cushion tassels. Our first conversation sees us ploughing a familiar furrow: cooking (what else?). Peter has heard stories about my recipes and he has long wanted to meet with me.

"I rarely get to meet my fellow chefs, not since I left Berlin," Peter explains. "Frau Brecht's news of your latest recipes makes me feel as if I have not been abandoned." He tells me about his training with Milos Botticelli, the city's legendary konditor. "Everything you have eaten in here has been created using one of his recipes," he explains. "I write them down in my notebooks."

He produces his latest notebook from his greatcoat pocket. I recognise the handwriting from my chocolate boxes. I broach the subject, but he is instantly shy again.

"You've visited us many times, Fräulein Rosenbaum," Peter begins again, this time more hesitantly. "I remember you bringing two lobsters in here and we had to put them in a champagne bucket."

"A new recipe I was experimenting with, Herr Schwarz. And please call me Esther."

Peter speaks with his head tilted down, but I'm not disheartened. Maybe he can't look at me directly. Too much colour to absorb, but if he did take a look? I would be flushed through, the colour of a rose petal. He seems to read my train of thought.

"My eyes are weak, but my sense of smell more than makes up for them," he says. "Some smells explode inside me; others are more subtle, like your hair, Esther."

He takes a curl between his fingers, as he speaks. A sudden and intimate gesture that startles me. I wonder if he smells desire on me too? His gesture inspires me to be as bold as the racecourse prostitute. I lower my head and kiss his fingers. I want to move gracefully, but I'm aware the ratios between us are hugely out of kilter. A hunger has flared up inside me. I know its source, but I'm nervous. I'm a virgin and fragile as china, even though I stand seven feet tall. But Peter is fragile too. He lifts his head up and exposes his red eyes to my full stare. I kiss his eyelids, which are as pale as cream. He presses his nose into my neck, unbuttons my blouse and inhales the sweaty crack between my breasts. I smell him too – vanilla, marzipan and orange blossom essence. My arms wrap him in close, his tongue licks my skin. Desire will be translated into a new language, flesh pressed against flesh, but not yet. Peter has a train to catch. It doesn't matter. His lips must taste of me.

"You'll come to the house when Frau Brecht is next at the races?" I ask him, my voice shaky with all this new emotion. Peter nods and puts his eyeshade back on. There are instructions to be given and tables to be cleaned. I must go home now. The rain has stopped, so has my life, caught up on the tip of this man's tongue. Excitement makes my limbs careless. I glide home inside a body that has been tasted by another. When is he going to come to me? I lie on my velvet cushions and pray for Frau Brecht to go to the races. She has been little of late, because of a bad cold. I want to confide in her, like her grandson does, but I'm afraid. Frau Brecht was once a woman of the world. But what a liberty that would be, a cook revealing her sexual desires to the woman who pays her to bake apple strudel!

When Frau Brecht recovers, she tries to persuade me to return to the races. I tell her I've caught her cold. I sniff loudly for impact, far too loudly. She knows I'm lying and it upsets her. She even leaves her binoculars behind. I quickly order Mimi to go over to Café Voltaire to tell Erich to tell Peter that Frau Brecht has gone to the races. I time her with an old stopwatch of Frau Brecht's. She's barely away for a quarter of an hour, but I convince myself that Peter won't come, that he will have thought me too forward during our meeting over coffee in Café Voltaire. When Mimi turns up alone, my fears are confirmed. Mimi takes her time coming up to the attic where I've hidden myself, distraught at being stood up.

"Herr Schwarz is finishing boiling some chicken bones," she reports. "He'll be over when he's made his stock."

The door closes behind her with a loud bang. I sit bolt upright on the cushions which I threw myself on top of just minutes before. He has time to boil chickens whilst I wait like an over-excited child for Christmas morning. Bertolt puts in an appearance next. He's got the truth out of Mimi and is quick to act. He pokes his head round my bedroom door and wags a warning finger.

"That Albino is not what he seems," he says. "Don't trust a man who puts chicken bones before your own."

He disappears before I can throw something at him. When Peter does finally show, I'm on the verge of ordering Mimi to say I'm out, but I haven't the heart. I'm edgy as a scalded cat, but he is calm. He inspects my room, moving in on things closely to absorb their detail and smell. He's like a dog sniffing out new territory. His inspection finished, he asks me to undress slowly in front of him, a request that surprises me so much I just go ahead. Peter studies me through Frau Brecht's binoculars, as I undress. I realise he's trying to cut down my giant's scale.

"They say you have to taste a city, before you can belong to it," he pauses. "Maybe it's the same with your lover?"

He puts the binoculars down and undresses too. He's a long white needle of a man, no flesh on his bones either. We'll rub together and whoosh! we'll catch light like two sticks igniting a forest fire. His hands are white petals curled round the edges of my breasts; he slides over me, like a small white marble across a white marble floor. Our first time is full of strange gestures that I've not even imagined when studying myself in the mirror. We twist and turn like eels. We don't hear Frau Brecht return, even though doors probably slam shut and voices call out greetings as they always do when someone arrives home. Peter's fastidious nostrils give the game away – they quiver violently for several seconds and then he sneezes. He rushes for his clothes, but already there is the sound of footsteps mounting the stairs.

"It'll be Frau Brecht," I whisper as loudly as I dare. "Quick! Hide behind me."

Peter slips down behind the velvet cushions and I wrap myself up in my dressing gown. It's cut from a theatre backcloth, so there are harlequins and troubadours skating over my damp skin. Frau Brecht knocks (although I don't know why she bothers, she always walks into a room without waiting on an answer) and I fall back on my cushions feigning illness once more. Frau Brecht's nose wrinkles on entry, but she doesn't ask any awkward questions, opting to walk straight back out again. Peter follows shortly afterwards, tiptoeing down the stairs with his boots in his greatcoat pockets. He escapes only because Frau Brecht has registered everything.

"I was young myself," she chides me. "You deserve love, Esther, of course you do, but don't you dare go neglecting my kitchen garden!"

malkeston's

So, my affair with Peter begins. He is my first love – but his first love is cake making. I can't compete, but I'm not disheartened. Peter can teach me his culinary secrets, as well as advance my sexual know-how. It feels like a good deal, particularly when I finally conquer the art of creating an Arctic Albino. It's Peter's trademark dish and as complicated as anything I've yet devised. An Arctic Albino is built up from a perfect pastry square. A hard layer of iced white chocolate is put on top of the square, layered with soft cream and then another layer of white chocolate popped on top, followed by a crisp bed of vanilla flavoured pastry. And there you have it. I begin to understand why Peter is so obsessed with cake making – it is impossible to stay uninvolved when learning about its architectural possibilities, let alone the transformative powers it grants the person brandishing an egg whisk.

"Cooking has been my life for so long, I forgot there were other pleasures in the world," Peter admits. "I've only ever really liked one other woman, you see, a kitchen maid at Café Botticelli. But she always ignored me."

"What about your customers?" I ask, curious to know if I am the first to be tasted by the maestro of the whipped cream extravaganza.

Apparently not. A woman propositioned him once in a note written on top of the tablecloth at Café Botticelli. Peter filed the experience like he does all others: by its relevance to his all consuming profession.

"As I recollect, she had a back covered in moles," he says. "She looked like a sponge cake filled with raisins."

When I first met Peter, I made the mistake most people do. I assumed he was an invalid. In truth, he has the strength of three men. The army medical board was despairing when they had to turn him down, because of his eyesight – he could lift a tank out of the mud. But instead, he's required to bake cakes and he sleeps with me in Frau Brecht's attic. She couldn't give a pfennig for what I get up to on my Salome cushions. What concerns her is my seeming indifference to the world beyond. Frau Brecht tries to inject a flavour of that world into my attic room: a place in revolt where people are hungry – starved not just of food, but of the possibility of any meaningful change in their lives. She leaves stacks of leaflets in my room written by members of an organisation called the Spartakus Bund. The Bund opposes the war and Frau Brecht backs their cause. She has been arguing for months with Herr Braun, our butcher, about the conditions of surrender being negotiated at Versailles. Blame is apportioned, as neatly as the corpse of the cow Herr Braun chops up with his knife.

"You can come up with any number of treaties, Frau Brecht," he says. "You can sit over cigars and port and cut up an atlas, but what does that mean to the Bolsheviks and the Communists in our midst? They plot to steal what is ours. Then there's the Jews…"

Frau Brecht cancels her standing order and we start eating more vegetables. I don't understand the intricacies of the arguments waging around the Treaty of Versailles, but I do understand that the armistice will bring peace and an end to the terrible flow of telegrams that have destroyed our neighbours' lives. But wars don't end cleanly, like a full stop at the end of a sentence. Returning soldiers are spat at in the streets, because they are blamed for losing the fight. I see them walk past Café Voltaire, ravaged, men in name only; they have gaping holes where their perfect mouths once sat, their facial scars are stitched up so roughly, they resemble cheap rag dolls. Frau Brecht says the government is failing to deliver to these men, and to the dismal wretches who sleep five to a bed in Berlin's slums. I knew families like that in the Scheuenviertel, but I have tried to forget them; I prefer to wallow in the luxury of baking my lover's extraordinary recipes, or of spending nights with him tucked into the fold of my hip, like a snail inside its shell. Frau Brecht disabuses me of my illusions.

"Old soldiers beg in the streets, Esther, and what does the

government do for them now they are crippled and blind? There is talk of revolution. People want action, not words. And why not? They work their fingers to the bone for little reward."

I remember the refugees from Auguststrasse, their terrible, sad eyes; their daily survival based on little more than trading out of the contents of their coat pockets. They were ostracised and broken down by their poverty. Peter the Albino eats and breathes a sweet-flavoured world a hundred miles distant from the dispossessed. Frau Brecht has no time for such sugary sentiments. At her favourite café, Malkeston's, the legendary Rosa Luxemburg is to put in an appearance. Red Rosa, the head of the Spartakus Bund. Apparently she has one leg shorter than the other.

"A lady mind, always keeps her hat on. She makes you believe you can exist beyond the place allotted to you in this world. I think you should meet her, Esther. You would have a very different impression of what the Bund is trying to do then, I'm sure."

Certainty is a commodity I would dearly love to possess – it's in shorter supply than shoe polish these days – but I find myself weakening, in contrast to my indomitable employer. I discover Frau Brecht has been employed as a courier for Thomas Tucholski, one of the key figures in the Bund. She shifts piles of leaflets and newsletters around, like a hyperactive fly. She settles nowhere for long, it would seem: Munich, Augsburg; the café, the canal house, the kabaretts. Round and round she goes, making drops here and drops there, her illicit literature stowed away in any number of racing binocular cases like so many portable bombs.

I'm impressed by her energy and by her contacts. Not only is Thomas Tucholski a notorious opponent of the war, but he's also Kaya Tucholski's lover, the same actress who so impressed me when I was painting my lopsided backcloths in the Scheuenviertel. I confess this is the prompt which finally gets me over to Malkeston's.

"It's not just old birds like me propping up the bar, you know," Frau Brecht wheedles, sniffing up my interest in the Tucholskis and their ilk. "There are musicians playing every night who have to compete for their slots, so it's all high quality entertainment. Oh, and Bertolt performs there too."

"Bertolt knows the Tucholskis?" I'm hooked now and Frau Brecht knows it.

"We sent Herr Tucholski food when he was sent to prison back in 1916," she says, almost boastful. "Eighteen months in the Moabit for daring to speak out against the evil of war. Herr Tucholski stood up in Potsdam Square in Berlin in front of thousands of people and spoke out. Not a single shot was fired, but he secured a victory – hundreds of people tore up their call-up papers that day. What does that tell you about the true agents of change?"

Here in Augsburg, I only remember Michael the Tailor's more conservative clients praying for the Kaiser and his soldiers on the front line. The Malkeston circle prayed to overthrow a discredited military elite. Malkeston's regulars were often arrested. It's 1919 now and even with the war finally over, things have got worse still. People on the streets talk of betrayal, but not by the Allies at Versailles – no, the betrayers are the socialists and the Jews who sit in café-kabaretts like Malkeston's and plot revolution. The Freikorps, the government's shadowy force, raid such places and people get beaten up as they sit eating their supper. The streets beyond our canal-side retreat are literally on the move – set into motion by hundreds of marchers' feet. They find people dead on the cobblestones, nuns improvising prayers over them. This is our new life, Frau Brecht argues, not lovemaking in a cushioned hideaway.

Then Red Rosa is drowned in a canal and the revolutionaries want blood – or at the very least a chance to write up their own laws. Everything is topsy-turvy. It is Bertolt who reveals to us how things stand. He materialises at breakfast one morning in April after several months of absence – unshaven, his favourite red shirt torn at the collar.

"The government has gone into exile," he reveals, wolfing down mouthfuls of semmel rolls and chunks of cheese. "We run the world over coffee and brandies. Tucholski has sent word. You must come and join us, Oma. There's work to be done."

Frau Brecht is studying Bertolt through her binoculars. She tut tuts over the ruined shirt.

"I've waited a long time for this day, Bertolt, but it's come a little late for me," she says finally. "You will take Esther with you. She can't possibly stay stuck in my kitchen at such a time, can she? Both of you: get to Munich. Find out what's happening and report back. Oh, if I was forty years younger, I'd be there on the barricades with you. But I'm a lame duck now. "

She's lying. She's a spring chicken and more than capable of making the trip, but she wants me to make my debut at Malkeston's. So, another journey is plotted: I'm off to catch a train to Munich to celebrate the Bavarian Republic's coming of age in the company of balladeer Bertolt. He's adopted a new outfit for the occasion: concertina trousers and a battered leather jacket and matching cap. I wear a velvet cape which Frau Brecht has made for me out of yet another theatre backdrop. This one is adorned by silver paste stars and shiny pieces of broken mirror. I glint and gleam like a dozen moonbeams. Peter is horrified at my choice of wardrobe – and by my destination. He has heard of Café Malkeston and isn't impressed by its reputation.

"The head chef is a slut with no gift for pastry making," he points out. "The clientele must have been born without tastebuds. You shouldn't be mixing with such people."

"Look, I'm not going for dinner. I'm going to meet with the Tucholskis. They're film stars, Peter. Don't you think that's a step up?"

"Idiot!" he hisses. "They are just troublemakers who envy what other people have and think they only have to stamp their feet and they'll get it."

In Munich, I wonder if Peter's judgement hasn't some grain of truth in it. I'm surrounded by swarms of drunken partygoers, who flood the streets in all directions. It's as if a party is taking place in every courtyard with people either dancing knee high in dead cherry blossom, or lying flat on their backs in dried-out, ornamental fountains. Malkeston's itself lies hidden away in a courtyard off Türkenstrasse, lurking behind walls overgrown with twists of ivy. Inside, the café is as big as a railway station, lit by green glass lamps hung from long metal chains. The walls are covered with bill posters, calling cards and newspaper articles detailing the activities of the café's regulars. Props from revue shows are nailed around the archways that divide up the basement: Valentin's bicycle wheel and trombone; wax corpses modelled on murdered women from a freak show, and dozens of shoes donated by the singers who appear in the kabaretts.

My arrival hardly raises an eyebrow. Seemingly, there are more marvellous things to see than a giantess in the new Bavarian Republic. Herr Suschke, Malkeston's proprietor, wanders over to us. He wears a new apron and carries a tankard of sekt in each hand. He drinks from both intermittently.

"The Kaiser never deigned to drink with me, but Herr Tucholski does," he shouts out. "I've been photographed for the newspapers. What do you think, Herr Suschke as Minister of Food, perhaps?"

To converse, we have to battle against a thick wall of noise provided by the entertainment on a small stage. A young woman with bright pink hair dances up there, like a dervish, her dress as transparent as glass.

"It's Sissi Finck," Bertolt shouts up at me. "A regular. Sleeps with everyone in here. They carve her naked on the bars of soap in the toilets."

Herr Suschke pulls at my cloak. He's after an introduction. I stoop down and take one of the tankards offered me.

"You must try my wife's sausages, Fräulein Rosenbaum – a speciality of the house. Frau Suschke would be most obliged to you for a recommendation. You are, of course, more than welcome to just sit and enjoy our little party, but there again, maybe you would like to sing? We're always looking for new talent in here."

I turn down both offers. I'm still nervous about this escapade and I don't feel like eating. Besides, I can't sing a note. Bertolt pulls me onwards in to the thick of things, pointing out Thomas Tucholski and his colleagues. They are sitting opposite the stage, up on a landing that stretches out along one side of the basement wall. The revolutionary leaders sit in leather armchairs beneath a portrait of Herr Suschke.

"Do you see what it's made out of, Esther?" Bertolt shouts. "Hundreds of matchbox tops. No counting the number of people who have scribbled their autographs on that portrait. It's a ritual for first timers at Malkeston's. You'll be asked to add your signature tonight."

I only half-absorb Bertolt's explanations, because I'm busy studying the group of men sitting beneath the portrait. I guess which is Tucholski – the name he is always known by – without further prompting: his colleagues lean in towards him, holding onto his words like they would a climbing rope on a mountain. Tucholski's time in prison has left him looking lean and haggard. He has receding, pale blond hair and a stooped posture that suggests too many nights spent in too many café-kabaretts. He's thirty-six, according to Bertolt, but he looks much older. He encourages me to head on up the stairs to meet him. I make my way carefully up a spiral staircase, but just at that moment Tucholski is up on his feet addressing the crowd below.

"Tonight is all about our victory, comrades," he shouts down to them. "But we must stay vigilant. The forces of opposition are gathering. The government-in-exile is funding the war veterans. They are setting up military clubs as a front behind which they will operate a policy of repression. Our demonstrations and rallies will be targeted. They will try to overturn our successes…"

Tucholski is interrupted by a barrage of catcalls and hisses from his audience.

"The bastards couldn't get it right in France, so what hope here when we know where to find them?" yells one man, his face already disfigured with bruises delivered in some street brawl.

"Arses!" responds the man next to him. "Couldn't even find a stopper in a bottle."

Tucholski silences them with just a wave of his hand. I begin to imagine what he must have been like on Potsdam Square in Berlin, facing down the soldiers and police with nothing but a few well-chosen words.

"March down one street, the tail end of a counter-demonstration sneaks round the next corner," Tucholski continues. "Left, right; radical; conservative. I don't care about the label, just the need to build on what we have here, tonight. And that is your cue, comrades. Our work starts tomorrow. A Republic to erect, no matter what is thrown against us."

Shouting, applause and toasts collide like packs of noisy street dogs. The thrill of those early hours of popular rule! As he returns to his armchair, Tucholski sees my head pop up in the direction of his table and he stops in his tracks. Many have heard of me, no doubt, but my appearance can still shock. I smile and wave, but both seem inappropriate gestures. Maybe I should have wrapped a Spartakus Bund flag round my body? I realign myself once I'm out of the stairwell and discover I'm on eye level with Herr Suschke's portrait. Bertolt's signature is scrawled across his nose.

"Esther Rosenbaum?" Tucholski asks, but it's for form only. "It's good to see you here – and tonight of all nights," he adds, holding his hand up to me. We shake hands and Tucholski makes way, so I can prop myself up on a chaise longue close to the table where he sits alongside his comrades. He darts between that table and the chaise longue for the rest of the night. I'm impressed in spite of myself. My reservations are watered down by bottles of sekt and a style of rhetoric I last heard my father deliver, dressed in a newspaper wig and a tapestry cloak. Tucholski writes many of the pamphlets delivered by Frau Brecht to secret addresses. (I flinch: I've only ever used them to light fires in my bedroom).

"I've never doubted the anti-war protesters, Esther," he explains. "Nor has Kaya, my companion. You will have heard of her, I expect, if you go to the movies."

"Kaya Tucholski? But of course I have heard of her. She's the toast of Berlin's film world." I slug back another tankard of sekt. Kaya Tucholski is a star in a December night and she is this man's lover. It seems even more incredible after meeting him in these odd surroundings – a far cry from the fabulous sets of the Bebelsberg Studio. But it turns out she's even further removed from those surroundings than I gathered – since Tucholski's imprisonment, her own character has come under attack.

"Ach, you know her. Of course you do,' Tucholski continues. "But she has learnt a new role since I ended up in prison. In short, she is a smuggler, just like Frau Brecht. She distributes the Spartakus Letter in her vanity case. She's away on a mission at the moment. A shame. I would have liked you to meet."

"It must be dangerous, this smuggling," I reply, recalling his earlier stories about prison beatings.

"Well, yes it is, but the people who support this cause are not a handful of losers sitting in a broken-down bar waiting for punishment," he points out. "They are a moving mass, stretching out across our towns and capital city. You must join us and see for yourself how things stand." I'm incapable of sitting at this point, let alone anything more active. I giggle into my tankard. Tucholski doesn't seem to mind my lapse in manners. He slips me another drink and a newsletter.

"Tell me, Herr Tucholski," I demand. "Is Frau Brecht a heroine?"

"She's an idealist," he confirms. "We all are these days. But I like her, because she looks out for us and she expects so little in return. She wants to serve the cause, nothing more, nothing less. Our dreams for the future protect us, you see, Esther. We get drunk on our hopes and expectations."

It's not a reprimand. Tucholski has kind eyes behind his steel rimmed glasses. His eyes swing it for me. I realise I do want to get involved, but I'm not sure if I have the stomach to face down the Freikorps.

"I could distribute the Spartakus Letter in Augsburg, if you like," I offer. "I have contacts at Café Voltaire. They could hide your newsletters in their cake boxes."

"It will be a pleasure to work with you, I'm sure," Tucholski says, taking my hand and planting a kiss on the back of it.

Bertolt joins us at this juncture. He winks at me from across the table and I wink back. My inhibitions have suddenly lifted – I even ask Sissi Finck to teach me some of her more daring dance steps. I'm too tall to shimmy, but I improvise as best I can. The table shakes and the newsletters get scattered to the ground, but everyone just laughs and Tucholski proposes a toast: "To a giant success!" he calls out.

My head the next day is as heavy as a bath weighed down with coal. I can't even lift it from my pillows. I fall asleep with the door to my hotel room left wide open, because my legs are too long to fit in the box-sized room, and on waking discover the manager has had them covered with bedspreads to spare the other guests' blushes. I've just come round when Bertolt comes charging into my room. He hurdles over my knees and lands on the far side of the bed.

"There's been shooting this morning," he says. "And someone's nicked Suschke's portrait."

"Freikorps?"

"Looks that way," Bertolt replies, stuffing random pieces of my clothing into my carpet bag as he does so. "We're really in the shit this time when you think of the names that have signed that portrait – yours included. You can't stay a minute longer, that's for sure. The Tucholskis have left already. They've found refuge in Kaya's old convent school, tending beehives."

"How do you know that?" I ask, intrigued at the detail – and the image it conjures up of Tucholski in a wimple.

"I helped them. And I'm going to help you too. I suggest you go back to Berlin. Augsburg is unsafe now the authorities suspect Tucholski's distribution network has reached there. We've heard rumours to that effect, anyway."

"Informers?"

"Don't ask, just move as fast as you can," Bertolt says, his assertive manner surprising me out of my drunken stupor. "The trains are still running."

"But what about your grandmother? I can't just walk out on her. And then there's Peter…"

"You must go back and collect a few things, but you must leave the same day," Bert orders. "Oma will understand, trust me. Besides, I shall look out for her, as always. And God knows, Peter is in love with his bloody cakes, not you."

Once Bertolt has finished my packing, we make our way through side streets to get to the station and all the while we are conscious of the sound of gunfire and strange shouts and cries. Bertolt safely stows me away in a train compartment and disappears again. He won't tell me where he is going – or what he plans to do.

As the train limps off towards Augsburg, I mull over the evening's events. Bertolt is right. It might well be time to go back to Berlin. Peter's descriptions of the time he spent training at Café Botticelli, the best patisserie in the city, have long whetted my appetite for new challenges. I'm good enough to work in such a place, after receiving Peter's unofficial training, and Botticelli is, apparently, an improviser in his kitchen, just as I have tried to be. Peter claims that Botticelli can turn pears into swans; he even pipes icing into intricate designs that challenge those found in nature's snowflakes. But is this the right course of action in the circumstances? Revolution has broken out, the dogs of retribution are on my tail and I'm off to beg a job from a man who makes imitation snowflakes? Besides which, Peter has been kind to me: he's even offered me his recipes, which is like giving blood for a man like him. That's where his heart lies though, not with me or any other woman.

Ach, it's no good. Up the revolution, but down with the revolutionaries. Peter's talk of Botticelli and his pastry wonders have started up a new hunger inside me – and it's not to turn gadfly and deliver Tucholski's newsletters. I want to stake my claim where I belong. I was wronged by Frau Stein and her cabal after the storm and I want to turn the clock back. I want to act the revolutionary, but on my terms, not those of the Bund. I want a stage to appear on, but it must be a kitchen as legendary as any kabarett so that my story-recipes can finally make the headlines.

But my hopes are squashed when I arrive back in Augsburg. I arrive, but I fail to depart as instructed. In fact, I don't set foot out of the door for days, not after the Freikorps bring the Bavarian Revolution to a bloody end. Frau Brecht brandishes the newspapers in front of my face. She can't bring herself to ask the questions she longs to ask. Malkeston's has been plundered; I hide in the attic and the Tucholskis move silently amongst a convent's beehives, but what neither of us knows for certain is the fate of Frau Brecht's other comrades in the Spartakus Bund – or that of her ballad-singing grandson.

cooking up a storm...

The weeks pass and there is no word from Bertolt. I doctor the newspapers's reports and provide Frau Brecht with pared-down versions that avoid the bloody statistics of a civil uprising. Her worried face staring across the breakfast table ensures I also fail to mention my planned exit when things quieten down. She's not eating and takes to her bed for days at a time. She doesn't even read the racing news. I take her dishes of soft-boiled eggs, plates of grapes and slices of homebaked bread covered in poppy seeds, but I know it's Bertolt she really wants to see at her bedside.

"His friends will contact us, if there's been a problem" I soothe, as if he's out for a leisurely day's hike, rather than risking his life sidestepping bullets. "Besides, he's resourceful. He helped others get away from Munich. He can look after himself."

"Ach! Sacrificing his life for what? A new anthem and a silly flag. Why do they always do this to me, Esther?"

"Who?" I ask, puzzled at the idea that Frau Brecht knows anyone with a penchant for flag waving.

"Men and their preposterous ambitions, that's who."

I kneel down beside her.

"Is that what you felt for your Junker, Frau Brecht?" I ask cautiously. "Bertolt mentioned him to me. What happened?"

"What do you think happened?" Frau Brecht snaps. "He was cut down by a sabre in another long distance war that no one remembers now. But I've never fogotten him. Let me tell you something: keep Peter safe. You mustn't live with memories alone." I don't know what reply I can give. I no longer feel very sure about anything, or anyone. Spartakus Bund members not only drank in Café Voltaire but received their newsletters in the café's cake boxes courtesy of Frau Brecht. Peter has let panic overtake him. He's a spider trapped under glass, clawing at its edges. Although I took no active role in arranging the distribution, Peter nevertheless decides that I've betrayed him by allowing the Bund to use his boxes as cardboard courier pigeons. Frau Brecht notes my hesitation in replying.

"Peter might well have marzipan under his fingernails, Esther, but what's inside his heart?"

She prods me gently, as if hoping this will get me to explain myself better. Frau Brecht is tired of life's battles. She wants a happy ending, but I'm about to make a tragic opening. I lean forwards and take her hands between my own. Her fingernails curl into her palms; her skin has the texture of a dried-out house plant.

"I want to go back to Berlin," I confess. "In fact, it was Bertolt who suggested I go. It's too hot for me here. I'm linked with Malkeston's – and with Tucholski." I am blushing because it's Tucholski's name which comes to me first and not my lover's, but Frau Brecht doesn't notice. "Peter is too afraid of reprisals to ever let me visit him again," I quickly add, anxious to rectify things.

Frau Brecht inspects my face with her binoculars. I have got used to this habit of hers, but this time it feels as if she's probing inside my heart with her ivory-trimmed antennae.

"Is that why you've been dropping plates and shouting at Mimi? You didn't know how to tell me? Oh, Esther. I think we have been friends long enough to understand we both want the best for each other. If it is the right move, make it."

"I don't want to hurt you, Frau Brecht. I'm indebted to you, after all. When everyone else turned their backs on me, you gave me a job and a home. But I'm nineteen now. I should go and discover new things. But who will look after the garden? And who will cook for you? Mimi can scarcely boil a potato."

"Maybe Michael the Tailor has another orphan I can steal from under his nose?"

It's almost like old times. Frau Brecht agrees to take a look at the racing pages – she even asks me to place a few bets. "If I win, it means

Bertolt will be coming home."

The next day, I place her bets. Frau Brecht is surprisingly calm before the races begin. She goes out and sits in her herb garden, whilst I make her cups of hot chocolate to pass the time. She doesn't move from her chair, even when the telephone rings. Mimi takes the call out in the hall. I hear the receiver crash on the tiled floor and rush as fast as I can out of the kitchen.

"Esther! It's Bertolt!" Mimi cries.

Frau Brecht has seemingly won her bet, the wise old bird. Mimi picks up the receiver and hands it over. "Where are you, Bertolt?" I shout down the line. "Are you safe? Why no telegram, or message…?"

"Apprentice beekeepers must be careful they don't get stung, Esther…"

"Oh God, is this some kind of code?" I ask interrupting his infuriatingly cryptic response. "You must speak to your Oma. She's been desolate without you. We all have…"

"Where is she?" Bertolt interrupts me in turn.

"In the garden. I'll go and get her…"

"No, Esther. Another few minutes won't kill her. I'm at the station. I'll get a cab."

He's that close. It really is a miracle. I rush out to the garden to relate the news, but find Frau Brecht has fallen asleep. Back in the kitchen, I start preparations for a celebratory supper. We have beef, potatoes and sprigs of rosemary picked from the herb garden. I'm interrupted by the slamming of the front door and, suddenly, there is Bertolt: gaunt, filthy, but triumphant. He welcomes me by throwing a handful of dead bees at my head.

"In case you didn't believe me, Esther!"

"You should have brought honey," I reprimand him, but only because it stops me from crying.

He's here and that's all that matters. A rush of guilt, because I'm not really thinking about Frau Brecht's joy, but my own. Bertolt sweeps past my snivelling self and heads out to the herb garden. I give him quarter of an hour alone with his grandmother and then I let myself out the back door. I close it quietly behind me, but there is no need for such consideration – the four horsemen of the Apocalypse could gallop by and Frau Brecht would still fail to notice anything. Bertolt kneels beside her, clasping her hands. She holds her last betting slip, which I'm supposed to have cashed in. I stand frozen by the door completely unable to take in this spectacle. Bertolt catches sight of me, at last.

"Please leave us alone, Esther."

His cheeks are wet with tears. Frau Brecht's demise is not our only burden in these troubled times. In keeping with tradition, she lies in state in her coffin the night before her funeral. The coffin is set out on top of trestle tables in the parlour. Visitors come and go, but I take up a twenty-four hour vigil by her side. Frau Brecht was a gregarious woman and the idea of her spending her last night in her home without constant company seems wrong to me. Bertolt drops in and out too. He can't seem to settle in the presence of a dead woman – or a living one prone to bursting into tears for minutes at a time. Eventually, Bertolt reveals another reason for his grasshopper behaviour: he warns me again to leave Augsburg. He wants me to seek refuge somewhere he deems more liberal than Bavaria. His concern outweighs his grief momentarily and he fills me in on what has been happening in Munich since his absence. The Freikorps have emptied Malkeston's cellars. Franz Suschke has lost a drastic amount of weight – and many of his clients.

"There are still a few who speak out," he adds. "Kaya Tucholski for one. What a woman. She borrowed one of Franz's suits and sang her defiance from the top of a table."

This is not hard to imagine. But what has happened to Thomas Tucholski?

"He must lie low," Bertolt reveals. "The Chief is top of the wanted list."

I'm probably wavering somewhere at the bottom of the list, but it's dangerous all the same. I've signed Suschke's portrait, so I'll definitely be blacklisted by the Freikorps. Bertolt's signature condemns him too. He believes it's essential that we put distance between us – my leaving for Berlin will give us that opportunity and we'll be able to keep our enemies from jumping to conclusions.

"Lie low and let the dust settle," he says.

We are standing on either side of Frau Brecht's coffin. I want to offer some kind of gesture that will show my friend my gratitude, but he holds himself rigid and gives nothing more away. I think he wants to be left alone to make his final farewell to his grandmother, so I leave the room to give him the opportunity. On my return, I notice that he doesn't seem to have moved from the spot where I originally left him. Bertolt leaves shortly afterwards for his father's house, but repeats his warning a second time before closing the front door. It's only later, when I make my farewell to Frau Brecht, that I see something has been tucked in under her hands, which lie folded on top of her breast. I dig out a photograph, which shows a man in a Junker's military uniform.

The day after the funeral, Peter takes a detour on his way to work and comes to hunt me out at Frau Brecht's old home.

"What have you got yourself involved with now?" he challenges me. Peter has come to issue me a warning too. He is frightened of associating with a revolutionary – but even more indignant that my antics in Munich have meant I missed a chance to learn to bake a perfect Bienenstich, a "beesting" cake. I am never to cross the threshold of his café again. I'm a rebel with a lost cause (in his opinion), worse, I'm a chef who put revolution before recipe learning.

"You're a cook, not a politician," he hisses at me.

But my konditor training has come to an abrupt end. I realise I'm an optional extra to a man like Peter; I'm an over-oily salad, or a flat beer, not a flesh-and-blood (and bones) woman. But then, I don't grieve over him as such, just a missed opportunity to create a new cake. Bertolt shrugs when I tell him.

"Maybe you don't want to love anyone," he suggests. "Maybe you just want to be loved? Achje, Esther Rosenbaum, the cook who relies on raw men's hearts to fuel her."

Bertolt helps me to pack and walks me to Augsburg station. Our goodbyes are made on a rain-splashed platform where he slips me the address of a contact in the Moabit.

"He'll rent you a room really cheap," he calls up to me, as the train pulls out from the station. "So no more excuses, Esther Rosenbaum. Go to Cold Chicago and cook up a storm."

I'm forced to pawn Frau Brecht's binoculars – bequested to me in her will – to pay my first month's rent in advance. The two-room apartment I get in return is situated in a dark basement, close to Artimius Market. The market, in turn, is not far from Moabit prison where Tucholski and his comrades served out their sentences during the war. Anti-war protesters were treated badly, because they were seen to be cowards, traitors and spies – a view shared by many of my new neighbours, the majority pieceworkers hired by the surrounding clothing factories. I listen to them pedalling their machines night and day, a noise punctuated only by the crying of babies, the coughing of the dying and the racket made by rotten window frames splintering as they are pushed to their limit.

My new home is a dark cave. Its rooms stink of onions and damp and the ceilings sag, the result of leaks from the broken pipes upstairs. My incompetent landlord has stuck up a riot of plaster mouldings in a bid to hide the botched joinery of his carpenters. They are shaped like swags of fruits and I pretend to eat them when I'm hungry. And I'm often hungry those first few weeks in Berlin, because I hear no word from Herr Botticelli after I send over a note of introduction. Bertolt writes and tells me to visit the tiny bierkeller at the end of the street where survivors of the Spartacist revolt meet, but I have no heart to see anyone. I'm still reeling from the loss of Frau Brecht.

I manage to nurture my hopes of joining a world class kitchen – and I discover the irrepressible Frau Schneider. She is a widow who lives in the next-door apartment. She dresses in her dead husband's clothes – "*waste not, want not*" is her motto – and runs the courtyard which we look out over. Her late husband was shot dead by the Spartacists, right under her bedroom window. She claims she doesn't know why, or maybe she just prefers to hold her own counsel in such times. In turn, I keep my recent past under wraps. Frau Schneider is proof that it is possible to endure the ugliness and volatility of city life; she is someone I think I can trust as a guide, so I start to invite her in for coffee and offer her what scraps I can from my meagre dinners.

Frau Schneider rates practical efficiency above all other qualities; she takes in piecework from the factories to make ends meet, stitching a blouse in seconds, although her fingers are thick and raw with chillblains. Friendship to her is an exchange of skills. When I'm offered an interview at Café Botticelli, she offers to patch up my old peacock skirt. Yes, I finally get the nod to turn up for an interview with the legendary konditor six weeks after arriving in Berlin. On the morning itself, I wake up with a ladybird on my cheek.

"It's a lucky omen, Esther," Frau Schneider crows. "Your mission can't fail."

Café Botticelli is not the sort of place Frau Schneider, or any of our other neighbours, would ever visit. It's a place where "society" gathers: politicians, celebrities, and high ranking government officers all eager to taste Botticelli's latest recipes, which are written up in the newspapers. I scent a master who can teach me something new and maybe provide me with a means to establish my worth in the volatile world of Cold Chicago. When I was younger, I heard time and time again in the synagogue about the *"woman of worth"*, one whose price was beyond that of rubies. I knew I could never match such a woman, particularly after my bones grew all funny and I was exiled from the world beyond my courtyard's borders. My price was never going to match that asked for even one tiny ruby ring, but with a world-class konditor's training under my belt? Achje, hope fills me up like a soufflé.

I arrive at the café just before midday. The place is every bit as imposing as its reputation suggests, even for one of my stature. Giant statues of naked women line the facade, vines twisted in their hair, their toes perched above a blue and white striped canopy sheltering the downstairs café tables. The patisserie is found on the first floor and here I'm greeted by a huge glass cabinet lined with familiar looking cakes, including the willow trees Peter made for me in Café Voltaire. The waitress serving behind the cabinet catches sight of me and a slice of marmokuchen slips from her spatula on to the floor.

"I have an interview with Herr Botticelli," I quickly reassure her. "Will you let him know I've arrived? My name is Esther Rosenbaum."

"You're here for the job then?"

The waitress fails to hide her surprise. She collects herself long enough to direct me out on to the balcony, then she scuttles off to the kitchens where I can hear a general uproar greet her story. I step out on to the balcony. It's a place of great charm: there are eight tables lined up beside window boxes filled with blue and mauve geraniums. The walls of the covered balcony are lined with tiny blue and white Delft tiles. In spite of my surroundings, I find myself getting nervous. What if Botticelli refuses to offer me a job when he catches sight of me?

"Fräulein Rosenbaum?"

I turn round and find a man who I would recognise anywhere as Botticelli. He's round as a frog with bulbous eyes the size of golf balls. Botticelli sidles around me, shy of the sweep of my hair, which has got caught up in his shoes. He sways violently and is about to fall when I put out a hand and catch him, as easily as I would a bouncing rubber ball. He looks startled, but then he bursts out laughing. Soon, we are conversing like old friends. I grow more assured as we discuss how things have improved generally for the café since the lean pickings of the war years. Botticelli waves my letter of introduction. He is delighted to hear I have "trained" with Peter the Albino.

"Peter is alive and still cooking. This is a relief, Fräulein. I've had the tummy aches thinking what might have been. We get the pops going, yes? We celebrate?"

He orders a bottle of sekt and then he suggests we lunch as well. He is affability itself, but I remain cautious about revealing my whole life story. I sense that to explain certain details of my life in Augsburg might be unwise. Instead, I tell him that I have only recently arrived back in Berlin after the death of my former employer – my excuse for having no references.

"The only reference you need is what you can cook," Botticelli replies. "I'm going to send you down to the kitchens to prove what you can do and then we shall eat."

I anticipated such a request and have devised a new pea soup recipe for the occasion. Botticelli's kitchen staff provide me with the ingredients: shelled peas, sour cream and a silver chased dish shaped like a bunch of knotted roots. Curiosity soon overcomes their surprise at my appearance in their midst. They hover as I mix up my ingredients, asking me questions and offering assistance with various pieces of equipment. The first (and only rule) of making and serving a dish at

Botticelli's is: that it should be a work of art. Botticelli is thrilled by my soup and promptly offers me a position as a trainee konditor. My delighted agreement is swiftly followed by early afternoon tea, served up by Botticelli himself. It consists of a parade of pastry baskets, each one moulded to fit into the palm of a hand. The baskets are filled with a mix of pistachios and strawberries, but most cleverly of all by dozens of wafer thin chocolate layers, sandwiched between strips of cream, some no wider than a hair from Botticelli's head.

"You know, Fräulein Rosenbaum, I think you can help me in a very particular way. I would like you to work on my pastry towers. They have won me a reputation."

"I've seen the reports, Herr Botticelli," I reply.

"Then you know I can make towers as tall as you are out of nothing more than vanilla pastry and whipped cream," he says proudly.

I forgive him something as paltry as boasting when I realise that for the first time in a long while, my ridiculous height will serve a purpose.

The day after my interview, I'm set to work on the top layers of Botticelli's cakes. We are soon tethered together by skeins of spun sugar, skilled as climbers on our pastry mountain. I often work from dawn to dusk alongside my employer, the days slipping through my fingers like flour. The more I get to know about Botticelli, the more intriguing I find him. He likens cake making to architecture; the foundations are everything. Whether making pastry, or icing a baroque motif around a square of sponge, every technique deployed has to be mastered before moving on to the next challenge. He holds seminars on the correct construction of an icing bag, or the correct temperature to roll out pastry on a table top. He has the most extraordinary hands, which he protects as carefully as any concert pianist, performing exercises each morning to keep them supple. A konditor's hands are his life's blood, he explains.

"Sometimes, you touch, like you are a fly bouncing down on the leaf," he confides to his enraptured staff. "At other times, you must pull hard, like in a tug-of-war."

We become accustomed to his impromptu musings, often delivered from the top of a table for added emphasis, because we know they serve his one ideal: that the culinary arts are to be ranked with the greatest achievements in literature, music and drama.

By December, I'm asked to run the downstairs restaurant at Café Botticelli. My reputation slowly begins to challenge that of my master, as I let my imagination loose devising new menus. This task preoccupies me and I don't find myself missing Bertolt. He sends me letters from Augsburg and Munich via Tobias, my landlord, but ballad-singing poets with purple ink stained lips seem a league away from my new world. I have rooted myself in Botticelli's kitchen, I am proud to have inherited something of my mother's skill which I can share with so many others.

Stories about my innovations begin to make the headlines. I flavour ice cream with real rose petals; make pigs' heads out of roasted almonds and toffee and I create Heart-of-the-Deer, a nest of songbirds baked inside the stomach of a deer and served up on platters drenched in sauces made out of cranberries and plums. Rumours of my achievements travel the city and I'm the subject of table talk all the way from the Wannsee back to Friedrichstrasse. Amazingly, Botticelli shows no resentment. He sniffs good business and gives me my head, trusting me like a jockey would his prize-winning racehorse.

"To give is to share, Esther," he claims.

He even offers me a partnership in his enterprise. He dreams of building an empire. He's going to buy up the neighbouring premises and expand the operation. We will be as close as twins in a womb. So much has changed for me, I find I rarely have time to observe the traditions I was brought up to observe, remembering only to light my Sabbath candles. I even fail to visit the Scheuenviertel to find out how Benjamin and Esau have fared, because I let myself be distracted by my new neighbours instead. They sniff out my talent by sticking their noses through my open windows to breathe in the wonderful odours I'm creating, like a prize perfumier.

In what seems no time at all, temptation overcomes them and they walk through my door. I serve cups of coffee and display my tapestry skirts. The banquet tables stitched onto them are weighed down with boars' heads, quails and chickens. I tell them about these rare meats, which I cook at Café Botticelli, and they shake their heads. They taste a pig's trotter on Sundays, if they are lucky. Frau Schneider tells me they sell their stories to Herr Bloch for twists of tobacco, which they chew on to stave off acute hunger pangs. Herr Bloch is a travelling entertainer in these parts. He tours the courtyards, a harlequin's hat on his head, singing songs about killer brides and one-eyed mad generals. He sings the news of the day and what he saw in the trenches of France. His voice was cracked in some awful gas attack, so his lungs wheeze and sigh like his rusty barrel organ. He also sings the songs of the uprising, but Frau Schneider claims she can't recall any of the lyrics. She's too busy denouncing Kaya Tucholski, who apparently sits smoking with her husband and his cronies in the bierkeller Bertolt recommended to me in his letters. I'm excited at the thought of meeting with both of them again. Frau Schneider is not so enamoured of the former Bebelsberg beauty.

"They say this Kaya Tucholski was once a great film star, but she's nothing more than a fat drunk as far as I can see."

Frau Schneider takes me under her wing. "You are what you cook, Esther," she points out. "You aren't just some man's lover. That's victory enough in a place like this, trust me."

I do trust Frau Schneider. She invites me into her apartment and I meet her grandchildren. The youngest, Cornelia, becomes something of a pet. The rats in the courtyard make her cry, but I don't have whiskers, or a tail, so she eventually feels brave enough to stand on my table where she plaits my hair with straw. In return, I make her snowflakes out of the finest choux pastry. One day, her brother Gunter drops by in her place. He hands back the pastry snowflakes I offer him.

"Keep them, Esther. Cornelia's ill. Let's give them to her when she's better."

But little Cornelia dies, one of the many victims of influenza in a cruel winter. I bake pies for her funeral cortège, which wends its way past my window in solemn procession.

"Such times," mutters Frau Schneider, her eyes red with crying. "And to think we hoped the war ending would change things for the better."

snowflakes & gingerbread hearts

berlin, 1919–1920

I'm one of the invited: Frau Schneider has asked me to join her cronies in the courtyard on carpet beating day. The gatherings take place in the cobbled yard that lies behind our mietskasernen in Turmstrasse. It's built on a slightly larger scale than the courtyards in the Scheuenviertel, which is a distinct advantage. Out in the courtyard, tucked away behind rows of carpets, friendships are made and enmities forged. It's a cabal; it's a gala.

Frau Schneider hasn't organised a gathering since Cornelia's death back at the start of November. The sight of her carpet beater hanging abandoned on its peg by her door was a sad reminder of how hard grief had struck a woman of such relentless activity. Christmas comes and goes before she so much as puts her nose outside her door. The other women in the courtyard claim the sight of her dusty carpet beater nearly unhinged her all over again, but her fiercely practical nature had won out. The event is safe ground to discuss with Frau Schneider, who resolutely refuses to talk about Cornelia, except for an unguarded moment when she confessed to me that she bit her hands raw trying to stop herself from crying. But there are carpets to be purged of fleas and other grime. Frau Schneider picks up her carpet beater, as if it were a sword and she were about to do battle with Death itself.

"Just don't go displaying anything too shabby unless you want to be talked about," she warns, striding towards the courtyard.

I have just the one rug, which I exchanged for a basket of fresh eggs – part of my wages from Café Botticelli – so I feel confident of avoiding criticism. By the time I reach the courtyard, a dozen women are already in place hitting away at their raggedy rugs in unison, singing one of Bloch's tunes as they go. Big clouds of dust obliterate the mietskasernen beyond. Eyes stream; foreheads are corrugated in concentration. The buzz of activity only stops when somebody starts coughing loudly.

"Who's that?" Frau Schneider demands to know.

Her sleeves are rolled up, revealing big sacs of purple skin that hang down to her elbows. She's so red in the face, she looks like she might lay an egg at any minute.

"No one in the line, Frau Schneider," one of the other women calls out.

It's a rule that they stop if someone has a bad coughing fit, because no one wants to aggravate lungs already damaged by our damp apartments.

"It's coming from the next courtyard along," shouts another.

We all turn and stare in that general direction and discover a man leaning up against the courtyard's doorway. He wears an old-fashioned frock coat, his glasses are pushed back on top of his head and, even amongst all the dust and debris, I recognise Tucholski.

"Herr Bloch's barrel organ has better lungs," Frau Schneider shouts over to him. "And where is Frau Tucholski today? No carpets needing cleaning?"

Tucholski flaps his hand by way of reply. "She is sick, ladies. She has indulged and must be indulged. Ach, how she suffers." He rolls his eyes in feigned distress.

"For shame – and you left to hold the carpet beater, is it?" Frau Schneider jokes.

The other women laugh, but I'm unsure how best to respond. I've not seen Tucholski since the night we celebrated the Republic's coming of age. Aware that it's probably best not to draw attention to such a connection, considering what occurred to Frau Schneider's husband in this very courtyard, I try and hide myself away behind the line of carpets.

"No, she won't be joining you today," Tucholski eventually replies, after another dreadful bout of coughing. "She's got a hangover. One of many this week. No pity should be wasted on her, truth told. She's not at death's door, merely a regular at Bacchus' table."

Frau Schneider snorts, rolls up her carpets and trots back to her apartment, giving me an opportunity to finally greet Tucholski. I see at once that he is even thinner since we last met back in April, his hips as narrow as a child's. His face is pinched and drawn, only his deep-set grey eyes are as vivid as ever.

"Ach, it's Fräulein Rosenbaum!" he exclaims, noticing my scrutinising look and wanting to distract me from comment. "I was just coming over to see you, as it happens. Bertolt told me we were neighbours. My apologies, I should have come sooner." Tucholski sweeps my brow with the flat of his hand and sighs, as if genuinely remorseful. I touch my forehead where his hand has rested and, suddenly, I feel much better than I have done for a long time.

"Is it a trick of some kind?" I ask him.

"The touch of human kindness is no trick," he replies, bowing low.

His charm wins me over again – this time to the idea of hosting my first ever dinner party in Berlin. New Year is upon us and I decide I will celebrate. I invite Tucholski on the spot – and I ask him to bring Kaya too. It's only later that I get nervous. To me, Kaya Tucholski is still a legend; what can I cook for such a woman? Botticelli comes to my rescue. He hustles me into his larder and picks out a selection of cold meats, even a startled looking salmon – a pile of food he gallantly offers as my year's bonus.

"This man Tucholski, he's a composer you say?" Botticelli is impressed. He tips up his prized spice jars and eeks out vanilla pods and powders, which he then sorts into little paper bags.

"Well, he's not Verdi, Herr Botticelli," I reply. "He writes for the kabaretts."

"Music is the food of lovers, yes? To write this music and let people eat it, ach, a special talent I don't think either of us possess, Esther."

He can speak for himself. I'm determined on aiming as high as I can with my first banquet in Berlin. I leave my shift that evening weighed down with a goose, a salmon, a bag of potatoes, red cabbage, flour, raisins, vanilla and nutmeg. I don't own a table, but Frau Schneider lends me one. She even brings round a pile of leafy greenery to stitch into garlands to hide the table's cracked joints.

1920 arrives on a cloud of hailstones, the size of small plums, and I'm convinced we'll have to take refuge under my borrowed table. The Tucholskis descend on me early, their heads hidden under their coats. The smell of the bread I have been baking, filled with raisins and cinnamon, has pulled them out of their apartment early – or so they claim.

"It's a treat to smell something other than stale cabbage," Tucholski points out. "Let's face it, Kaya, nobody ever loved you for your cooking." His words carry a sarcastic undertone, but Kaya doesn't rise to his bait. She sits down on the window ledge and buries herself in her fur-trimmed evening coat. I'm not disappointed by my first impressions of her in my candlelit room – she seems the true film star. Her coat is mint green, decorated with gold couched weave embroidery and a collar and cuffs made from red fox fur. She doesn't say anything, just bites her nails.

"You want to draw blood just for the sake of it, don't you?" Tucholski's tone is accusatory and there is no missing the tension between them. Catching my eye, he slips into the character of genial guest. "We're not being polite, Esther. I'm so sorry. Please let me introduce you to Kaya."

I shake the hand she holds out to me, noticing her fingers are still wet from her mouth, and then return to my baking. Suddenly, Kaya is up on her feet. She strides over to me and runs her fingers through my hair, before I can do much about it – both my hands are full of sprigs of rosemary for I'm about to seal the potatoes in their paper envelopes ready for cooking.

"We didn't get you a present, Esther, and it's New Year too," she says.

I'm surprised by her deep voice. She punctuates her words with odd pauses, which I assume might be the result of her theatre training.

"I'm ashamed, really I am, but we are under such a strain at the moment." She tilts her head upwards, as if seeking a spotlight, before resuming the conversation. "Did Bertolt tell you that we live in exile and we can't get work? In Munich, it would be easy – all my contacts are there, you see, but here I'm just another fish in a cold, dark pond. And Tucholski," she sighs, her hand flitting briefly against her heart.

"He can't find backers who are not afraid of his past catching up with him."

"All the more reason to enjoy yourself tonight, Kaya," I reply, but I'm no actress and my words sound clumsy. "And please don't worry about a gift. I haven't bought you anything either."

"You offer us food and friendship. That is more than we have been given by anybody in months. Thank you." She pauses. "Look out of the window," Kaya demands next, waving her hand in the direction of my closed shutters. "You'll see there all you need to see to understand that things have not changed at all. This is what Tucholski writes about and his songs cut to the bone. I sing them in the kabaretts that still dare to hire me and I see the effect they have on people. It's these songs that get us picked out of the crowd."

"Are you still in danger?" I ask. Her dramatic tones finally make an impact on me – a piece of salmon escapes my grip and lands on top of my boot.

"Yes, along with thousands of others who trusted an ideal," Kaya explains, choosing to ignore the fate of the salmon. "People like Frau Brecht. Ach, we miss her badly, Esther."

I realise I have failed to put the goose in the oven. It is the centrepiece dish for my banquet: a roasted goose served up on a nest woven out of ribbons of red cabbage and twists of orange peel. Luckily, my guests don't mind waiting. Tucholski offers to read our fortunes. Back in their apartment he has melted a small piece of lead specially for this task. He hurries out the door to rescue it and returns within minutes, the melted lead swimming around violently on top of one of my white dinner plates, which he thoughtfully took with him. Tucholski places it on top of my table and we all crane over to inspect the patterns left on its surface. I think I can see a gigantic snowflake, but Tucholski insists it's an egg.

"Take a look, Kaya," he demands. "Don't you agree?"

She pokes her head towards the plate and concentrates hard.

"If it's an egg, it means wealth is coming our way," Thomas adds, his voice slowed by the effects of the winter cold. He coughs and tucks the ends of his muffler in to the top of his shirt. I try and build up the fire, but the wood is damp. "The truth is, I can't perform this trick as well as my mother used to," he admits. "She could see a whole panorama in every blot and streak. I'm struggling to give you a single wish."

"Why is an egg associated with wealth?" I ask.

"Who knows?" Tucholski replies, rather wistfully. "One of my mother's many superstitions, as Kaya would no doubt inform you, if she could avoid stumbling over her words…"

"But I like superstitions," she interrupts, rattled by his gibe. "I like them, because they aren't dependent on what is happening in the here and now. I mean, we see an egg and we think we can be rich this time next year. It's a wonderful con trick. Why didn't we think of this before? We could have gone out on the streets and demanded money for our visions. We'd fit in after all. We look like beggars."

Her retort is greeted with another awkward silence. There is some truth in what she has said. Now I can see her in close up, I notice that her elegant coat is very dirty and ragged. The fur on the neck and cuffs is matted with grease and some of the embroidery on the silk sleeves has come unstitched.

"You exaggerate as always, Kaya."

"If you really looked at me for a change, you'd see I'm a mess," she counters. "We shouldn't have come at all, Esther. I'm ashamed at how dirty we are."

"Oh God, that's rubbish! I washed you myself tonight, Kaya. I filled a dish from the pump; I even heated it on the stove. I put your favourite perfume in. Can you smell it, Esther?"

I don't know what to say. My banquet seems to have turned into a backdrop for a horrid ritual. Kaya has started crying. Her tears drip down her coat and on to the table. She cries with great gusto, hitting the table with each choked sob. The plates dance up and down.

"*If I had one penny in the world, thou shouldst have it to buy gingerbread,*" Tucholski says, reaching out to grab Kaya's thumping fists.

It's as if he has mended a broken tap for Kaya immediately stops crying, wipes her eyes on her coat sleeve and then blows her nose on the edge of the tablecloth.

"I'm sorry, Esther," she says. "Tucholski is right to change the subject. I know, I'll tell you a story."

Kaya squeezes her lover's hand, throws off her tatty coat and stands up as if she was about to walk out on a kabarett stage. She's wearing a beautiful green dress, which shimmers like the gilt beading on a Tiffany lamp.

"Christmas was a special time for my family too," she explains. "There was the tradition of the gingerbread hearts. Mama cooked them for me every year and hid them in my shoes whilst I slept. They represented St Nicholas' heart, you see, and every year they were passed into my keeping. Such responsibility, you can't believe! Then Mama died. I was nine years old. There were no more gingerbread hearts. I was sent to a convent school where traditions like that were frowned upon."

Kaya strikes a tragic pose, as her story turns a new chapter. I pass her my handkerchief and she smiles distractedly, pressing it to her eyes.

"It's all right, Esther. I don't need this talisman any more, not now I have Tucholski's heart to look after."

She turns to look at him and it's as if the black cloud that has wrapped them up since their arrival has disintegrated. Tucholski stands up and puts his arm round her bare shoulders. It is an opportune moment to serve up my festive Goose-sat-on-a-Nest. The Tucholskis whistle and applaud as I remove the dish from the oven and deliver it to the table. (Tucholski has rather unceremoniously dropped the lead and my precious plate onto the floor.) He offers to carve, but Kaya intervenes.

"You can't even slice bread. Leave it to me."

They wrestle with the carving knife and fork but Tucholski gives way. He's coughing badly again and needs to sit down. I hand him a glass of water, whilst Kaya attacks the belly of the goose. She carves messily, but the job is soon done. We eat in a protracted silence. Kaya is as messy an eater as she is a carver; tendrils of orange peel litter her breasts and gravy stains her chin. She is a woman of fierce appetites; she almost disembowels her dinner with her knife and fork, she's so keen to wolf it down so she can pile on a second helping. Thomas picks at his food and takes only a few mouthfuls. I follow the goose with a plate of gingerbread squares. I've used real ginger, a rare ingredient which I hope my guests will savour, but it's not to be.

"One day, I'll make a gingerbread heart for you, Kaya," Tucholski says, holding up one of my squares and gazing at it with a disappointed look. "I'll use the ginger that Marco Polo discovered when he travelled to China. It will be the most wonderful New Year's gift ever, so much more valuable than a coat that falls into holes the minute it's worn."

I realise the black cloud has fallen again over my table. Kaya freezes. She pushes Tucholski's arm away from her and, standing in close, whispers in my ear, "The same tired promises, Esther. He makes them every year, you know, and every year he fails to do what he promises."

She's whispering secrets Tucholski doesn't want me to hear. He calls my attention back to the lead, which is hardening on the floor by his feet. We all shift up close again and watch his fingers trace over it.

"It looks like a woman painted by Rubens, don't you think?" he asks. "Ach, he would have painted you if he had known you, Kaya. I would bet on that, if I had a spare dollar."

I ask him what my future might hold.

"You will cook up your own fortune," Tucholski replies. "I don't need a piece of lead to tell me that. Botticelli wants to make you a partner, but I think you should look to Schorns."

"That's a stupid idea!" Kaya interrupts him. I catch the look on her face and I'm surprised. She seems furious. "Schorns is hardly a place for cuisine. Any chef hired there will be better off training first as a juggler."

"On the contrary, Leon Wolf wants only the best chefs in the world to cook in his restaurant. He's hunting high and low. Esther should make her pitch. She's the best we have in Berlin, isn't she?"

"I've seen the advertisements on the litfassaüle in Friedrichstrasse," I interpose, "Is it true Herr Wolf is going to hire Josephine Baker for his opening night?"

"And the rest," Tucholski replies.

He knows a carpenter who works on site and he has spoken of an interior that will make Zoo station look minuscule in comparison; there will be fountains in the foyer and an army of commissaires in blue and silver uniforms parading around them. A florist will also be in residence at the foot of the spiral staircase leading to the showpiece restaurant. The shop will sell enormous chrysanthemums as mementoes to the diners – the petal heads alone will be the width of my head. And that's not all: the whole place will be lit up by a staggering one thousand electric light bulbs, an unheard-of extravagance in the Moabit where we have to make do with a few smoky tallow candles of an evening.

"You really think I should go for an interview?" I ask, not a little stunned by Tucholski's description of this wonderful restaurant.

"Wolf will make a stage for you to appear on," he answers with conviction. "And quite right too. You're a performer, just like Kaya and myself."

This comment galls his partner – she very obviously hates sharing a spotlight – and this might account for her squashing the idea of my going for an interview. But it's just the opening shot, before the gunpowder kicks in. Job creation schemes are the theme of the evening – if I'm to go to Schorns to improve my employment prospects, then she will take up an offer to give a private recital to the Tucholskis' bank manager.

"He's begging me and we need the money, Tucholski."

"Bored with only acting one, you have to play a prostitute for real?" he asks, viciously. I make a start clearing the dishes, but my discretion is ignored – I'm completely invisible to the Tucholskis who continue their argument.

"I've slept with him already," Kaya taunts. "So why these objections?"

"I'm leaving," Tucholski announces abruptly and is off out of the door before anyone can say anything else.

"Oh, God, Esther, I've messed up again," Kaya wails, falling against me and sobbing bitterly. I hear Tucholski's footsteps stamp down the hallway. Kaya clutches at my arm and refuses to let go. "But we need every pfennig we can get – wherever it comes from," she continues, evidently determined on putting across her argument. "You tell me what else I'm supposed to do, Esther? Climb into my pockets, if I'm to sleep at night? We've no money to buy wood for the stove. That's why I went the first time. It's so unfair. I had a contract at the Schall und Rauch last week, but Francine will be back soon and she gets all the work because she's so wretchedly thin. I've got better songs – I mean, Tucholski writes them, there's none better – but I look like a truck driver alongside that bitch. Shit, I'm going on, aren't I? But there's so little work and then last night, I slept on the bierkeller floor, because we had another bloody row…"

Tucholski materalises in the doorway. He's waving her coat like a matador would his cloak in front of a bull.

"You'll leave *now*, Kaya," he orders.

This couple seem so full of hatred, confusion and jealousy. Kaya struggles into her coat while I cry unregarded, my eyes dripping like a pump. I turn my cheek to the wall and fail to see my guests leave. I just hear the door slam shut and then voices raised in fierce argument. My head dances. I'm drunk on sekt and pain. I've been abandoned and only the open sky races above me. Everyone falls away from me eventually, like dead flower heads: my parents, Frank, Frau Brecht, Peter the Albino – and now the two people I thought I might be friends with in Cold Chicago. Black spots cover my vision, like dozens of migrating birds kicking up from the rooftops. I stumble over a fallen chair and hit the floor hard. Hours later – days later? – I hear a voice close to my ear. It sounds like a piece of music filtering in from the apartment next door, a rhythm that nudges open my eyes and only then do I understand it's a living voice.

"Esther? Are you hurt?"

It's Tucholski, sponging my forehead with ice cubes. I come back round to greet the world and he helps me up on to a chair. He waits for a few minutes for me to say something, but I've simply no words left inside me. He holds my hands and offers a few of his own to fill up the silence.

"I must apologise for what has happened, Esther. I've had a fierce row with Kaya over the whole business. She's remorseful. She always is after these displays of hers, but it's not good enough…"

"I don't suppose it's all her fault, Tucholski. It's hard for you both at the moment. For all of us in the courtyard come to that. No one can love, or trust, or believe in anything." Saying this, I feel as if I have turned my heart out of my chest and placed it in Tucholski's hands. I sink back down on my knees. "I don't know," I whisper almost to myself.

"It seems worse than ever before and we are supposed to be at peace."

"Well, you can always trust me," Tucholski says, gripping my shoulders and giving me a little shake. "And Kaya too. Achje, she's not all bad, whatever the impression she might like to give people."

"You mean the banker?"

"Ah, she mentioned him, did she?" he says, his tone giving nothing away. "Well, in a way, yes it is. But he's a whim. Kaya proves her love for me in a rather unconventional fashion. She sleeps with other men, but she always returns to me. That is how I know I'm the one she really loves. Don't try and understand her behaviour, Esther. I accept it, which is what counts. We stay together, so who is harmed? Survival is a cruel game, but like I say, you can trust me. I promise you that – and I always keep my promises."

He leaves shortly afterwards and I finally get to bed. My head spins from the multitude of impressions I've received since the previous night. In the end, the New Year rolls in on the back of a terrible storm. It's colder than anybody can remember, even Frau Schneider whose memory is prodigious. My quilt freezes on my bed as the winter frost settles inside the walls of the apartment. I take the chill off with jugs of hot water I boil in saucepans on the stove and then pour down the glass. A month passes. Kaya tucks a bunch of flowers into the iron grille that curves over my window boxes, but they die in an overnight frost, before I find them.

I wrap up in my quilt and wait out the worst of the weather passing by my cracked windows. As I lie in my freezing room at night, I give way to one appetite only – one that has been whetted by dreams that lie far beyond my wretched cave. Numb with the terrible cold, I still cling to a giant-sized hope: I've decided I will win an interview with the infamous Leon Wolf, determined that his magnificent restaurant will give me the chance to scale new heights.

the Jugendstil room

Never Year comes and goes. February arrives and so does
Bertolt. He holes up in Eislebenstrasse, Ice Life Street.
That's where we are all living these days. But I find myself
confiding in Tucholski rather than in my old friend, partly because
we have experience of exile in common, and partly because Bertolt is
distracted by wine, women and endless wheeler-dealing with various
theatrical managements.

There are differences between my situation and that of Tucholski,
of course. I remember Pappa's stories about my ancestor who emerged
from the ghetto at the end of the nineteenth century to shake hands
with the leading figures of the haskalah reform movement. In spite of
what he achieved, in the eyes of many, I should remain in a ghetto. I
might not choose to recognise its geographical boundaries, but a cruel
mix of superstition, contempt and ignorance continues to restrain
me. This attitude has hardened in recent months. Even I can't help
but notice that the world is something more than just a giant recipe
book.

"There's talk of another war. Do you think it's possible, Tucholski?"
I ask him one night.

"There's a war being fought right now," he replies. "It's not being
fought in the street. No, it's something a lot more dangerous. You see
it there in people's eyes. They are twisted up with anger and shame.
Guns don't threaten us, the way starvation does..."

"Surely it's different now? We remember what went before, don't
we? Look how people took to the streets and brought in a government
that reversed the bad old days of the Junkers and the Kaiser? Lessons

have been learnt."

Tucholski sits on the floor, his back against the wall. He rests his hands on his knees. When he's stuck on a particular point, he clenches his fists and hits the floor. He doesn't agree with me.

"But we fail to speak of this at the right time and in the right place, Esther," he says, his rasping voice threatening, although he means only to enlighten me. "People are standing up and saying terrible things against peace and against the reparations demanded at Versailles. They go unsilenced, because so many of us have invisible threads tied across our mouths."

Tucholski is an exception, as always. He continues to speak out against the people who dragged us into a world war and berates the Weimar Republic for not standing up to the forces of the right. He is wearing himself to a thread with the long hours he keeps, but he has little time for his health. He puts everything into his work – and when he's not working, he's trying to explain away Kaya's behaviour. She has been badly affected by his course of action and I should bear this in mind before I judge her, he says. Her relationship with him is both curse and celebration.

"Kaya was dismissed from the Bebelsberg Studio because she stayed with me," he points out. "She was heading for great things – film producers were even calling her the new Asta Nielsen. She had got that far when I gave them reason to suspend her contract. I refused to enlist, you see, and after that, we were reduced to living out of suitcases. Circumstances have chiselled away at her and she's been broken. Haven't we all been broken in some way by what has been? Ach, Kaya and I have gone through so much, but we're still together. It's like a miracle. That's what I hold on to."

Jealousy taps at my heart. The Tucholskis might well have experienced prison, unemployment, hunger, exhaustion (even stage fright), but their love has mapped their lives into an unbreakable whole. They have made love on grass soaked in a storm's rain; they have slept on restaurant tables rolled in their coats; they have made love in shop doorways and warmed their chilled bones in the early morning sunlight. This is what they have given to each other. I am lucky to see out a night of experimental thrills with someone made curious by my strange looks. But Tucholski has another tune to play; he is pushing me to apply for an interview at Schorns.

"You have market value, Esther, and you should use it to shore up a better future for yourself," he argues. "Wolf knows this so you must make demands, even though you're a skinny Jewess with too open a heart!"

He orders me to eat more – and not just cook – and he orders me to dress up. He lives with a mobile fashion plate and must look upon me as a terrible imposter of femininity. He tries to rectify matters as best he can. He sneaks brooches and bracelets from Kaya's ever-growing collections and brings them round for me to try on. He helps pin up my hair and then decorates it with the brooches. He even smuggles out one of Kaya's favourite shawls – a huge piece of black velvet, printed with tiny silver circles.

"Good," he mutters, as I strut around my tiny kitchen. "If you could just put on a little weight – only a little, mind – you would carry this off so much better."

I hesitate a while longer before making my move. I'm busy experimenting with dishes I hope might appeal to the tastes of a man who won his restaurant from a war hero's widow in a game of cards. I've walked past the building, a former department store, thousands of times. It stands on the corner between Friedrichstrasse and the Weidendammer Brücke, defiant in its design even though the plaster is patchy and pigeons have roosted on its window ledges. Most of my neighbours can hardly buy an egg with their wages, but Leon Wolf has bought up an entire building and spends recklessly on the new art that is scandalising the city's headline writers. They claim Schorns is going to be the grandest restaurant our city has ever seen.

One morning, late in March, I arrive at work and find that Leon Wolf himself has come to breakfast in our café. I smell him, before I catch sight of him because he favours the spiciest of aftershaves. He is parading around downstairs when I make my entrance, dressed in a black leather coat, buttoned up over his pudgy bulk. It gives him the appearance of a very stout penguin, but he's evidently as vain as his photographs in the newspapers imply. His thick dark hair curls up over his temples in a succession of brilliantined waves; his polished button boots are like mirrors. His large question mark of a head curves its way out of his collar, attacking everything it swivels towards by either biting down on it very hard, or by posing some outrageous demand. He has already reduced the waitresses to tears and torn up the breakfast menu. Then he spies me.

"Fräulein Rosenbaum," he calls out. "I need rescuing!"

His hand flutters over his heart; his eyes roll towards the ceiling. I burst out laughing at his preposterous stance and then fall silent again, just as fast. There's no telling what this man might do next. He squints at me out of the corner of one eye.

"Good. A sense of humour. Now, bring me brioche, before starvation leaves me cold, stone dead on top of this floor."

He throws off his leather coat and settles himself down on a very fragile looking chair. I signal to a cowering waitress to bring brioche and eggs. Leaning forward to spread a napkin over Wolf's knees, I nearly topple as he grabs hold of my face between his highly scented hands.

"Your bone structure is very good, Fräulein," he remarks. "You look like one of my Colombian wall hangings. Do you know where Colombia is?"

"No, Herr Wolf. Is it in Germany?"

His turn to laugh. He honks as loudly as one of the zoo's sealions.

"I'll buy you a globe," he finally answers. "You really must see more of the world, Fräulein, even if it just spins under your fingers. You should keep up to the minute, but how can I blame you for falling behind working in a place like this?"

He shudders and gives a cursory nod to his surroundings. I notice Botticelli has slunk out of the downstairs kitchen and is now standing by the kasse waiting on events. I cast a sideways glance at him and see him glaring back at me. Judging by his sour expression, he must think I'm hatching a takeover bid with his rival. Wolf is completely indifferent to his presence, however. He has finished his brioche and is now spearing scrambled eggs up on his fork. He switches subject without effort, forcing me to concentrate hard in order to catch salient details about my interview. He suggests we meet at seven thirty that very evening on the front steps of Schorns where I'm to apply for the position of head chef. HEAD CHEF! I can barely pour his coffee out straight when he indicates I should refill his cup. Tucholski has told me chefs from all over Europe have written begging letters to Wolf asking him for a place in his kitchens. I'm so excited, I bob down in a curtsey.

"Bravo, Fräulein Rosenbaum," he chortles. "You know it makes sense not to hide your light under a bushel, particularly as you are made to stand head, shoulders and torso above the common man. Botticelli has wasted a great opportunity, in my opinion. You were served up to him on a plate and all he's done is put the dish cover back on again. He has not exploited your unusual potential as much as he could. He hasn't maximised on the public's fickle attention span. I can rectify this and you will oblige, if you are as astute as I think you are."

Botticelli has moved away from the kasse, his eyes starting out of his head like two poached eggs. He is also wielding a vicious-looking chopping knife in his left hand.

"You make a pickle of your life, if you go work for this showman, Esther," he shouts. I try and deflect Botticell, but he skips past me and the chopping knife lands on Wolf's table. The splinters fly up like gnats and crash-land in to his dish of eggs.

"I should challenge you to a duel, Wolf," he shouts out, full of rage. "You steal my livelihood."

"All's fair in love, war and business, *Herr* Botticelli," Wolf replies, after carefully wiping stray egg from his waistcoat. "And no more talk of duels, please. I have no inclination to get up at dawn for anybody. Sudden volition at such an early hour does terrible damage to one's looks, don't you find, Fräulein Rosenbaum?"

At the next table, a man's false teeth have fallen out when he screamed in shock at the sight of Botticelli's carving knife. His teeth have landed near my shoes and I notice there is still a remnant of salami clamped between them. A long pause follows Wolf's rejoinder. Botticelli concedes defeat first and storms back to his kitchen, but not before he has kicked the teeth out of the reach of the shocked diner. I scoop them up in a napkin and discretely return them to their owner.

"Seven thirty it is then, Fräulein," Wolf laughs. "It will be my turn to rescue you then."

We both make a quick exit. I can't face Botticelli's wrath. I'm about to land myself the job of the century. Risking losing any job to come back to, I hurry to the Moabit and get the brooches and the scarf out of the blanket box where I have been storing them.

"A jewellery box on legs," Wolf announces when I finally stumble up the steps of Schorns and into a foyer that is framed by colonnades of huge pillars, all shaped like giant lilies. The foyer itself is lit by clusters of lights which resemble half-opened rose buds. Their long green stems fold back into the stucco ceiling to form dozens of ribboned rosettes. The walls are lined with mirrors in ornate silver frames and the floor is tiled with a thick green marble that echoes the mossy floor of a storybook forest. Commissaires in blue dress coats with silver braid stand on duty between each pillar.

"All Englishmen," Wolf explains, noticing where my gaze has landed. "And none of them is under six feet in height." He whisks me through a door concealed behind a palm tree. We walk down a short flight of steps and into a warren of kitchens and larders that lie in the basement. The kitchens have been built into what was once a huge vaulted cellar. I am close enough to see how the whole roof resembles an upside-down market garden, featuring row upon row of enormous hams, strings of venison and boar sausages and ropes of fist-sized onions. There are also hundreds of copper pots and pans nailed up around the walls and laid out ready for use on dozens of wooden tables, as scarred as the one Mama used in our old home. Each kitchen has an enormous fireplace complete with spits and a variety of iron pots, as well as one wall given over entirely to shelving filled with dozens of spice and herb jars. The noise is overwhelming: orders are bellowed from the depths of the next kitchen along, pans clang against stoves, hot fat hisses. Faces are disfigured in the mists that emerge from numerous cooking pans. Small children dash between the stoves and the tables, trying to sweep up the debris before it becomes dangerous underfoot, or they tend the fires and the spits, crouched on their heels like little devils overseeing hell's cauldrons. To my left, a fat cloud of feathers flies high as a row of women pluck away at dozens of poultry corpses. Next to them, a group of trainee cooks gut and truss up the birds ready for use. In the far distance, a table full of chefs is engaged dressing cooked fish, popping peas into eye sockets and trimming fins with intricate blobs of sauce and jelly.

"Over one hundred and fifty chefs, kitchen hands and waiters are going to be working here, Fräulein Rosenbaum," Wolf shouts up at me. "This is the advance shift. They are preparing recipes for our opening night menu."

There is another clang on a dumb waiter's bell and a peacock, its tail feathers sweeping over the edges of a silver dish, is rushed past us into a gaping hole in the wall. We slip back through the palm tree door and find ourselves once more in the crowded lobby. Wolf leads me on up the staircase to his extraordinary restaurant. It is known as the Jugendstil Room, although it spans the length of a ballroom and is spread across three floors. I glimpse over the stair railings and find my nose is on a level with a fantastic mosaic floor. It's like falling upwards into the bottom of the ocean.

"Everything that can possibly be fished and eaten is set down on this mosaic," Wolf says, tapping his booted foot on top of a particularly beautiful tropical fish.

The diners will sit on polished church pews; their tables will be fashioned out of the ornate metal stands of Singer sewing machines. My eyes are drawn to a giant cake stand, which nudges the ceiling. It's filled with pastries and cakes set out on frosted glass shelves, like dozens of Fabergé jewels. Benjamin would have loved this display I think, recalling his last Purim gift of a sweet pastry palm tree. In order to reach the top shelves, the waiters have to climb up a set of wheeled steps, which Wolf nimbly demonstrates.

His apartment leads off from an art gallery on the fifth floor. The rooms we pass through are all stacked with paintings and statues, including a giant toucan bird with glass eyes and what appear to be real human teeth. Wolf escorts me into his study, lined with pink and green silks set between carved wooden frames that resemble the sinewy outlines of water plants. The ceiling lamps are flying fish, carved out of silver and glass, the chaise longues carved to resemble lily pads.

I desperately want to walk in this world. It would be the backcloth to meet all backcloths and a chance to really let my dishes take centre stage. We drink several cups of coffee, but Wolf is slow coming to terms. I begin to panic. Maybe he's going to let me down and I'll have to go back to Botticelli and gorge on humble pie? Wolf puts his cup down for the umpteenth time.

"I have heard great claims made of your culinary talents," he finally says. "However, I must have a taste of those claims. I'd like you to prepare a dish worth serving on one of my menus. The job of head chef is yours, Fräulein, if you succeed in taking my breath away."

He throws himself back in his seat and fixes me with a long stare. It's a histrionic gesture, rather like a pose adopted by an actor in a film, but I daren't smile, let alone laugh.

"Go, go!" he urges, waving me in the general direction of the apartment's front door.

It's only at this point I make my final decision about what I shall cook for him. All the experiments, the dithering, the hesitation of the last few weeks count for nothing – I shall make him a dish of my pea soup. It's my lucky recipe, after all. I spot a tureen decorated with four tree frogs on top of a cabinet and request it for a serving dish.

"It's from Java," Wolf says rather suspiciously. "You will be careful and not ruin it with anything untoward?"

"I'm making pea soup, Herr Wolf."

"*Peas?*" he replies, his tone betraying his disappointment.

I assure him he won't be disappointed but he's still crestfallen when I return a couple of hours later with the frog tureen filled to the brim. Wolf sticks his spoon in, as if expecting another frog to jump out of its creamy depths, and eats in silence. After a short while, he puts his spoon down and gazes intently into my eyes.

"Food of the gods," he pronounces. "I picked up this spoon and I tasted my childhood, my hopes. You're a genius, Fräulein. You have overcome the most vicious of hungers by pampering my stomach – and with peas, no less! Die Suppe Rosenbaum is a worthy addition to our menu – and you a more than worthy addition to my kitchens."

In one sentence, I have had a dish named after me *and* I've been offered the job of head chef – but that's not all: I have a gift. It's a handcarved spice box, shaped like an oak leaf. I glimpse inside and discover dozens of tiny chocolates, each one nestling in a seashell.

"Herr Wolf, I'm grateful for your generous offer. But my conditions are these and they are not negotiable: I won't work on my Sabbath and nor will I wash any dishes."

He shakes my hand, walks over to his desk and produces a contract written up in the most exquisite copper plate handwriting. He takes a seat behind his desk, and busies himself picking at his teeth with a little silver toothpick, engraved with two intertwining initials: "H" and "L."

"From Hans," he sighs rather melodramatically.

He stabs at a piece of pea skin, spitting it out in triumph in the direction of his ashtray, but it falls short – on top of my contract. But no matter, I must celebrate my success. (And my pay rise – two hundred deutschmarks a day – and he says he will pay me in dollars). For the first time since arriving in Berlin, I feel a moment of great pride. I want to share this and I make straight for the Tucholskis' apartment, forgetting that Kaya might well be at home too. But it's Kaya who opens the door. She looks terrible. Her hair is down, tangled up like a big thistle, and there are red rings round her eyes. I can't work out if she's been crying for weeks, or is the victim of some ghastly eye condition. Tucholski is not far behind her. "Esther! To what do we owe this unexpected pleasure...?"

"I got the job, Tucholski. I got the job at Schorns. I start next week. It's just as you predicted."

"You'd better come in," Kaya cuts across me. She struggles to light a cigarette as she opens the door wider, but the draught from the hall defeats her. "I really am sorry, Esther," she says, offering me her cigarette. "You were trying to be kind and all we did was ruin your New Year."

I accept her apology, but not the cigarette. I have a bottle of sekt to chill, after all, and Tucholski has beer stored in the kitchen, screened from the rest of their room by a quilt nailed to the ceiling. While he busies himself behind the quilt getting glasses, bread and cheese, Kaya confides that her banker is becoming too demanding.

"You'd think he was the bloody Kaiser the way he orders me around, but he did give me this." She steps behind the canvas screen that blocks out the room's solitary window and returns a few seconds later, dressed in the most wonderful toffee coloured coat. "I know Tucholski doesn't approve, but what choice do I have?" she moans. "Ach, he'd be better off with you, is what you're no doubt thinking. How has he ended up with such a slut? You must really despise me."

I can't meet her gaze and I find myself blushing at her insinuation (yes, I do have a guilty conscience). But in some ways, I admire Kaya. I mention the newspaper photographs I used to hoard and how excited I was about meeting with her at Malkeston's.

"But you'll get your photo in the papers now," Kaya says. "And you'll be even more famous once you start working for Wolf."

Kaya flops down at the floor by my feet. For a moment, I see something of the vulnerability that Tucholski has warned me about. Kaya reminds me of a tired child who needs cajoling into eating and sleeping. I wonder if she doesn't envy me in some way. A woman of her ilk feeling jealousy for a lovelorn pastry chef? I dismiss the thought.

"My mother used to work for Amalie Rosenblum, a milliner in Friedrichstrasse, and they always needed models," I tell her. "You could get yourself hired for the next season. Frau Rosenblum will know of other designers who might take you on. You could make a fortune."

"That's perfect, Esther! I'll earn real money, but I'll be free to work the kabaretts at night." She throws her arms round me and kisses me. "And goodbye to all bankers then," she whispers in my ear, as Tucholski reappears from behind the suspended quilt.

We are reconciled and it feels as good as it did when Wolf offered me the job of head chef. We have soon knocked off the bottles of beer and the bottle of sekt. I stumble back home at three o'clock in the morning. I'm drinking a final toast, before heading for bed when there's a fierce knock on my door. It's Tucholski. Someone has been looking for me in the courtyard, he explains, and there's a message. I rip open the envelope he hands me and discover a note written in red ink. For a minute, I assume it's from Wolf, maybe something he's forgotten to mention in the interview, but then I check the signature. It's from Frau Frankl, the baker's wife who used to haggle bags of

Purim spices for tickets in the synagogue. She has, apparently, been trying to track me down for some time. There is news of Benjamin, but it's not news I can drown with a bottle of sekt. Benjamin never even went to war, Frau Frankl reveals. He hanged himself from a lamp post, shortly after I left for Augsburg.

"They think it was the shock of discovering your Pappa's body the way he did," Frau Frankl continues in her untidy, red scrawl.

She begs me to go back to the Scheuenviertel, but in the weeks that follow I'm scarcely able to put one step before the other out of my front door. Even Tucholski has to knock a dozen times or more, before I answer him. Our roles reverse. He cooks and I eat like a sick child, too absorbed by grief to even taste what is put before me. Kaya also visits daily, sporting a dizzying succession of designer hats. She tells me that Wolf sends his condolences and that he intends keeping the position of head chef open for me.

She also manages to winkle out of me my guilt over abandoning Botticelli. I have got it into my head that this news of Benjamin's death is retribution for my ingratitude. Kaya sees a drama unfold around her and immediately finds herself a role to play. She shoots round to Café Botticelli and acts as intermediary between me and my former employer. Goodness knows what stories she spins, but the very next day a hamper containing various culinary delicacies handmade by Botticelli himself is delivered to the courtyard. I don't believe I deserve this gesture of magnanimity and end up feeding the food to stray dogs.

"I was beaten in prison," Tucholski reminds me, "but now I'm praised in the kabaretts. Change will happen to you too, Esther. Take up Wolf's offer. Challenge your demons head on."

I'm in confrontation with the world once more. Confrontation is a tobacco stinking prostitute standing on a chair; a Frau Stein with dagger eyes and spitting mouth. I'm no match for such rivals.

"I'll argue with you until you give in, Esther," Tucholski warns. "That's a promise. All the while you're angry, you know you're still alive."

"To what end?" I snap back.

"You bake the most wonderful apple strudel. I'm no match."

I look askance at him.

"No, I'm being serious," he protests. "You have a rare gift. Exploit it. That's how I survive, when it boils down to it."

What neither of us needs to say is that I must work, if only to avoid being evicted from my room in the Moabit. So, I make amends with Botticelli first, sending round a sugar spun Gothic tower. Next, I send Wolf a telegram explaining I will start work within the week, but first I intend returning to the Scheuenviertel.

bakery of lace

err and Frau Frankl survived the Great Storm of 1915 relatively unscathed. At the time, Frau Frankl claimed it was down to the power of prayer, but Herr Frankl conceded it was more likely owing to their taking refuge under the table where he rolled out his bread dough. Their only regret was that they had missed Pappa – and Benjamin's – last Purimspiel. The Frankl's bakery in Gipstrasse has always fascinated me. As a child, I rarely saw anything beyond the doorway that led up to their apartment, so I had always assumed the couple were permanently engaged baking and selling. The reality is like walking into the centre of a huge white spider's web, for every surface in the apartment, from floor to ceiling, is covered with intricately woven pieces of lace.

"Carrying such a large bag and so near the Sabbath!" Frau Frankl cries out, as I stoop through the doorway. "I haven't so much as a lipstick weighing down my pockets. I observe the law, Esther. Ach, but you should ignore my ramblings. What need has someone like me for vanity on any day of the week? I'm past such nonsense as you can see. There is nobody going to walk me under the wedding canopy, but my husband. You do remember him, don't you?"

Frau Frankl is eloquent, which is just as well, as I've been reticent in speaking my mother tongue these past few years. I walk into the hall, remove my coat and she's still not paused to draw breath. On the side table in the hall, two braided hallah loaves sit beneath a fringed cloth. The tray underneath the loaves bears the traditional inscription: "*Eat your bread with joy.*"

"Oh, but how he suffers with his stomach," Frau Frankl gallops

109

on. "May Heaven throw water on the fire in his bowels. Either that or I must find a doctor who can put up with his temper. I'm a fuse lighting gunpowder whenever I speak to him about his condition. Ach, I bear it, as best I can. If God wills it, so be it, but it's a curse. He has to tiptoe up to every breath of his and catch it unawares otherwise it's a like a red hot snake twisting in his belly. Imagine! May you outlive his bones." She peers up at me, her sheitel slipping at a dangerous angle over her right eye. "Ach, Esther. You have been away for too long. And now you are a woman." She skims her hands lightly over my hair. "I remember when you cut all this off because you wanted to be a boy," Frau Frankl sighs. "It so worried your mother, that you would never be happy with anything unless you could change it first. You took her millinery scissors and chopped off your plait in one go – like this!" Frau Frankl turns her fingers into snipping blades and clicks her tongue. "Your mother sold it to Agnes, the flowerseller, so she could have a false hairpiece made."

"Ach, such sorrow for us all," she continues, dragging me back to the present. "They say Benjamin lost his mind, after seeing his friends crushed up like eggshells. What a night that was, but I need hardly remind you." She halts for a second, no more, before sliding on to a new topic of conversation. "Now you must look at my lace collection. Esau buys up bits for me wherever he goes."

She flings open a pair of double doors and we walk into her parlour. Swags of frothy lace billow down from grimy windows, shutting out the dullness of the day beyond. The room itself is a symphony in lace and polished silver – there are even small lace ribbons tucked around the dozens of silver photograph frames. Frau Frankl steers me across the corridor and into the bedroom. The room is dominated by a pavilion made up of lace streamers, which hold in their flimsy embrace a large metal bed. Moving in close, I feel as if I'm walking into the heart of a picturesque waterfall. We are still discussing the quality of Esau's fabrics when Herr Frankl unexpectedly joins us. He has just finished his shift before the Sabbath begins, his arms and shoulders covered in flour, so he blends in with the strange white landscape. Herr Frankl wears a singlet and large blue trousers tied up with a thick leather belt. His arms are surprisingly slender, like a dancer's. He has come to change.

Frau Frankl fishes out a jacket from under one of the drapes and helps him into it. A soft coating of flour manages to stay on him. Returning to the parlour, it dissolves into the velvet armchair where he sits.

Removed from his world of yeast and flour, Herr Frankl is largely silent. He sips coffee from his china cup and smiles at me and his wife in turn, as if reassuring us that he is perfectly satisfied with this state of affairs. Indeed, it's Frau Frankl who launches the attack.

"You might think we view the world through a gauze, but you would be wrong," she warns. "What I'm saying is this: we are concerned about you. We are concerned at how far you have travelled since leaving the Scheuenviertel."

"It has not been easy, Frau Frankl…"

"And it will get harder, if you continue to deny all that you were once taught."

Frau Frankl had butted into my confession, like an overkeen puppy. Herr Frankl lays a restraining hand on her arm.

"Ach, patience was never one of my virtues. I would make the flour rise before the yeast were added, if I could be sure of making a quicker sale. However, it's not your job that is the problem, Esther, but the man who has just employed you."

I wait, expecting to hear the usual litany of complaints about Wolf's profiteering on food stored in his warehouses during the war, but I am unprepared for the revelation that follows.

"You remember the storm, of course you do," Frau Frankl begins. "But do you remember what was said at the time about the condition of the hostel in Auguststrasse?"

"I remember Frau Stein thought I had brought it down around our ears, but it was an act of God wasn't it?"

"An act of God? Herr Frankl did you hear that?"

Her husband shakes his head and a little shower of flour falls on to the velvet armchair. Frau Frankl recovers her powers of speech first.

"Ach, it was no act of God. The landlord's agent didn't keep his property in good repair. It was an insurance claim, you understand? You see him now, that same man driving in the streets in one of his fancy cars without a single care for any of those souls he let be taken so cruelly from us. Thirty-three people dead and he buys a new car!

111

And your parents amongst them, carried out on a stranger's front door, like two sausages on a butcher's tray. It was Wolf's agent who was to blame. May fire burn in his evil, black heart."

I've never doubted the rumours about Wolf's illegal activities, but that he might in some way have brought about my parents' deaths – even at one step removed – is quite incredible. I ask Frau Frankl more questions about the incident. What has she heard and from whom? Had the authorities ever been brought in to investigate? Frau Frankl laughs at my questions. Nobody ever showed a great deal of remorse for a group of penniless refugees, she points out. Compensation, justice? Swept under the carpet, like dust.

"You're saying that my employer's agent as good as murdered my parents?" I ask. "And does that mean Herr Wolf is guilty too, although he might not have known about the insurance claim?"

"We mustn't forget poor Benjamin Stein," Frau Frankl interrupts, not overly pleased I've put forward an opposing point of view. "That agent's blatant contempt for his victims' fate must have swamped his reason."

"But what on earth am I going to do? I've left my old job and I'm destitute without my new one. It's a huge gamble to turn down Herr Wolf's offer without knowing all the facts. And I've no one else to support me."

Herr Frankl puts a floury hand on my shoulder and squeezes it gently, as he speaks.

"You have your friends, Esther," he reminds me. "Please don't forget us."

"Exactly," Frau Frankl continues. "And you must listen to us. What can we tell you? That you are young and you are strong. You can make changes in your life. You don't always have to bake to the same recipe."

She's building up to something, I can tell. She threads her hands together and taps her toes expectantly. Herr Frankl takes up where she has left off.

"You will have control over everything that goes on in the kitchen at Schorns?" he asks.

"Yes, I'll be organising the rotas, hiring and firing the kitchen staff. Devising the menus and ordering the food and taking care of its disposal. I'm unlikely to find another position that would suit me so well…" I hesitate, aware that my arguments must sound selfish in the circumstances.

"You will oversee the disposal of waste food?"

Herr and Frau Frankl exchange looks.

"Well, what does the law tell us about that?"

Herr Frankl's question throws me completely – there are laws about the disposal of waste food? He prompts me with a quotation: "*You are not to gather the gleamings of the harvest. You are neither to strip your vine bare nor to collect the fruit that has fallen in your vineyard. You must leave them for the poor and the stranger…*"

Hearing these words again, my memory unfolds, like a bolt of silk across a polished floor. I was taught their meaning by Pappa on holiday. It came about after a miscarriage Mama suffered when I was five years old. The doctor said she had to recuperate away from the city, so we set off for a short break in the countryside where one of his pupils lived. Our stay with the Katzbergs, just outside Naumburg, was the only time then I had ever left Berlin.

The Katzbergs grew many different kinds of fruit. Even the house they lived in seemed to blossom and ferment according to season. Everybody joined in the rituals of harvesting and preserving. I played my own part. I collected windfalls and added them to the heaped piles that squeezed out any other presence in their tiny kitchen. I breathed fruit, ate fruit and at night time, I smelt the flowering orchard trees in my dreams. I often slipped away to go and eat windfalls in my hiding place behind the farm's outbuildings. I sat with my back against an old well, shaving apples of their peel. One day, Pappa interrupted me. He sat down and gently pulled at the peel caught between my hands.

"This is not right," he said. "The fruit that falls from the trees must be left for the poor."

"But where are the poor, Pappa?"

"Everywhere."

I looked around for some shabby beggar hidden amongst the trees.

"Look up, Esther," Pappa continued. "See all that fruit up there, more than enough to fill our stomachs for the rest of the winter and beyond. So, what need have we of these extra apples? We can let them go, because too much is not right. We should be generous instead and leave them, as our law tells us, however little we may possess ourselves. For one day, we might be the hungry beggar who has to search the ground for fallen fruit."

The drowsy heat of that long forgotten summer day seems to blur with the warmth given out by Frau Frankl's little fire.

"What are you trying to say?" I ask the couple.

"A lot of food goes to waste in that restaurant of yours, no doubt?" Herr Frankl says. "And there are some who will scavenge for those leftovers in your bins, like rats. You should leave them out for the poor, but not in bins. These people should eat as if they were seated at a banquet. They should not be made to feel ashamed of their hunger."

This idea appeals to me: what Wolf's shameless agent has taken away with one hand, I can give away with another! This is, no doubt, what the Frankls have plotted all along. Better still, Benjamin would have approved of such a scheme. He was always giving away his dinner, or his sweets, in spite of Judith's rebukes.

"You think by doing this I can atone for what has happened, Herr Frankl?"

His eyes gleam in the light of the coal fire.

"The distance was not as great as I first feared, Esther. You might yet prove to be your father's daughter."

I develop my plan still further, after taking up my post in Schorns. I decide to serve my Die Suppe Rosenbaum, my signature dish, when I set up shop in the restaurant's courtyard. The Frankls lend me some spare trestle tables from the bakery and, by September I have a thriving soup kitchen. Word spreads quickly about a service like this being run out of the city's most prestigious eating establishment. It even reaches the ears of Bertolt, who writes a ballad about my soup kitchen. The ballad becomes a hit and I discover just how far Bertolt has come, his dramas winning him huge praise, and more lovers than I have bread loaves for my diners.

The Frankls help me meet demand by sending over batches of loaves whenever they can spare them from their day's orders. They frequently accompany their donations with requests that I return to the synagogue of my childhood. I turn them down, however, convinced I can better serve my faith by running my soup kitchen. Rituals are little more than empty gestures unless they connect with the life lived beyond a synagogue's teachings. Each repeated gesture can become guardian to a certain kind of truth: the windfalls of apples, the challa loaves, the fingers dipped in wine, all are sensory experiences that stand in for harsher truths. People are blind to those who can't afford to eat. People like Wolf, who eats to excess every day. I decide I can't do much about the shadowy business deals conducted by his agents, but I can redress some of the injustices they perpetrate within the boundaries of my soup kitchen. I know I can also honour – in part – the rituals of my faith, even if I do distort them by employing kitchen ladles and storm lamps instead of a silver yad, or a menorah candlestick.

Needless to say, Wolf sniffs out my plans in a matter of hours. He tells me I can run my soup kitchen on his premises on one condition: I supply his restaurant with new recipes that will stun the critics. He is not unaware that my out-of-hours commitments attract good publicity in some quarters and, ever anxious to stroll in the spotlight, he lets me go my own way. It seems a generous offer on his part, but I have to work twice as hard to keep up with the many demands being made on me. The responsibility to cook up new menus for the Jugendstil Room takes me to Wolf's crowded bookshelves where I ransack his antiquarian tomes for recipe ideas.

I'm different to the common run of restaurant servants, Wolf claims, and so not subject to the same laws he imposes on his other employees. I know it already: in my ivory tower, pressed in by the peeling walls of my steamy kitchen, I flourish like a flower growing in a swamp. My colouring is too strange and too vivid to be shown out of doors in daylight hours. It's a fact, but it's also a news story. The city's restaurant critics swallow it up as fast as they do bowls of my latest innovations. Over the next twelve months, they digest my legend and embroider it. Wolf feeds them gossip and I provide the rest in silver bowls and tureens. In this way, we call a strange kind of truce over the events of 1915 in the Scheuenviertel. When I do raise the subject of the illicit deals done by his agent in Auguststrasse, Wolf feigns ignorance. With so many men sent to the front, he could barely pick and chose his employees, he points out.

One evening, my boss brings a stranger to my soup kitchen. He has picked him up outside a club in downtown Nollendorfplatz. Wolf often goes there at night, moving like a blind old fish, his feet made unsteady by the Forget-Me-Not he takes alone in his apartment. This latest conquest has a terribly damaged face: his inflamed eyes run with some foul coloured liquid. Wolf whispers he is cheap, but it is his repulsiveness which really attracts him. I ask to hear the stranger's story, but he has difficulty speaking through his puckered lips.

"Write the words down," I suggest, hunting in my pockets for pen and paper. He shakes his head and, painfully, mimes to me that he is illiterate. Then he motions me to take his hands. Our fingers lace together and he makes a series of gestures with them.

"You have to talk with your hands?" I ask him.

"Essential in his line of trade," Wolf mutters under his breath.

The stranger smiles and his burned skin pleats up, like an accordion's belly. His face has almost been destroyed in a terrible factory fire. When he finishes his story, he gently brushes the air around my head in a mockery of an embrace, before making a crude gesture signalling he has to go back to work. He pulls out a pocket handkerchief and unknots its corners to show me he has earnt only a few stained banknotes that evening.

"Your clients are very mean," I commiserate. He gives Wolf a significant look, but he chooses to ignore it. This man no longer means anything to him, but each night, I leave a bowl of soup aside for him. He never comes back though.

Tucholski often visits my soup kitchen for inspiration and the stories of its regulars. Other clients follow him from the kabaretts. Truth telling, they are not that far removed from my diners in terms of their finances.

The soup kitchen up and running, I take time out to visit Esau Jakoby and am relieved to find he is still living in his old apartment in Linienstrasse amongst his mountains of old clothes. Esau tells me his eye for a bargain remains undiminished, even though business is slow.

"I've not been to a house sale in months, Esther," he reveals. "People hold on to their bargains. We wear them to threads these days and what use are threads to anyone but your mother? I still miss her. Such fingers! How she could sew!"

Esau sighs. His only lucrative trade, he reveals, is in army uniforms. His supply comes direct from the battlefields of Europe, washed and mended en route by another army of near-starving widows. Wolf has set him up in this trade. (It would appear he has the monopoly on employing the Scheuenviertel's inhabitants.) Our talk of uniforms puts me in mind of an idea I have been mulling over. It is difficult for me as a single woman to go out late at night to find my diners. But I remember how Kaya met such a challenge in the aftermath of the ill-fated Bavarian Republic in Munich. She put on one of Tucholski's old suits and performed her cabaret act on top of café tables. She had been invincible – and she had set a new dress trend among Malkeston's circle. Maybe a well-cut suit will win me some of her chutzpah, as well as offer me a useful disguise in downtown Berlin?

"I'd like you to make me a trouser suit, Esau," I say.

"A *trouser* suit?"

"Yes, that's right. I need to make myself less visible."

"Less visible? With those feet?"

"Esau! I've come for advice, not insults."

"Let fire burn my tongue, if I've offended you," he apologises quickly. "But a suit. Let me see now."

He forages amongst the piles of clothes around him, pulling out a jacket here and a pair of trousers there. He has a lady friend, he claims, who can make me a suit from a dozen cast-offs.

"Frau Meyers is almost as good a needlewoman as your mother, Esther. She can sew with all seven fingers, certainly. She lives close by. I can make an introduction, if you like."

"Tomorrow?" I suggest, anxious to make a start.

"If need be," he says, but he doesn't sound too sure. "Ach, Esther, you have become impatient, like the age we live in. That is not what I had hoped for when I saw you leave for Augsburg."

"You wanted me to turn into a country girl with apples cheeks and barn-size hips?"

Esau throws back his head and laughs. He rescues his kappel from the floor where it has fallen, before writing down Frau Meyer's address.

"What was I thinking of? This is where you belong." He means the Scheuenviertel. He begs me to return to the quarter. The old rumours have died down and new ones sprung up in their place. He tells me that Judith has left the neighbourhood and gone to stay with relatives in Bavaria; Benjamin lies buried close to Mama and Pappa. He clasps my hand and tells me my return to the city would have meant a great deal to Benjamin. He was devastated that I had to go, he adds.

"It's the past, Esau. We must look forward."

I take my own advice. The very next day, I meet with the tailoress. Frau Meyers is a squirrel of a woman whose tiny hands move like darts around her various pieces of needlework. She's curious to hear about my life in exile and so I tell her all about Frank and Wilhelm and the wonders of the synagogue they helped to build. I soon learn that Frau Meyers's faith is like a giant embroidery, stitched out of a thousand stories and rabbinical sayings.

"There is nothing more whole than a broken heart, Esther. How can you love without also knowing despair?" So Frau Meyers consoles me, after I talk vaguely about an unrequited love for a man I don't dare name. I'm superstitious in my old neighbourhood – if I say the name out loud, it will bring bad luck. I spin out my story like rolling a cotton reel and reveal that the man I admire is a balladeer – and married.

"I didn't really know it before now," I say, surprised at my own confessional tone. "I admire this man, because he puts me in mind of my father. The same gift at telling an anecdote, or writing a choice phrase."

Frau Meyers listens without prying, or contradicting. She hops from chair to window sill and back again. She props her truckle bed up against the wall, so that I can sit down on the floor and stretch out my legs.

"We must get the measurements exact," she points out. "A tailored suit, those were my instructions from Herr Jakoby. Nothing slipshod."

She measures me up with tape and string. She draws her pattern out on top of several pieces of brown paper glued together with paste and brush. My two bodies – one a living, breathing mass, the other a silent paper shadow – squash Frau Meyers into a corner of her room where she begins to cut up the suits given to her by Esau for the enterprise. My pinstripe suit is going to be cut with sharp-edged lapels; the trousers will fall in neat folds. Frau Meyers takes two days to stitch her miracle: she lines up the pin stripes from a dozen suits so effectively, it's impossible to tell where one jacket starts and another ends.

"A work of art," Esau declares. "Even your mother would have been proud of such a suit." Frau Meyers blushes. She drops her needle and lets her hand come to rest on Esau's shoulder. They are in love, I see, as they stand before me admiring the herringbone stitches. I feel as cold as a pebble. Their shy display of affection tears my heart wide open. I stand apart from such happiness. Nor will this suit lend me the glamour of the woman who inspired it, or bring me any closer to her lover.

suiting myself

Late November and the rain comes down so heavily, the streets outside are reduced to a filmy mirage. I'm interviewing for a new kitchen hand, Bertolt Brecht is coming to dinner with a posse of admirers and I need extra help. He's riding high professionally following the successful staging of his play *Drums in·the Night* in Munich. I've not seen him for an age and I'm delighted things have turned out so well for him since he was holed up in Ice Life Street. Kaya has brandished the reviews for his play under my nose. She knows Bertolt, of course, from their Malkeston days. She says she's going to toady to him in the hope of winning a role in his next play. I just panic about what to serve up for such a disparate group of people. Maybe we should stuff an elephant with cloves and be done with it?

I sit on a stool by the tradesmen's entrance and wait on my last interviewee. Karl Schmidt is over an hour late. The minutes tick by; the rain pours down. When he does finally arrive, he's not only soaked but terribly nervous. He apologises over and again, dropping his hat and then crashing into one of the stoves, sending three chickens spinning. He's very young, maybe fifteen, sixteen. His blonde hair is trimmed so close to his skull, it looks like a second skin and his grey-blue eyes are fringed with thick blonde lashes. His posture is defensive. I try and put him at his ease by offering him a chocolate from my spice box. Karl looks startled at the sight of such beautifully wrapped sweets.

"Can I eat the shell too?" he asks, trying to raise his soft pitched voice above the crash of the rain. He pauses. "Fräulein Rosenbaum, might I ask you something else?"

I'm intrigued at this role reversal between interviewer and interviewee.

"Go ahead, Karl."

"Why are your boots so old?"

I glance down at my feet. He's right. These boots, made for me back in Augsburg really are a disgrace, all cracked and stained by winter snows and rain.

"You're Jewish aren't you, Fräulein Rosenbaum?" Karl perseveres. "We couldn't meet the other day, because it was your Sabbath and you weren't at work."

I nod, intrigued.

"Well, my father tells me that all Jews are rich, but here you are working in a kitchen."

"There are rich Jews and there are poor Jews, Karl," I say, choosing my words carefully. "I suppose I'm one of the poorer ones, but I don't see it like that: I have a gift which I treasure more than money."

"But you earn a good wage as a chef?" Karl asks bluntly, despite his timidity.

"Enough," I laugh, "But still not enough to repair my boots, it would seem. Poverty is not discriminating, even if many people are."

I hear all about his father's vindictive talk after I take Karl on. He tells me his father was invalided out of the army, his face torn apart by a mortar shell. We are sharing the graveyard shift which proceeds the first of the breakfast servings.

"The field surgeons sewed him up, but it was a botched job," he reveals, stopping to wipe his hot cheeks on the back of his shirt sleeve. "Just the one glass eye to suggest a human being in there under a ladderwork of blisters."

He rummages in a wicker basket, finds a few pieces of wood that are not wet with sap and flings them into the stove. His eye catches mine, as he turns round.

"I don't like the idea at all, do you? Dying in a wet ditch, I mean, like he nearly did and most of his friends. He beats me when I say things like that. I try and run away, but it seems wrong, him being blind and everything. But I don't want to fight."

"Armies have catering corps," I suggest, but only half-heartedly. "We could always join up as frontline chefs."

We take a sly look at each other. Neither of us wants to go to war, even if we could roast, baste and grill our way through the carnage. A week later, Karl turns up for work, his face swollen by a big, black bruise.

"I told father I liked a Jew and he hit me."

Friction enters my world, bold and direct as an arrow. First, prejudice and then Bertolt Brecht who wants his lover, the singer Marianne Zoff, to come to the dinner but Kaya has kicked up a fuss. She thinks Marianne will try and stop Bertolt hiring her for his next play and who can blame her? Poor Marianne has got a rival and a half on her hands. Kaya is being head-hunted by Fritz Lang, a new director in town and one seemingly not put off her by her recent revolutionary zeal. There is also talk of her being rehired by the Bebelsberg Studio. Bertolt likes successful people around him and there's none more successful than Kaya Tucholski right now.

In the end, she arrives at Schorns – without an invitation – accompanied by a scrum of reporters and photographers. Marianne is absent from the line-up surrounding Bertolt when he makes his entrance. Wolf is ecstatic. I'm to create a banquet from scratch, he orders. I play safe and do a variation on my jugged hare recipe – but served up inside hollowed-out toy drums. Eventually, we have things under control (and Wolf banished from the kitchen), and I risk creeping upstairs to catch a glimpse of my old friend, as he tucks into a plate of Hare-in-a-Drum.

Craning through the bannisters, I see him seated in the middle of the restaurant, like a God in Parnassus. Wolf sits on his right hand side, Kaya on his left. Surrounding them is a motley crew made up of Bertolt's theatrical cronies. Kaya looks a mix of sophisticated socialite and down-at-heel vamp. Her lipstick is smudged and the flowers in her corsage have wilted, but the cobweb threads of her chiffon dress expose her every curve. Bertolt is attentive of her, I see that much at once. He's up to his old tricks. He kisses the ear poised towards him. Kaya takes it all in her stride, as if it has been scripted to her own design.

"Here she is at last, Bertolt," she calls out, above the general uproar. "Your wicked grandmother's protégé."

"Esther Rosenbaum," he yells, jumping up to his full height on his chair. "But who else could it possibly be up there amongst the cobwebs?"

A passage is made for me through the tangle of chair legs, upturned glasses and abandoned plates that surround the glittering circle. Bertolt kisses me and hugs my neck. Tears choke me. The Jewish actor, Alexander Granach, offers me his chair to sit on. He sweeps a low bow, but bangs his head on the edge of the table causing the designer Cas Neher to spoil the image he has drawn on the tablecloth.

I'm still reeling from Granach's praises when I return to my kitchens to check on Karl's progress. He's as delicate as a child and I'm terrified he's going to cut off his fingers as he chops vegetables. Bertolt follows close on my heels, eager to share a cheesecake and to chat privately.

"We have both done well, Esther," he reflects, "particularly when you think what might have been, after the revolution."

"It's the past, Bertolt," I reply as he looks around him, taking in the shadow-filled, cavernous kitchens. "We have to keep looking ahead, if we are to stay sane. But talking of the future, what about your next play? Will you cast Kaya? She's desperate to work on the stage again."

"Who knows? But I'll need to walk carefully."

"Why's that?" I ask.

I think I know the answer as well as he does, so what he reveals next really does surprise me.

"I'm a married man, that's why."

A man married for precisely two days, but already in trouble. Rumour has it that Tucholski is kicking up rough about some notes which he found hidden in one of Kaya's old hat boxes. Notes penned by one Bertolt Brecht.

"We flirt over business," he says airily when I quiz him further about Kaya and the state of his relationship with her. "It makes it a less dreary event for the both of us."

He tries to change the subject after that, compliments me on my cooking and says he's going to move to be nearer my cheesecakes.

Then he's off somewhere else, I suspect the Tucholskis'. Early the next day, Tucholski knocks on my window. He's called round to say he and Kaya are travelling to Potsdam the very next morning – filming with Lang at Bebelsberg is due to start within the week. They are going to rent an apartment near to Park Sanssouci. He adopts a bright and breezy tone, but he's anxious below the surface. I wonder if the suddenness of this departure has anything to do with a certain late night visitor?

"You must come and visit," Tucholski declares, as he takes another lap around the kitchen. "We'll get the studios to send you a car. You'll be a film star too. And you can throw away your aprons!"

God knows, I'm going to miss him. I want to share my feelings, but I can sense how preoccupied he is with this move to Potsdam. He circles me once more, before finally giving in to his suspicions: "You'd tell me, Esther, wouldn't you, if people were talking about me and Kaya?"

"What talk?" I act the innocent – but I'm no Kaya Tucholski.

"I don't know, really," Tucholski admits. "That's why I'm asking you. I mean, I already know about the poems in Kaya's hat boxes. That's hardly significant, is it? To be honest, I thought they were very second-rate for Bertolt. He's capable of much better."

He's bluffing now. Tucholski has always been afraid that Kaya will fall in love with another writer. Actors, cameramen, cab drivers, bankers, waiters; he never worries about any of them, only those individuals capable of replacing his words with their own.

"This move to Potsdam will give us a chance to put some distance from the Schorns crowd," he continues. "We can get on a better footing. Stop rowing so much."

What to say? I saw the way Bertolt hung around Kaya in the Jugendstil Room the other night. I know he has been sniffing around her ever since their Malkeston concerts together. A distance is opening up, but it is between me and him. I don't feel brave enough to step over it and offer the words of comfort he craves to hear.

After the Tucholskis depart, I head off in my pinstripe suit on one of my endless walks through the city, searching for the hungry to invite to my soup kitchen. When I arrive back at Schorns, Wolf is still up.

I burst through the tradesmen's entrance, my hair tied up with parcel string and my suit jacket over my arm, and there he is propped up against the wall, wielding a new toothpick carved out of ivory and engraved with the initials "E" and "W." They stand for Etienne Weiss, he explains, a neighbour from the Moabit. I'm unlikely to meet him, however. Weiss has collapsed in the street, weak from hunger, and has been admitted to the Charité Hospital. Wolf was sitting with him, but now he wants an early breakfast before retiring to his apartment upstairs. Well, this is ostensibly his excuse for lying in wait for me.

"It's like the war all over again, Esther," he says, moving to and from the larder to the butcher's block where he piles up his edible spoils. "People just dropped down in the streets from hunger and stayed where they fell. We knew we had lost the fight, I suppose. Ach, the streets were filled with survivors who ached like broken teeth…"

"I think you'll find they are still out there, Herr Wolf." I interrupt him a little too sharply, but then I'm always made uneasy when Wolf makes reference to the war. There are many who despise him for his black market activities. Did he so much as sacrifice his hair oil during the crisis that followed Germany's surrender? He made a lot of money in the war and he has used a great deal of it to fit out Schorns.

"What I meant to say was, people are angry at anybody they see stepping above the general misery," I try again, but I've hit a raw nerve.

"I don't see why I should deny that I'm successful!" Wolf snaps back. "I work for it and so do you. The people who complain about me do not, I notice, say "no" to the dishes you serve up gratis to them every day of the week. Yes, I've seen you do it, handing bowls of pea soup over to these troublemakers who call themselves artists. Do I make them pay? No. And what then? I have to suffer the indignity of listening to them denigrate our state opera!"

Wolf casts around him for support of his stance, but finds only Karl Schmidt. The rest of the kitchen hands have sloped off to the local taverns, but Karl doesn't drink. He prefers to dust down eggs with an old pastry brush. I realise suddenly how much he is around and wonder if he has, in fact, got a home to go too. There's no time to make enquiries, because Wolf is angling for my attention again. He's

125

prodding at various tartes with his toothpick and discarding some by throwing them over his shoulder.

"But Herr Wolf, those troublemakers, as you insist on calling them, they earn you your headlines."

My employer freezes in the act. Karl stands behind him ready to catch the remains, probably because he understands what real hunger is.

"I confess, Esther, that's why I turn a blind eye to what often goes on in here," Wolf says. His tone makes me wary. He sounds amiable, but I fear a backlash. "I know I get a good return on this particular investment. As for you, if it makes you feel good, then you must continue, but please remember that I'm not a charity. You may feed some of your friends, of course, like the beautiful Kaya Tucholski, but the rest must fall by the wayside."

He sweeps a dish of eggs to the ground. The shells crack loudly on the slate floor. I signal to Karl to leave us alone.

"You want to play the Good Samaritan, then throw away your apron and good luck to you, Esther," he says, turning to face me and avoiding the yolks. "It's a jungle out there. You mustn't become distracted by that which doesn't touch you…"

"I don't agree, Herr Wolf –"

"I've never asked you to agree with me," Wolf quickly cuts in. "If memory serves me correctly, I hired you to provide my diners with culinary splendours. Demand grows and I'm proud of you, in spite of…"

Here, he breaks off and begins picking at the edges of an apple tartlet. I stand stock still, hardly daring to breath. I might have gone too far by openly criticising him, particularly as my own behaviour is hardly beyond reproach. It is illegal for women to walk outdoors dressed in male attire after eleven o'clock at night.

"In spite of the rumours about you that have reached me. A certain somebody tells me that you have long adopted this disguise. You undoubtedly carry it off rather well, but there are some out there who would not be happy to see you dressed in such a costume."

"It's not a costume, Herr Wolf." I realise this meeting is no chance encounter, but an opportunity carefully orchestrated to warn me.

"We shall not, I hope, quibble over mere detail," Wolf continues, in a slightly more conciliatory tone. "The facts, however, are these: you wear men's clothes at the wrong times and in the wrong places. Out there, where they can bay for your blood and get it, if you are not careful. I respect you greatly, Esther, as you know, and so I'm concerned about you. I must ask you to be more circumspect in the future."

"I don't take risks, Herr Wolf."

This is not the answer he wants to hear. Wolf throws the remains of the tartlet on to the floor and grinds it under his heel. Karl hops back into view with a mop and bucket in his hand. I indicate with a nod of my head that he should leave again.

"Ach, have you taken your brain out to stuff a goose?" Wolf shouts.

He notices that the stewed apple from the tarte has found its way on top of his polished boot. He wipes it off with a tea towel and then continues his sermonising, but his tone is less angry than before.

"Seriously, Esther, it just won't wash with the police," he wheedles. "You break the law, even though you do look rather wonderful in the process. Let me put this another way: do I risk wearing a frock in the Friedrichstrasse?"

"It's not the same thing at all, believe me, Herr Wolf."

"I do believe you, but there are few enough people like me out there willing to accommodate your strange ways," he points out. "We shall have no more arguments about this, but I promise when Etienne recovers I shall ask him to paint you dressed in your suit. We can pop you into one of his portfolios of special drawings. No one will see you there, not unless I give the say-so. What about it?"

I don't feel like appeasing him, however. I wave him on his way to his apartment. There is worse being done in my world. Worse by far is the fact that Bertolt has betrayed his old friend and colleague Tucholski. I confess, I envy Kaya, largely because she has Tucholski in her life. She is loved, but she turns her back on her lover. And he is the man I want more than any other. Achje, Wolf would have done better to caution me as to where my heart lay, rather than the cut of my suit.

the house of clocks

berlin, 1923

I receive the odd letter from Tucholski whilst he's away in Potsdam over Christmas and New Year, but he writes only about Kaya. She's working hard, he says, and everybody has fallen in love with her, even the carpenters who construct the trees she walks under in a fairy tale forest. He also reveals they are planning a move when they come back to Berlin – he hopes before Spring. Kaya is sick of turning her heels on our courtyard cobblestones and wants somewhere grander to live. As usual, she's not doing anything by halves: she's set her sights on the Kurfürstendamm district, so can I keep an eye out on any properties coming up for rent?

This is a blow, I must admit. I don't want to lose the Tucholskis as my neighbours, but there is no way I can afford to move to such a grand district on my wages. In truth, I earn little enough in monetary terms, but there are things more valuable than cash in hand in these volatile times. Galloping inflation has been affecting our city this last year, introducing a brutal existence to many of us – whatever our class. Working for Schorns has protected me better than most – Wolf pays in dollars, or food. I frequently opt for the latter and share my spoils with Frau Schneider and some of the other women machinists in the Moabit who lose work when they get too weak from hunger to stitch to order.

I start making a few enquiries whilst I'm out walking late at night. The Moabit is crowded as a matchbox but being shoehorned into a box is a luxury to many who have been made homeless in the post-war years. Frau Schneider tells me of one war veteran who lives on the doorstep of a bank in Friedrichstrasse, only minutes from Schorns. I take him soup, but he's proud. He insists I knock on the pillar flanking the steps and request permission to enter his "one-room mansion" before he eats.

One night, after serving the man at the bank, I find myself close to Fasanestrasse, a street filled with turn-of-the-century villas. I'm particularly struck by one that stands halfway down, a narrow, six-storey building with a pointed turret stabbing at the skyline above a parade of lime trees. On one side of the turret, there is an elegant porch with some very lecherous looking gargoyles. The basement windows feature heavily carved fretwork, which puts me in mind of Frau Frankl's lace collection. On the other side, above a large rosette window, there are four more storeys, each one decorated with a balcony and stone relief carvings, topped by a large brass clock.

This is a fairy tale house created by a magician's wand to accommodate someone with ridiculous overgrown bones: in fact, the very place I should live. I return to Schorns and plan how I might breach the front door. The next day, my luck seems to be in – I've hardly stopped in front of the porch before a very rotund gentleman bounces down the steps in some agitation at the sight of me. I hold my ground; the stranger holds a large fob watch, as if it were a grenade about to explode.

"Have you been sent by the agency, Fräulein?" he demands. "We were expecting you *two hours ago*. Herr Handke's schedule is timed to the last minute and here you are causing chaos. I suppose you still expect us to let you look at the room, in spite of this breach of manners on your part?"

I cunningly apologise for my bad time keeping and plead for a chance to look round the house. The stranger relents. He introduces himself as Herr Rolf, agent to a Herr Handke.

"I've handled all his business affairs since 1882," Herr Rolf continues. "After we met at the city Zoo, as it happens. I was its finance director and I commissioned Herr Handke to make a clock to mark the retirement of our lion keeper." He pauses momentarily, to put his fob watch back in his pocket. "I must ask you at this point a question of the greatest importance, Fräulein. What are your views on clocks?"

"I quite like them, although I've never owned one."

Herr Rolf frowns.

"Herr Handke is a very special artist," he explains. "He makes the kind of clocks that run for centuries, clocks that are taller even than yourself, clocks that you could quite easily worship. Yes, worship. Ach, the gold, the jewels, the gems, the precious beauty of them all! Which reminds me: cotton wool for the striking of the hour."

"Cotton wool?"

"For the sake of your ears, Fräulein Rosenbaum. The noise in the house can be quite unbearable to some, particularly when the hour strikes. I shall act as your interpreter with Herr Handke, by the by."

"Why do I need an interpreter?"

"It's straightforward enough: when you visit the workshop it will be unlike any other experience you have ever heard – or imagined. There is, as you will discover, the most unique rhythm running throughout this house: it is the combined noise of ten thousand clocks. Yes, really *ten thousand clocks*. Herr Handke has made them all. Before the hour strikes, however, you *must* take precautions. I suggest to all visitors they make a set of ear plugs for themselves with the cotton wool."

"But how will I hear you, Herr Rolf?" I ask, puzzled by his odd request.

"You don't hear me, you *watch* me," he says, with just a hint of exasperation in his voice. "I use sign language with Herr Handke."

Herr Rolf walks into the house and straight up the first flight of stairs. I rush after him and soon find myself distracted by the sight of dozens of cuckoo clocks flanking the staircase's cobalt blue walls. "Miniature birds of paradise nest inside each clock," Herr Rolf points out. "They wait for the quarter hour to sound and then they fly. I decorate them with real feathers from antique hats I buy up in job lots from Herr Jakoby. He is a clothes dealer living in the Scheuenviertel. You might have heard of him, Fräulein?"

He doesn't wait for an answer, but holds his fingers up and counts out the seconds. As his thumb curls down, hundreds of tiny birds appear to fly out around my head, their coloured feathers spinning to create a kaleidoscopic blur. The birds' noisy serenade completed, we continue on our way to the clockmaker's workshop on the second floor. There are more clocks lining our route. I catch sight of clocks curved like women's bodies, each with tiny nipple-pink jewels lowered into their grooved numerals. They lounge between Augsburg Clocks, sculpted with stories from the Bible, Blinking Clocks featuring animals whose eyes move in strict time with the clock's hands, and a Crucifix Clock modelled in the shape of a giant tear.

"Herr Handke's mother posed for this clock, Fräulein," Herr Rolf explains. "He made her cry by stuffing green onions under her nose."

The Cruxific Clock is mounted on the door of the workshop itself. I'm about to meet Max Handke, but I pause, made self-conscious by the delicate mechanisms all around me. Herr Rolf indicates with a nod that I should enter. I take a deep breath and walk into the workshop. It is a long, narrow room, lit by four enormous stained glass windows. I see Herr Handke bobbing up and down amongst his clocks like an animated cherub, his round cheeks flushed with pleasure. I walk over and kneel down on the floor by his side, so that I can better observe him at work.

Herr Handke is seventy-eight years old, but his nimble fingers can still breathe life into the most complex arrangements of wheels and cogs. I watch as he lowers a number of tiny motors and springs inside a watch's case, which he holds secure in his right hand. Many of these tiny pieces of machinery are just a hair's breadth from each other. Herr Handke cleans each part gently with a soft brush, before finally lifting a tiny jewel in a pair of tweezers and placing it in the heart of the ensemble. It's an exquisite piece of work, even though it only measures the width of my thumb nail. Herr Handke points to my jacket lapel and I realise that the watch can also be worn as a brooch. He shows me the silver pin attached to its back, curled like a tendril of ivy, and a small gloved hand clasped over the pin's end for safety.

Herr Rolf hops up to his employer and taps him on his shoulder. They stand and sign to each other for a couple of minutes and then Herr Rolf translates. He wants to show me the room which has been advertised for rent. He leads the way, gesturing vigorously with his hands. The room is located behind one of the balconies, spacious, but with very little in the way of furnishings. There's an old mattress propped up against one wall, a cabinet with tiny oak drawers that once held medicines for zoo animals, and a shabby basket chair. Surprisingly, there are no clocks. The room is very tall, if a little cramped, but filled with light and painted a pleasant creamy yellow. A huge archway leads over to the window, at its centre a carving of a very cross looking Bacchus. He is the spit of my old friend Benjamin Stein and I know at once that this is a sign I should take the room.

We return to the workshop to negotiate my contract. Dusk has fallen and Herr Handke is lighting the oil lamps that stand between the clocks laid out on his work bench. He doesn't seem to have noticed our return. Herr Rolf has to tap him twice on his shoulder, before they fall to discussing business in a series of hand waves, reminding me of the merchants who used to trade outdoors in the Scheuenviertel. Herr Rolf beckons me over to deliver his verdict.

"You have the room, Fräulein Rosenbaum," he announces, "and on very good terms indeed. You don't need to pay cash, because Herr Handke would prefer you to cook in exchange for your board. He recognises you from the papers. He's heard good things about your cooking."

"All meals?" I ask, worried how this might clash with my duties at Schorns.

"Herr Handke eats like a bird," Herr Rolf confirms. "He's in his workshop by seven and rarely stops to eat before eleven at night. He's happy to pick at whatever you can conjure up from ingredients I will buy myself – the black marketeers allowing. Ach, such times! They tell me a dollar is exchanged for four billion marks these days. I don't have dollars, just the odd fob watch to barter."

These are terms I can happily accommodate with my work at Schorns – and, who knows, maybe I can muster up a few spare ingredients from my own larders? Hardly daring to believe all is going so well, I turn to accept and find Herr Handke mouthing an order at me: *"Ear plugs!"*

I push the cotton wool Herr Rolf has given me into my ears and wait for the clocks to strike the hour. The floor of the workshop shakes as ten thousand clocks start chiming and I grip the workbench. Herr Handke is completely oblivious to the racket. He continues to sign his questions via Herr Rolf. He asks me what I think about his clocks. I tell him that I think they are quite remarkable. Herr Handke explains how he started to design such wonders, his moving fingers translated into a story on Herr Rolf's lips.

"I visited the fairgrounds when I was a boy. I loved all the different rides, particularly the carousels. All that frenzy and colour, winding up and winding down, like the pocket watch I was given by my father on my sixth birthday. Time I could clearly see was motion. And so I decided I would try and match those rides with the most spectacular clocks possible."

He chuckles to himself as he recollects his distant boyhood, his several chins brushing up against the collar of his impeccably tailored Norfolk tweed jacket.

"We lose hours and minutes, like coins from a hole in the pocket, Fräulein," Herr Handke continues. "That's why I create all of these clocks – I don't want my pockets to empty too soon."

He turns his attention back to the task of winding up the clocks in the workshop, his white head moving down the room, sometimes just centimetres away from the huge pendulums that swing above him. Why don't they knock him down? Instead, they seem to part as he walks reverently through their midst. Everything receives his closest attention: from the whorls in the raw wood that will be planed into the clock cases to the polished brasses that will later be engraved with his signature.

Not until Herr Handke draws out his silver fob watch do I realise it's time to get back to my soup kitchen. Outside, an early scattering of snow falls on to my lips and I have to bite them hard in order to bring the blood flooding back into my frozen skin. Back at Schorns, I celebrate my impending move with Karl and a few of the other soup kitchen workers.

I arrive at the House of Clocks two weeks after my interview, on a cold February evening. A heavy downpour of sleet soaks me to the bone, but I'm anxious to make my mark with my new landlord. I have purloined a chicken pie and some carrots from Schorns' larders which I cook and serve in his workshop.

We soon establish a routine: I take up snacks on a tray before I leave for Schorns, then I return to cook Herr Handke's supper, before setting up my soup kitchen. If I'm too busy, I send over one of my staff with the dish of the day. Working in my soup kitchen sets me thinking about all those who can barely afford to buy a loaf of bread, never mind one of my landlord's extravagant clocks. But Herr Handke points out his craft is not a superfluous one, but a course of action every bit as considered as the one I adopted when I opened my soup kitchen. He begins his explanation as I kneel by his side, my coffee cup held up against up my cheek to keep me warm in the late evening air. My eyes flit between his hands, as they move between tasks with their usual fluid speed. One blue eye. One green. Lapis lazuli and emerald. I watch him prepare the pieces of stale bread which he uses to clean the watches' pivots. He dries the bread in the corner of his apron and then roasts them for a few minutes over a gas flame on the tang of an old file.

"This was my first job when I became an apprentice," he explains. "It took me a long time to learn just the right texture for the bread, to make it less sticky. And then you must find another consistency all together when you clean down the pivot. Try it yourself, Esther. Put a piece between your thumb and finger and knead it with some of this oil here."

He hands over the perforated tin box in which he stores the prepared bread. I break off a crumb and soften it with a little oil, whilst Herr Handke begins cleaning a pivot with some oil stone dust. The bread is used to wipe away all traces of the dust. I begin to understand how making a clock demands knowledge of a thousand recipes – Herr Handke even collects rain water in old beer barrels to mix up with ammonium carbonate for his special cleaning lotions – and the correct application of any number of skills, from enamelling to engraving. The House of Clocks is a place of inspiration and in time I find myself experimenting alongside my landlord – but in the kitchen, not the workshop. The kitchen in my new home might only be the size of one of my larders at Schorns, but it is a bright, airy space where I can work uninterrupted. Herr Rolf brings in a carpenter to make cabinets and worktops to my exact specification. I suspect he uses wood salvaged from houses where the owners have gone bankrupt. The cabinets are made out of a variety of woods with any numbers of elaborately styled door knobs. How many different histories combine in my kitchen? I find myself daydreaming about who might once have lived behind a door of chestnut wood, as polished and shiny as my rope of hair, or who used to open doors with little handles shaped like bow strings.

History is also important to my landlord, that is to say, the kind of history that leaves its story imprinted in a clock. Everywhere you go tells you a story, he claims, but it's how that story is kept alive that marks out the vision of a community. For Herr Handke, that history is soldered into every pinion and click spring. He shows me a rare seventeenth-century Apple Musk watch, named after the pomanders that people once carried to ward off the stench of insanitary streets. This watch is his inspiration, for in spite of its pocket size, it embodies many of the mechanisms that he has adopted on a larger scale in his elaborate kinetic clocks.

"You must keep your eyes fixed on the lid, and it will reveal its miracle," he explains.

He holds the watch out to me and I stare hard at the embossed silver lid. A heavily jewelled griffin emerges from its centre, its tiny wings opening and shutting, as if it is about to take off in flight.

"It's like something from out of a fairy tale!" I cry.

Herr Handke and I travel the four continents in our many discussions about clockmaking. We exchange stories, which later find their way into new clock designs and dinner recipes. I tell Herr Handke about a basket of stolen pears I was given by a woman who wished to secure immortality by being named after one of my dishes. She stole at night from the kitchens of big houses and by day, slept between the floorboards of an empty apartment to keep warm. I create Lotte's Pear Tree Cake in her honour, and, later, Herr Handke makes a clock in the shape of a tiny silver pear tree, which shivers and drops its fruits when the hour strikes.

In turn, my landlord tells me about King Alfred, a British king who discovered a way of mastering time with clock candles. That a king should have invented something so humble surprises me. Then I remember he was a cook of sorts, even though he burnt the cakes he had been set to watch over. His clock candles burnt too quickly in

England's wintery draughts, so he devised a lanthorn to protect them. A lanthorn was a wooden frame with sides made out of pared-down animal bone. Eventually, I create my own tribute to a king with a love of horology: clock cakes made out of pastry moulded into the shape of a candle, flavoured with raisins and nutmeg, served up in dishes made out of translucent bone.

Slowly Herr Handke's workshop comes to inspire most of my new Jugendstil dishes. In return, I get a private viewing of his kinetic clocks, kept secreted in the turret room from the prying eyes of horological rivals. Over the course of several evenings, he sets into motion the most fantastic of parades with the turn of a key. I watch enthralled the clockwork antics of troupes of dancing women, prides of leaping lions, gilded men-at-arms and flocks of rampaging unicorns, as they squeak and turn on top of their glittering pedestals. Herr Handke explains that they are all prototypes for the city clock tower he plans to build in Berlin, a clock tower so grand it will outshine the legendary Strasbourg clock. Descriptions and drawings of this clock survive, but little else. And what descriptions! They inspired Herr Handke to think on a grand scale, even before he had mastered the art of filing. The Strasbourg clock was situated inside the city's cathedral and measured thirty-four feet in height. Its frontispiece alone consisted of an entire Nativity scene, acted out by life-sized clockwork figures.

"Imagine what it would be like to restore clockmaking to such an art, Esther," Herr Handke says. "Imagine turning the clock face into a living stage for the most enduring dramas of our age. But there is more: I want my clock to be built from the treasures donated by the very people who will use it to check the time."

It must have been years since Herr Handke spoke so personally on a matter so close to his heart. Such trust and faith. I remember Pappa's description of the *"woman beyond worth"* and realise I might be catching her up – at last. I tell Herr Handke stories from my soup kitchen and from the Scheuenviertel and he plans how he might use them as he designs the different sections of his clock tower. Each storey is to feature a different city district, marked out by the trades of its inhabitants – the cake makers, the factory machinists, the artists – even the animals in the Zoo.

"My ambition is to see this clock tower grow so tall nothing will ever be able to fell it, no disaster born of either man, or nature," Herr Handke declares. "And I shall use you, Esther, to measure the height of each storey. They shall be as tall as you are in your stockinged feet!"

theater hoffmann

Life is sweet: Tucholski has moved back to Berlin. He has been hired to direct *The Calling*, a new play that will launch Theater Hoffmann, situated within walking distance of Schorns. And I'm hired to feed the company in rehearsals. Kaya has been given a leading role and Theater Hoffmann is just the kind of place she likes to perform in: it boasts an extraordinary interior filled with original hand painted wallpapers and plaster nymphs, who race around its elaborately gilded ceilings armed with bows and arrows and garlands of flowers.

"Himmlischen kitsch," is Wolf's verdict. He's not far wrong. For Tucholski, the design of the wallpaper is immaterial: his appointment will establish his reputation as a director – and not just as a communist troublemaker.

"It's my first real job since leaving prison," he admits when we meet in the Jugendstil Room on his return.

I raise my glass in a toast. Tucholski reveals more as we down our glasses – the theatrical impresario Dr Heinrich Richter is the producer and he is a long-standing ally of both Tucholski and Kaya. The latter is back from Potsdam too, but busy furnishing her new home in up-and-coming Luisenplatz. She has declined my lunch invitation in preference to shopping for curtain rings. Tucholski reveals she is jealous of my new abode in the illustrious Fasanenstrasse. Nor did she like the the fact that I moved into a grander home before she did. I can't understand her reasoning: the Tucholskis' new apartment is a very plush three-bedroom affair, complete with a housemaid and cook. Tucholski will work in a glass conservatory tacked on to the side of the apartment building, overlooking the River Spree. It is quite a distance from Theater Hoffman but Kaya has organised a chauffeur to bring her to rehearsals as part of her contract.

The producer Richter arrives, turning heads. He is dressed in a beautifully tailored suit and a yellow silk shirt, such a contrast to Tucholski, who is dressed like a dandified tramp. Following on Richter's polished heels are Walter Mundzeck, a failed mathematician-turned-poet, and a tiny stranger in huge workman's boots who looks as if she is about to hoe a field, rather than sit down and dine. Tucholski leaps up to greet her. Mundzeck is like a busy red ant hissing around the edges of a very fine sweet cake in our company, and yet he has already wheedled his way into the stranger's affections. When I discover that the heavy-booted mouse is no other than Eva Schlinsog, the writer of *The Calling* and Richter's latest discovery, I realise why Tucholski is so attentive.

"Evie is shy in coming forwards," Mundzeck cuts across Richter's introductions. "And that's never an advantage when you need a cheque signed, is it?"

Richter raises his eyebrows at this little gem, but there's no response from Fräulein Schlinsog, just a quick glance up at me which reveals her extraordinary eyes, the colour of sea-washed glass. This newcomer with her badly cut hair and workman's boots hasn't been eating too well, if her pallor and fragile wrists are anything to go by. I encourage her to order, as Mundzeck treats the rest of the gathering to anecdotes about his university career. He has absconded from his mathematics course to write a novel, or so he claims.

"Spinster auntie provides my daily bread, but she demands I show her my weekly accounts, doesn't she, Evie?" Although Mundzeck turns to his girlfriend for confirmation, he gives her no time to answer before launching into the rest of his diatribe. "She wants to calculate exactly where her investment might be going," he continues, flicking at a pair of very beautiful cufflinks, which I assume he has bought with his aunt's funds. "Then she accuses me of drinking all the ink I'm buying. She'd rather I do that than write a novel. The idea that a Mundzeck would ever write a novel is not to be tolerated, apparently – she thinks writing is the occupation of wasters."

"Then he has found his true metier at last." This from Richter, who has finished his lobster bisque and is hungry for a conversation not dominated by Mundzeck.

"Well, well. You sniff a hit, don't you, Richter?" Mundzeck ploughs on. "There's going to be money in this play and I warn you all now: I'm not going to see Evie done out of a fortune. It happens all the time, I know, but I shall be keeping my eyes peeled for any Jews that try and fleece us."

I swallow hard on my glass of water. Richter visibly freezes. Eva stares down at her feet.

"No one is remotely interested in anything you have to say, Mundzeck, " Richter finally replies, his voice cold. "Your opinions are irrelevant. Please shut up and let Fräulein Schlinsog speak for herself. Unlike you, she has the talent to put words to a very good use."

"On the contrary, Richter, my opinion has value with the very person you seek to exploit," Mundzeck retorts, his cheeks turning a shade redder than his hair. "I'd advise a degree of caution, before you insult me again."

"Please, don't let's us argue, Walter," Eva intervenes. She's shaking in her horrible boots, but she perseveres. "Dr Richter and Herr Tucholski have been very generous..."

"And what is expected in return, Evie?" Mundzeck erupts. "You're such a child. You don't know how these things work. We could have got Brecht to direct for us and then we would really have hit the mark..."

Tucholski knocks over his chair getting to his feet. He takes off his glasses and slowly wipes them on the tail of his shirt, always a bad sign, but Mundzeck fails to heed any danger. He continues to rant on about Brecht, until Richter is forced to thump the table and bring him to a halt.

"Leave us, Mundzeck," he hisses at him. "Walk out of here, whilst you are still capable. Eva, you stay put." ·

Everything happens rather quickly after this point. Mundzeck spits at Richter, Tucholski thumps him on the nose and then Wolf materialises, as if on a set of castors, banning Mundzeck from the premises. Eva hunches up on the pew bench beside me and bursts into tears. She's no longer concerned where she is, but where she hurts most: in her heart. The wrong love is a vicious thing to have running around in your bloodstream – as Tucholski would probably explain, except he's busy bandaging his fist up with a cloth full of ice having taken a swipe at Mundzeck. The latter staggers down the stairs, closely pursued by Wolf and one of the commissionaires, who is loudly complaining to his boss about getting blood on his uniform in the general mêlée. Richter starts putting on his overcoat, but not before he issues a warning to his weeping "discovery".

"Mundzeck knows you're a more lucrative meal ticket than spinster auntie. It's as transparent as the window here, but you've got the blinds pulled down." Eva is childishly sucking on her thumb and doesn't seem to be taking in anything Richter is saying. "Ach, Esther," he sighs. "You must look out for Evie for me."

"Of course, Herr Doktor," I reply, but he's already moved on.

Glancing down at Eva, I can't help wondering how she's going to survive the backbiting and chaos that will almost certainly accompany rehearsals at Theater Hoffmann, but she unexpectedly rallies when Wolf's Pig Nose arrives, a vol-au-vent stuffed with six different types of mushroom, topped with truffle shavings. The truffles were dug up by a pig's snout in France and brought to Schorns overnight by train. The dish is a favourite of Wolf's, because the pig has been named after him. A pig called Wolf. He finds it amusing, so why argue? Eva wins back my attention with her revelation that she knows me already for she often saw me lunching with Frau Brecht at Café Voltaire. It turns out Eva Schlinsog is a native of Augsburg and has only recently moved to Berlin in order to further her writing career, abandoning a teacher training course along the way much to the chagrin of her parents.

"It's not been a huge success as yet," she admits. "Maybe I should go back to my course next term, or just say I will, and then Pappa will send me an allowance again? I can live on that, until my commission comes through from Dr Richter. That's what Kaya suggests anyway, but what do you think?"

I think this advice reflects Kaya's cunning mind admirably, but then again, Eva probably needs more of this commodity if she is to survive in our world. She's as fresh as a newly sprung crocus.

"When are you going to get paid?"

"Dr Richter says very soon."

"Well then, wait," I suggest. "No point in telling some elaborate lie that will just complicate matters still further, is there?"

"That's what I was thinking, Esther, but I'm not too good with money matters." Eva has carefully banished all the truffle shavings to the side of her plate and is concentrating her attention on the mushrooms. Ach, she has a lot to learn about our world. "That's why Walter is so obsessive. He knows I don't have much money, so he fights my corner."

And his own, I think, but I don't want Eva getting upset all over again. I switch the topic back to her life in Augsburg and discover we know many of the same places and faces.

"It's odd finally meeting you, after all this time," Eva admits. "I mean, you were such a sensation in Augsburg. Everyone was a bit frightened of you, to be honest. Catch your eye and we thought we might catch whatever it was that made you grow so tall."

Eva falters as she realises what she has just said. I'm rather surprised too. Since when did being over-tall count as a contagious disease?

"Sorry," Eva apologies, almost immediately. "That was rather tactless."

I wave such tactlessness away. I'm curious to hear how the good citizens of Augsburg came to terms with having a giantess in their midst, particularly one they feared might spread her misfortune to others.

"Nobody knew why you had grown so tall, so they just made things up, I suppose," Eva continues. "Actually, it was the whole household in Hinterer Lech that people talked about. I mean, there were so many rumours."

"Rumours?"

"Frau Brecht is a gambler; Esther Rosenbaum is a whore; Bertolt Brecht, a general disgrace..." Eva counts off each rumour on her fingers, giggling. "Please don't be upset, Esther. I never agreed with any of it, certainly not after I met Frau Brecht. She was so proud of Bertolt, wasn't she? She sent me a signed copy of his play *Baal* and I memorised every line. I wanted to live under the sky just like Bertolt's rebel and drink red wine, but Mama kept interfering with my day dreams. She said if I dreamt for too much, I'd never be happy."

"And?"

"I went on dreaming. And I spied on Bertolt in Café Voltaire. He was amazing when he sang, wasn't he, even if he did wear those horrible shirts with frayed collars. Do you remember them?"

What I remember most clearly is standing alongside Bertolt in my old kitchen, whilst he read his poems out loud. I'd leave dough to rise overnight in the kitchen and the smell of it mingled with my memories of Bertolt's crazy words for days afterwards. His words often worried me – his poet murderers were not the kind of people you would want to meet on a dark night, but they have become heroes to a new generation of writers.

"Anyway, Bertolt told me to write about the miracles in my life," Eva continues. "But before I met Walter, there were very few miracles. I used to make up the world from things I overheard on the trams, or in the market. I wrote in the cemetery. Walter told me incredible stories about his life in Munich. I'd never left home, what did I know of anything?"

Poor Eva. Wracked by her dreams and bamboozled by Mundzeck's self-promotional litany, he had landed her like a fish amongst the headstones of Augsburg's great and good. I laugh as she tells me how she lost her virginity to such a loser. She acknowledges he's no great writer, but insists he has hidden talents, encouraging her to write *The Calling*. Unsurprisingly, it is set in a cemetery and tells the story of three young women who fall in love with a group of army engineers who arrive in a small town to build a bridge. But Eva has started doubting miracles and mentors now her purse is running on empty.

In a bid to move the conversation away from troubled topics, I ask Eva where she is staying in Berlin.

"In a hotel in Kantstrasse. We live in a ballroom, next door to Frau Heckel and her nine children. It's a nightmare, to be honest. The noise and the smell, but Frau Heckel reads my palms and she tells me all sorts of things about the future. You should come and visit, Esther, have your fortune told too."

I know the hotel Eva refers to – it once welcomed members of the Habsburg royal family, but now its rooms have been sectioned off, leaving a catacomb of dingy holes for rent. I arrange to go round on my next day off, but the porter who lives on the ground floor is unsure of where I can find a "Frau Mundzeck" until I describe her in some detail.

"Oh, the mousy bitch living over the brush with the ginger joker?" he mocks. "Second floor up. There again, you could just stand outside and peer in at the window. You'd save yourself a climb."

I stumble up two flights of filthy stairs to reach the ballroom, now reduced to a mess of improvised corridors. I squeeze through its narrow length, watched over by a cupid with a bow and arrow. The rest of the celestial entourage is screened by the cheap wood partitions dividing up each lodging room. Eventually, I find Mundzeck's door. My third knock finally rouses him. I demand to know where Eva is, but he simply slumps down to the floor and throws up in response. I march inside, uninvited, and discover a very small, very cold room dominated by an old mattress, covered in rags. There is an unlit wood stove in one corner, and a table with two chairs pushed up against the wall by the door. Underneath the table, a tin basin and a full chamber pot. The only other decoration in the room are the postcards that line the walls, mostly pornographic postcards dating from the previous century. Mundzeck rolls over on his side and seems to be about to go to sleep, when I land him a hearty kick.

"Where is Eva?" I demand.

He still doesn't reply, but then I catch sight of spots of blood on his shirt. There's more blood on the mattress. Something is terribly wrong and I'm about to lay into Mundzeck again when someone calls my name from outside in the corridor.

"Is that Fräulein Rosenbaum, we want to know?"

I hurry back out and find a woman standing in the corridor, her unwashed hair caught up on her head with a large toasting fork. The stranger isn't much older than I am, but her movements are slow, impeded by her many rolls of fat. I smell drink on her breath, but she's sober enough when she speaks.

"Fräulein Schlinsog wants to know if it's Fräulein Rosenbaum shouting. Is it?" I nod and the woman beckons me over to her doorway. "She's in here, duck, and in a right state," she reveals. "You've come just in time."

I walk in and the first thing I see is a bloodstained blouse laid out on the floor, surrounded by a group of squabbling children. They fall silent when they catch sight of me. One lad, braver than the rest, asks me if I've fallen down from the ceiling. He touches me with his fingertips. I ignore him and head over to Eva who is lying asleep on a truckle bed by the window, her lower lip and right eye swollen with bruises.

"Stupid girl, she is," Frau Heckel declares with a sympathetic tone. "That oaf next door is a lost cause. Told her so myself, Fräulein Rosenbaum, time and time again when I finds her in the corridor, naked as one of my own babies. He stuffs paper in her mouth. Can you imagine? I don't have to tell you why he needs to gag her. Happens all the time. Many's the time we've been sat in here and she's started screaming. I took a fair few knocks from Herr Heckel when he was still living here. What I tells her is this: find a new life for yourself, quick. I looks at her palms and I saw what's what. A tall figure under a star – that's what I said only the night before last, didn't I kids? And here you are. Palms out, duck, and we'll see where to go from here."

Frau Heckel makes coffee and sits me down on her floor. Her children crowd round, now that my height has been so radically shortened. They touch my hair and my cheeks. Frau Heckel takes my palms in her hands and turns them over and over. Then she wipes them down with the flat of her palm and begins her spiel: "Ach, gott! It's like trying to read a tramway map, Fräulein. You've that many lines, you could be eight people all at once!"

"I want to be rich, Frau Heckel," I prompt, but my fortune teller is not swayed by such antics.

"Well, I don't see none of that, Fräulein. What I do see is a life that won't unfold neatly, not like no laundered napkin, oh, no. It's going to be a right old maze…"

But Eva wakes and jumps up out of bed. She reaches out and I grab her hands.

"What shall I do?" she wails. "Herr Doktor wants me to rewrite the final scene, but last night…Walter…Walter tore it up and he made me eat it."

I tell Eva she must come home with me at once to the House of Clocks. Eva takes some cajoling, but lets herself be persuaded. Luckily,

Herr Handke is happy for me to have a friend to stay in the guest bedroom. Helping my friend to undress later I see her body is covered in stale bruises and cigarette burns.

She sleeps on and off for three days, but when she finally gets up I learn more about the nightmare that was life with Walter Mundzeck. Eva's flame-haired "angel" pressed iced glasses against her wrists to keep her from fainting when he raped her with his nicotine stained fingers. He made her pose naked, for his cocaine-dealing friend Johann, just like the women in his postcard collection. Johann tied ribbons round her neck and ankles, drawing them in so tight she fainted. Eva tells me she survived being drugged and bound and tortured like this, because she had her play to rescue her. I'm not so sure. Tucholski is anxious over interference from Richter. He implies Bertolt – or Bert, as he now styles himself – is scheming behind the scenes and, demands his own rewrites from Eva behind his back.

Bert might be away in Munich, but his presence still makes itself felt daily. I can see how Eva has not given up on her idea that Bert Brecht is her knight in a shiny red shirt. She defers to him on her rewrites, just as Tucholski fears, and won't listen to reason (or to me). She accuses me of being ungrateful towards Bert, who, she claims, "saved me" in the days of revolution.

"Bert wants a commission for himself," Tucholski tells me the day before the read-through.

It is August and flies are swarming in their hundreds over the empty dishes in the soup kitchen where we are sharing white beer and sliced apples. Tucholski tries swatting at the flies with a rolled up playscript. I assume it's one that Bert has seen fit to tamper with.

"I think Evie should watch out," he says, squashing a fly dead on top of a plate. "Richter and Bert have twinned up like a pair of dominoes."

On the day of the read-through, I find myself coinciding with Eva on the theatre steps, a basket full of homemade bagels and conserves on my arm. The company waits for us backstage when we finally step behind the gilded front-of-house doors. Walking into the rehearsal room, I'm confronted by two apparitions – my own reflection bounced back at me from two mirrors that have been rescued from an old wardrobe and left propped against the wall. I see my torso and my booted feet, but my head is guillotined from the top of my body by the edge of the mirror. I'm wearing a quilt cloak that Frau Schneider made for me and can see various patches have come loose. I turn from this tatty apparition to a sea of faces which only gradually materialises into somebody I recognise: Kaya.

"Come and sit with me, you two," she calls over.

She sits with her long legs stretched out across the rumpled pages of Eva's manuscript, dressed in a loose muslin dress with one of Tucholski's waistcoats worn over it. I can smell her Nuit de Noel perfume. Richter sits opposite her and beside him is Tucholski. Kaya delivers the opening monologue, but is soon interrupted by a late arrival: Bert. He waits ostentatiously by the door until one by one the company acknowledge his presence. He wears a filthy, distressed leather jacket and his steel-rimmed spectacles are adrift on top of his head.

"Who has persuaded Eva to come up with this nonsense?" Bert thunders. "As if I couldn't guess. It's a disaster. All this fine falutin' poetry. I'd grind it up under my cigar, if I could."

Tucholski is up on his feet, his face red. Various members of the company immediately start to argue about the script's freshly perceived failings. Richter walks up to Tucholski and places his hands on his shoulders.

"Let me tell you something and then we can have a fight," he says. "I've asked Bert to act as script adviser. He has a won a prize for his work. He knows what he's talking about."

"And I don't?" Tucholski is dumbstruck "This is intolerable, Richter. Am I in charge of my own rehearsals, or aren't I? Next, you'll be telling me that Bert is food-taster for Esther's breakfast bagels!"

Bert leaves the actors bickering amongst themselves and moves in on Eva. He whispers something to her and they make an abrupt departure. I'm not slow to follow, because I have lunches to oversee at the Jugendstil Room, and that's where I find them, wrapped up in curls of cigar smoke, ordering carp and pear strudel with raisin ice cream. I retreat to the kitchen. After all: "*if your enemy is hungry, give him bread to eat*". Old habits die hard, but I can't forgive Bert what he's just done to Tucholski. Bert stays over at the House of Clocks that night and seduces Eva. He creeps into her room on feet that are soft as a cat burglar's, but I still hear them making love.

It's a game, not an affair, the chief casualty my friend Tucholski. He is convinced Bert not only wants control on *The Calling*, he also wants to keep Richter dancing to his tune until he comes up with a new playscript himself. Rehearsals over for the day, Tucholski calls by to seek solace and soup. Professional rivalry is putting a rift between my two oldest friends and I have no words of advice. I can help one person, however: Eva. I try and warn her not to take her affair with him seriously, but she's hooked.

"You must take more care," I insist. "Bert demands you compromise all the time, but for him the word is one of infinite meanings, particularly when it applies to his own actions. Listen to what he has to say by all means, but get a second opinion. Talk to Tucholski. He is the director of the show, after all."

But she won't listen, just digs her heels in and waits on Bert. She has a long wait. Bert travels up from Munich on and off throughout rehearsals, but he prefers to spend time with Kaya, if he gets the opportunity. I've seen them leaving rehearsals together on my way to and from work, climbing into taxis arm in arm. Bert pays Eva just enough attention to keep her hoping. I sense Eva's pain, because it is one I share. I yearn too, but have never been rewarded with even the slightest hint of physical intimacy. In some ways, I feel I should just let Eva be; she has a degree of affection from her lover – why hunger for more? Maybe it can be enough – and it is much more than I can ever hope for from Tucholski.

I walk further and further afield as I head out to find new diners, the Musk Apple watch in the pocket of my suit. I can see how another kind of hunger has folded itself around my city, corrupted by senseless excess. How change this? How deal with a world where your friends are on the brink of disaster, a loaf of bread costs 201 billion marks and a shave at the barber's two precious eggs?

I beat a retreat. Unlike my namesake, I find words dry up on my tongue. I hide under my quilts and hold myself as still as can be. I clench up against the cold that invades my skin, but I refuse to take any sustenance – not even my pea soup. I must conquer the pain of denial and hunger. The world can take care of itself and I'll learn to control my overgrown mess of bones. It's bizarre, but I feel much stronger, as my body slowly reduces in size. I can control its shape, if nothing else: I will be the giantess with the pygmy appetite. I must convince myself that I can stomach all that's coming my way. I check on Eva regularly, curled up in bed, her hands clenched so tightly together I'm unable to slip my fingers between them to comfort her. God damn Bert and his lilac-tongued lies. But God help me, how I envy his lack of scruple at chasing after the one thing he thinks he most wants.

ghost boy

The opening night of *The Calling* draws near and I'm walking on eggshells. Wherever I turn, there is confrontation. Richter frequently rings up, begging me to go over to Theater Hoffmann to sort out some dispute. Ructions occur daily over the allocation of lines in the script, or the precise colour of a costume. There's even a dispute over the type of material used to make a dress, which runs on for over a week. On the day of the dress rehearsal, Richter rings earlier than usual and I discover that catastrophe really has struck. I walk over to find the theatre has turned into a battle zone. Bert lies smoking on the stage, unperturbed, but everyone else around him is shouting and bickering. There is no sign of Tucholski. Eva looks particularly awful, her hair and clothes unwashed and her new hat squashed down like a pea under her feet.

"It's really very simple, Esther," she shouts, the minute I step out of the wings. "Everybody has been making demands on me, so I thought why not make demands on them for once?"

Richter hovers close by, armed with a brandy bottle. It appears Eva has threatened to sue him for allowing her play to be rewritten in rehearsals without her express permission – and in rehearsals that have not been overseen by Tucholski. Tucholski has already walked out on the proceedings and threatens not to return. I don't need to guess who might be responsible for either the impromptu, illegal rehearsals or Tucholski's disappearance. He lies supine at my toes, close to a wobbly-looking bridge. Bert's calm demeanour is matched only by that of Kaya, who sits in a garden swing – part of the set – gently rocking herself to and fro. She looks glacial, dressed in a white linen, three-

150

quarter length frock coat. I can't believe she's not intervening to defend Tucholski. I would have had Bert banned from the premises.

"It's always been your problem, Eva, right from the off," Bert drawls, hoisting himself up on his elbows. "You should take life by the throat, not pray for bloody miracles all the time. Tucholski is no miracle maker, is he, Kaya?"

She just smiles at Eva's tormentor.

"What do you pray for Bert?" Eva shouts back at him.

"Well, I don't trust in miracles," he replies, his voice irritatingly calm. "Only in revolution."

Bert puts on his mock philosophical expression, which goads Eva still further. Kaya lights up a cigarette and carries on swinging her garden chair, its chains creaking. I prop myself against the bridge, anxious to stay out of Kaya's field of vision. I catch her eye, I might be forced to act. Kaya's cruel indifference towards Eva goads me more than Bert's posturing. I want to knock her off her wretched swing, but Eva is shouting again.

"So what should I in trust then? Something I read in one of your boring newspaper articles about revolution?"

Revolution, eh? Poor Eva has been pinned to the barricades by Bert, her only armour her handwritten manuscripts. No wonder she's fallen so far and so fast. Richter calls a halt to the dress rehearsal and disappears with the brandy to his office. I decide to rescue Eva from this mess and take her home. Over hot chocolate, she tells me how Bert has touched her with hands as hot as tongues. Her circulation is bad, and her skin is often blue as an iris, but he has turned her into a pink flame of longing. Of course the bastard has. But there is worse: Tucholski is still absent on the first night of *The Calling*. When I confront Kaya before curtain up, she claims she has no idea where he is.

"This is supposed to be Tucholski's comeback," I argue. "You must put Bert to one side and go and find him."

"You don't understand," she snaps back. "Bert has the connections, not Thomas, or Richter. Yesterday's men, the pair of them."

"Thomas worships you – "

"Ah, there's the rub! You're jealous, Esther, jealous."

She's barely ruffled by such an idea, because she knows full well

I can never mastermind an affair with her lover, a man who has loyalty running through him like a second backbone. If it weren't for Tucholski, I would walk away from the wretched production without a second's thought. But Richter invites me to the first night party and I feel it would be churlish to decline. Besides, I still hope Tucholski might show. I join the company at the Blue Piano in the Tiergarten, a gaudy place filled with men with elaborate toilettes who call themselves by the names of their favourite female film stars. I sit between the owner, Hans, and Eva on a red satin divan. Kaya keeps her distance, flirting with Bert at the bar.

"I used to be Liesl Brun," Hans explains. "You know, I can change everything, ladies, except my birth certificate. That still insists I'm a woman, but what of it? It's a piece of paper. Here, there and everywhere else, I'm what I say I am. You should demand the same."

"It's different for me," Eva chimes in.

The rapturous applause that greeted her play has built her confidence. She's wearing lipstick and a racy top that dips towards her navel, revealing her nipples. Hans has already expressed admiration for the quality of the lace.

"We all think we are different, Evie, but under our skins we all cry and we all despair."

"What I mean is, I simply thought I might write under a man's name so as to be taken more seriously by publishers."

Eva is trying to converse in a logical fashion, but Hans is unimpressed.

"Serious is not allowed in here," he interrupts. "Bert has decreed it and what he decrees is usually conformed to, yes?"

He's laughing at Eva. They are all laughing at Eva, even Bert who sits with Kaya at the bar leaving her to merciless Hans. I go over to Bert and persuade him to join us for the toasts, but he is being deliberately provocative. When Richter declares Eva is without question the "saviour of Berlin's theatre", he knocks a carafe of red wine over his cream linen suit. Bert then disappears; Kaya tries to swab Richter down with paper napkins and Hans asks Eva to dance. He smirks and touches her nipples under the pretext of examining her Brussels lace and Eva is incensed. I make my exit unnoticed. Life is short and here

I am friends with a bunch of hysterical egotists.

I quickly get lost in the deserted streets surrounding the club. Piles of evil smelling refuse spill out of the doorways of tall buildings which have been shoehorned together. I walk for a long time, taking reckless turnings, chasing my elusive goal of reaching Schorns in time for the first breakfast servings. Eventually, a light shows up in the far distance. I hurry towards it; I can hear laughter and the sound of a piano. I trust the place's visibility in the otherwise dark street. The club I've just left was built underground, keeping its secrets hidden from anybody not directly invited into its plush interior. The café I now stumble on is alive with extravagant display. I order a beer at the bar and ask the man serving me the quickest way back to Friedrichstrasse. He laughs at my question.

"Long way away, Fräulein," he reveals. "You walk?"

"Yes," I reply, shifting to alleviate my feet in a new pair of lilac boots with silver heels.

"Well, I help you, okay?" the barman offers. "You wait ten minutes?"

He is about nineteen years old with a strong accent I can't quite place. His hair is shorn close to his head and his brown eyes are as round as tea cups. His sleeves are rolled up to his elbows and I can see how the veins have knotted themselves under his skin. I'm attracted by his open manner, even though I know he's probably only chancing his luck with me. What the hell? I think. It's been a long while since I've risked being picked up by a stranger – and there's been precious little in the way of offers from within my culinary circle – so I tell him I'll wait by the door. I take the opportunity to pull off my shoes and I find several weeping blisters on each heel. The barman comes up to me, as I'm inspecting the damage. He crouches down and lifts each of my feet in turn. He shakes his head and delivers his verdict.

"You're in trouble, Fräulein," he says sadly.

"Yes. I'm in trouble," I agree.

"Well, everybody has some trouble sometimes. You must not worry, but your skin, it's… it's… kaputt!" We laugh when he finally hits on the words he was struggling to find. He picks up my shoes and stows them away in his pockets. "No alarm, please, Fräulein. I save your skins."

"My feet. You want to save my feet?"

"This I can do, okay?"

"Okay. But if you do that, I must at least know your name."

"My name is Juan Ruiz."

The name makes me feel as though I'm breathing in a wide, open landscape, swept by pampas grasses and palm trees.

"And I'm Esther. Esther Rosenbaum. Where are you from, Juan?"

"Portugal. I come to Berlin to work."

"And to save women with bad feet."

He laughs. His teeth are surprisingly white and they're not crooked. I'm conscious of my ugly yellow fangs. I turn away from the brilliantly lit interior of the bar under the pretence of studying the view beyond the door. Dawn is breaking. A sliver of pink light is peeping up over the rooftops opposite the bar. Juan leans up against the wall opposite me, his hands dug in the pockets of his gaucho-style canvas trousers.

"You speak good German, Juan," I say, which is the truth.

His accent is good and his grammar catching up.

"I have lived all over the world, so I must speak a little of every language I hear. One day, I go and live in America. I find my brother there and we make a fortune."

"It's a good plan."

"Yes, it is," Juan replies, a small frown appearing between his eyebrows. "You have to find a plan, I think."

"I don't have one."

"But you have a lovely name, Esther."

"Shame about my feet."

Juan doesn't pick up on this. I think he's busy trying to think up the words he needs to explain his next move.

"I give you a help, okay?" he offers, waving at my disfigured feet. "To the tram. Then we go home?"

He moves back inside the bar, which confuses me for a minute.

"Juan, I can't walk," I call after him. "My feet are a disaster."

He waves away my fears and busies himself improvising a pair of shoes from out of a torn tablecloth so no more harm can be done to my feet. I try on my cloth shoes, crouching in the doorway. Juan towers above me and makes a joke about this, but he's not being unkind.

"In my country, I think you would be some kind of a saint," he says. "So tall, so... so tiny."

He rings my waist with his hands. His thumbs overlap just above my navel. I have kept strictly to my decision to stop eating and the results are beginning to show. As we make our way to the tram stop, he tells me more about his dream of sailing to America. At the stop, we sit on the kerb and I lean into him, as if searching for warmth in his words. Juan circles my arm with his fingers. I fold back his jacket sleeve, tracing his knotty veins with my fingertips.

By the time we clamber off the tram, we are walking hand in hand. It's still early. A light drizzle falls, but the streets are full of people and cars. We flit between them like dancers. I decide to head for Schorns. I lead him straight out to the courtyard and into its darkest corner. I lie down and he mountaineers his way up my body. He tears my blouse open and my breasts appear like white globes. He bites hard on my nipples. It's like a strange dream, being caught up in the blackness of the yard, a stranger growing inside me, until I scream with a pain I have never really experienced before. My head knocks on the ground, but I'm hardly conscious of that, just lost in the exquisite agony of this stranger taking me. After we have made love, Juan helps me dress with the gentleness of a mother, tying up my torn blouse before heading back to his bar. I even begin to wonder if he might be a ghost.

Autumn passes and I spend my few free hours alone at the House of Clocks, a pot of coffee going cold beside me. Eva thinks I'm mourning a lost love, but she can't guess it's Tucholski, who I love but cannot help. I can't confide in Eva, because she's in thrall to Bert too, and is in any case returning home to Augsburg. Although her play won applause, it hasn't earnt her very much money, particularly after Mundzeck tricked her into getting the profits and has drunk them dry.

Kaya writes to me from Munich where she is now working with Tucholski on a new revue show commissioned for Bar Grossenwah, a stone's throw from the celebrated Kammerspiele. So far, so good. I read on. Bert is also in Munich, directing a production of *Edward II* – for the Kammerspiele. This is not so good: both shows are to open on the same night next April. There is also news of Tucholski's original leading lady: Francine has been set upon by a group of men whilst she was out at the market. Once Kaya's rival, she is now reconciled to her foe who has had her nose and jaw broken in the vicious assault.

"And all because she was wearing a man's suit, not unlike the one Frau Meyers made you," Kaya writes. *"Tucholski is frantically rewriting her songs to suit my vocal range. We work together in close animosity in a room above a bar, kippered by cigar smoke. I really can't tolerate much more, but it's not just poor Francine who worries me. Tucholski and Bert argue constantly. And then only the other day, martial law was declared in the city. Can you believe it? We were sitting drinking coffee in Malkeston's and our world turned upside down all over again. There has been an uprising in a bierkeller, but this time the man who led it is no friend of ours. I fear the past has come back to incriminate us all and the sight of the barricades has done nothing to comfort me. Disaster strikes at every turn. You must come down, Esther. Please, please do come down. You will save the situation, I'm sure of it. And Tucholski needs you on his side. Forget everything else, please."*

I'm aware that Kaya has sent me an SOS. Having survived the suppression of the Bavarian Republic, I feel qualified (to a degree) to enter the fray again. I plan carefully my return to scenes of revolutions past. First, I have to persuade Wolf to release me from my duties at Schorns. Although I have had no holiday since starting work, he's still reluctant to grant me a fortnight's leave. Eventually, he relents, but there's a catch.

"You must research new recipes whilst you're away," he orders. "And you can wire them to Karl who will take charge of cooking them in your absence."

In addition to the political intrigue mentioned in Kaya's letter, I'm curious to see how Tucholski is faring in the face of his lover's volatile emotions. Is this maybe the moment I can convince him of what *I* feel? I instruct Karl on his new duties and pack for my trip. In spite of the dangers, I fold my pinstripe suit up in sheets of tissue paper and add it to my little leather case. Who knows, but I might need a disguise to weather this new crisis in our lives?

Arriving in Munich by train, I find the Tucholskis in Malkeston's, along with Bert and Edward II, alias the actor Erwin Faber. Erwin is a thin, delicately built man with strange dark blue eyes. He holds his shoulders back, as if pinned in a vice. Erwin is relating news of the Bürgbräukeller uprising which took place just days ago, the incident Kaya wrote to me about. Erwin hardly draws breath from his account to stop and shake my hand.

"It was just like standing in a boxing ring," he continues. "This Herr Hitler plays his audience like a professional. He reminds me of a clown I saw once, nearly as tall as you are, Fräulein Rosenbaum, who pretended to saw a bump off his head and eat it. That shook me out of my boots, I can tell you. Well, this man is a similar kind of illusionist. We believed in everything he had to say, things every bit as incredible as that clown pretending to swallow his own flesh."

"What kind of things?" Kaya asks.

I notice she has bitten her nails raw. One of her false eyelashes has fallen off and landed in her plate.

"It boils down to very little really," Bert replies. "He wants to establish some kind of Utopia where all those damned papersellers in brown shirts can roam around unchecked."

"And what will women do in this Utopia?" I ask.

"Breed for their country, as usual."

Bert gives a deliberately dismissive reply, but before either Kaya or myself have a chance to protest, Erwin jumps in for the defence.

"It was Herr Hitler's supporters who attacked Francine, remember? You don't have to stray very far to be labelled a deviant in their eyes. Forget Utopia, Bert. You should be inventing another kind of theatre – one that challenges these people."

Erwin picks up his hat, ready to return to rehearsal. He waits for an answer, but Bert is intent on lighting a cigar. Erwin changes tack with his departing comment.

"My congratulations, by the way, Kaya."

There is another awkward silence. Kaya's head stays pointed towards her shoes, but I can see tears escaping out of the corners of her eyes.

"Congratulations?" I ask nervously.

"Tucholski and Kaya are getting married," Erwin replies.

"Surely you've noticed how everything is always back-to-front with the Tucholskis?" Bert interjects. "They get married, but only *after* their relationship is over."

I'm stunned by this news. I'd assumed the Tucholskis were already married, but apparently they were only masquerading as man and wife to avoid scandal with the studios. And then there was my secret hope of winning Tucholski for myself. I can scarcely believe how gullible I've been. My head is a whirl, but there is simply no time to catch up. Tucholski is on his feet, fists clenched at his side, and Bert is up too, brandishing a beer bottle and shouting the odds. Tucholski begins coughing violently and then falls back into his chair, as if he has already been punched by his tormentor. Kaya rushes to minister to him. Erwin shrugs and makes his departure. Bert is still tormenting poor Tucholski, in spite of his racking cough.

"So, you find a couple of poems," he shouts at him. "What's the point of getting married, just because you're pissed off by a couple of verses? They don't mean anything." Kaya puts her head in her hands and starts crying. "This is the crisis she must have told you about, Esther. That's why you're here, isn't it? For the wedding? A wedding, mind, which is only taking place in order to appease Tucholski's stupid pride."

"Shut up, Bert!" Kaya hisses at him through her hands.

"My poems have unnerved him. He thinks he can best compete by buying a ring. I can't believe you are going along with this farce, Kaya."

"Don't you have a rehearsal to go to, Bert?" I interrupt.

Bert picks up his cap and leaves without another word. He's made his point. Tucholski leaves shortly afterwards, crawling down the stairs with Herr Suschke acting as support. Kaya is still sniffling behind her hands.

"Oh God, Esther. What a disaster. But Tucholski gave me an ultimatum and I was cornered. The registry office is booked and Franz has offered us a reception in here. And we would like you to be a bridesmaid and witness."

"*What?*"

"Please, Esther," Kaya is almost begging. "Tucholski threatens to ask Bert, if you don't do it. The witness bit, I mean, not the bridesmaid. But if you come, and Erwin acts as our second witness, at least I can avoid that humiliation."

I slump down on the chaise longue opposite Kaya. What on earth has been going on in my absence? Kaya pushes her plate to one side, leans in to the table and fixes me with a steady gaze. There has been no affair, she promises me, but Bert has been putting the pressure on. He slips love letters into her bag when they drink in Malkeston's and Tucholski has read them. As she talks, my thoughts run riot. All these years I have been holding back my feelings for Tucholski, partly out of the belief that to interfere in a marriage would be wrong. (The teachings of my childhood rear their head at the most unexpected moments.) But the Tucholskis weren't married; they were lovers. Would I have acted differently had I known this earlier? It's a quagmire and I should sidestep it instantly. Kaya interrupts my thoughts with another warning.

"And the love letters are the least of it," she points out. "Tucholski's revue show isn't going to have the impact Bert's play is going to have. I've sneaked into a couple of rehearsals and, you know, it's quite brilliant. Erwin's just extraordinary. Shit, what a mess. I can't seem to put anything right."

"Isn't the wedding supposed to be doing that?"

"I doubt it, Esther. But look, we can't talk here. Let's go to the apartment. We'll have coffee and I'll fill you in."

It's the best offer I have had since leaving Berlin on the night train, so we set off on foot to the apartment the Tucholskis are borrowing in Akademierstrasse. We pass through long streets lined with picturesque pavement cafés, jeweller's workshops and second-hand goods shops. I glimpse displays of eighteenth-century dancing shoes, filled with pearl necklaces, old editions of *Simplicissimus* hung from brass hinges and a silversmith with an eyeglass busy working at a bench in his shop window. There are also a large number of papersellers out in force, brandishing copies of a newspaper called *The Stormer*.

"The trick is not to catch their eye," Kaya warns me.

Her advice isn't hard to act upon. I'm easily a foot, or so, taller than the papersellers, something which wins me a lot of contemptuous looks and insults. Kaya is not so lucky. The papersellers push forwards and stare into her face, demanding her attention.

"Come and hear Herr Hitler speak soon, pretty Fräulein," one man shouts out. "A new rally is being organised. You should come along and see him for yourself, why not?"

Kaya ignores him as best she can, but he's persistent.

"Friend of yours? The freak?"

She turns as if to respond, but I beckon her on, as I've just caught sight of a group of men drinking in a café close by. They wear brown shirts like the paper seller and watch our confrontation with him a little too closely for comfort. It's a relief to discover we are only minutes away from the apartment block where the Tucholskis are staying. The tall, pink apartment building is covered with black plant stems, which thread their way up and down the plaster walls in a variety of intricate patterns. A large blue door takes us into a small courtyard. Kaya heads up the nearest stairwell and I limp after her, circling its length like a bead on a wire until we reach the attic apartment. Kaya leads me straight into the sitting room where a piece of rope has been nailed up along the length of the far wall. Dozens of sparkling dresses hang from this improvised clothes rail, each with a luggage label pinned on its sleeve explaining its destination in the show. Kaya unearths some large cushions from behind the piano, my bed for the next two weeks. My sheets and blankets will be selected from the show's costumes hanging on their string rail. I settle on the cushions whilst Kaya makes us a pot of coffee, which she pours out into big china bowls, so we can warm our fingers.

"I usually run outside to keep warm," Kaya confesses. "I chase the moon between the rooftops."

"What about the Brownshirts, Kaya? Aren't they on the watch?"

"Yes. And sometimes they follow me," she admits, her voice tailing off momentarily. "They broke our windows a month ago."

She leans forward, conspiratorially. Enthusiasm finally leaks through her drawn face.

"Ach, I so want to make a stand, like you have with your soup kitchen, Esther. Actually, I'd like your advice on something."

It's no good. I lean forwards too, drawn into her web, anxious to hear what it is that has inspired her this time.

"I've been meeting people through Erwin who have told me extraordinary things," she explains. "They are artists from Russia.

They have shown me maps of their new country. What we only talked about in the Republic, they have made happen in people's everyday lives. A mediaeval social order has gone and painters and film-makers are at the vanguard of change."

I listen to Kaya with some interest. Her renewed enthusiasm for politics is evident enough, but I feel it is underpinned by something else. In a matter of days, I've put my finger on it: Kaya's renewed commitment to the Communist cause is simply another wedge she's planted between herself and Tucholski. Far from encouraging her, he has strongly voiced his opposition. They have switched sides since arriving in Munich. Kaya has come out fighting and has joined the Communist Party, whilst Tucholski has torn up his party membership card.

"I promised I would never expose you to danger again, not after we were forced to hide in that bloody convent," he argues, his voice weary with dispute. "I've not forgotten the fear of waiting to run, waiting on nothing more solid than a stranger's whistle."

We are sitting late at night, smoking and drinking, stretched out on the floorboards under the row of cabaret costumes. Unusually, it's just the three of us. Another sign of trouble between this couple is their habit of filling their living space with other people when they want to avoid talking to each other.

"Esther says you should turn your anger into defiance," Kaya retorts.

"Ach, so you're responsible for this latest act of rebellion, are you?"

Tucholski looks over at me with an expression mixing spite and sadness. He thinks I'm siding with Kaya but, in truth, I know as much as he does about her new ambitions. I also feel awkward being described as a rebel. All I've done is step back into the shadows and watch out for my friends; I've not even unpacked my pinstripe suit, let alone dared to wear it.

"I want to bear witness to something, Tucholski," Kaya pleads.

"You can do that in Berlin," he replies, his eyes still fixed on me. "Bavaria is getting too hot for us and I've no desire to turn beekeeper again."

"In other words, we're going to admit defeat…"

"No, Kaya! I've got to go back to see a doctor about my lungs. I hardly think that's asking too much, is it? I need to go home and get the treatment I hope will keep me alive." I'm thunderstruck: I had no idea Tucholski was so ill. "The pressure of living here has made my condition much worse," he says pointedly.

What he refers to are his battles with Kaya, I realise, not the practical difficulties of rehearsing and opening a new show. He suspects Bert of encouraging her in her new ambitions in order to deepen still further the rift between them; worse, his suspicion has been extended to all who come into his orbit, including me. The confidences we shared in our Moabit days have all but dissolved. Tucholski is convinced I'm just another link in the chain that is wrapped round Kaya, dragging her away from him. "I never thought you'd betray me, as well," he says a few days later.

He is sitting smoking in Malkeston's. The smoke is torturing his already weakened lungs, but he's ignored my counsel to stop smoking.

"Please listen to me, because I have always valued you and what you stand for," I plead. "You're the only constant in my topsy-turvy world."

It is the first time I have ever dared give voice to how I really feel about our friendship, but Tucholski barely registers my heartfelt confession. I feel sick with disappointment when he just shakes his head and ploughs on with his list of grievances.

"Forget constancy," he sneers. "It's much overrated in these times. Better understand short-sightedness, selfishness – betrayal."

Even as he kills my hopes, I try and keep the peace.

"Let me act as arbitrator between you and Kaya," I urge. "I've always felt I've shared your fate in some curious way."

"If push comes to shove, you will follow Bert, just like they all do."

With this accusation, he snaps our relationship between his hands like a stick. He truly believes I'd turn my back on him and support his rival Bert. I hardly know what answer to give. Anticipation of something very different brought me here, but in just a matter of days those hopes have been blasted. Tucholski can't even bear to share a drink, or a cigarette with me, let alone a confidence, or (God help me!) an embrace. The pain he inflicts in just these few sentences leaves me hollowed out like an abandoned shell. I don't try and argue with him any further. I remember the prostitute at the races and her sneering comments; later, Kaya's cruel put-downs of my admiration for her lover, but worse, far worse, I now have this terrible memory of Tucholski's dismissal of my pathetic hopes.

In truth, I don't yet fully realise that he is a dying man. And if I had, would I have ever let him drift so far, so recklessly, without speaking to him about my real feelings? But it's Kaya he wants. His hopes are as futile as my own: Kaya is more likely to don a brown shirt and sell newspapers than sacrifice herself to his cause alone.

under violet skies

In the days following my botched confession, I avoid the attic apartment and head over to the Kammerspiele to watch Bert's protracted rehearsals. It feels like safe territory, after my humiliation in Malkeston's, but not long afterwards I see a man thrown through a plate glass window in Türkenstrasse. I'm so close, my skirt is pinpricked with dozens of pieces of bloodstained glass. Three men, dressed in brown shirts, appoint themselves stewards to the scene. They stretch out their arms and signal to those out walking in Türkenstrasse to move on. There is only one woman demanding an explanation. She wears a beautifully tailored black silk suit, with a moss coloured lining, the exact match of her crocodile handbag.

"Who is he?" she asks repeatedly, until one of the stewards finally gives way under her persistent questioning.

"A tailor," he confirms.

"But why has he been attacked?" she asks.

"He's a Jew, apparently," says another of the Brownshirts. "But he's dead now."

The shock of hearing such casual dismissal of a life makes my spine tense up. I stumble over to the Kammerspiele and watch in silence Bert's company rehearse another brutal murder. The dungeon where Erwin's King Edward lies imprisoned is little more than a grimy cubicle, separated by a metal grille from the seated audience. At periodic intervals, Erwin hurls himself against this grille, like an animal wracked in the most terrible pain, his mouth a silent "O", his body in anguish. Except I find myself watching not Erwin, but the tailor I have just seen land in his bed of broken glass. His twitching, bloody

164

body superimposes itself over Erwin's each time he hits the grille. That street murder was a calculated desecration too: the severed flesh and the split skull paraded before viewers too shocked to remember the man, the son, the lover, or the husband.

The numbed feelings I have been shutting out since coming to Munich only now begin to stir. That creature's ugly breathing creeps across the streets; it has come right into the Kammerspiele where an elaborate pretence is being constructed out of another century's murderous violence. The horror of the tailor's torture blends into the stage ritual, so how separate out the two bodies? I'm edgy and can hardly recognise anything of what I see, or hear around me.

In the weeks following this rehearsal, I undertake long negotiations with Wolf to take more time off. I plead exhaustion and general low spirits. Wolf probes and I confess my despair for my friends and what is happening in Bavaria. He offers me a "sabbatical" only on the grounds that I do return. Karl Schmidt is working wonders in my absence, but there are limits.

"And we miss you, Esther Rosenbaum," Wolf adds. "No one has written about us for days. The critics are in uproar. We had to serve the same menu twice in a row earlier this week. We're little better than a run-of-the-mill café."

I smile to myself, as Wolf mourns the loss of newspaper column inches. He frets and fumes and even threatens to close down the Jugendstil restaurant. I promise to return once the shows open, armed with a new batch of Bavarian culinary wonders, and Wolf is temporarily appeased. But hopes for a swift return of the prodigal chef are soon scuppered – rehearsals for both productions drag on interminably. The Kammerspiele management is convinced bankruptcy lies ahead if Bert doesn't soon complete his play. Erwin asks me to help him learn his lines – an impossible task as they seem to change each morning.

Thomas is struggling too. He is creating a new alter ego, Thomas the Doubter, the latest in a long line of such characters, but this time he plumbs new depths of cynicism, his fear of losing Kaya feeding into nearly every line, like a bitter herb poisoning a dish of meat. Thomas the Doubter will make his debut at Bar Grossenwah: a self-effacing, rather ridiculous man who mocks his body, his intellect and his presumptions about women and the world. In spite of my hurt over what occurred between us in Malkeston's, I know I can't abandon my friend entirely. I sneak into Bar Grossenwah and watch him at work in the smoky bar. I notice how he wheezes badly even after the shortest of monologues. It's no good. I know I must protect him. I stood guard once before back in the Moabit and and kept Kaya from drifting too far from Thomas. If she ever leaves, he will finally collapse. It's as simple as that, so whatever my heart dictates, I must watch over this couple like a hawk would a wandering pair of mice.

The New Year comes and goes; one morning in late February I'm invited – along with a small group of other Malkeston regulars – to sit in on the dress rehearsal for Tucholski's new show. I find it an uncomfortable experience, but everyone else applauds his monologues with gusto. They don't even flinch when Kaya comes on stage and sings songs that underline Thomas the Doubter's cynicism.

"*Thomas the Doubter falls down dead, if he is shot at by a well-aimed heckler. Thomas the Doubter makes edible money to cut out the black marketeers and their inflated prices; Thomas the Doubter rides his bicycle on parade ground to save the. leather of his boots. The figure of a doubting man captures the spirit of our times, don't you think? If you mistrust everything, nothing can ever surprise you again.*"

· Not even the knowledge that he wants to marry Frankenstein's bride, I can't help but think? I *feel* cruel thinking such thoughts, but Kaya *acts* on them. A week before the revue show opens, we hold a small birthday party for her in the Akademierstrasse apartment. She is twenty-five years old. Erwin's guest for the evening is his pet wolfhound Boris, a huge snuffling beast intent on tying himself up into furry knots around his owner's bony knees. Bert has been banned from the apartment by Kaya. His crime? He is sleeping with another actress: Helene Weigel. Kaya is furious she's being upstaged by someone she believes to be a "dwarf with a giant's ears". She rants on about "the impossible creature" and before long she has created a full-scale blazing row with Tucholski. He presents her with a small statue carved by Etienne Weiss, but she throws it back – narrowly missing his head. It hits the wall behind him, breaking its arms as it goes.

"Would you break my arms too?" Tucholski asks, his voice cracked.

"If you ever stopped wanting me, I would," she shouts in reply. "Yes, definitely."

"It would make you as angry as this, if I ever stopped wanting you, Kaya? No other emotion, but anger. That's interesting."

"Maybe you should try getting away from all these exact meanings, Tucholski," Kaya responds, her voice shrill with exasperation. "Maybe we wouldn't fight so much then."

"You nearly kill me, because I use the right words?"

Tucholski shifts his glasses up his nose with one hand and with the other he picks up the broken fragments of the statue. Boris plods over to Tucholski and starts snuffling around the statue's fragments. Tucholski brusquely knocks him away, before stuffing the statue's remains into his coat pockets. He slams out of the apartment and Boris starts howling. Kaya joins in the chorus by collapsing on to the chintz armchair and bursting into tears.

"Oh, God! I've got to get away."

I'm shocked, because I have never really been able to imagine the Tucholskis split down the middle (even if my desire means I have often hoped for the contrary).

"What about the wedding?" Erwin asks, rather too pointedly.

Kaya seems to consider his question, but her answer betrays where her thoughts on the matter really lie. "He's very ill, you know, Erwin. The visit to the doctor in Berlin is just a formality. He's suffering from pulmonary tuberculosis." She glances over at me, timing her next sentence with all the precision of a great tragedienne. "There's no cure."

Her words hit me like stones. I can hardly believe Tucholski would keep something this important from me.

"Well, let's not forget that Tucholski's as good as ignored you since you turned up," Kaya says, noticing my distress and seemingly keen to prolong it. "Oh, but don't take it to heart, Esther. Don't waste your sympathy on him. He's not as open as so many of you seem to think he is. It's just loyalty is such a hard habit to break, isn't it?"

I know she's addressing me with that comment. Who is the true loyalist in our relationship, after all? I have no claim to the title, not really. Tucholski was given a death sentence by his doctor, but he

167

didn't think me worth consulting with on the matter.

"And I'm going to marry Tucholski regardless of everything that has been happening recently," Kaya adds.

"So, you're getting married just to spite a rival?" Erwin asks, his surprise making him a little careless with his remark.

It really is too close to the bone. Kaya doesn't give him a direct answer. She shifts position on the armchair and leans back, exposing her swan neck as if she were awaiting execution. I'm feeling more than awkward, because I feel she has picked up on my true feelings for Tucholski. But what exactly is *her* ambition: surely she wants more than a snatched rendezvous with Bert in a hotel down the road?

"There's no point in going on at me, any of you," Kaya sighs. "I'm a lost cause. Abandon me."

"You're my friend, Kaya," I object.

"It's Tucholski you want as a friend, not me," she says, again rather sharply.

Erwin gives me a very searching look, which I do my best to ignore.

"You are my friend too, Kaya," I repeat, trying to keep my voice from betraying my nervousness. "I can't ever give up on either of you."

I breathe in the perfume of stale coffee grains and feel panic surge through me. My world is shaking still. I can only respond by changing the subject: I tell everybody still present about the terrible fate of the tailor of Türkenstrasse. It seems important to keep a perspective. The Tucholskis may be struggling, but they are still alive. Erwin kisses my hands. He has been attacked by the Brownshirts too. There but for the grace of God go us all.

"Ach, ladies," he cries out. "Nothing is unbearable, all the while you can still dance."

He waltzes with Kaya and I hold on to Boris in my corner. On and on they spin, until Kaya kicks off her shoes and dances her feet raw, picking up splinters from the floorboards with each spin of her heels. The dancing gets crazier and crazier. I pluck the kabarett dresses from the string rail and pile them up in a corner to create more space. Boris breaks free and hurls himself on top of the clothes. The pile slips and Boris with it. Soon, he's tangled up in silk dresses and scarves. He snorts and snaps and I risk losing fingers trying to detach him from a mermaid tail evening dress. Etienne and Kaya dance on, totally oblivious to the couture carnage happening an earring's throw from their dancing feet.

Close to dawn, they fall down on top of the wrecked costumes and Boris paddles over to Erwin and licks his ears. Kaya waves her ruined feet in the air and begs for an ambulance. Erwin and I tend her sore feet with bandages made out of handkerchiefs and the remains of her kabarett dresses.

The wedding finally comes, the day before Tucholski and Bert's rival productions are due to open in the city. The organisation is, as a consequence, a disaster. Erwin has been caught up in extra rehearsals and I'm the only one who can stand witness. Kaya and I manage to cajole a passing stranger to join us in the registrar's office, before Tucholski can act on his original threat of offering the job to Bert. Nothing else goes to plan, however much we try and catch up with ourselves. Tucholski hasn't bothered to dress up for the occasion. He wears the old frock coat he used to wear in the Moabit and a wrecked top hat, which I'm sure Boris chewed the night of Kaya's party. I look at his shabby exterior and feel a kind of rage that he can't assert himself more than this. To upstage Bert, he needs more than an empty ceremony like this one promises to be. I shouldn't condemn Tucholski, certainly not on sartorial grounds alone. In all the hoopla of the past few weeks, I am reduced to wearing my (very) faded tapestry peacock skirt and Frau Schneider's quilt cloak. I have to ask the stage manager at the Kammerspiele to glue the ragged hem up just minutes before heading to the registry office.

But it's going to take more than a strong glue to fix this couple's marriage together. As Tucholski starts his vows, he's overcome by a furious coughing fit, brought on by the scent of the stocks Kaya carries in her wedding bouquet. His eyes stream as he tries holding back the coughing fit, but it's no good. He takes to his heels and runs out of the door, leaving Kaya, the stranger and myself facing an astonished registrar. Kaya leads the way back into the vestibule to wait on his return.

I watch Kaya shred her bouquet to pieces and wonder whether we should cancel the whole sorry business. I feel this unexpected delay is a bad omen, but I can hardly raise my objections sat beside the bride-to-be. My feelings on the matter are no more straightforward than Kaya's. I glance over at her. The folds of her caramel slip dress are filled with torn petals. Her hair is slicked back with oil and she has painted her lips a very odd shade of orange. She reminds me of a tawdry Byzantine icon. The bony stranger with a face creased up like an old purse criticises Kaya for not wearing a hat. She's crosser still when Tucholski returns, sniffs up Kaya's hair and declares it's probably been slicked down with cooking fat from one of Frau Suschke's pans. He claims he can smell roast pork every time she turns in his direction.

The couple manage to complete their vows without any further interruptions, although they both look dreadful. Malkeston's Herr Suschke has insisted on hosting a party, even though both bride and groom are reluctant to have any kind of public celebration. He insisted that it was the least he could do after Kaya and Tucholski saved his café from ruin when the Republic was crushed. And so the party goes ahead, Erwin the first to shout out his congratulations as the small wedding party arrives. He leaps on to a table and drinks our health – once, twice and a third time, before falling back into the arms of friends. Tucholski abandons the party early, claiming he's still not feeling well, but Kaya stays on. I see how her spirits recover in his absence; it's possibly the scotch she's drinking, or the many dances she's asked for by a steady stream of admirers. I minister to Erwin, pouring him several cups of thick black coffee and eventually he recovers his powers of speech. He wants to know why I've not been back into rehearsals.

"You bring me luck, Esther," he points out. "I remember every word perfectly when I see you sitting out front."

"Oh, Erwin! It's all gone wrong."

"Has it? I was thinking how much Kaya seems to be enjoying herself at last."

He sits on the table in front of me, cross-legged. He is trying to make light of my woe.

"She's drunk, can't you tell?" I snap back at him.

"Is that really such a crime?" Erwin brushes my cheek, like he would a crying child's.

I know Erwin is a good listener, so I confide in him my fears for our circle of friends. I tell him I've been avoiding rehearsals, because I'm frightened they will bring back the nightmare of what I saw happen out on the street. Erwin understands.

"We must put his poor ghost to rest," he says. "Will you join me in a drink to the tailor of Türkenstrasse?"

We drink several glasses of sekt in quick succession. I laugh for the first time in months, but the dangerous undercurrent of the evening remains. We have a gatecrasher in our midst. Bert has turned up, armed with a knife. I first see him silhouetted in the entrance to the café-kabarett, the pointy collar of his leather coat turned up so that he looks like Nosferatu in the horror movie. He storms up to Kaya and pushes the blade against her cheekbone.

"With this knife, Kaya, you can kill one of your lovers!"

He's drunk, so drunk I feel I can take my time in reaching him. Bert, meanwhile, leans in even closer to Kaya.

"What do *you* say?"

"Talk to me another night, Bert. I can't say fairer than that," she replies, surprisingly calm given the circumstances. "I've just got married. There's no time for your games right now."

Bert's knife has drawn blood, but it hasn't cut too deeply. He lets the knife drop, seemingly transfixed by the sight of blood trickling down her cheek.

"I'll wait for you, Kaya."

Then he loses his balance. He sways forwards and the knife gently pierces Kaya's bare shoulder. Bert falls flat on his face and Kaya runs out of the café. I apologise to Herr Suschke and set off in pursuit of my friend. Outside, cracks of light filter down from the skylights arching above my head. My anxiety increases as I draw nearer to the atelier. I walk as fast as I can up the stairwell. My key turns in the lock and my heart jumps. Inside, all seems peaceful. The small porthole window reveals a patch of sky the colour of a violet. Somebody is awake and moving around in the room that leads off from the vestibule. I open the door and there is Kaya settling down on the floor with a cup of coffee. She's wearing an old dressing gown, torn across the sleeves, its hem unstitched. The cut on her face has dried and her scar now looks like a broken vein tracing her cheek.

"Esther?"

God knows who else she thought might have followed her tonight.

"Are you all right, Kaya?" I ask, walking up to her and putting my arms around her neck. "I was really worried."

"Because of what Bert just did?"

She's anxious and jittery and all because of one man. She's fixated on him despite there being so much else tipping upside down in our world.

"No, not just because of Bert," I say, sinking on to the floor. I should shake Kaya, but she won't listen, unless I'm talking about her desire for Bert.

"Ach, men! Why do we go through this pain for them, Esther? Look what I've been reduced to now."

She holds up a parcel, which she has retrieved from its hiding place behind the piano.

"Who's it for, Kaya?"

"Bert," she says, simply and without further explanation.

"But he's staying just down the road. Don't be ludicrous, Kaya."

"He won't be there this time tomorrow," she reveals. "That's what he told me tonight. He's got a job with Reinhardt back in Berlin. Oh, Esther, I so want to be with him. This is what I thought: I'll send him my nightdress then he can sniff me up in its folds at least. Look, I've even soaked it in my perfume."

"Kaya, this is crazy."

I rip the brown paper parcel open and pull out her nightdress. The stench of her scent in the shuttered room is hideous.

"It's hot with my dreams, Esther. He can't ever forget me."

She stoops towards the floor as she says this, her voice barely more than a whisper. Her pathetic stance inspires only irritation in me.

"You know he can and he will," I answer, ruthlessly.

I'm angry with Kaya, because there is to be no reconciliation with her newly married spouse, just another stand-off with me playing giraffe-in-the-middle. I'm sick of the arguments, the complications and all the nonsense that is drowning us here in Munich.

Erwin is my only true ally now and so it is I agree to be his guest at the first night of *Edward II*. He says I'll be stepping into history when I walk into the Kammerspiele's auditorium and he's right: on the evening of the premiere – 19 March, 1924 – excitement and anticipation hit the air like moths. Tension lifts and I want only to enjoy the moment. I wear my pinstripe suit and a garland of lilies and ferns, which creates quite a stir when I walk into the theatre foyer, but for once I'm proud of my towering bearing.

The play is every bit as engrossing as it was all those months ago when I first saw Erwin in rehearsal. The grim set, the perfunctory delivery of an horrific killing, the refusal to conform to any theatrical niceties is breathtaking. I'm back on Türkenstrasse watching a man breathe his last, his killers as ordinary as the men portrayed on stage, but for the blood on their hands. There are angry discussions behind me about the way the play unfolds, even a few boos when the actors take their bow, but overall it's a hit. (I suspect Bert would only count the boos anyway and ignore the applause; he's positively relishing a chance to have a stand-up row in the aisles.) I sidestep the audience and make my way backstage to see Erwin. He lies on the floor of his dressing room where one of the stage managers is busy tending the cuts and bruises on his torso – the result of his literally hurling himself against the metal grille of the set. Boris watches intently from his basket under the dressing room mirror.

"It was a success, wasn't it?" Erwin asks, wincing as the youthful stage manager dabs at a particularly ugly looking wound on his stomach.

"Someone in the audience tried to hit Bert on the head with their umbrella at the end," I say.

"Then we have made it into the annals of theatrical history," Erwin laughs. "I might even get paid."

"Don't hold your breath," mutters the stage manager, with the kind of rasping voice that should belong to someone at least twice his age.

Far too late in the evening, I learn the fate of the rival show that opened at Bar Grossenwah. The front-of-house manager delivers a message to me during the backstage party, the majority of which I've

173

spent ensconced in Erwin's dressing room, Boris wrapped around my feet.

"Herr Tucholski's revue started and finished in ten minutes flat," the front-of-house manager hisses in my ear. "Apparently, he keeled over after his opening number. Frau Tucholski says to go home immediately, please."

I detach myself from Boris as best I can and hurry back to Akademierstrasse. Bursting through the apartment door, I find most of the revue company assembled on the floor cushions. Tucholski is in bed and a doctor is attending him. I can hear Tucholski's weak, persistent coughing. By the time dawn breaks, most of the guests – and the doctor – have departed. The door to the bedroom opens and Kaya finally emerges. She stands in the doorway chewing her nails, looking out over the debris left by her visitors. Her hair is a bird's nest of collapsed curls; her dress as creased as a winter leaf. She puts her hand out to me. There are no words, not at first. Eventually, we find ourselves able to talk. Kaya tells me the doctor is advising Tucholski to go to a sanatorium in Davos. We both understand the futility of this advice. Tucholski will never stop working. He has been up on a stage practically every night since he was twelve years old. How can he stop now, even with death catching at his lungs? Kaya slumps down at my feet and rests her head against my shins. Impending tragedy has made her less hostile towards me.

"He found the nightdress, Esther. He thinks I've as good as left him already."

I rest my hand on top of her head, as if trying to still her thoughts. The dawn chorus arrives, as we sit waiting on the morning's newspapers. We read there the rumours hinting Bert's play will shortly close because the Kammerspiele is facing bankruptcy after the protracted rehearsal period. I feel this is probably the true explanation for his sudden departure from Munich. We find the news of Tucholski's collapse on stage in just one short paragraph at the bottom of an inside page.

spitting cherrystones

I n the days following Tucholski's collapse, Kaya and I are thrown together for hours at a time. She encourages me to wear my suit during our vigils at Tucholski's bedside. In this way, I act defiance, even if it is only between our four walls.

Wolf has reluctantly given permission for me to extend my stay in Munich – with the proviso that I continue researching new recipes whilst playing nurse – but I find myself sitting beside the tulip wood bed where Tucholski sleeps, chain-smoking away the hours with Kaya. Her husband sleeps under the lettuce-green quilt they have owned since moving in together. An embroidered cloth she bought from a Russian émigré in a street market is nailed above it, along with framed manuscripts of Tucholski's most popular songs. The room stinks of the blue smoke from our *papyrossi*, the long, thin Russian cigarettes we have developed a taste for in our self-imposed exile.

Kaya's passion for Bert is weighing her down, like a pitcherful of water. She finally gives in and sleeps with him during a brief reappearance in Munich. Kaya tells me everything, like a schoolgirl revealing a precious secret. She tells me that they had their rendezvous in the broken down hotel close to the train station. That first afternoon, two crows flew in through a broken window and fought in the hand basin. Bert had turned up to talk to the Kammerspiele about the fate of his production of *Edward II*. He moved on a day later and she has heard nothing since.

"It's not as I imagined, Esther," she confesses from her side of the tulip wood bed.

"Is it ever as you *imagine?*"

175

I'm disappointed by Kaya's revelation. It was always lying there in the shadows, along with many other stories and affairs I've uncovered over the years, but now it's out in the open I find myself incredulous. Surely Kaya sees through Bert and his ways? Doesn't she remember how he abandoned poor Eva?

"It's no good scowling like that," Kaya defends herself. "You're only jealous, because you never had the guts to act like I have done. And you've got fat chance of doing anything now, the state Tucholski is in." I start to deny her claims, but she silences me. "I'm not criticising you, Esther. I just thought you of all people might understand. My mind is fixed on Bert, even if it's like living in the centre of a whirlwind."

"And Tucholski?" I hiss under my breath. "How is he surviving the whirlwind?"

"He's still with me…"

Kaya's voice trails away. We both cast a nervous look over at Tucholski, but he's deep in sleep. I don't know why I'm being so hard on her. In many ways, we share the same predicament and contradictions, and not just because we fall in love with the wrong men. I'm the cook who doesn't eat; Kaya is the beautiful film star who promotes her politics, not her looks, and certainly not her affairs. She drinks with me, and with theatre and film directors, but she rarely lets anyone glimpse the confusion of her private life.

A few weeks after Bert's latest disappearance, Kaya confides in me again. She times our confessions to avoid Tucholski's waking moments, which are few and far between. When he is awake, he tends to ration his speech, even though he realises another day is slipping from his grasp, unmarked by a choice word, or phrase. He is too weak to even sit up in bed and write. Kaya sometimes tries to cajole him into speech, offering to act as amanuensis, but he declines.

"Have you never wanted to have a baby, Esther?" Kaya asks pointedly that evening, but only after double checking to see that Tucholski is still asleep between us. "You will ruin your chances, if you don't eat." She tries pinching the skin around my ribcage, but it's glued in tight against my bones. "I can't believe you don't get hungry any more. I eat loads, have done ever since we left the Moabit.

176

I suppose I want to make up for all the meals I didn't eat when we were so poor and shabby."

"What chances?" I scoff, anxious to steer the conversation away from my ribcage. "I realised long ago I would never be a mother. I mean, how can I provide for a child, as well as myself? Besides, what man would want me?"

"There's always someone," Kaya says, refusing to give way. "You can't rely on Tucholski, so what about that kitchen boy of yours?"

"Karl's father would kill me before he would let his son give me a baby," I joke, although I'm actually stunned she can ridicule her husband's physical frailty at such a moment. "Besides, Karl's not what Mama would call a good catch – as if I have a chance of catching anything, even a cold."

Kaya smiles, but she's lost in thought. "There are always so many obstacles, aren't there? I really want a baby, but I know I can't bring one up alone." I think we both know she's not talking about having a baby with Tucholski. She admits he's never made her pregnant. "And then there's our farcical wedding vows. I can hardly invest in them, can I? I want to be free to go where *I* want, Esther."

It is like a little bud of hope quickening inside her to think another might root himself inside. Snag is, the potential rooter is married and already a father. I look over at Tucholski, asleep in bed. His rattling lungs betray him – he is a gambler playing his last, unplayable card. Cold mornings, stifling afternoons, it makes no difference – death speaks to us in each of his long, drawn-out breaths. Kaya distracts herself by rereading Bert's love letters and poems, which she hides in her hat boxes. Despite his nature, Bert seems determined to keep her in the fold. Kaya hands over the odd letter for me to read. They consist of long lists of crazy words.

"*What impressions do words make on our senses, Kaya?*" Bert writes, the night he leaves for Berlin. "*You are ice, a revolver, a cherrystone. Eaten fruit; a shining deadly thing; drowned and frozen. You are close, standing by my shoulder, but I don't speak of these things. Why? I must spit out the cherrystone. B.*"

Kaya reaches into her hat boxes and pulls out a tangle tent of emotions and lies. She's ripe for a new dream: Berlin can't hold her, any more than Tucholski can. The city is as restrictive as the combined width of her outspread palms. She doesn't mention this to Tucholski, because she knows he will never move. He is Berlin born and bred. "Stay too long on its streets and you can never be free of the place," he once warned me.

In my case, I can never be free of Wolf's demand that I return. I have run out of excuses and he seizes his chance. By Easter, Tucholski's health has improved a fraction and Wolf is immediately on the phone offering up the services of his chauffeur to drive the invalid back home – and his runaway chef. On Good Friday, Tucholski manages to leave his bed for the first time in nearly six weeks. A few days later, the car turns up and Kaya installs Tucholski on the back seat. At the very last minute, she makes a switch in plans. I'm to take the night train, which she was originally booked on, and she will take the front seat in Wolf's car. She's recovered her poise – she's en route home *and* she's been offered a lead role in a new film by Georg Pabst.

Folded up in a too small train seat, I can't help but approve Pabst's choice of leading lady. Kaya is taking on the role of a woman who sleeps with a butcher in return for miserly cuts of meat in our inflation-torn city. She won't have to try too hard to act that one, I think, my ears deafened by the snoring of the obese man opposite. Kaya will now be able to hire a maid and a nurse specially for Tucholski, who she is convinced will recover now he is back in their Luisenplatz apartment. Her optimism and her concern for Tucholski put me to shame.

I mark my return to Schorns with a menu packed with Bavarian delicacies – suckling pigs, boar steaks, curling twists of red cabbage and huge apple tarts. I haven't been able to cook on a grand scale since leaving Berlin and I realise how much I've missed the challenge. Kaya is guest of honour at my Bavarian Banquet, along with Pabst, which ensures the cameramen from the newspapers turn up. Wolf is so excited he barely eats a morsel. He changes outfit three times during the meal and even insists on a photocall with the pigs speared on their roasting spits down in the kitchens. At the end of the evening, Kaya asks me to help her interview candidates for the new maid-nurse she wants to hire to look after Tucholski whilst she's filming.

"You know just how he likes his hollandaise sauce," she points out. "They can try and make a sauce to your exacting standards as part of their interview."

I wonder if she's trying to present me with a consolation prize? Tucholski has not asked me to visit since we got back and Kaya, showing an unexpected sensitivity towards my plight, has tried to come up with a plan which will sanction my presence at the Luisenplatz apartment. I have my doubts about getting involved, but in the end it proves a sensible strategy. Kaya has had an application from a young Russian girl called Saskia Jurowski. Her ethnicity has already sold her to Kaya, even before we host the interviews around her kitchen table.

"Just think," she muses, as we wait for the first of our candidates to arrive. "A generation ago, Saskia would have lived out her life as a serf, bought and sold by her masters like a market egg. But now, the workers in Russia assert themselves and help write government policies that will benefit them, not their bosses."

Shortly after taking on Saskia, Kaya tries establishing some rules in her relationship with Bert, but they always collapse like dented pastry cases. He's a sly man with too many words at his disposal, but Kaya isn't ready to believe this. Over the summer, she works hard for Pabst, but she is living beyond her limited means, just like the rest of us. Kaya starts borrowing and trading mercilessly on the hopes of still hungrier rivals. One such is the woman who plays opposite her: Greta Garbo, a woman of outstanding glacial beauty. We meet briefly on set where I have gone to deliver some apple tartes – Kaya's sweet tooth has not been affected by lovesickness. Greta slips her arm through mine and whispers: "Kaya is not playing shame, Fräulein Rosenbaum. She *is* ashamed."

I flinch when I hear this: Greta has hit the mark. She knows scarcely any German, beyond what is written down in her script, and yet she teases out Kaya's secrets in a moment. Reality and fiction interlock in an ugly way throughout filming – and in the Luisenplatz apartment. Berlin is tightening its hold on Tucholski. He is literally choking to death on its grimy, noisy air, but Kaya doesn't want to fight the city any more. She dreams only of escape, not compromise, and she has a new partner: Sergei Romanov. Only Kaya can decide to challenge the competing demands being made on her by two different men by involving a third, one who even claims to be a blood relation of the late Tsar of Russia.

Kaya has been haunting the Bayrische Viertel ever since we all returned from Munich. The area is home to a growing community of Russian émigrés and it is here Kaya finds herself eavesdropping on a seductive language. She also remembers Erwin's two old college friends who have set up a theatre company in Russia, devising plays for the workers who have reshaped their lives in a revolution. Kaya is inspired to create a new fiction: she will sail to Russia, away from Tucholski, away from Bert, away from the whole sorry, sad mess. In her sleep, she walks up and down gangplanks of cruise ships, whilst by day she drinks glasses of hot lemon tea with Sergei and his compatriots in Bayrische Viertel's open air cafés.

Sergei speaks an erratic German, which is charming because he has an instinct for picking up the vitality of a sentence. He throws out words and hopes his listeners can patch them into sentences, his bloodshot eyes always hopeful of understanding. His hands are terribly scarred and he has a bullet wound on his shoulder. He only really smiles when we go to Ufa Palast am Zoo, one of the city's more exclusive cinemas, because he claims its luxurious interior reminds him of his old family home in St Petersburg. Kaya is horrified to think he once lived in a house with one hundred bedrooms, but relieved to hear that after the revolution they were handed over to needy families. Her homesick lover says he is not against the revolution as such, but simply fears a world where tradition fails to get a toehold on the imagination.

"Me, you doubt?" he asks, his brow wrinkling up like a newborn puppy's. "Think: one night, Tucholski he drinks champagne. Month moves on. Nobody listen to him any more. Silence in his head. No good voices any more, you understand? Friends? Ach, they are bad friends now?"

"Tucholski will be successful, but within a month he will have detractors wanting to pull him down," I translate. "All will change and he will be left doubting. Like you were, Sergei?"

He grabs my hand and kisses it, which I take for a "yes". Kaya gets sniffy. She knows, just as I do, that Sergei's thumbnail sketch of her husband's future matches the fate of many of our friends in the kabaretts. One minute, everybody speaks to them and trails in their orbit; the next, they are a crumpled publicity photograph. Kaya pushes it from her mind and returns to more comforting illusions and who in a way can blame her? She drags us off to see any number of films, but the real treat is shuffling our feet through the cinema's thick wool carpet. This inspires Sergei to reminisce about his splendid former home.

"Can you be homesick for somewhere you have never been?" Kaya asks Sergei. "You might never have been there, but you know it's the place where you should be?"

If he understands her question, he chooses to ignore it. I soon realise Kaya views Russia's immediate past from a vastly different perspective to her lover, but she's hungry for even the smallest of details that will bring her closer to the shores of her dreamland.

Even though Tucholski has refused to see me since our return to Berlin (he remains convinced I threw in my lot with Bert and betrayed him), I determine on staying loyal to my old friend, and keep Kaya within her husband's orbit. It's not made easy by Wolf's new habit of hovering outside my kitchen door, stopwatch in hand. He's jealous of any time I spend away from Schorns; he has even clocked up the hours I spent away in Munich and is determined I repay each second. I bribe Karl to stand in for me whenever I can and slip away to join Kaya and Sergei on their travels around the city. We often find ourselves sitting in the dark brown velvet womb of the magnificent Palast cinema. Sergei joins us because he is shocked to discover we would otherwise spend the afternoons in there alone.

"No escort? No man?" he grills us one afternoon.

"No man," we lie.

"Not good. No man. I buy you."

He means he'll buy our tickets for the afternoon screenings, but we laugh anyway. I laugh hardest of all, as I've no man at all. Kaya's is frail, forgotten and housebound. Poor Sergei fares no better. In the Russia he comes from, women are glittering people who emerge from one hundred-room mansions to be paraded in fairy tale sleighs, not revolutionaries like Kaya with unwashed camisoles and dirty fingernails. Day after day, Kaya and Sergei walk around the city gardens, up and down avenues and into restaurants where chandeliers rustle above their heads. Sergei tries to teach Kaya Russian, because he's so lonely. Occasionally, they invite me to join them, maybe because I only sip from glasses of water and that makes me a very cheap chaperone.

"Speak, Kaya," Sergei begs her. "One more time. Then eat, please."

And Kaya struggles through her few sentences, watching his eyes all the while. If his eyes close and he remains silent after she finishes her little speech, she knows she has achieved the near impossible. She has sounded, briefly, like his past.

"Actress. So speak very good," is Sergei's highest accolade.

I see how Kaya burns with pleasure, sensing escape close by, but this expires the minute she walks back into the Luisenplatz apartment where Tucholski waits, jealousy burning up inside him. He is not jealous of her Russian prince, but jealous of the wider world which will finally take Kaya away from Berlin. He finds books about Russia hidden under their bed. He is finally provoked into taking action. He rings me at Schorns early one Autumn morning and begs my advice.

"How will I find her, if she starts walking down streets we've never shared together?" he asks.

Tucholski calls a truce, inviting me over to supper where I see for myself how far Kaya has changed.

"Do I speak Russian in my sleep, Tucholski?" she provokes him.

He takes his glasses off and starts rubbing them clean on the tail of his shirt. Kaya looks at him coldly. She's not afraid of him any more. She will push him to the limit.

"I don't know," he finally answers.

"My Russian prince listens to me."

"He's no more a prince than I am. They all lie about their origins for pity, or to wheedle money."

"That's unfair."

"Does Sergei ask you for money?" he demands next.

"Sometimes, but he pays for our cinema tickets and the teas afterwards."

Tucholski scents betrayal in the air. "How much have you lent him, Kaya?"

"I don't want to see him thrown out of his room," she replies, a touch too hastily.

"You pay his rent? Why, Kaya, why?"

I fiddle with my coffee spoon. This inquisition is becoming painful for all of us.

"Yes. I mean, yes, I pay for his room."

"Why? What on earth do you get in return? Half a dozen words and dogged devotion? That's a cheap deal."

"I like him, Tucholski. Besides, if…"

"If? If what, Kaya?"

We all know what is coming next, the revelation that will leave Tucholski stranded on his side of the room. Kaya is going to admit that she wants to make a journey, and he knows it's one he can never make with her.

"If I go to Russia, he can provide me with introductions to his friends."

"They are probably all dead, or else they will be beggars."

Kaya throws herself down on the floor in exasperation. Another truce is needed.

"Stop arguing about this for a while and let the dust settle," I suggest.

"For two days, or two months, Esther? Or shall I make an appointment to speak with my wife?"

"She's right, Tucholski," Kaya intervenes. "Don't bite her head off. We're all so tired. No more talking for tonight, at least. All right?"

In fact, the Tucholskis barely speak after this, even though they continue to lie together under the lettuce-green quilt. Their lives fall apart, like the loose pages of a manuscript. Tucholski waits; Sergei waits; Bert waits somewhere between here and Munich. And Kaya is watched by them all, like an animal in the Zoo.

stockings and stars

A terrible winter of never-ending fogs and dirty snow is salvaged by a very special invitation. Herr Handke is keen to share his extraordinary vision with a few trusted friends and so it is that Kaya, Leon Wolf, Etienne Weiss and myself are invited to a private view at the House of Clocks. Arriving in his workshop, we find several dozen prototypes for the clock tower laid out on the benches, each spotlit by a carefully positioned candelabra. Herr Rolf darts around keeping a careful eye on the dripping candles, ensuring no wax falls on his employer's creations. The stained-glass windows have been blocked out by large canvas screens onto which Herr Handke has hung framed copies of his designs in pen and ink. The assembled company agree that the prototypes and the drawings which have inspired them reveal a masterpiece in the making.

The devices Herr Handke plans to bring the different sections of the clock tower into life will rival those of the great master clockmakers of the past. Even the signs of the Zodiac will be animated: summer will be announced when a lion paws the ground in the Zoo, and a shoal of fish swim up the Wannsee; autumn will be signalled by the twitching of a scorpion's claws. Passers-by will not only see this visionary clock tower, but smell it! Twice a day – at noon and at midnight – scents will be released from each storey, each distinct perfume linked to a particular district. The Scheuenviertel will, of course, reek of Purim spices. Herr Handke has barely started on his explanation about how all this will be achieved when he's interrupted by Wolf. He has broken away from our little group to leaf through the stack of portfolios, which have not been put out on display.

"Ach, you can almost taste the drawings in here, Herr Handke," he calls out.

He's found drawings depicting the city's pastry makers, including my old boss Milos Botticelli. "And here I can definitely see an opening for myself," Wolf adds. "The kabarett scene, Herr Handke. I could be popped in here between Thomas Tucholski and Frank Wedekind. No, no, I run ahead of myself. I provide the most wonderful patisseries through my management of Schorns, so maybe I should stand up there with Herr Botticelli? What do you think, Esther?"

Typical of the vain old peacock to haul me into his argument.

"You can only plump for one storey, Herr Wolf," I reprimand him. "You can't be everywhere at once."

"But that I fear is the case. What a dilemma. You must resolve it, Herr Handke. You are the artist here, after all."

Well, of course, that sets Etienne off. He bristles up, angry no doubt at what he perceives to be a slight on his professional reputation. Etienne stands close beside me at Herr Handke's work bench. He wears his hair brilliantined down on to his scalp, revealing the odd shape of his narrow skull. Purple semicircles shadow his eyes, making him look like one of his own barbarically coloured paintings. He's no more animated than a dying weed, except for the glitter of colour on his knuckles. Etienne wears a huge collection of jewel-crusted rings on each finger. I'm amazed he can lift his hands at all, but he's been drawing away since he arrived in the workshop. He holds out his left hand and I see he's sketched my portrait, using just a couple of heavily exaggerated hollows. I'm disappointed by it – although it's true to life. In recent months, the weight has dropped off me.

"I don't flatter," Etienne says, catching my look. "This is hardly the time for flattery, is it? It's a time for truths. What you hear said bears little relation to what we see, not if we look out of our windows, or out of our hearts."

I feel something similar when I host my soup kitchen. I ask him if he would like to come and draw there one night, but he says he would like to ask a very different kind of favour. I'm instantly on my guard. I've been propositioned many times before now on account of my strange looks.

185

"I just want to paint you," he reassures me. "My old model has let me down. She's got fat." Etienne only paints people as jagged and sharp as the contours of our collapsing city; men-like-women and women-like-men, hunched up in the picture frames like so many dessicated leaves. I will pass muster in such androgynous company, particularly if I opt to wear my suit in my sittings. Only the other day in Schorns, a delivery man asked me what I was, even with my hair loose and my favourite skirt on – a fishtail number stitched by Frau Schneider out of an old theatre curtain. Without a woman's curves, it flapped sadly around my hip bones, which stick out like door knobs. I told my enquirer I was a human being, just like himself, but of the female variety. He prodded at my chest and laughed.

"Could have made you out of kindling wood myself," he said. "Nothing to relax on there, is there?" Jab, jab, jab. Each dig of his finger and another bruise bloomed. My skin is stretched so thin, I'm surprised it doesn't tear like tissue paper. Only a man like Etienne wants a woman like me. He will paint me dancing wantonly, or drinking or having sex, his usual subject matter and as such highly combustible to the sensitive demeanour of the city's gallery-goers. Etienne's paintings are often confiscated from exhibitions by the police. His reputation casts a long shadow on such occasions and now it casts itself over me. He watches me with dilated eyes, as if he's about to carve me up on a canvas that very instant. I take a deep breath. There's something very seductive about Etienne's look – although it's not the kind of look a man generally gives a woman. It's something a lot more dangerous, because it implies a set of rules played out within boundaries I've yet to experience.

"And I'll pay, Esther," Etienne whispers. "Stockings. Silk stockings. I've got boxes of them up in the studio." Silk stockings for free is not an offer to be dismissed on the grounds of modesty alone. Besides, I can always insist on keeping my hat on, so I accept and we agree to meet later that same morning at his studio. It is very close to Artimius Market, situated at the top of a disused factory where the silk stockings Etienne plans to pay me with were once manufactured. When I walk through the studio door, I find myself surrounded on all sides by dozens of boxed-up orders standing ready for a delivery date that will never arrive. The only furniture in the studio consists of a wood stove, a battered cane armchair and two trestle tables pushed together, covered in tubes of paint, cans of linseed oil and bundles of torn rags.

Etienne welcomes me dressed in a paint-splattered singlet and a pair of torn trousers tied up with a pair of stockings. He's all bone and vein. His arms are peppered with needle pinpricks, which he makes no attempt to disguise. He shows me sketches of his previous sitters who are all naked; not so much as a pair of earrings between them. I recognise Etienne's favourite model from the Jugendstil Room. He drew Eloise O'Donnell countless times before she reached puberty, usually from angles best appreciated by a gynaecologist. I'm thinner than Eloise, even though I'm probably twice her age, and we both have red hair, floods of the stuff. So, what's there to be modest about, after all? My breasts are mere shadows, out-matched by the curve of my rib cage; my backside is as flat as an outstretched palm. Maybe if I were a real flesh and blood woman, I would blush to show off the fact?

"We've got the whole day ahead of us, so don't panic if you feel odd at first," he advises. I undress as he prepares his colours and papers. First, he asks me to curl up on my side, my hair stretched out around me like a big fat halo. This is how I fall asleep, so it feels almost natural – except for the absence of any bedclothes. Etienne takes his time watching how the light shifts against my skin. He plays with my hair, stretching it out across the floorboards, until it resembles a long red tentacle. He draws the crack between my legs, the hollow echoes of my once fleshy buttocks and the sacs that were my breasts. He draws on the move. He paces around me, holding his pencil up against my hip and my shoulder to correct their proportions on his, surely, too small page. He tries to understand my folds and creases, like he would a strange kind of engine. He is not interested in my sex, except as a pattern of colour and shadow which he jots down in washes of orange and pink gouache. When dusk falls, we continue by candlelight. I'm grotesque again. My limbs turn into shadowy tree trunks that wrap up Etienne's body. I consume the light, like a giant, licking tongue. Etienne eventually throws down his sketch pad and collapses on the floor beside me.

"I should be paying you with wheelbarrows full of marks," he says, wrapping his arms in my hair and snuggling up to my side. "You're a natural." I don't mind about the money at all, I want to say. I just want to feel his eyes moving over my distorted body, turning it into splashes of extraordinary colour. I'm genuinely excited by Etienne's sketches. He's not restricted by what came before but is happy to crash-land into the future and paint its debris. I turn artist too – indirectly. I scoop up armfuls of stockings and dye them in vegetable juices taken from Schorn's leftover dishes. Soon, I've got dozens of orange, green and purple stockings hanging out to dry in my bedroom. When they are ready, I twist them up into my hair, or wear them with my tapestry skirts, bunched up at the waist so their daring colours can be admired. I get mocked by people on my way to work, but I don't care. Etienne is keen to exhibit his paintings of me at one of Wolf's notorious Art Balls and word gets out. How many of the dull, grey characters who shout after me on the streets, waving their umbrellas in disapproval, have my experience to boast about? Surprisingly, Kaya seems to share their reservations, although she never tries to hit out at me with her parasol.

"Surely that's a step too far?" she asks, but I think she's just jealous that Etienne refuses to paint her.

"Cow hips and big lips," he declares. "Yuck."

Etienne is the only man alive not to be taken in by Kaya's beauty. That makes him as much of a freak as I am. We become thick as thieves. I borrow his rings and he dresses up in my tapestry skirts. It's quite a while before I finally catch up with Bert again. Large numbers of people are pouring into Berlin for sanctuary, the majority running away from the recent upheavals in Bavaria. Bert has also joined us in the city for good, his pockets full of cheap detective novels. How do I know? Because I bump into him en route to Gipstrasse. Something's cooking, because he has a fancy new wardrobe: gone the awful old trousers and cap and in their place a red silk shirt, matching tie and a trilby hat. He even owns a cigarette case. Some things don't change, however: he's full of weasel words of apology about neglecting to call round, but he's not really sorry. He's going to see his tailor and then Kaya, so there is little time to spare on a giantess in blood orange stockings.

There is another surprise in store: Bert's tailor in Gipstrasse is none other than Michael Jakoby! He's arrived here too – his old business in Augsburg having come under fire from Herr Hitler's supporters. He now rents the ground floor of an apartment block close to my old family home. Apparently, Michael no longer needs to tighten his belt; he wears it loose under a swelling paunch. Business is good, he confirms, when I follow Bert into his new premises which look much the same as those he rented in Augsburg. "Another black wool coat, is it, Herr Brecht?" Bert looks sheepish too. A double act! What's going on?

"For you, half price. She's my old apprentice, after all."

"Why is he haggling with you?" I ask incredulously.

I see a half-finished black merino wool coat standing on one of the tailor's dummies. A mad idea pops into my head as I inspect the neat tailoring on the coat, the idea that Bert might have a whole army of women marching around in matching black coats. Could he be worried that he might fail to recognise them otherwise? Then another idea dawns: Michael the Tailor must think I'm wound up on Bert's chain of command too.

"So, that's the deal, is it? Sleep with the legendary Bert Brecht and get a cut-price coat into the bargain?"

My questions reveal to Michael that he has got hold of the wrong end of the cutting scissors and he hastily drops his sales pitch.

"It works a treat, usually," he confesses. "Herr Brecht informs the lady concerned how much her investment in him might cost her, before arranging a fitting. I make a discount, depending on the status of the client. I mean, someone like Kaya Tucholski can bring me a lot of a publicity when she's photographed wearing one of my coats outside Schorns."

"Michael, I need to speak to Bert – in private."

Michael the Tailor suddenly remembers he has stocktaking to do in the back room and I'm left alone with Bert, who inspects his fingernails and avoids my hostile glare.

"Does Kaya know about this scam? Have you even considered what might happen when she bumps into another woman dressed in the same bloody coat?"

"She doesn't suspect a thing. Why should she, Esther? Head in the clouds – or a map of Russia, which comes down to the same thing, if you ask me."

I stare out of the window. Delivery boys pull handcarts along the road, the odd car scrapes up against the pavement and a woman walks by dressed in a red, high-collared coat, a Dalmatian dog trotting at her heels at the end of a matching red lead. Such elegance, but what place can it have in a world where men like Herr Hitler walk tall, lining their listeners' ears with the honey tongue of borrowed power?

"Why have you come back, Bert? Is it for Kaya?"

He looks up at me. "Who knows, Esther, who knows."

"Is it worse than before? I mean, the Freikorps were bad enough, but are the Brownshirts more dangerous?"

"I wanted a change of scene."

His blithe response provokes me more than the business with the coats. I realise I want him to dismiss what is happening in Bavaria. I want him to deny he has finally settled in Berlin, because he's afraid like the rest of us would appear to be. I want him to offer up the challenge that Tucholski can no longer make in his ballad writing. But he kicks up a fuss at the role I try and cast him in.

"Why do you expect *me* to sort everything out?" he barks. "I'm just a writer."

"Because you have a talent with words, Bert. What if you used that talent to defeat people, like this Herr Hitler? You could do it, except it would mean pulling the plug on all your affairs. And I doubt you'll ever do that. You'll lose commission on all Michael's bloody coats for a start!"

Bert slips down from the work bench. He's furious, because at last I've hit a raw nerve. He will have more than one reason to settle in Berlin, so why should I object because he offers one like this? It's simple enough. Many strut about in times of trouble – Herr Hitler for one – but a lot more of us cower as words of reassurance and tolerance dry up. I've never thought of Bert as a coward before. Me, yes, but then I'm rootless in a way he can never understand. My nationality doesn't come with a passport, but a curse; I'm not an Orthodox Jew, but nor am I assimilated into the busy heart of the capital. Bert, on the contrary, doesn't appear lost. Distracted, maybe, but he could still put up a resistance that would count for something.

"Bert!" I call out to his departing back. "Kaya's as good as left you. She's as good as left us both. Ignore her, but don't ignore what is happening outside your bedroom door, please." My warning floats after him, useless as a big fat soap bubble. A few months later, I'm proved right, but it's no satisfaction to find we are not immune from the threat that has forced Michael the Tailor and my friends to flee Bavaria. It's suddenly brought home in a most visible and ugly fashion in a chilling message scrawled in pigs' blood across Schorns' facade: "*Die Jugend sind unser Ungluck*".

So, it is we Jews who are bringing bad luck to the world, is it? Wolf is summoned down from his apartment to inspect the damage and arrives scrubbed and scented, like a bar of pink soap. (He has been warned in advance by his servant boy that there are newspaper photographers circling the restaurant steps.) Karl is in the process of collecting up saucepans of water to wash away the outrage, but Wolf brings him to a halt so that he can take part in a photocall.

"The work of maniacs," he booms to the reporters clustering around him. "But we shall open tonight, regardless."

"I don't think we should court further attention from these people, Herr Wolf," Karl whispers. "Surely, it's just asking for retaliation, behaving like this?"

Wolf forgets to mention the fact that he employs any Jews at all in his establishment, even when asked this question by more than one reporter, which makes me feel distinctly uneasy. I'm not convinced by Wolf's bravado. I intended going out later this evening in search of new diners for my soup kitchen, but now I fear the thugs who defaced the restaurant walls might be lying in hiding for me. Karl seizes his opportunity to protest further when Wolf briefly pauses for breath to pick up a rose that has fallen out of his buttonhole.

"The world has gone mad and maybe we have gone mad too, Herr Wolf? We should pay heed to this warning."

"I don't think I'm mad, Schmidt, and nor do I think Esther is mad," Wolf replies. "She's a cook, a genius. You worry too much, Karl, but I won't hold it against you. It seems to be the curse of our times.

Nobody can bear to rise to a challenge any more – all they do is worry. Take this act of desecration on our doorstep, for example. There was no style in its execution. A great pity. No, a great tragedy."

Wolf breaks off from his monologue at this point, carefully observing the effect he is having on the crowd of intrigued reporters. They hold their pens aloft, ready to scribble his musings.

"People used to rise to a challenge," he continues. By this point, he is no longer addressing Karl, but the assembly and beyond that, the world. "Yes, a challenge used to be delivered with style, gentlemen. A kid glove would be thrown down and a duel announced in the language of the poet and not that of the sewer rat. The poetry of these rituals is gone. It has been lost, and yet it was the ritual that made the impact, never the bullet, or the thrust of a sword. But where can we find such style these days? Here, in this very restaurant, we have had a challenge written on our walls in something as *crude* as pigs' blood. And the smell!" Wolf pauses again and glances at the faces surrounding him. He bends his head towards his lapel and breathes in the soft fragrance of his rose buttonhole. "I know of only one answer to this outrage, gentlemen. We must pack Schorns out every night this week and only with people scented to the nines! Schmidt will be in charge of turning away anybody without a decent perfume, or aftershave on them. Do you hear me, young man?"

This characteristic gesture of Wolf's of calling in the trivial to answer the absurd leads everybody, except Karl, to burst into a round of applause. The call to perfume is not a sufficient means to calm his by now overstretched imagination.

"Herr Wolf; gentlemen. You smell danger today. Yes, danger."

Wolf reacts furiously to such a blatant contradiction of his views. He rummages in his jacket pocket, extracting a bottle of aftershave from its torn lining. He pulls out its stopper and flings the contents over his shoulder. The overpowering scent of oriental spices makes our eyes water – it's as pungent as the whiff given off by days-old fish.

"A man may litter my doorstep, but my God, he shan't tell me about scent!" Wolf roars, shifting his bulk from the step and descending on his renegade kitchen hand, like a brimstone ball of fury and anger. "You lack the spirit I expect from my employees," Wolf whispers to him, out of earshot of the news reporters. "You must leave here at once. I shall see that your wages are made up to the end of the week and you can collect them from Esther later this afternoon." He then swings back to the company, raises his voice by several decibels and continues his diatribe: "Were you born a fool, young man? There are countless other people who would give their eye teeth to do the work that you do, and yet all you give me is contradiction and a spirit of defeat. Is it cringing behaviour like this which will make our country a great nation?"

I can see Karl's stunned senses revive at this last comment. Wolf must sound remarkably like his father does when he lectures his friends over a swastika-draped table in his courtyard. He waits for a moment or two, as if expecting a fierce blow to land, but Wolf's hand comes to rest instead on the shoulder of the reporter nearest to him, a conciliatory gesture and one which seems to say: "look what I have to put up with nowadays and in my own restaurant!" The unknown reporter nods his head in sympathy, sucks at the top of his pen and begins devising a headline. For my part, I'm furious that Wolf has sacked Karl without asking my opinion on the matter first. I follow Karl back to the kitchens and promise I will have a word when Wolf is out of hearing of the newspaper reporters.

"You know how it is with the boss," I try and reassure him. "He was just making a scene for the press. He'll soon realise how much we need you down here."

Karl is not to be appeased. He has worked hard for Schorns ever since he began his career with us as a kitchen hand. He's been humiliated in front of dozens of journalists and it smarts. He bangs out of the tradesmen's entrance vowing never to return. I hope this is for effect only and refrain from calculating what we owe him in back wages. But I'm distracted by a new arrival: Kaya has heard about the incident, and is keen to be a part of our protest. She's been tapping her sources in the Communist Party and has further bad news for those of us hoping to wait out the worst of this latest political storm. She shows me an article in *The Stormer* newspaper announcing the appointment of Paul Goebbels to the post of district leader for the National Socialist Party in Berlin. He's been interviewed at his home, photographed against a bush of extraordinarily fat rhododendrons dressed in a sharply cut, navy blue suit. His looks combine the glowering attraction of a matinee idol with those of a quizzical ferret.

"I wouldn't underestimate such a man," Kaya says. "I met him at Schorns a couple of months back and he asked me to dance. I turned him down though. He terrified me, although he was charming with it."

In the article, Herr Goebbels speaks of the great task that lies ahead of him, primarily the pressing need to increase the party's representation in the Reichstag, but at the same time he is mourning the loss of his favourite cook. I recognise the name: Maximilian Sagebrecht was another member of the army of sous-chefs at Botticelli's. His speciality was cooking fish. Goebbels is bereft without his haddock kedgeree, it would appear. How, he asks in the article, can policies be formulated on an empty stomach? Kaya pulls more newspaper cuttings out of her coat pockets and I read them with a sinking heart. Bert has taken my attacks on his courage literally – calling in an essay for a new "totalitarianism of the emotion". The killing of the "outsider" is to be celebrated – act outside the law for a greater good. I think of the refugees in Auguststrasse and my soup kitchen clientele. Kill them and what do you gain? I'm furious at Bert's blinkered vision. I'm almost tempted to write to him and suggest he take up the tailoring of his bloody merino wool coats instead of indulging in hateful policy making.

"It'll be Elizabeth Hauptmann writing on his behalf," Kaya surmises. "She's the new woman in his life, Esther. Very clever by all accounts. She agrees to be published under his name, because it's the only route open for her in our wonderful democratic press. Yes, you can have all the views you like in this world, except if you're female."

Kaya fidgets with her gloves. She's not happy, but what am I saying? She's been ousted from her throne, so of course she's not happy. I slice up an Apfelkuchen and pour out glasses of Weisse mit schuss – a light white beer with a dash of raspberry juice. Goebbels can starve; my friends will dine in the splendour they deserve. For Kaya has shown herself to be vulnerable and that makes me feel sorry for her. She's not invincible, after all, for all her advantages. Kaya gives me a rueful smile – she knows she's a fool.

"So what is Bert's game this time?" I ask.

Kaya shrugs. She's put on weight, but it doesn't harm her looks.

"He's a *dompteur*," she finally replies. "He'll break this Hauptmann woman, like he's broken the rest of us. We should join a circus. We're as wretched as those sealions who play trumpets out of tune for a handful of coins."

Green Phoenix

berlin, 1927

Kaya rings me early one morning in November. Tucholski has collapsed again and she wants me to come over to the apartment in Luisenplatz. I have only just come in from one of my walks and am still dressed in my pinstripe suit, but I snatch up my greatcoat and head straight back out. As she opens the front door, Kaya fills me in on what has happened in an urgent rush of words.

"Saskia found him, slumped over his papers in the conservatory," she says, pulling me in by my coat sleeve. "There was ink everywhere. He's thin as my finger, Esther, but I could hardly move him. He was a dead weight…"

. I ask if I'm to go straight into the bedroom. I still think Tucholski can order me off the premises, if he has a mind to, for we have never recovered the ease of our early days together in Cold Chicago. Kaya waves me on and I encounter him for the first time since leaving Munich. The noise of his choked breathing fills the bedroom. He watches me intently, as I kneel down beside his bed. Without his glasses on, his eyes flicker like underworld creatures exposed to brilliant daylight. I wonder if he really sees me at all for I'm as brittle as one of his forced breaths. And the crumpled suit and rain-stained trilby hat don't help. Just then, Tucholski heaves up another terrible breath and, instinctively, I reach out to touch him. It hasn't sunk in that he can't speak any more. I had expected to hear anything rather than this ugly clatter. He breathes like someone exhausted after tunnelling in a quarry. I fold my hands around his ribs, binding his bones in a ring of flesh. His face is as flat and pale as a stone. I can't begin to imagine how he must be suffering, trapped inside his huge, cracked breaths.

Kaya has followed me in, carrying a jug of water. She puts it down on the window ledge and then takes up her place opposite me.

"He's asleep," she says, lifting my hands away from Tucholski and placing them up against her cheeks. I glance back. She's right – Tucholski has dropped off faster than I blink.

"Don't worry about it, Esther. The doctor says he must sleep as much as possible. He's very weak now." Her voice trails away. We sit and listen to the dislocated beat of Tucholski's breaths. The shrouded room amplifies the sound, like a seashell filled with the roar of an ocean. Kaya seems happy for me just to sit and listen to her.

"I never know if he's in pain, Esther, or if he's just asking me for a drink. I have to second-guess everything."

"Hush, you're upsetting yourself."

I'm stalling her, trying to avoid the conversation which I know she really wants to have. Tucholski is dying and she wants to absolve herself from any responsibility of having pushed him to the brink. She can best do that with a witness, and who better than me? What don't I know about these people's tortured past?

"You know I deserve it," Kaya replies in a harsh tone. "You know how much I've hurt him over the years."

She's pushing me to a denial that will convince her of her innocence, but I can't think of the right words. I fall back on the usual sentiments expressed at such times.

"I know how much you have always loved him, regardless of anyone else. Tucholski knows that too."

"I've cheated him of his dreams."

"I don't think so, Kaya."

I'm aware that she's really begging me to express the forgiveness Thomas can no longer bestow on her.

"He was always so proud of you," I try again. "He never stopped writing for you, did he? And you're still together…"

My feelings overwhelm me. I know how much I loved Thomas and I never tested that love – not like Kaya did. How many men did she leave to come back to him? How many did she have to leave, before even he said enough was enough?

"I've always been so jealous of the trust you share," I whisper.

197

It's a simple statement, but what lies behind it is complicated. Kaya ignores my revelation and plunges on with her own script, which I've departed from in this unusually frank admission of mine.

"It's all just words," Kaya says, cutting in. "Judge me by my actions, not by words, and what do you get?"

I'm unsure how to answer this one. Do I start with the banker and move on from there? It seems cruel in the circumstances, besides I have this strange feeling that Tucholski can hear us, although he's still fast asleep. Kaya gets up and removes a battered suitcase from under the bed. She pulls something out and strips away its tissue paper cover. It's a black merino wool coat. Kaya puts the coat on and parades before me, as if I'm a dressing room mirror.

"Here's evidence of what I've done, Esther, in spite of warning everyone about Bert — even you, on occasions," she says, wistfully. "You know, he advises us where to buy these coats and even how to wear them. I mustn't button it ever, but hold it in close to my body, like so, my elbow over my stomach."

She sinks down on the end of the bed, careful to avoid Tucholski's feet. Explanations fall out of her.

"When I first slept with Tucholski, I felt safe," she confides. "Then, I was resentful of his protection. Bert comes along and…"

"And?"

"I feel as if all the excitement in the world lies just out of my reach, that I have to move forwards and grab it…"

I touch Tucholski's feet under the lettuce-green quilt. We're still here, I'm trying to tell him with this gesture; more to the point, Kaya's still here.

"But Bert was dismissive of me. Excuses and explanations. You know how he is. So, back I come to Tucholski. His trust in me cancels out Bert's ignoring me. Ach, God, it's no way to treat him, is it?"

I assume she means Tucholski, but who knows? Kaya has been ricocheting between two men and their competing demands for a long time now. She reminds me of one those broken-down statues in churches, which people kiss so often the carving is rubbed away. Bert and Tucholski have kissed her to dust.

"I love him, Esther, in spite of what you must think. I've always admired his courage…"

"And when he dies?"

I just blurt it out, which is stupid of me, but Kaya has unnerved me. She looks away. She plays with the button on her coat. The tears spring to my eyes. What has she gained by this affair of hers, exactly?

"Are you still seeing Bert?" I ask, rather too bluntly but I need a straight answer.

Kaya shakes her head. He's not called round in weeks to see his old rival, in spite of her repeated calls and messages. This indifference to Tucholski's plight is the final straw, as far as I'm concerned. I won't spare her a thing.

"Bert is stealing my time too, Kaya," I point out. "He's after my soup kitchen stories. He's been in to see what's going on after hours at Schorns. He's been asking my diners all kinds of questions. He even offered to buy me a coat, like yours. He's says I look worse than the beggars at my table."

"He's up to something?" Kaya doesn't understand my anger. She's sniffed the hint of a new production in the making; she has no interest in how that play might arrive on the manuscript pages, just that she gets first choice of any role. Oh, Kaya, can't you change for one minute? She doesn't waver, however strong someone's objections might be. So clear and direct, even if she does prance about in one of Bert's stupid bloody coats.

"Of course," I reply, after a short pause. "I think he's planning to make a drama out of my soup kitchen. Without my pea soup, he couldn't write."

It's true enough. Bert has been coming by for weeks now with Elizabeth Hauptmann to write down his musings. Although I was happy for Tucholski to find inspiration in my soup kitchen, I find it hard to extend such a feeling to Bert after his recent behaviour. It seems wrong that he should profit at my diners' expense – whilst Tucholski falls sick by the wayside. Ironically, it was Tucholski's ballads written about the soup kitchen that alerted Bert to its dramatic potential in the first place. Kaya doesn't pick up on this, only on my revelation that there is to be a new play from Bert. She even ignores my reference to Hauptmann (rumours abound in Schorns that she is his mistress and not Kaya) and asks me – just as I guessed she would – if I've heard about any forthcoming auditions.

"Oh, God, Esther," she cries, tearing at her cheeks with her fingernails as she realises what she has just asked. "Tucholski is dying and all I want to do is audition."

Kaya is too shattered to even cry. For once in her life, guilt overtakes her. After that encounter in Tucholski's death chamber, I often come across her alone in her apartment kitchen. The maid Saskia reveals that she sits in there motionless for hours at a time, dressed in that cursed black coat. I join her in her vigil whenever I can spare time from Schorns. I know I'm largely doing this because I want to be near Thomas, even if he can't speak to me. During these vigils, Kaya claims she will help me in the soup kitchen when Tucholski gets better. How long can we trust such fictions? As long as it takes Tucholski to die. January 1927 arrives in a blaze of copper-coloured light and he draws one last painful breath against its unseasonal heat. I'm awake, but Kaya is still asleep. There is no time to stretch over and shake her. As Tucholski closes his eyes for the last time, he releases a small explosion of air into the otherwise silent bedroom. I hear it and try to imagine what word it might have formed if he was still capable of speech. I hope it was Kaya's name. When she wakes up, I tell her as much. Half asleep, she only catches part of what I tell her. She's convinced that in his final minutes on earth, Tucholski was able to talk again. Her eyes shine with a sad gratitude.

In truth, there was just the one voice in that sun-filled room. My voice. It sounded odd reverberating around the walls. Tucholski's eyes had never lost their terrified stare for a minute. I wasn't forgiven; Kaya wasn't forgiven. What must that have felt like at the end, to have been surrounded by the two women who he thought had betrayed him? Bert doesn't even send his condolences in one of his wretched notes.

Tucholski is buried in a wind-whipped graveyard with myself, Kaya and Eva in attendance. The priest intones the words of the funeral prayers and yawns without restraint as Kaya throws handfuls of soil on top of Tucholski's coffin. She curses the Catholic church and the priest. Tucholski had abandoned his faith long ago but Kaya has never completely abandoned the religion she too was brought up in. She frets about Tucholski's soul – and about the cost of a red satin lining for the coffin.

"It has to be red," she told the undertaker, whose habitual expression of sad repose had been jolted by her odd request. "Red, because he was a communist and a man of passion."

The undertaker's eyebrows had shot up at the words "communist" and "passion". Kaya had then threatened to cut costs and bring along the handles from her own kitchen cabinets, until the undertaker surrendered and offered to throw in a set free if she bought the satin at full price. They had haggled on, as I inspected a brochure full of dull looking ceramic saints. Kaya had drawn the line on "papist fripparies" but the undertaker had insisted on the coffin itself being painted black and not red.

In the days following that bleak funeral, I take to my bed. Erwin, though, turns up trumps. Arriving on the tail of the newspaper obituaries, he spends hours listening to Kaya's jumbled apologies and accusations. Gradually, she finds her way back to the world – or rather that corner of it she has long set her heart on visiting: Russia, a land currently being mapped by Erwin's friends, Herren Gruber and Poelzing.

"Their stage is improvised wherever they happen to be," he explains. "A factory floor, a street, even a barn. It's like the Republic all over again, but it's official. I can put you in touch with them, Kaya, if you like. It will be such a coup for them hiring a Bebelsberg goddess."

I have invited them to afternoon tea in the kitchen at the House of Clocks. It's evident that Erwin has helped Kaya recover in recent weeks, but at this point she stalls. After all, it's one thing to dream of escape, quite another to find someone else has drawn up the map to achieve it. She's evidently nervous of Erwin's challenge.

"But can I really do it?"

"What have you got left to lose?" Erwin replies. "You need something and why not my friends? They're both very good looking, very charming, very dedicated – and they pay on time, or so they claim. What more could you possibly ask for? You'll be able to boast on the Day of Judgement that you have lived your dreams. How many people can make a claim like that?"

"Did Tucholski live his dreams, do you think?"

Erwin pauses, before replying.

"He came close. After all, he lived with you, Kaya."

Erwin strokes her cheek with the back of his hand, which seems to quieten her. I'm jealous of that tender gesture. I feel a terrible urge to jump up and shout about my grief, but I must mourn Tucholski alone. The only time I haven't mourned alone recently, come to think of it, was when Tucholski shared my pain after I learnt of Benjamin Stein's suicide. Tucholski kept me alive, feeding me from a spoon and giving me words of encouragement. Tears well up in my eyes. It's been a long time since I was touched by a human hand – let alone by someone like Tucholski. Erwin has turned to ask me something and catches my look of despair.

"Esther, are you all right?" He leans forward and seems to be on the verge of taking one of my hands when Kaya bounces back into the conversation.

"The trouble is everyone will claim I'm going into exile," she interrupts.

"Well, they'll be wrong, won't they?" Erwin says, shifting in his chair to turn his gaze on Kaya once more. He measures out each of his subsequent words very carefully, as if it were a medicine for a sick child. "You've wanted this for a long time now, haven't you, Kaya? So, your trip will be made from choice and not necessity. Besides, people in Russia are hungry for stories told in the theatre, Gruber has written to me about it. He says they speak to people who not only want change, they have fought for it on the streets and won their battle. Exciting times, that's his promise."

"I get on a boat and go? That's all there is to it?"

Kaya is disbelieving and hopeful all at once. She hops up and down from her chair. I take this opportunity to wipe my eyes and compose myself. This is no time to exhibit emotion – Kaya is holding centre stage.

"Take a cruise; make your entrance like Cleopatra on her barge," Erwin encourages her. "You stay here, you'll just get wrapped up by the studios, like a novelty parcel."

"But I've made so many mistakes in the past," she says, sinking back down again. "How do I know this isn't another one? I've not got Tucholski here to advise me any more."

"I think you're afraid, because you're near to achieving what you really want," Erwin replies, after only the shortest of pauses. "Sensing fulfilment close to hand makes cowards of us all. And it takes one to know one. I'm on the brink of achieving a long-held ambition, you know. Pabst has summoned me. Oh, yes, and so has Bert. He's writing something new. Rumour has it, it's a musical."

Erwin surveys the room in a suspiciously casual fashion. The mention of Bert's name has me back on guard at once. "I'd like to visit your soup kitchen too, Esther," Erwin adds, looking over to me and smiling. "Taste a bowl of your famous pea soup. I hear Bert has been sniffing around there for research."

"Please come and dine at any time, Erwin," I reply, anxious to try and keep the subject away from Kaya's erstwhile lover.

I realise he's probably digging for information on how the land lies between Kaya and Bert. (Isn't everybody?) Kaya decides on a cautious response, which suggests to me she is really rattled by his name being mentioned.

"Bert ran riot in your kitchen, didn't he, Esther? But he didn't give you anything in return. Typical."

"Maybe a donation from his profits, *if* he is to get any. But tell me, Kaya, have *you* been asked to audition yet?"

"No, not yet," she snaps back. "I'm in mourning, remember? Anyway, his silence might be for the best. I still have my dreams to explore, after all."

"Which makes you luckier than most," Erwin acknowledges.

Some of us are not so lucky. Saskia is resentful when I move in to Luisenplatz temporarily to keep Kaya company. At first I think she has seen through my guise as loyal friend – in truth, I've moved in to keep close to what is left of Thomas's world; his writing materials in the conservatory, the vague scent of his shaving cream in the bathroom, even the sight of his old frock coat hung on a hook by the front door. But Saskia is, in fact, just annoyed at my lack of status. She is accustomed to dealing with the film stars and celebrated communist agitators who usually flock through the Tucholskis' apartment doors. If I wasn't so distressed over Thomas's death, I might well argue with her. After all it was my praise of her hollandaise sauce that won her the wretched job in the first place.

Grief slows me. I sleep for hours at a time under the lettuce-green quilt, hooked into Kaya's arms. We are like fairytale babes in the wood. A fortnight passes before we set ourselves the task of searching through Tucholski's old papers. We are kept busy for several days, before Kaya stumbles on a discovery that threatens to throw everything off course all over again. She thrusts under my nose a page of jottings in Tucholski's handwriting. The paper is headed "Green Phoenix". I read on: *Green Phoenix – the Hanged Woman of the Sung Dynasty. Commits suicide after being caught out betraying her lover with another man. GP's ghost meets and marries a fox-spirit. Decides to betray him too with servant of county magistrate. Fox-spirit swears revenge and puts curse on GP. Doomed to lead many men to their suicide, but NEVER wins place back in world of living. Her search is wild and terrible. She destroys endlessly…*

Curiosity turns to shock, as I finish reading. Here is evidence surely of Tucholski's feelings towards Kaya's adultery? He had revenge in mind at the end, even if he hadn't been able to express it. This is not how I want to remember him, however. Kaya feels the same way. She's already wrestled with this revelation and has resolved it true to her own spirit: she's going to make a drama out of a crisis. To be precise, she's going to get Eva to finish writing the script and she's going to ask Richter to stage it posthumously at Theater Hoffmann.

"Tucholski always promised he would write me a great role one day and I'm sure this is it, Esther," she points out. "Bert will be jealous."

Ah, that last remark gives the game away. She is still smarting at his continued silence and the fact that he has not yet invited her to audition for his latest work. But Kaya ignores my warnings and deals with this emergency as she does most others by entering a whirlwind of activity, which sees us sitting in Richter's office at Theatre Hoffmann within the hour. He sees the value at once of putting on *Green Phoenix* with Kaya in the lead role, but he is less sure of employing Eva to finish a work by the legendary Thomas Tucholski. Richter hesitates just a second too long for Kaya's nerves to stand. She springs up and hauls him from his swivel chair with her bare hands.

"You think I'm a heartless bitch? Well, the way I see it, it's my punishment. I have to do it!"

"Kaya, please!" Richter yells. "You misunderstand me. I'm simply speechless that you can move ahead so fast at a time like this. Most women would be content with their prayers, but then, you have never been like most other women, have you? Please, let us stay calm. I didn't mean to hurt you. I admire your resolve. But what is all this about punishment?"

Kaya falls back in her chair. "I will be crucified when the play's produced, Heinrich. Tucholski makes certain revelations in his play that touch on our relationship. You understand?"

He certainly does. Over the years, rumours have nibbled away at the edges of the Tucholskis' lives like busy little mice.

"Well, if you are sure, Kaya, then so am I," he concedes, rubbing cautiously at his bruised neck. "We can trust each other, I think."

"Yes, Heinrich, I do trust you," Kaya says with as much conviction as she's capable of acting out in the circumstances. "And I trust Eva as much."

"Then we are agreed," Richter says, smiling for the first time, "we can sign the paperwork and get going!"

Kaya gives me a frantic look: we haven't got around to asking Eva if she will finish the play. All could yet be lost. I stall Richter by suggesting we settle the deal over supper at Schorns the following night. He's enchanted by the idea, as I knew he would be.

"No good ever came of working out deals on an empty stomach, eh, Esther?"

But it's no joking matter from where Kaya and I are sitting: we have less than twenty-four hours to convince Eva of our plan and it isn't going to be easy, for she believes Tucholski to be the best writer of his generation. The idea that she should complete his last play will probably seem like a sacrilege of his memory. However, I know we have bait to hook her. When she came back to Berlin for the funeral, she had hinted she was reluctant to go home. The reason? Dieter

Haussmann, the new love of her life and a champion swimmer, has not made up for the disaster that was life with Bert Brecht. The day after Tucholski's funeral, Eva pulled open the neck of her blouse, revealing a vicious scarlet burn.

"Didi threw an iron at me," she had admitted.

If Richter commissions Eva to write *Green Phoenix*, I'm convinced she will jump at the opportunity to return and avoid her violent suitor. Kaya pulls out all the stops when she telephones Eva with our proposal, weeping real tears whenever she hesitates. I grab the receiver from Kaya and add my own half-pfennig's worth.

"But how can I hope to finish what Tucholski has started? I'll be second-guessing and I'm bound to make a hash of it."

"Nonsense. Besides, Kaya will be on hand to guide you. She does know what he wanted; her disadvantage is she can't write as well as you."

Eva weakens under our persistent badgering and within the week she's back in Berlin and we are unearthing a dead man's ambitions. We arrange a number of safe houses for Eva to live in whilst she works on the manuscript. I've seen the evidence of Didi's bad temper, so we cover her tracks as best we can. She writes at the kitchen table in the House of Clocks, setting to work each morning on sheaves of her favourite lined manuscript paper, which Kaya seems to have bought by the barrowful. She pores over the bare bones of Tucholski's outline for several days, before starting to make progress. There are certain experiences which made this story important to Tucholski, Kaya points out, and Eva needs to hear them. She recites her many affairs; she even throws open her hat box collection.

"I'll give it my best shot," Eva promises.

"I'll open the sekt now!" Kaya shouts excitedly, but Eva declines her offer and settles for bowls of Die Suppe Rosenbaum to sustain her in her task.

I find her still sitting at the table when I come back from my late night walks, or from my modelling sessions with Etienne, shadows under her eyes, ink blots all over her hands and blouse. We share a jug of coffee as dawn breaks and Eva reads out her latest dialogues. I'm surprised at how close she comes to understanding the complex betrayals of the Tucholskis' past. I tell her this one morning and she just laughs.

"I was betrayed too," she points out.

I enjoy watching Eva write. She attacks the page with her pen nib like an angry bee, stinging meaning into each carefully worked phrase. Eva writes and rewrites each page with an energy that matches mine when I stride the streets drumming up new trade. I create a special dish in her honour: a ginger and lemon consommé, which I serve up in old ink bottles. I've not invented a new recipe since Tucholski died, so this is a breakthrough. I celebrate with another creation – this one for my dead love. Whilst we were sorting through his office in the Luisenplatz conservatory, I smuggled away his favourite fountain pen in the pocket of my peacock skirt. Tucholski never made a will and Kaya never actually asked me if I wanted any keepsakes. I didn't think she would miss an old pen and I was right. I find a new use for the pen nib when I create my recipe for Tucholski. I detach the nib from the pen and press it down into thin slips of saffron-flavoured pastry to create dozens of little pastry nibs. These nibs are then inserted into little hollow hearts made out of chocolate. To eat the Pen Nib Hearts, I instruct people to tap the edge against their plate and break it open so each pen nib can be nibbled on at leisure and not swallowed in one go. They are an instant success. I send up tray after tray to the Jugendstil Room.

I'm almost distracted from my grief, but the world continues on its destructive course regardless. Etienne disturbs us one morning, shaking with tears and rage. The Brownshirts have broken into the Artimius Market studio and slashed his canvases with carving knives. They left one of the knives plunged into a portrait of me, slicing down my belly as if I were a fish to be gutted. The proposed exhibition of my portraits at Schorns is cancelled indefinitely.

"I don't know if I can carry on working," Etienne says, munching distractedly on a Pen Nib Heart. "I can't even buy a roll of canvas, but the bastards are on my doorstep shouting the odds. My landlord says I've got to leave – he doesn't want to get on the wrong side of those imbeciles."

"Maybe Herr Rolf can find you somewhere?" Eva replies,

applying herself to the dictionary. "He's keeping me safe from my ex-fiancé."

"One man," Etienne points out coldly. "One man, but I'm confronted by a hundred at least. Daily."

It sounds like the kind of odds Etienne would once have relished, but his life has taken a desperate turn. He spends more time at the Jugendstil Room than in his studio, reduced to drawing on the tablecloths, which he then folds up to the size of a book and smuggles out tucked under his greatcoat. It would be comical, except the Brownshirts keep up their vigil. They even abduct one of our laundry baskets, convinced they will find Etienne's latest "unspeakable" art works hidden amongst the gravy-flecked tablecloths. Wolf is indignant – but fearful. He orders Etienne to stop drawing on the premises – unless it's in a notebook. The rows between them are fierce and uncompromising. Etienne fails to draw very much for quite some time.

Kaya is absent from our circle in Schorns, which I put down to her decision to observe the rituals of widowhood – but she also keeps her distance from the House of Clocks. I think maybe she doesn't want to distract Eva, but a chance encounter in Friedrichstrasse tells a different story. Bert has finally been in contact, she reveals. She hands me a note he left pinned to a dried-up sunflower on her doorstep, the day after we commissioned Eva to work for us: "*Why can't you of all people understand?*" he writes. "*My mouth kisses you, but in my dreams. Everything keeps me separate from that which I hold most dear. B.*"

Kaya is fuming, because there is no reference to Tucholski in the note, no indication of either grief, or remorse.

"Just what kind of monster have I been dealing with, Esther?" she seethes. "Ach, he'll get his reply soon enough, but not the one he's been expecting."

mrs kowalke's wedding dress

April, and the rehearsals of *Green Phoenix* are underway. On stage, I watch Kaya inherit a fictional woman's tortured personality, betraying many aspects of her own character. It is an extreme test of her emotional strength. Exhaustion slows her and at times she simply looks too old to play a siren. In spite of this, the newspapers have picked up on her story and she's praised to the skies for her bravery and her devotion to her dead husband's name. Very few of these journalists question how easily she inhabits her role.

Fame brushes against Kaya like a dazed moth. She is bombarded with dresses and jewellery by the city's leading couture houses, but her favourite gown for the publicity drives remains the one designed by Poiret out of nothing more than a handful of emerald green scarves and dozens of strings of tiny beads. It's so soft, I'm able to lift it with one breath. When she wears this dress, Kaya really does transform into Green Phoenix. I help her dress for her public appearances, dusting her shoulders with talcum powder and curling her hair in scraps of rag.

"It's like wearing a flower petal," I say, preening in the mirror, the dress held against my hips.

"Keep it."

"And where would I wear it? At the butcher's? Maybe I could wear it to Schorns and roast meat in it?" I put the dress down with a sigh and fiddle with the powder puffs that litter Kaya's dressing table top. "Here you go again," I reflect out loud. "Dressing up as some ghostly femme fatale, but what's it in aid of? Memories aren't going to be exorcised, just because you take this tack, you know. You wanted to set the record straight, but as far as I can see it's only gone and got more crooked. You need to find a new life for yourself, away from Richter – and Bert."

My warning is too late. Bert has already been alerted by the press coverage to what is going on to revive Thomas's name as dramatist, so it comes as no surprise that he starts sending messages to Luisenplatz asking Kaya to audition for his new play which Erwin has already mentioned.

It has caused uproar, even before rehearsals have been pencilled in, largely because of Bert's choice of composer. Kurt Weill is considered an enfant terrible, but the choice of Kaya to play the leading lady has met with the producer's approval. Bert has given her to understand that her character's costume is already under the cutting scissors and Weill thinks her voice ideal for the part he has in mind. As a consequence, the atmosphere in rehearsals for *Green Phoenix* worsens considerably. Tension flies everywhere, an invisible lightning force ripping up the company's confidence. Kaya withdraws from the rest of the cast. She stops eating and soon we match up like two withered sticks. I suspect her long silences have something to do with the messages she has been receiving from Bert. The day before we open, Kaya collapses in her dressing room. I help her onto the little sofa that stands by the dressing table and sponge her forehead with cold water. I fear her collapse is possibly the result of some vicious verbal assault from the Brownshirts who gather on a daily basis outside the theatre. Tucholski's play is in their sightlines, because they believe it slanders "German womanhood". Kaya is German, female and, I thought, unshockable by anything, let alone accusations of slander. But she lies shaking in my arms, her face as pale as a stripped bone.

"He wants me back, Esther."

It's what I've been fearing for weeks: Bert has turned up on Kaya's doorstep; they have eaten together and they have slept together, but words failed Kaya the minute she really had need of them.

"I should have got rid of him, but I didn't. God knows why. I cooked him a chicken instead. He'd brought some of his script along, saying he wants me to audition. Day after tomorrow."

Of course he does. Bert wants to sabotage Tucholski's last stage work, although what can be the point of such rivalry now?

"Maybe you should just lock your door until after we open?" I suggest. "Concentrate on this show and nothing else, Kaya. The regrets can come later, not now, not after everyone's hard work."

She squeezes my hand and thanks me, but I think she's probably beyond my advice. There is no time to discuss alternative strategies, for the opening night of *Green Phoenix* arrives shortly after Kaya's confession and it's a headline-grabbing event from the off, exposing everybody in its spotlight, whatever their role. Schorns relocates to Theater Hoffmann – Wolf and Etienne turn up in matching waistcoats and cigarette holders; Eva wears a new dress that shows up her startling eyes; Richter is in black velvet frock coat and red silk scarf and Herr Handke and Herr Rolf don plus fours and cravats covered in tiny, ticking clocks. I wear a new suit stitched by Frau Meyers and my hair is tied up with a collection of dyed stockings from Etienne's studio.

Everyone who is anyone is present on the night: theatre critics and feature writers from the film magazines; actors; directors; writers and politicians. We all enter the mysterious world Eva has created in her second play and come out stunned by Kaya's performance. It is a haunting and complex portrait, with Green Phoenix revealed in monologues that capture the essence of the woman I have known for so long. The tormented ghost spirit-woman moving from man to man, but destined to settle nowhere. The critics are united in their view on the matter, falling over themselves to unearth new superlatives to praise Eva's characters and interpretation. They also praise her inspired reworking of Tucholski's legendary, disjointed prose style. Not even the baying protesters outside the theatre can ruffle our feathers tonight.

And yet by the time I get to Luisenplatz the following morning, the impact of these delirious few hours has evaporated. Kaya's back with her melancholy thoughts. She's not even changed out of her stage costume. The reviewers talked at length about her "incandescent beauty"; for more than one moustachioed, portly scribe she seemed like "a Greek goddess personified". The goddess is soiled goods by the time I reach her with the first of the reviews. She is slumped on her chaise longue, her face drawn and mean, like the fox-spirit she has only recently transformed herself into, though the mask is lying by her feet. I try and rally her spirits, but she barely glances at the overnight reviews.

"Stay, Esther," she pleads.

I curl up tight beside her, under the lettuce-green quilt. Kaya places her hands around my neck and attempts to sleep, but she's far too jittery.

"You risk loving a thief, Kaya," I warn her. "Be careful. Bert nets people and then transforms their desire into a knife. You only end up hurting yourself, if you try and use that knife against him."

Kaya promises she will stick to her contract with Richter. She has no intention, she claims, of failing him, or Eva. I smile into her tired face and wonder how it has come to this: betrayal and cowardice bind us together. Except I *like* Kaya. So, what harm if I make one more mistake and stay her friend? The harm is this: Kaya is obsessed. She wants revenge on the man who has no idea that geography might finally enable her to desert him. He thinks he can play her like a poacher does a fish on his bait, but Kaya has other plans. She reveals them to me at a photocall in the theatre auditorium later that same morning.

"I'm going to buy a ticket away from all this madness, Esther. Bert is nothing more than a liar and a thief. That is the truth we should be putting up on stage: a man who cuts purse strings and heart strings, like he would an animal's throat."

Kaya sends word she will audition after her photocall. She asks me to go with her to the audition, which I discover is to be held in the backroom of Michael the Tailor's workshop. We are welcomed by Bert himself, who darts out from behind stacked bolts of cloth the minute the shop bell rings. He greets us both as if nothing of any great significance has happened since we all last met, least of all a friend's premature death. He has brought his maid along to prepare coffee and cakes – his only apology is delivered to me and it relates to the standard of fare on offer.

"Hardly in the league of the legendary Esther Rosenbaum, but we had to make do with the shop on the corner," he says, before pulling Kaya to one side to talk her through her lines. "Take emotion out of your speech," he advises. "And remember, the dirt on your skin is your only coat…"

Kaya follows his directions to the letter when she addresses Mack the Knife, who will play opposite her; a man who will slit open her belly and tear out her soul for the price of a beer. Except someone else has already beaten him to it. Kaya's voice is emotionless; all hope has escaped like rainwater from a broken shoe. There can be no emotion, remember? But Kaya remembers and I remember. The silent telephone. The empty hat boxes. A black wool coat stroked into threads. Kaya recites Bert's words, like she would the contents of one of her maid Saskia's shopping lists, but inside there's another page waiting to be read out loud. It's not a text Bert would care to hear, because neither has he written it nor rinsed out its raw emotions. Kaya is not so disciplined, however. She loves and hates in one breath. Bert doesn't pick up on any of this, just offers her the role of Polly Peachum as he always planned to do.

To accept, or not to accept? That is not really the question. The role in *The Threepenny Opera* is a surface detail to Kaya, as she plots and schemes. She succeeds in getting Bert to delay rehearsals until the run of *Green Phoenix* is over. When she finally turns up at Schorns in late August to start rehearsals, she looks extraordinary. Grief has whittled down her fleshy contours and she now boasts the clarity of line of an Egyptian tomb sculpture. She wears her favourite diaphanous green gown and more than one person present comments on how she really does look like a triumphant phoenix. Ernst Josef Aufricht, the producer of Bert's new piece, is on hand to squire her round. He is a small-boned man, dressed in a sapphire blue shirt and workman's trousers with a high waistband held up by braces. He is evidently smitten with Kaya; actually, the whole world is smitten, but she has a secret that beats all this adoration into a cocked hat.

Kaya makes her entrance into the company on a day of aborted rewrites. There has been yet another fierce argument in the Jugendstil Room and Aufricht is desperate for guidance from a source not linked to the troubled rehearsal room.

"We eat words, dear Frau Tucholski," he sighs. "Maybe you can see a way out? Everything has gone to seed and I am no gardener. You have green fingers, I hope?"

Kaya sits and argues with the best of them. She also makes a great exit, outraged (allegedly) at the reallocation of some of her lines behind her back, and she's not even started rehearsals yet! I learn more later when Herr Aufricht rings me from the Schiffbauerdamm where the company rehearse. Day one of her contract and Kaya is already refusing to co-operate until her "stolen" lines have been restored.

"What to do, Esther? You're her best friend. She'll talk to you, won't she? Come over, please."

My instinct is to tell him to hire someone else if he wants peace of mind, but old habits die hard. Kaya needs me to play support, so be it. I pull on my boots and head for "The Schiff". It's only a short walk from the Jugendstil Room, but by the time I arrive a fresh crisis is waiting to greet me. A frazzled stage manager directs me to one of the dressing rooms where Herr Aufricht is closeted with Frau Kowalke, the costume maker. There are problems with the various show budgets, he reveals. My heart sinks. Money troubles, actress troubles. This is going to take more than a bowl of pea soup to sort out, except the costume maker has an idea how to bring Kaya back into the fold.

"Frau Tucholski is one for the finery and the fuss, is she not, Herr Aufricht?" Frau Kowalke says.

I look at Herr Aufricht, but he is studying Frau Kowalke's intriguing appearance. Her shoulders are weighed down with tape measures and pieces of half-finished costume giving her the appearance of the old street pedlars in the Scheuenviertel.

"What of it?" Herr Aufricht replies.

"You must show her Polly's wedding dress, that's what. It's a beautiful gown, even if I say so myself. She will die before she gives up an opportunity to wear it. Besides, it would be a crime to see such silk go to waste. Bought it myself in the market and never would I get a bargain like that again. You must bring it back without so much as a speck of dust on its hem. I beg you: take care of it. We have no time to restitch anything. You understand?"

"Well, Frau Kowalke, I really can't think of a better idea," Herr Aufricht admits. "What about you, Esther? You women always understand each other best, don't you? What do you think?"

I ask if I might see the dress for myself.

"Promise me, Fräulein Rosenbaum, you won't sneak it away for your own wedding?" begs Frau Kowalke.

I snort with laughter at such an improbability, but nonetheless I promise. Frau Kowalke ushers us into a second dressing room, which is, in fact, nothing more than a long, narrow store cupboard lined with wobbly shelving. Here are stored the costume designer's treasure trove of oddities: piles of solitary gloves suggesting the discarded limbs of an over-zealous surgeon; boxes of crusty pancake make-up and dozens of plumed hats.

"Decorated it myself with the tiniest of seed pearls and stitches of silver thread," Frau Kowalke points out. "It's the crowning glory of my career. I guard it from my assistants' prying fingers with my life."

Herr Aufricht and I agree that the gown is as stunning as the woman destined to wear it. She carefully lifts it off the dressmaker's dummy and parcels it up inside its cotton wrapper.

"This will surely do the trick?" gasps the false bridegroom.

"Mind what I told you, Herr Aufricht. It would be a sin to damage such a dress. You must return it tomorrow morning at the latest."

Herr Aufricht kisses Frau Kowalke's cheek which is dusted with dressmaker's chalk, and then he turns and asks me to accompany him to Luisenplatz.

"I'm so excited, Esther, I don't mind admitting it," he enthuses. "I feel as if I'm wooing the lady for myself!"

We drive up to Kaya's apartment in Herr Aufricht's open-top car. The dress sits in the front seat, whilst I drape myself as best I can across the back seat. I feel as if we are at the centre of our very own film. We stride up to Kaya's apartment with our offering of peace, but here the soft focus film splutters to an abrupt halt. We are kept waiting as Saskia makes a great show of going to announce our arrival to her mistress. After a delay of rather too many minutes we are shown into the conservatory where we find Kaya lying on a chaise longue, wrapped in the lettuce-green quilt. I see an actress at work and so does Herr Aufricht. He quickly adopts his role as penitent, blustering his apologies for Bert's behaviour and promising restitution of her lines by the very next rehearsal.

"What more can I do, Kaya?" he begs. "Achje! To think we could have lost you from our company! I'm mortified, but I have brought

Polly's dress with me, hoping this might tempt you to forgive us all. Yes, it's quite a creation. There will be women travelling from all over the country to take a look at it. Parisian couturiers will be jealous of its every detail and *you*, dear lady, will be wearing it. Think of that, I beg you."

Kaya was probably hoping to let Herr Aufricht sweat it out for as long as possible, but the sight of the dress when it's delivered from its wrapper is too much for even her mercenary calculations. She jumps up from the chaise longue and snatches it from his arm.

"I shall need time to consider your offer," she bluffs. "But in the meantime I'll try the dress on. It's made to my measurements, you say?"

"Yes, indeed. We always had hopes, you see, even when you said you were leaving us."

Kaya stops Herr Aufricht in mid flow and invites me to help her try on the dress in her bedroom. Only when we are out of earshot does she reveal how vulnerable she is under her pose of outraged actress.

"If I wear the dress, I take on the role of a bride, but I'll be a fraud, won't I?"

"Are you still planning to take your revenge on Bert?" I ask, wondering if this new fragile Kaya will upstage her earlier conniving self.

"Wait and see."

In the end, Kaya returns to the conservatory still wearing Polly's wedding dress. Herr Aufricht hops after her, anxious she doesn't catch the lace train on any of the furniture. He nibbles his fingernails and waits for the verdict. I feel sorry for him, because I know he waits in vain.

"Is there no other message, Herr Aufricht?"

Kaya is concerned that Bert is not pleading for her return in person. She really wants to rub his nose in it! Herr Aufricht shuffles through his pockets to show willing, but there is nothing else in there he can produce for Kaya. She was hoping for another note at the very least. I watch the pantomime and keep silent.

"I shall be back in rehearsals tomorrow, Herr Aufricht, because you have asked me; no other reason than that. Please report back to

Herr Brecht with this message."

"Kaya, I'm honoured. I can hardly describe my gratitude…"

"Then don't insult me by failing!"

Kaya packs up her train and exits the conservatory in a whirl of cream silk and fabricated outrage. I realise my friend really was born to play Revenge.

"What message was she expecting?" Herr Aufricht asks in perplexed tones.

Saskia ushers Herr Aufricht back through the front door, and I hunt Kaya out in her bedroom. She's still dressed in Polly's wedding gown and stands swaying gently to and fro in front of her dressing room mirror. Her hands trace over her flat stomach in a gesture that makes even my cynical self feel sorry for her. Death can do that to a person, I know. It can make them want to achieve something, to have it in their arms where they can protect it from all the bad things in the world, but maybe Kaya isn't ready for such a gesture yet? What she is ready for is Stage Two of her Revenger's Tragedy. She resigns from The Schiff's company just two days before the opening of *The Threepenny Opera*. It is a cause célèbre in the newspapers and the critics rush to analyse such extraordinary behaviour. The consensus is *"women's fickleness compounded by an inability to face widowhood at such a tender age"*. Kaya snorts her derision. Tenderness has never been one of her chief qualities, after all. She refuses to read any more, but does linger over a photograph of Bert burning Kaya's copy of his manuscript. The picture caption claims he has *"returned the phoenix to its ashes"*.

"I can't believe how simple it was in the end, Esther," she declares in triumph.

But will anything ever be that simple in our lives again? I head back out to the streets to recruit for my soup kitchen in a bid to stem my worries. In recent weeks, I've got into the habit of wearing several layers of greatcoats to disguise my thin frame – and my trouser suit. I hide my face under the brim of Tucholski's old top hat, the one he wore for his failure of a wedding and which I found in his office after he died. My drastic weight loss means I stoop badly, closing in round my shrunken belly and protecting my bones which rattle with each step on the district's uneven cobblestones.

The night after Kaya's theatrical coup d'état, I find myself in the Moabit and decide to visit the courtyard of my old mietskasernen. It's dark, but this doesn't deter Bloch, the travelling song merchant, from giving one of his legendary performances. The eerie darkness makes his Moritaten songs of murder and deceit all the more powerful to his impressionable audience of machine workers and their families. I'm standing in shadow, listening intently when someone unexpectedly calls out my name. To my amazement, Kaya materialises beside me, still wearing Frau Kowalke's wedding dress. Even in the murky light, I can see that the train is torn and quite filthy; one of the sleeves has come loose and trails behind her like a false limb.

"Herr Handke has asked me to learn up one of Bloch's tunes," she explains. "He wants his mechanical Bloch to sing it exactly the same way. He said he can't trust you with the job, because you've got tin ears."

"But in that dress?"

"I've nothing else to wear."

I'm about to dismiss this blatant exaggeration, but am shushed by a disgruntled bystander. Bloch picks up on the disturbance and calls out in the direction of my big, black shadow:

"Who are you?"

He hasn't recognised me under my top hat and several greatcoats – he's probably mistaken me for a shadow given out by a large rubbish heap. Kaya is also heavily disguised under her dirty bridal finery.

"We're collecting songs," I reply.

"A thief, you mean?" Bloch sneers.

"No. Collectors."

"*Collectors?*"

Bloch lays an unpleasant stress on his last word and the crowd around us laugh nervously. People are frightened by this exchange. There aren't many who dare challenge what they don't know, but Bloch has always been the exception to this rule. His scarred face indicates an unwise curiosity in the lives of strangers he meets with on his travels.

"We'd better leave, Esther," Kaya says, stretching up and pulling at my coat sleeve.

"Is that Esther Rosenbaum? The Jewess?" Bloch shouts out, catching my name as it drifts towards him on the evening air. "I might have known it! You'll steal my blood next. No, what am I saying? You take my songs, you steal my life's blood already. What a bitch!"

Saying this, he stoops and picks up a lump of crusty mud and throws it at what he takes to be my head in the dark shadows before him. Others follow his example and Kaya and I are soon running for safety to the street outside. There, it's still light and our eyes contract painfully in the unexpected glow of a late evening sun. Kaya is distraught.

"What's going on, Esther? Bloch was a friend to us in the past."

But the world has moved on. Herr Goebbels and his Brownshirt cronies have been busy in the Moabit. The stories they have to tell are not overly friendly towards people like Kaya and myself. We see bill posters advertising meetings in bierkellers that echo the demands of the men who crowded around Herr Hitler in Munich. It's as if the terror following the defeat of the Bavarian Republic has swept back here. Kaya is so shaken she has to grip my coat sleeves to steady herself on our walk back to Fasanenstrasse. Herr Handke helps us clean up with old rags. He's concerned at the reception we have been given, but even more concerned to think Kaya might not have had time to gather up a song for him. It is Kaya who recovers her wits first. She sits down on a stool and sings the ballad we heard, before being set upon by our old neighbours. Herr Handke asks her to repeat it over and over again, until he gets the rhythm for himself, tapping away on the side of his workbench with a small file.

Long after day breaks, I leave the workshop with Kaya. The incident at the Moabit has finally caught up with me. I sit down on the bottom of the stairs and find that my hands are dancing on top of my knees, like a stringed puppet's.

"I don't know what else I can do, Kaya. I'm weak as a piece of string."

"Then you must come to Russia with me," she replies with an air of such finality I'm unnerved. "The troupe will need a cook and a storyteller. You can manage both, just as you have done here for Herr Handke and Herr Wolf. Besides, I need you out there. You're my only friend. I can't go without you."

Exile myself to Russia? It sounds incredible. I imagine a country filled with sleighs and huge mansions, Sergei lookalikes brandishing whips and unvarying vistas of snow, white as the inside of an egg shell. Where on earth would I fit in? Besides, haven't I shivered enough here in Cold Chicago? The motive to leave has never been stronger in some senses: so much has changed since I last packed a carpet bag. Tucholski's death has left a hole inside me; my whole body aches when I think I will never see him again. Bert is on a crusade like Kaya, but the detail of the course he is taking disturbs me. He seems as relentless as the forces of opposition. Take away compassion, as he keeps demanding in his newspaper articles, and what is left? The strident statements of a Herr Goebbels; Etienne's paintings slashed with a knife in Schorns' gallery; a woman like Kaya reduced to pinning her hopes on a mad dream – that's if she can't have the mad man who prompted it in the first place.

Catastrophe is imminent; it prises and teases me open. I know instinctively that my response to Kaya's offer to join her in Russia will be the biggest decision I have yet had to make.

potatoes & pomegranates

berlin, 1928–1929

Eva has gone into hiding, because Dieter Haussmann has come up to town determined on frog marching her back to Augsburg. Kaya and I must find more hideaways for our friend, who is determined to stay a writer and to hell with her frustrated lover. He is indeed another *"dompteur"* like Bert Brecht has proved to be – a man who must control, if he is not to explode. As for me, I am only able to assert my authority in the kitchen. It is my sanctuary, my eerie; I'm like a big old crow determinedly fashioning its nest as the storm clouds brew ahead. Wolf is worried that I work too hard – and that I don't eat.

"See reason for once in your life, Esther," he begs. "But what am I asking? You can't swallow reason any more than you can a grape. A wilful woman, God help me, a wilful woman to placate."

I don't respond and he skulks off to Etienne's studio. I no longer model for him, because I'm too thin even for him.

"You must watch yourself," he warns, in turn. "You get thinner by the minute. He flicks up a rope of my hair, which stretches from my head to the kitchen floor. "The only thing that thrives is your hair. It's just getting longer and longer."

Etienne is in trouble with the Nazis. They don't like his pictures and they don't like him. When he comes to visit, he must duck and dive like a spy in a film. He knows every doorway from here to the Moabit and back again.

"Just as well, because I might soon have to live in one," he claims.

Wolf accompanies him on his journeys occasionally, but doesn't like getting his velvet coats spat upon by passers-by. Wolf makes pomanders out of spices stolen from my kitchen and wafts them in front of the noisy ragamuffins, but he can't block out their threats and taunts about his relationship with Etienne.

"If you're not even tempted to eat your own dishes, what else can possibly revive your appetite?" Wolf asks one evening.

He has threatened to tie me to a chair with my hair and force-feed me.

"You'd get grease on your waistcoat," I retort.

"That's true," Wolf realises, with a shake of his carefully pomaded head. "A terrible sacrifice. Ach, the world goes upside down and we just paint ourselves!"

Or we buy a one-way ticket to Paradise. Kaya has bought her ticket and is pushing me to do the same. She makes a tour of Russia sound like an idyllic stroll in the countryside. There will be no potholes, crummy hotels, argumentative drivers, appallingly behaved actors – nor writers. She will accompany a merry band of troubadours along the length and breadth of a country that has made revolution come alive for the masses. Kaya knows how to tell a good story, and she repeats her stories over and over again when she comes over to the House of Clocks to help me wash. I might have brought my wayward body under control by refusing to eat, but it means I need assistance to bathe. My bones now poke into me like dozens of little knives and the task requires a sensitive hand. Kaya obliges, because she uses our bath times to extend her campaign to get me out of the country (and she encourages me to try eating again). She brushes soap against my skin with the tips of her fingers, but still I bruise up like an old plum.

"In Russia, things will be different, Esther. No more sidestepping the Brownshirts. You'll have audiences eating out of the palm of your hand."

Kaya perches on the edge of the bath, lost in thought. The water turns cold and the soap dries on my skin, but I don't like to distract her. She's happy when she's lost in the highways and byways of her imagined Russia; happier than she's been since Tucholski's death. I'm aware that this is a troubling bond between us. Tucholski is dead and buried and finally I understand just how much I loved him. He

222

stayed constant, which is a rare achievement in our world. When he fell ill, he was instantly dismissed by the likes of Bert, who wants only to build his own myth with the right kind of people around him. Sick and dying, Tucholski was never going to be invited to the writing sessions Bert holds in his attic apartment.

Gambling has paid off for Bert, however. *The Threepenny Opera* has been hailed as the best theatrical event of the Weimar Republic. I think Kaya is secretly furious she ever walked out on the production. She is *persona non grata* with Bert's clique and they rule Berlin's theatreland thanks to the antics – and songs – of his most famous characters: Mack the Knife, Polly Peachum and Pirate Jenny. But if Kaya really wants to honour Tucholski's memory, she must continue to be frozen out by his rival. I try and convince her that comparisons are pointless at this time. Who knows what is going to survive the muddle of our Republic? A couple of playscripts, a restaurant, or a corrupt elite fuelled by bigotry? Copies of the *Völkischer Beobachter* are left in Schorns and I read there what Herr Goebbels thinks of people like me and Kaya. Berlin's Jews are little better than the Bolshevik revolutionaries in Moscow. We all need to watch out.

Kaya flicks open her compact and checks her appearance. She may well be one of the people, but she ensures her false eyelashes stay in place. She studies her face long and hard. Her beauty is a mask. I think she mourns Tucholski more than she does the loss of her part in Bert's play, but I don't know for certain. I, meanwhile, grieve in a way I can't express to my closest friends and it keeps me silent. I take time to work on new dishes. Herr Goebbels' followers have started hanging out in the Jugendstil Room and there are daily confrontations over the menus – but it's not my dishes that are under discussion. Occasionally, fights break out. Wolf is compromised, because these visitors offer him ingredients that rarely make their way onto the menus of rival establishments. He only agrees to swallow his pride when I point out that we can salve our consciences by using some of the contraband goodies we receive from the Brownshirts in my soup kitchen.

Kaya – ever the chameleon – weaves between the two camps, picking up intelligence for our kitchen conferences. One day, she alerts me to another potential crisis: Dieter Haussmann, Eva's former fiancé, has been appointed Goebbels' right hand man. A violent individual, he has without doubt the right qualifications for the job but his presence in our midst is deeply unwelcome. Eva's hideways are cold, dark places and she's been using the restaurant as her unofficial office. Wolf had no objections, because she made a name for herself by writing *Green Phoenix*, but when he learns of her relationship with Haussmann he pales and suddenly finds his love of literature waning.

"We can't afford another scene," he argues. "Haussmann has great influence. He could have us closed down overnight."

We must find a new home for Eva. We end up back at the Moabit on the advice of Herr Rolf. Herr Handke plans to unveil the first storey of his clock tower in our old courtyard and has been wooing our one-time neighbours for donations to help in its creation. According to Herr Rolf, many have forgotten the ugly mud-throwing incident and are offering what they can to this unlikeliest of projects. Kaya is convinced their change of heart reflects the world beyond the tenements where Berlin is once again on the brink of change.

"It's like it was in Munich during the days of the Republic," she argues. "Don't you think so, Esther? Everyone's clutching at half-understood ideas, trying to plot a way forwards. It's showtime again and the stage is a politician's platform."

Kaya momentarily forgets about her escape plans, caught up in the drama of the clock tower's launch and the chance to spread word of revolution amongst new recruits. The machinists and the servant girls welcome her. They know her from her film appearances and they are enthralled at the idea of a famous actress taking time out to speak to them. She makes their dreams come true on the silver screen, so maybe she can pull it off in real life too, exchanging their shabby lives for a brave, new world? Sitting cross-legged on the cobblestones, Kaya reads out leaflets promoting new visions for our city. (There are many living in the Moabit who are barely literate.)

I am appointed head of catering for the courtyard construction workers. Each morning, I plan three menus: the Jugendstil Room's menu, which reflects our new diners' taste for Bavarian cuisine, the soup kitchen dish of the day and the cakes, pastries and breads I take over to the Moabit. Kaya drives an old hearse these days – she thinks it provides a cunning cover for her political activities – but it is also the ideal size for transporting the food I prepare for the Moabit run. Kaya is flourishing in this odd world we find ourselves in: one minute, dining on pigs' heads with Haussmann and company, the next hot-hoofing her way over to a battered old courtyard where a miracle is planned. Loaves into fishes? Strike me dead to say it, but Jesus had it easy. I must make bread out of turnips; dandelions and nettles grace my salads; steaks are cut out of the body of a knacker's yard horse that collapses in the street and, more recently, from a whale's belly (Wolf did a deal with a contact of Haussmann's). Everything I have ever learnt, I draw on now to keep my trio of menu planners as fresh as the printer's ink on our daily newspapers.

Eva isn't immune from what is going on, even if she does live like a mole in a hole. She persuades her neighbours to dig up wasteland behind the Artimius Market and grow vegetables. She ensures a percentage come over to Schorns, which I can then use to bribe the Brownshirts from making too many enquiries into the market garden that has suddenly sprung up in the middle of nowhere. I learn more than ever how much a cook must create: who would believe there were a hundred different ways to cook a potato? I know them all. I've invented most of them. Potatoes cooked in a smudge of butter, spruced up with winter herbs I jealously guard in my window boxes; potatoes fried in goose fat and trimmed with thyme; potatoes cut into wedges, rolled in thick black pepper and roasted; baked potatoes wrapped in newspaper, handed out from Kaya's hearse to the factory girls.

After emptying the hearse of our contributions, we often head over to Eva's and listen to her read out her latest stories (Brecht, sniffing a rival, has had the city's producers blacklist any plays of hers.) This is a strange comfort in our otherwise ugly world. We drink mulled wine and nibble on my latest confectionary triumph: Kiss-of-Hope, tiny vanilla creams mounted on sweet pastry heart bases. Eva plans to grow fruits in the summer, which she will send over to Schorns so I can create desserts that will whet tastebuds grown stale on stewed apples. She plans rows of soft fruit and whatever else she can tempt out of our unpromising soil. She lives in a stinking labyrinth like everyone else in these courtyards, but she stays optimistic. I take courage and tramp down alleyways I once knew as well as the lines on my palms. The winter rains lie frozen between cracked cobblestones, my elbows graze against narrow walls and I have to bend down double to fit under the low archways dividing up the courtyards of the Moabit, but wherever I go I find someone who is in need of sustenance at my soup kitchen. I issue invitations faster than leaves drop from trees in the parks.

Ach, but what would Tucholski have made of it all, I can't help but wonder. How would he have stood up to people like Haussmann and their poison? He would never have left, because he was Berlin born and bred. *Stay too long on its streets and you can never be free of the place.* Even if this city is rushing to meet its destruction.

"Tucholski would have written a song, you can bet on that," Kaya argues with me one night. "But I want to survive. What's the tune for that?"

"You know full well I'm tone deaf. But I suppose if all else fails, you can always dream of perfection, even if you never get to live with it."

"Do I take it from that you're not coming to Russia with me, Esther?" She fixes me with such a serious look, I find it hard to look her in the eye.

"No, I won't be coming." I pause, because I can sense that she's waiting for more. I take a deep breath. "I'm sorry, but this city is where I was born. It is where I belong – if anywhere. I can't really explain better than that."

She smiles, but it's a wry one. I sound like Tucholski and we both recognise the fact. It's my last word on the subject of buying tickets to Russia and she accepts it, although I think she thinks I have let her down. I love this city, even as it fails me. Eva is of my opinion. She idolised Tucholski too, so I find myself confiding in her rather than in his ex-wife. She's observant, is our Eva. She soon picks out my secret, like a bird winkles a snail out of its shell. Tap, tap, rat-a-tat tap. *Et voilà!* I'm revealed to be a woman suffering from unrequited love.

"Well, nothing very remarkable about that," she says, munching on a Kiss-of-Hope. "What are you going to do about it, that's the question."

I shrug. What can I possibly do? Tucholski is buried six feet under so do I hold a seance, tattoo his name on my shrunken belly, or recite his poems and his plays on street corners? Eva laughs.

"You're being too dramatic, Esther. But it's the fault of the times. Have you seen the crazy parades the Brownshirts get up too?"

Dieter Haussmann is the king pin of their proceedings in the Jugendstil Room. His boots are polished to the sheen of a brand new silver teaspoon and his uniform is ironed into sharp creases. He is as unpredictable as he ever was. He knows about my job at Schorns and so far has not rocked the boat by ordering my dismissal. I know – and Wolf knows – he's in a position to do just that. I crisp up pigs' ears in my frying pans, because he likes to snack on these when he's meeting with his cronies in the Jugendstil Room.

Besides, Dieter is distracted: he's taken a real shine to Kaya and fills the gap Bert has left in my friend's Fan Club membership, after the *The Threepenny Opera* stand-off. He provides her with free petrol for the hearse and presents her with jewels which I don't think he buys in any shop. For once in her life, Kaya is made uneasy by a man's attentions. She has no idea how to play Haussmann. In the end, she keeps the gifts of petrol so she can make her bread-and-cake run to the Moabit, but rejects the jewels.

"I have some standards, Esther, honestly. Besides, when I join the company in Russia, we will all be equals. I can hardly manage that with emeralds the size of conkers round my neck."

But it's no good. Kaya can't avoid the spotlight and the adoration that goes with it. A little boy in the Moabit makes her a garland of paper flowers, because he believes she's an angel. She wears the garland for quite a while. In Russia, the company tour in boiler suits and army boots, so I hope she'll receive plenty more paper garlands in the future.

Winter arrives and it's a bad one. The winds blow cold and ice forms *inside* the kitchens at Schorns. The door bolts freeze hard and I have to loosen them with hot water before we can set up the soup kitchen. 1929 arrives and catches us unawares, buried as we are under scarves and greatcoats, to-ing and fro-ing from Schorns to the Moabit in a dirty old hearse. Herr Handke has set the date for unveiling the first storey of his clock tower: May 1st. Activity in the Moabit reaches fever pitch. Herr Rolf supervises dozens of volunteers who go out collecting materials to help build the first storey. They hunt out old bike frames, mattress springs, string, rope, candlesticks, old pots and pans and even pieces of tree bark. This first storey will celebrate the world of the Moabit: it's chief attraction a life-size model of Herr Bloch singing above a platoon of sunflowers (each measuring seven feet in height).

Alongside Bloch, there is a new tableau showing Tucholski writing his ballads inside the Moabit prison. It's an extra scene I have begged Herr Handke to include by way of thanking Kaya for her assistance in recruiting machinists to the clock tower's cause. I'm not sure he doesn't see through my lie – Tucholski is shown sitting at a desk with a little peacock embroidered onto his prison suit, a copy of the birds stitched on my tatty old peacock skirt from Scheuenviertel days. The piece of paper underneath his pen nib records one of the ballads he wrote in my soup kitchen – *The Ballad of the Red Giantess.*

Hundreds of donations have been pouring in to Herr Rolf's office at the House of Clocks, including pen nibs, links of chain, tarry ropes, horseshoes, bird feathers, bricks, hair pins and necklaces. Esau is jealous of the rags and stalks the courtyard for anything he might salvage. Herr Rolf bans him from the site and he comes to join me in Schorns' kitchen to drink coffee and reminisce about old times. Esau is my one remaining link with the Scheuenviertel. He reveals that the Frankls have closed down their bakery and moved to Paris where Frau Frankl's sister lives.

Eva senses my loss and decides to write a story about my father to make me feel better. She picks my brains and cooks up a beautiful story about a man who wooed his wife under a chestnut tree and then turned his faith and his love of a world-class hatmaker into little dramas for a near-forgotten world. We make copies on the backs of old wallpaper strips, bind them up with parcel string and ask Etienne to illustrate them with little scenes. Our model is the Megillah of the Book of Esther, which Pappa used to read to me when I was a child. We sell them from the kitchen to raise funds to buy food for the clock tower volunteers. Dieter Haussman gets hold of a copy and summons Wolf to a dressing down in the Jugendstil Room.

"Imagine, Esther," he tells me later. "Pulled in to explain myself to that oaf. He wanted to know why I was associating myself with – forgive me, but I must quote him here – "maggot Jews". I asked him why he associated himself with people who fail to incorporate any sense of individuality in their choice of clothing. I'm afraid to say, we didn't part the best of friends."

Haussmann is offended by our little homemade booklet, but even more so by the rumours that have reached him of Herr Handke's clock tower. Wolf has been quizzed on this abomination too. I check with Herr Rolf. His view – and that of Herr Handke – is to push ahead come what may.

"The gauntlet has been thrown down," Herr Rolf says. "May Day it is. You will join us, won't you, Esther?"

Of course I will. All of us will be there to share in Herr Handke's moment of glory. For glory it will be – he is devising a beacon for a world where so much is being ring-fenced and denied. Hold out your hands and warm them on the memories of what was – Herr Bloch in full voice; sunflowers peeking through the solid brick walls of dim courtyards; a blind flowerseller selling blooms as bright as suns; Frau Schneider plucking lucky ladybirds from my cheek. And Thomas Tucholski stretched out on my floorboards winning me over with his words and his much-welcomed gifts of candles and soap. Herr Goebbels thinks I'm a maggot; that I can never be rescued because I pollute the purity of the German race. Impure and unclean. A woman who bruises when just a drop of water touches her skin. I'm a burden beyond burdens. I even start to believe that myself, and plan to stay at home on the day the Moabit storey is unveiled. I let slip my reservations to Kaya, who is slowly brushing soap down the mountainous expanse of my bare back at the time.

"If you're an immoral degenerate, we can only hope you breed like a rabbit one day," she retorts.

She's only half joking. Women in Haussmann's world are supposed to breed, cook and hop to and from church. We have to play him at his own game, she says, and challenge such nonsense by glorifying the role of the degenerate.

"Breed for the revolution," Kaya declaims, as she rummages for the soap which she has dropped into the bath tub.

I can barely manage to let loose a cough, let alone a baby, into this crazy world. Kaya is no doubt resting her hopes of impending maternity on some Russian actor. I doubt either of us will ever knock Haussmann off his perch, but at least Kaya hopes for something. Since Tucholski died, I haven't let hope nudge me. I'm afraid of hope, truth told. Hopes won't turn potatoes into pomegranates, or the Dieter Haussmanns of this world into poets. What do I have to lose if I go to the Moabit on May Day? I tell Kaya I've changed my mind and she punches the air in a victory salute. Oh, Kaya. I know why Tucholski loved you so much when I see you so triumphant. Your passion for life was your winning suit, but I opted for caution.

"There's something else you should know, Esther," Kaya says, as I begin to haul myself out of the bath tub. "The communists are planning a march on May Day. It's going to get lively out there."

This is not welcome news. If a march is planned, Haussmann and the Brownshirts will be prowling. It can only mean trouble.

"We have to show we mean business. I'm impressed by Herr Handke's clock tower, but it's hardly going to win us the war, is it?"

So, war has been declared. The skirmishes of the last few months have been nothing more than a prelude to a full-blown attack. I'm to be a foot soldier in a drama overseen by an actress and a clockmaker. I've known worse odds in my time. Kaya grins up at me. She's been denied a chance to appear on the stage ever since she walked out of *The Threepenny Opera* company, but what does she care about that now she has the chance to strut in front of a whole city. It's how Tucholski would have played things, had he still been alive. We both know that...

the city of confiscated memory

May Day arrives and we find our way into the courtyard off Turmstrasse. Spirits are high. We can see that, the minute we pass through the entrance porch. A hint of reckless abandon hangs in the air, like the tinge of frost on cheeks and lips. Kaya, Eva and myself join the throng and, immediately, we feel as if our very lungs are being squeezed of air. We all breathe as one and wait for the moment when Herr Handke will emerge and give the signal that the ceremony is about to begin. Minutes tick by and he finally appears from behind the row of sunflowers. It's one minute to eleven in the morning. His face breaks into a smile, as if to say: "*here is my magic, make of it what you will,*" and the hour strikes. A mechanical Herr Bloch eases his way out of his giant sunflower, clicking and squeaking his way over our upturned faces. As he moves, he sings the very same song we heard the night we were pelted with mud by our old neighbours.

The peals stop ringing after ten minutes and then the real Herr Bloch begins cheering. He stands right at the front of the crowd, admiring his musical doppelgänger.

"Why even the same teeth are missing. I'm a work of art!" he exclaims. "Achje, don't you agree, it's better than a play, friends. The drama of our lives is keeping up with time itself. It's a miracle!"

Bloch is trying to reach his cronies further back, but the bodies are packed in so tightly at the front of the clock that there is simply no room for him to shift in. He gets shirty and lashes out, but the confined space results in him whacking a small woman in the face with the tip of his elbow. The woman's husband starts shouting and then winds

231

up by punching Bloch. Now, everyone seems to be coming to blows. Within the space of a few minutes, it's mayhem all over the courtyard. We find ourselves surging forwards and backwards in the disturbed crowd, even though our legs aren't actually moving.

Kaya tries to keep hold of my coat tails, but she's spun away in the opposite direction – I see her face pushed up against one of the sunflowers so hard its petals cut deep into her cheek. She's rescued only when she reaches the rim of the sunflowers, carried away above the crowd's heads to the relative safety of the archway leading into the adjoining courtyard. I make propellors of my elbows, pushing and bringing Eva with me until we both reach her side. We shelter under the arch, as the crush of bodies beyond us oozes into every nook and cranny, like a troubled wave. We hear women crying out for their children and men screaming for an order they can't even impose on their wayward feet. It's some time before anyone else thinks of following us under the arch. Once the artery is opened, the crowd thins out a little, but already it's too late. An elderly woman has been crushed to death in the stampede, her face reduced to a mashed red poppy.

"Oh my God, Esther, look! It's poor Frau Schneider. I recognise her shawl," Kaya points out my friend from the Moabit carpet-beating days.

There are shouts of anger and distress all round, as her fate is relayed from person to person. Kaya rushes forwards and places her jacket over Frau Schneider's battered face, just as a group of young men enter the courtyard from the street outside. They wear an easy arrogance. Their uniforms and their bearing suggest violence, even for those vague about recent political developments. Shock soon gives way to panic, but Kaya chooses to ignore the new arrivals and kneels down beside Frau Schneider. She starts to say a prayer, but hesitates. Another neighbour runs for a priest.

"Is she dead, Frau Tucholski?"

I'd know that voice anywhere – it's Dieter Haussmann. He reaches Kaya's side and, slowly, he lifts the edge of her jacket to inspect the pulp that is the dead woman's face. He affects a shudder of horror and then calls his colleagues over.

232

"See what degenerates have allowed to happen here?"

Karl begins to pace up and down as best he can with the body at his feet and a crowd at bay, stopping occasionally to look with exaggerated distaste at the sunflowers.

"We've all heard about this clock tower and we know Jewish capitalists support its construction. Why? Because they like to celebrate and flaunt their filthy existence. Look here, you celebrate a man who sings of rape and murder. You wish *this* monstrosity to stand in your courtyard?"

Kaya finally looks up from the dead woman and sees the faces ranged above her. She sees how the mood of our old neighbours has changed. We shiver in the cold air. As the men in uniform smile into our fear, we remember the rumours we have all heard, about the shadowy justice being meted out on the streets.

"Well, we don't want any more trouble," Haussmann continues, as if reading our collective mind.

He comes to an abrupt halt in front of the sunflowers and stands for a while gazing at their decoration. The mechanical organ grinder has sensibly disappeared and only the flowers remain on view, lined up like so many Sunday schoolchildren in best bibs and tuckers. I can almost hear the crowd breathing out a giant sigh of relief at Haussmann's more reassuring posture. There is to be no more unpleasantness, no, these young men were simply hoping to sort out an unfortunate incident without fuss. Some people on the fringes of the crowd start to make tracks towards the stairwells, but Haussmann holds up his arm and everyone freezes again. Only Kaya moves, a daring act of velocity in the midst of an otherwise static group of onlookers. Haussmann holds her gaze, as she walks up to him.

"Call the police!" she shouts.

He ignores her and turns away to whisper something to one of his henchmen. Then he pushes Kaya out of his way and addresses the crowd once more:

"We are going to dismantle this outrageous insult. Has anybody any objections?"

Nobody dares say a word and the very next minute, a dozen young men leap into action on a signal given by Haussmann, who blows a silver whistle he wears around his neck. They have been lurking around the entrance porch where another group of Haussmann's cohorts have been surreptiously handing out sledgehammers. The operation unfolding around us has been well planned, I see that in a moment. Herr Handke must have been under surveillance since work in the courtyard got underway. The clash of metal against metal is quite terrible as the clock tower is smashed. The ground shifts under my feet with the impact of blows. Shards from the collapsing tower fall like metal snowflakes amongst us, darting off our faces and hands, leaving angry red cuts that nobody dares attend to whilst the destruction continues in our midst. Herr Handke manages to join Kaya, Eva and myself under the archway.

"I think I left it too late," is all he says, after watching the tower's disintegration.

"We must get out of here," I tell him.

Haussmann's men are spoiling for a fight; smashing up a clock tower is no compensation. And we are public enemies number one, two and three and four – what better target could they have? We are forced to slip out of Turmstrasse through back alleyways, like criminals on the run. But we are luckier than some. It's not only Frau Schneider who loses her life on May Day. The communists went ahead with their demonstration in the city as planned and many were killed after the police opened fire. We could have been arrested – or worse – if we had taken a more direct route back to the House of Clocks.

Once there, we discover Herr Rolf has already made it home ahead of us and is busy organising the evacuation of the workshop dedicated to the tower's construction. Wolf assists with the removal operation, standing at its centre in a new waistcoat, armed with a clipboard.

"It's too dangerous for Herr Handke to work here any longer, ladies," he calls out. "No, no, he must be moved on. All hands to the pump, if you please. Esther, those shelves over there. Can you clear them and pack the artefacts you find in the boxes by the window. Frau Tucholski, Fräulein Schlinsog, you will assist too?"

Before we know it, we are packing up boxes of buttons, pen nibs, ropes, pieces of pots and old pans that had been collected over the months.

"All that work for nothing!" Kaya cries out in dismay.

"No, Frau Tucholski, think of it rather as something that people will always will remember and not because they were afraid of it," Wolf commands.

It's probably his finest hour. He is at the centre of a web of intrigue: everything is being delivered to Schorns kitchen before being shifted to dozens of secret workshops. Herr Rolf is organising the venues, even as we speak.

"We must keep everything under wraps," Wolf admonishes. "That wretch Haussmann mustn't suspect a thing."

What impresses me most is the large number of volunteers who appear in these secret workshops over the coming months. They are a band of fellow scavengers, who set out to rescue keepsakes as each subsequent storey of the tower is built, only to be pulled down just as quickly by Haussmann's gangs. They trade their finds in my soup kitchen, treasures carefully hidden away in the linings of dirty, ragged coats. Wolf rotates amongst them, a gaudy beacon throwing light on the huge jigsaw puzzle being mapped out in his backyard. A piece of a sunflower here, a bread crumb there; sometimes, a mannequin's toes, or a scorpion's claw.

Day after day, the fragments are rescued by citizens anxious to see Herr Handke's city clock rebuilt, if only in their imagination. Sometimes, Kaya and I join in the rescue operation, using the hearse to ferry the larger remnants of the different storeys to safety. There are occasions when we ferry humans, not artefacts, because some of these brave scavengers are marked men – and women. Ironically, a sense of security is restored as more and more people are encouraged to join in. As their confidence grows, so too do the tales about the wonder of Herr Handke's clock tower. It's going to root itself like an oak tree in the heart of the city, spreading its boughs far and wide.

I'm one of many who share this vision. I still walk the streets, but this time I'm following the chequered progress of Herr Handke's clock tower. It is my new obsession and keeps me from regretting my decision not to join Kaya in Russia. Whenever we meet in these terrible days, she is clutching sheafs of timetables for any number of passenger ships and train companies. She calculates her impending journey like a mathematician, adding up and dividing metres of rail track or stretches of ocean. She is confused as to which journey to make; whether there is a short-cut possible, whether she needs to buy trunks, or travel with a knapsack and avoid undue scrutiny at border crossings. She spends hours a day hunting down different visas. Some are forged; some are real. She's not sure which are which. She rolls them up tightly and secures them to her thighs with garters. Visas are currency. Her legs are worth more than a brand new Rolls Royce.

One night, I'm confronted by a stranger as I walk in the Moabit.

"Where is it safe?" the stranger begs me.

I laugh and the wind whips my breath from out of my throat.

"A country so far away, you may as well fly to the moon."

The stranger quickly rushes away, frightened she might have chanced on a lunatic let loose in the streets. After this, the nights begin to draw in close. People hold their coats to their chests and wind scarves round their mouths and cheeks. My soup kitchen is suddenly closed down by the city authorities who claim it's a health hazard. Wolf is troubled by this turn in affairs.

"I can't risk my life's work for the sake of a bowl of pea soup," he argues.

He doesn't fight the order. He bolts the kitchen's back door and I'm requested to come up with even more extraordinary dishes for extraordinary times. Then Dieter Haussmann announces he will host a birthday party for Herr Goebbels in the Jugendstil Room. Such is Schorns' reputation, he demands something extravagant and memorable for the banquet table's centrepiece.

"But you must keep your head below the kitchen range," Wolf advises. "I'll keep you posted via the dumb waiter. Check for updates under the plate covers."

I have a strong suspicion that Haussmann is out to cause trouble, not host a celebration, but I can't resist cocking a snook at such a man. I plan to make a giant, sugar-spun Cuckoo Clock. Inside, a nest of tiny birds will lie dormant until the hour strikes for the birthday toasts and then out they will fly, each bearing a little card in its beak. The names of the people we know who have disappeared without trace in recent months will be inscribed on each of the cards. (Kaya's Communist Party friends have been keeping records and she will supply the names.) As the birds reach the full stretch of their mechanical flight, they will drop the cards in unison onto the plates of the diners sitting below. The birds will be made out of marzipan, their plumage a mix of coloured glazes and piped icing. My kitchen staff rally round the project and Kaya joins in too. She sits by my kitchen range writing the cards.

The night of the birthday celebrations underway, I realise just how dangerous my sugary concoction could be. All manner of provocations are thrown at Wolf who has been ordered to attend the dinner, culminating in Haussmann's demand that the entire restaurant staff gather to drink Goebbels' health. Wolf manages to send an SOS down to the kitchen, tucked under a chicken wing.

"Let everyone else come up, but you stay put, Esther."

I'm not inclined to disagree. The rest of my staff troop up, smeared in cooking grease and oil stains. I know what Haussmann is up to. Well, what of it? There are precious few talents to draw on in this benighted city of ours. As far as Wolf is concerned, a Jew can roast a chicken as well as the next man or woman, be he, or she, Protestant or Catholic. This is the only wisdom you need to run a kitchen, but Haussmann is a man obsessed. He's infuriated when he sees the rank and file kitchen staff, but no head chef. He demands to know where I am. Wolf prevaricates, makes up a story about me visiting a sick maiden aunt, but is suddenly interrupted by the shower of name cards, delivered by two dozen sugar and marzipan birds. An underling of Haussmann's has set the clock into motion too soon and the chance for a dramatic toasting of Goebbels is passed. The uproar that follows can be heard as far as the basement kitchen. Another note shoots down the dumb waiter.

"For God's sake, Esther. Hide!"

Maybe I should pop myself in the bread bin, or under the cheesecloth? It's four o'clock in the morning and there are few places I can tuck myself away in at such an hour. Luckily, another note follows swiftly on its heels:

"Panic not. He's pissed."

I turn my attention to supervising the washing up. It's a while before I become aware of the sound of raised voices outside my kitchen. I recognise Wolf's booming tones instantly, but the other man's voice eludes me at first. Then the pfennig drops – well, a rather valuable Colombian dish to be more precise. Wolf is arguing with Haussmann. He is trying to prevent him from reaching the kitchens.

"She'll have told you where she's going, Wolf," I hear Haussmann shout. "You're both freaks, after all. We're watching you…"

"Well, how very flattering," Wolf replies. "But do stick to my right side, please. It's my better profile."

There is another muffled exchange and I assume Haussmann is trying to get past Wolf. Good God, what is going on now? Karl rustles up a couple of my kitchen staff to barricade the door. Outside, there is the sound of a scuffle. Wolf is fighting for my honour? It's absurd, no it's terrifying. I grab a soup cauldron and hold it up, as if expecting a vat of boiling oil to be unleashed on my head. There's more crashing about and the door flies open. Wolf is revealed on the other side, red in the face, his waistcoat torn at the seams.

"We need to call the police," he says, his voice strangely muted.

I rush out into the corridor and find Haussmann lying at the foot of the stairs.

"Oh, my God, Herr Wolf. What have you done?"

Wolf sits down beside Haussmann: the man's neck has been broken in a fall. Well, Wolf assures me it was a fall. I remember all the crashing and banging going on earlier and the arguments that proceeded it.

"It was an accident, Esther, believe me."

I nod my head. Well, we have to trust each other in such circumstances, don't we? Wolf insists I leave the restaurant, before the police arrive. He doesn't want to risk them seeing me here on such a night. He's right, of course, but I don't like him being left on his own with Haussmann's drunken mob. Wolf promises to send word the minute he can and I'm left to flee to the House of Clocks. The following day, I sit and wait in Herr Handke's kitchen for news. It's a long time coming. In the end, it is Herr Rolf who is the bearer of mixed tidings. He happened to be passing Schorns, as Haussmann's corpse was brought out on a stretcher.

"So far, so good, Esther. They say it's an accident. Wolf is helping with enquiries."

Just how helpful will he be, particularly if they deny him freshly ground coffee and cognac? It seems that the scandal of my Cuckoo Clock has been ignored, preceding as it does the news of Haussmann's sudden death. But it will all unravel at some point. I fret. I bite my nails. I clean behind the stoves.

I'm on the verge of biting my fingers off all together when the telephone rings. It's Wolf. He's back at the Jugendstil Room and asks me to come over. The police have gone, but I'm still to arrive by the tradesmen's entrance. I find him upstairs, eating a stale apple strudel.

"Herr Wolf? Are you all right?"

He sighs. There are dark rings under his eyes.

"Where are we going to find refuge now?" he asks, despair scarring his voice. "Once, this restaurant was a sanctuary, but now Haussmann is dead and his followers are calling for blood." He slowly licks each of his fingers, before looking up at me. His eyes are red with lack of sleep. "They are calling for my blood, as it happens."

the banquet of Esther Rosenbaum

The present is a never-ending winter and a coldness seeps into all of our hearts. Schorns is an ice palace, even though it's summer. Theatres are being closed, books banned, and the Jugendstil Room continues to be ambushed by supporters of the National Socialist Party. They come to put flowers on the spot where Haussmann died. Wolf gets me to pinch him each morning to see if he might be dreaming such castastrophes, but no. It's real, all too real. I stay away from the Jugendstil Restaurant and tend to my stoves. What the eye doesn't see, it doesn't try and shoot. Haussmann's colleagues hound Wolf, but don't yet apportion blame. The world spins, but he steadies himself as best he can by dining in the kitchens to avoid undue attention.

Then Herr Handke is arrested in the Scheuenviertel for attempting to resurrect another storey of his now infamous clock tower and my two closest friends show an uncharacteristic air of defeat. Eva plans to return to Augsburg to live with her parents. Kaya decides once and for all to go into exile.

"It's now or never, Esther. If I don't leave within the month, I'll be joining Herr Handke in the Moabit."

"I'll bring you food parcels, just as I do Herr Handke," I promise.

She smiles. Kaya has finally booked her berth on a ship that will deliver her to her Russian comrades by the end of July. She shows me the ticket, which has joined the visa papers in her stocking garter.

It's only when I see that date written down in black and white that I begin to understand Kaya really is going. I try and argue with her: there is Tucholski's grave to be maintained; fresh flowers to be laid, the grass cut back. Theatre managements clamour for her presence in their shows; the kabaretts are still anxious to hear her perform her dead husband's songs. But Kaya is adamant on giving it all up. I remember how her affection for Bert oscillated like a weather vane and wonder at her new found single-mindedness. This is what fear has done to my friend.

Herr Handke was always set on one course and his arrest is no surprise, but I grieve to think what this extraordinary man has been reduced to shut away in a solitary, windowless cell. His once dexterous fingers are swollen with chillblains. He is unable to draw, or weld, or engrave. Herr Rolfe says he scratches ideas on the walls of his cell, but he misses terribly the actual construction of new timepieces.

"It's like watching a volcano getting ready to explode," he says. "The ideas are filling up inside him and there is nothing he can do about any of them."

Herr Rolf used to take along a clock or two for Herr Handke to tinker with whilst they sat in the visitors room at Moabit prison, but it was too painful for the clockmaker to see his old masterpieces. He smashed them to pieces with his bare hands. Herr Rolf carefully picked up each fragment and brought them back to the House of Clocks.

"He can restore them when he comes home."

Neither of us dare wonder aloud when that might be. I can bury the thought no longer: our little circle is beginning to break up so I shall pull out all the stops to mark Kaya's departure from Berlin. I will host a banquet for my friend – possibly the last such celebration I will ever hold in the Jugendstil Room, but there is a problem. Members of the National Socialist Party rarely budge from its tables and I have indirectly become Herr Goebbels' new chef, the one who lines his stomach so he can devise new party policies which will spell oblivion to my kind. Tucholski would have loved such irony, but the past is the past. I inform Kaya of what I am up to and she's delighted. None of us have partied for ages and this is a chance to rectify things, even if it's only for one night. She's also the one who puts the Brownshirts off the scent by recommending they drop into Uhu, a new kabarett up the road, on the night we plan to meet.

"A real dive, but the women dancers wear nothing but necklaces and you get free vials of Black Bear with each bottle of sekt," she tells them.

Consequently, the Jugendstil Room is empty the night of my banquet. Our dress code is more circumspect than Uhu's, but the menu will boast a variety of my story-recipes, as well as different sorts of bread, which I ask my guests to provide. This banquet may well be the last time all my friends will meet together under one roof. Kaya offers to help me set up in the Jugendstil Room but she arrives late, after being caught up in the aftermath of a disturbance. (Haussmann's gangs still roam the streets.) A man with a cut lip pushed by her on the Weidendammer Brücke where the street lamps are broken and she slipped on a piece of bloodstained greaseproof paper.

By the time she runs up the restaurant stairs, I have already shifted the cake stand. Herr Rolf has asked for a space to be cleared in order to display a special gift for us all and this seemed to be the best option. He doesn't give away much more, only that it is a gift made by Herr Handke before his arrest and he wishes it to be presented tonight. Illumination for the evening is provided by dozens of candles, reducing the Jugendstil's usually vast dimensions to a circle of tiny gold coins. It is so late the last of the regular diners have long since pulled up their coat collars and left. To ensure privacy, I close the old wooden shutters before dressing for the banquet.

I let my hair down and it reaches my heels. I'm going to wear a green dress cut down from a theatre backcloth featuring a forest scene, pinned in at the back to fit my vastly reduced shape. Esau and Frau Meyers have collaborated on the design and the sourcing of the materials used to make it. The dress is quite wonderful: tall, shadowy trees stretch up from my toes to my collar bones. Close to my navel, Pierrot and Colombine dance under a bronze moon in carnevale masks. My shoes are also of another century: ballet pumps with little red heels. Around my neck, I wear a key on a velvet ribbon that Herr Rolf has given me earlier, ready for the presentation later in the evening.

Kaya brings a dozen gingerbread hearts with her, baked to her mother's old recipe. Eva appears next, carrying six rye loaves topped with crunchy sunflower seeds. She is accompanied by Erwin and Richter, who offer a dish of plaited sweetbreads, covered in thick icing sugar. Esau and Frau Meyers present a basket of braided hallah loaves, as my banquet coincides with the Jewish Sabbath. The loaves are tucked under a hallah cover, hand-embroidered in gold by Frau Meyers. Finally, I welcome Erwin, Leon Wolf and Herr Rolf. The latter produces a box of breadcrumbs, the last to be bequeathed to the Clock Tower project by the Frankls, before they travelled to Paris. Destined to clean the clock tower's gearing systems, they shall now garnish a last serving of Die Suppe Rosenbaum.

My guests assemble around the candlelit table. In front of them stands a spice box filled with different flavoured tobacco and a glass full of purple ink. I explain that this tobacco and ink is a reminder of who, despite his failings, brought us all together: Brecht, a man with tobacco on his lilac tongue. What holds us together, however, is something a lot more valuable – my story-recipes and their gifts of bread.

I serve the first course. Over the years, my friends must have eaten literally hundreds of my bowls of pea soup, but this version they claim tastes different, as if all those other bowls were trial runs for this one last offering. Then comes the banquet: Hare-in-a-Drum, Wolf's Pig Nose, Heart-of-a-Deer, Frank's Apfelkuchen, Clock Cakes, Lotte's Pear Tree Cake and bowls of Kisses-of-Hope and Pen Nib Hearts. After eating a selection of the breads brought by my guests, I distribute my own gifts. I've baked hamantaschen to represent the special achievements of everyone present that evening, rather than the historic characters traditionally associated with Purim. Eva receives a cake in the form of a book and Erwin receives a cake shaped like a crown in recognition of his abilities to play a king. Richter and Kaya both receive cakes in the form of a phoenix. Richter breaks off a wing and chews it in a bid to distract himself from the tears that well up in his eyes.

"I'm so proud to be associated with you all," he says. "Your names will always be remembered for what you have done at Theater Hoffmann. And Herr Tucholski also, although he is no longer with us."

Kaya wraps her phoenix up in her napkin and puts it away in her embroidered evening bag.

"I shall eat my cake on the boat to Russia."

She sounds hesitant, as though she's still trying on the idea of escape. She glances round the table. There are tears in her eyes. Kaya Tucholski's bravado is wavering amongst her closest associates. I swallow hard. I smile at her through my tears and she smiles back. We have been conspirators on many occasions, so maybe we can survive whatever lies ahead? Our chances are as good as the next man or woman's. We live in a roulette wheel. Kaya dabs at her eyes and straightens her back.

"It's amazing, isn't it?" she announces. "I'm finally doing what I've always said I would do: I've booked my berth on a cruise ship. I'm joining Erwin's friends as soon as I disembark."

She grabs her flute of sekt and waves it in the air in a triumphant fashion. Erwin picks up his cue – ever the professional.

"Congratulations, Kaya!" he shouts and clinks her glass. "You will be missed, and not just by your friends here tonight. You will be missed by the whole city who know you as Green Phoenix. And by Bert. He's still fuming over that bloody wedding dress you ruined. Anyone would think it was the real thing."

Kaya shakes her head at his cheek, but she's not angry. Oh, no, she's moving away. Up the gangplank and goodbye devious playwrights with lilac-coloured tongues! Erwin kisses Kaya's hands and the rest of us applaud his little speech. Next, I present Leon and Etienne with their cakes, shaped like paintbrushes. For Esau and Frau Meyers, I have made two little figures dressed in wedding clothes. They both blush and feign surprise, but it can only be a matter of time before Frau Meyers walks under the wedding canopy. For Herr Rolf, I have baked a cake in the shape of a clock. He, in turn, has a gift for me – a rococo-style clock, built in the form of a miniature tower. It is – as to be expected – no ordinary timepiece.

This scaled-down tower, created just days before Herr Handke's arrest, stands in for what has been lost to Haussmann's gangs. Salvaged artefacts from the original masterpiece have been incorporated into its structure, including Lotte's Silver Pear Tree with its shivering boughs of heavy fruit and a dish of Pen Nib Hearts, amongst them Tucholski's own pen nib, cast in gold which I gave to Herr Handke to use in his visionary tower.

"The idea is for this clock to safe keep all your memories," Herr Rolf explains. "It will keep them safe, even after much else has faded away."

The clock carries our individual portraits, each one engraved in a turret on the small tower. Herr Rolf points out who's who: I stand tall in one, armed with my buttercup-yellow carving knife; Eva is pictured before her new typewriter, whilst Kaya has been caught in a theatre spotlight. The fourth turret portrays the rococo clock in pride of place in the Jugendstil Room with Wolf, Etienne, Richter and Erwin all recognisable amongst the crowd of diners in the background.

"In another century, someone will see this clock and they will want to know who created it and what was their inspiration," Herr Rolf continues. "I'm going to invite Esther to wind it up on our behalf."

Herr Rolf indicates a small door at the base. The key hanging around my neck matches its lock. I stoop down, open up the door and insert my key. Tick, tick, tick goes the clock, its rhythm matched by the sound of footsteps coming up the stairs to the Jugendstil Room. Who can it be? No one else has been invited. Eva and Kaya run over to the stairwell and discover Bert staggering up the stairs. He's very drunk. His body dips and sways dangerously and we're all convinced he's going to tumble. When he finally arrives in the restaurant, we discover he's incapable of forming a coherent sentence. The clock ticks on. I join Eva and Kaya and the three of us flank Bert in angry silence. He is soaked and his opaque eyes skid from one face to another, like two rolling marbles.

"Drink?" he splutters, before swooping down onto our banquet table, his arms held out in front of him in a desperate bid to balance himself.

I'm the first to reach him in one giant stride, but even I can't stop him from falling. He pulls the tablecloth down with him, overturning dishes and glasses. He lies unconscious at my feet, his body covered with flecks of tobacco and splashes of purple ink. One arm lies submerged under the tablecloth. Kaya shakes his coat lapels in a bid to wake him, but he is out for the count.

"What do we do now, Esther?" Eva asks.

"We'll leave him here to stew."

I'm determined to have the last word at my banquet, just like my namesake, but it is a shortlived victory. If I had known it was the last time I would see Bert, would I not have doused him in cold water and insisted on one final conversation? And if I had, what would I have chosen to say at such a time? That he made almost as many mistakes as I have done? If he had been courageous enough to take on Kaya, would that have stopped her walking that gangplank alone? What of the days when we sat and chewed over the fate of drama in our benighted country? It feels over a century ago, and I wonder whether any of that old Bert still exists.

The day after my banquet, Kaya sets sail for Moscow – and Wolf discovers Etienne's body in his studio. Wolf knows his lover has been murdered and that Haussmann's cronies are probably responsible, but he's powerless to do anything.

"We are living through dark and ugly days," he warns, his voice struggling to find its usual booming cadences. "Ghouls and sadists are out robbing and killing our angels."

Etienne choked to death, after being forced to swallow oil paints and turpentine. The paintings in his studio had all been defaced with graffiti, much of it abusive and directed at Wolf. Following Etienne's funeral, my boss begins to pack away his collection of paintings and sculptures. He arranges with Herr Rolf to have them removed to places of safety and gradually they are found new homes in abandoned barns, old shipping vessels, even under the mattress of a dying nun. I notice how Wolf begins to change with each painting that departs under cover from his apartment. Something is affecting him, and it is not just the fact that his restaurant is filled with shouting men dressed in brown uniforms. He's afraid for me. He's afraid that Schorns and all it once stood for will crumble up, like the bread roll sitting in front of him. He worries about Kaya traipsing around the Russian countryside in a boiler suit and army boots. We have infrequent tidings from her and we read entire novels between each sketchy line. Kaya is working hard – along with her colleagues she is improvising new dramas on a near nightly basis. Dramas about the agricultural revolution being initiated with new tractor designs, or record harvests delivered by the country's burgeoning collective farms. They make war against anti-Soviet sympathisers in their speeches – a brave new world is delivered in a brew of formulas.

"What's wrong with Shakespeare?" Wolf mutters. "Kaya was born to play Ophelia, or Rosalind."

Instead, Kaya cuts a swathe through rural Russia on a horse-drawn tractor. It's an image that troubles me, because I remember the German newspaper photographs of her in her ridiculous sable furs swanning around a military hospital ward. Preposterous, but life enhancing, as revealed in the admiring eyes of the mutilated heroes of the First World War.

"Achje, theatre is now a corn shed in the Urals," Wolf sighs.

A small miracle takes place in the Jugendstil Room, just days later. At first, Wolf thinks his head must have turned into a soufflé, but the fact is whenever the Rococo Clock strikes the hour, we smell baking bread. Various customers comment on this phenomenon and very soon the prime spot to be had in the restaurant is one within inhaling distance of the turreted clock. How appropriate that the one surviving scent should be bread. I've no idea how Herr Handke has managed it, but he has somehow captured the smell of the Frankls' bakery, the lingering odour of the mietskasernen stairwells and my last ever city banquet in one.

I'm staggered when Wolf fails to charge an extra fee for those wanting to book the coveted places, but this is how far he has changed. He lets his diners fight over the prize seats and opts to walk the streets instead. I stay put, whilst my boss dons my top hat and greatcoats.

There are many he meets on his walks over the coming months who are able to smell his clock. They tell him they breathe in its aroma and remember something long forgotten, maybe a chance word that lit up their heart, or a touch that left them shivering in the rain by a tram stop. There were others who felt as they did when the first rays of summer sun came in through the tenement windows, they picked up an apple and walked down to a café where coffee bubbled and people had time to talk about their small concerns, like the man growing seedlings for his neighbours' window boxes, or the girl in

247

the green dress at the tram stop laughing, because she was off to a party with her lover.

Wolf walks down the streets of his city for the first time in years, eventually arriving at the prison where Herr Handke and the kabarett performer Francine wait out their days in solitary confinement. Herr Handke is in prison for daring to imagine; Francine has been locked up because she stole a loaf of bread and she is homeless. Inside prison, hundreds of other people wait with them. Their calendar is the sky outside, or the changing temperature of their cell, possibly the growth of a tiny plant, which they are allowed to keep if the wardens turn a blind eye. On and on he goes, past the tenement block where I once made love to a ghost man who saved my feet. By the time he returns to the Jugendstil Room, Wolf has made a decision. He rings Eva in Augsburg and asks her if she will keep the Rococo Clock safe.

"It's precious, will you look after it?" he asks.

Yes, I have heard right. I have heard Wolf beg for something. We call on Herr Rolf to assist us and he promises to do all he can. The clock goes on its travels and so do we. It is no longer safe to stay at Schorns. Wolf is "discovered" with a minor, who turns out to be an old pal of Haussmann's, but it takes all his savings to buy his way out of prosecution. Then raucous mobs begin stoning the restaurant windows. What else to do, but save our skins?

Twelfth Night, 1933, we flee to a disused house in the Wannsee recommended by Karl, my old soup kitchen assistant. Many other people have found refuge there, sleeping under the floorboards wrapped in newspaper and old coats. Unlike me, Wolf still risks going walkabout. We have swapped roles and I find myself admiring his courage, rather than despising his corrupt nature (what is left of it). He even meets up with the carpet beaters in the Turmstrasse courtyard who remember clearly the giantess who once lived amongst them and the actress Kaya Tucholski. They have heard about her flight to Russia.

"A rat leaving a sinking ship," one of the women tells him.

How could any of us know her future will be as bleak as our own. A whole city holds its breath as fire cracks open the sky above the Reichstag. The fire burns and burns, then darkness. The flames are doused and the crowd pulls back. I'm present that night and so is

Wolf. I'm still taller than everyone else around me, although I'm badly stooped. My starving body, dressed in my old pinstripe suit, is covered in dirt and I've pulled out the remaining strands of my hair.

Why are we waiting in this city of confiscated memories? Because we are listening out for a story hidden in the mechanics of a wonderful clock. For a while, I think the wait is an abortive one. The day German soldiers march into Poland, Eva contacts Wolf through Karl to say the clock no longer smells of baking bread when the hour strikes. We are adrift once more. I think it will be safer if we split up. Wolf pawns his leather coat and buys a handcart, determined to set up in any improvised trade that comes to hand. He can forget all the pretty boys and the angels, because he's a survivor.

"We'll meet again, Esther, I'm sure of it," he promises me.

And then he's away, pushing his handcart over a horizon I will probably never travel. He doesn't look back. I must follow his example.

clocks and angels

epilogue

My story tells of a magical clock which measures time and the pulse of the senses. Of a clock that plays out the lives of its creators: *the metal from a father's belt buckle; feathers from an old woman's mattress; even a cheap candlestick that lit up a first love affair*... It notes the bricks and stones which I see Wolf trundle around the streets for the tenement women. They are rebuilding their homes with nothing but their bleeding hands for tools. I hear one of them call out to Wolf in Oranienburgerstrasse:

"Excuse me, but it's Herr Wolf, isn't it?"

He has spent so many months hiding from his shadow, he takes his time before replying.

"It's Eva Schlinsog, Herr Wolf. Don't you remember me? I was Esther Rosenbaum's friend. You sent me her clock."

I watch them embrace on a pile of bricks. Then they fall silent for some minutes. I wait on their words. Wolf is obviously terrified to ask the question uppermost in his mind. Eva understands that fear. She tells him the Rococo Clock is safe. Something remarkable happened the day that armistice was declared. The clock started to release the smell of baking bread once more. She decided to return to Berlin.

"Where is Esther's clock now?"

"With Herr Rolf."

"Dear God, he's still alive?"

"Yes, although Herr Handke himself died in prison a year ago," Eva replies. "Herr Rolf and his agents have hidden hundreds of drawings and maquettes all over Berlin."

The blanket bombing which has so transformed our city has not succeeded in destroying Herr Handke's vision – or the indefatigable Herr Rolf! It's an omen and it encourages my old friends to think to the future for the first time since war broke out. They sit down on the remains of an old chimney breast and plot. Eva will take Wolf to Herr Rolf's basement hideout and deliver the clock back into his safekeeping. He wants to reopen Schorns, he explains. He wants to revive my old story-recipes under the Rococo Clock on the site of his former restaurant.

"And Esther, Herr Wolf?" Eva asks. "What has happened to Esther, do you think?"

Her question brings Wolf's flood of words to a sudden halt. They both stare at the remains of their boots and can hardly bear to look at one another.

"There are stories of what happened outside the cities, Eva. Terrible places of exile..." The silence catches up with them, until Wolf brings his fists down hard on some loose brick. "I will wrong-foot the barbarians! I want to remember what went before, not all of this. You can help me, if you like, Eva."

"Another soup kitchen?"

"No, a new Jugendstil Room. Start at the top and move on from there. Ambition is the new currency for Leon Wolf."

I follow them at a discreet distance as they transport Herr Handke's clock back to Friedrichstrasse. It's tiring work and they ask for help from many passers-by. As they travel, Wolf makes a point of inviting all those who help them to join him for his first banquet in his new restaurant. Eva wonders if they will be able to cater for so many, but Wolf is adamant that his doors will be open to all.

"It is how Esther would have run things," he points out.

Schorns once stood six storeys high, but now it's flat as a sheet of paper. In spite of this, Wolf anticipates opening up between eleven and three each day serving from portable stoves. He knew many of my story-recipes by heart and works his memory hard to revive and adapt them for a post-war trade. Just as encouraging, Eva learnt by heart many of her stories, before the war broke out, stories that were first banned and then set on fire in the nightmare world we once inhabited. Wolf suggests she tell her stories at the restaurant tables. A dollar a story. Eva jumps at the chance.

I return each day to see how this new restaurant fares. Its interior is as glamorous as can be, designed with the limited resources available. Wolf has dusted down elegant furniture which he has salvaged from other ill-fated establishments, including Café Botticelli. The Rococo Clock is set up in the centre of a medley of tables and chairs which all originate from different centuries, but they help cancel out the eyesore of the scorched brick walls. One morning a stick-thin man with a discernible limp arrives at the restaurant. It takes me a while to place him for he has aged terribly. It is Karl, my old kitchen assistant. His brow is deeply furrowed and his mouth has twisted up like a corkscrew, so that he can no longer speak. Wolf does recognise him; he improvises a chef's hat out of a piece of sackcloth, and sets Karl to work in his al fresco kitchen.

It is Karl who becomes responsible for serving up my old story-recipes; clock cakes in dishes made out of old shrapnel; Frank's Apfelkuchen and bowls of Die Suppe Rosenbaum. Recipes that unleash memories of what has been, just like the carvings on the facade of the Rococo Clock. Diners will be encouraged to ask questions about the strange names of the dishes and who is represented in the clock's intricate tableaux. *Erst kommt das Fressen, dann kommt die Moral* – first comes the eating and then the moral. My old friend Bert Brecht got that right, at least, before he too went into exile. Rumour has it he went to Finland. He writes plays sitting on ice caps, like a penguin. Achje, rumours are this city's new history. Wolf ploughs on, relentless, implacable.

"We must check the weather forecast daily, Eva and then we can open our doors, in a manner of speaking."

And each morning, those invisible doors open to welcome the crowds which assemble from an early hour close to the mish-mash of tables and chairs and the legendary Rococo Clock. I watch my old boss stretch out his arms and embrace the crowd, and beyond that the ruins of his once great restaurant. He calls out his invitation to everybody standing within hearing distance:

"We have room for you all at our banquet," he declares. "Please join us."

Then he turns and opens up the first of the covers, as Eva tears up chunks of freshly baked bread and the hungry crowd edges fowards to join the al fresco banquet. I retreat back to the broken stage of Theater Hoffmann where the air is disturbed only by the soft whisperings of broken chandeliers. I close my eyes. One blue, one green. Scheherazade, who once fed imaginations as greedy as hollow stomachs. I am this story and nothing more…

A note on the characters

The majority of characters who appear in *The Banquet of Esther Rosenbaum* are entirely fictional, with the exceptions of Bertolt Brecht, Greta Garbo, the actor Alexander Granach, designer Cas Neher and long-suffering producer Herr Aufricht, who all appear as themselves. Grandmother Brecht was also a real person, but I've made her move house to Augsburg and developed her love of racing and Spartacist political leanings. She certainly adored her grandson Bertolt and caused a sensation travelling to the races with her cook. After that, fiction well and truly takes over. Cabaret legend Klabund, the actress Carola Neher and the playwright Marieluise Fleisser, contemporaries of Brecht, offered inspiration to the development of my fictional characters Thomas Tucholski, Kaya Tucholski and Eva Schlinsog respectively, but criticism of anything they get up to in the story is entirely to be laid at their doors and not at anyone else's.

Schoms is an amalgamation of many extraordinary eating establishments that used to exist in pre-war Berlin, chiefly the *House of Aschinger* (it once stood near Friedrichstrasse Station). Anyone passing by the impressive *Villa Grisebach* on Fasanenstrasse today will spot more than a passing resemblance to Herr Handke's *House of Clocks*. *Café Botticelli* is larger in scale, but inspired by the lovely *Café Leysieffer* in Kurf'damm. The *Schiffbauerdamm* was a real venue in Berlin and did stage the original production of Brecht and Weill's *The Threepenny Opera*; the *Kammerspiele* remains a working theatre in Munich, and it's also possible to visit the beautiful *Art Nouveau synagogue* in Augsburg.

Acknowledgements

Key sources used in my research include: *Bertolt Brecht: Diaries 1920–1922* (Eyre Methuen); *Drums in the Night, Baal, In the Jungle of Cities* and *The Threepenny Opera*, all by Bertolt Brecht (Methuen); *Cabaret* by Lisa Appignanesi (Methuen); *Brecht on Theatre* by John Willett (Part I 1918–1932); *Culture and Society in the Weimar Republic* by Keith Bullivant (Manchester University Press); *Bertolt Brecht's Berlin: A Scrapbook of The Twenties* by Wolf Von Eckardt and Saunder L Gilman; *The Jewish People: Their History and Their Religion* by David J Goldberg and John D Rayner; *Berlin 1675–1945* by Alexander Riessner; *Rosa Luxemburg: A Life* by Elzbieta Ettinger; *Art and Revolution* by John Berger; *Roman Vishniac Vintage Prints Exhibition*, HackelBury Fine Art (1998); *Die Busche der Pandora*, G W Pabst (1928); *Der Dreigroschenoper*, G W Pabst (1931); *Watch Repairing* by J W Player (Crosby Lockwood & Son).

Big thanks to the Arts Council of Wales for a travel bursary to visit Berlin, Munich & Augsburg; those inspirational people at *Llanos de la Luz, Andalucia*, particularly Hannah Davies for timely advice and encouragement; Phil and Maggie at The Bay Art Gallery; The Goethe Institute, London; Heidi, my German teacher at Howard Gardens & the very helpful member of staff at Cardiff Library who lent me his personal copy of *The Life and Lies of Bertolt Brecht* when it wasn't on the shelf. And a special thanks to Alcemi editor Gwen Davies for realising the potential of my novel and to Nia Davies who edited an early manuscript.

Last, but not least, *llawer o ddiolch* to my more culinary-minded friends who provided food, friendship – even a futon to rest my head – in the long months it took me to complete this book. I owe you, one and all.

Praise for Penny Simpson

"Alive... startling and original... quirky, unsentimental... funny... The writing flies off the page."
Tessa Hadley, Meic Stephens, 2007 Rhys Davies Short Story Competition Judges

"Penny Simpson is a born story-teller; she has created a richly-imagined tale of 1920s Berlin cabaret culture, written with a zest reminiscent of the best magic realism, but with a flavour all of her own."
Nicholas Murray

"Penny Simpson has a vivid imagination. At times it is as if it takes physical shape and goes down streets like a searchlight, a scalpel following behind. This allows her formidable talent to exercise itself on both the likely and the unlikely. It's best to listen in."
Alun Richards, *Planet*

"The short story is an ideal form for the telling glance into another world, but, as Hardy says, a story must be exceptional enough to justify its telling and when we read it, we like to feel we are reading something that is the fruit of a single incident in time. This is true of all Penny Simpson's stories."
Planet

"Simpson's art is to craft from very few words characters that actually make you feel something...As with all good short stories, each covers its topic sufficiently to be engaging yet leaves enough unturned for interpretation and assumption."
Big Issue

"Read [DOGdays] and be hooked."
Western Mail

"The settings for DOGdays' stories are evoked through extraordinary atmospheric details."
Buzz